CONTEST OF QUEENS

JORDAN H. BARTLETT

QCONTEST OF QUEENS

When you're on the edge,
your next step is to fly or fall.

CamCat
Books

CamCat Publishing, LLC
Brentwood, Tennessee 37027
camcatpublishing.com

Hardcover ISBN 9780744304985
Paperback ISBN 9780744304626
Large-Print Paperback ISBN 9780744304640
eBook ISBN 9780744304657
Audiobook ISBN 9780744304718

Library of Congress Control Number: 2021945837

Book and cover design by Maryann Appel
Map illustration by Andrew Martin

5   3   1   2   4

In memory of Poppa Roy,

for painting castles in the sky

and showing me the way to get there.

Your stories are sorely missed.

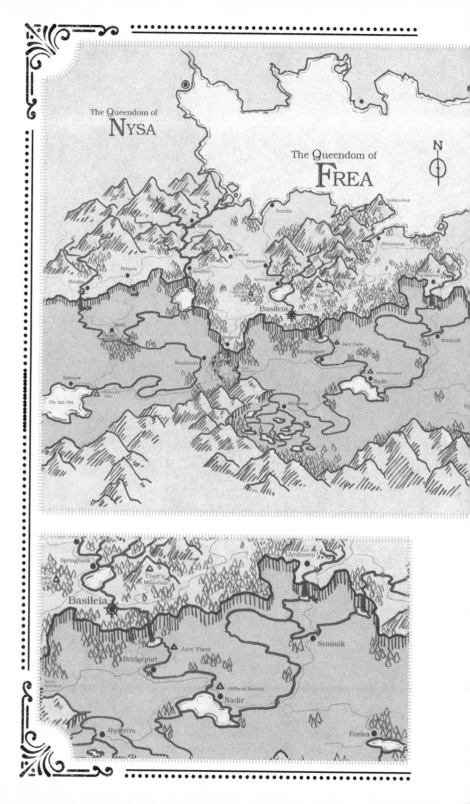

1

THE FIRST VOYAGE

"There's too many of them!" Iliana roared, her long black hair streaming behind her like a war banner. Connor's keen eyes studied the battlefield and he cursed, sweeping his hair from his face, the wind whipping the acrid stench of battle around him. Their eyes locked for a moment. Adrenaline still coursing through her veins, she grasped his waist and drew him in for a deep, passionate kiss. When she let him go, he took a moment to catch his breath. Eyes wild, smile flashing, she drew her sword. "But with you here, we just might have a chance." He stood up straighter. Her words burned in his mind, and the ghost of her lips lingered on his. He drew his sword and brandished it high.

"Let's finish this," he bellowed. Iliana's battle cry rang in his ears and they leaped forward as one. A light flashed across his field of vision, blinding him. He staggered back, his sword dropping to his side. Iliana looked at him, confused. The light flashed again, and he felt the world around him begin to fade.

Rolling over, he groaned. The weight of leather armor dissolved to the weight of featherdown.

The first fingers of sunlight crept their way through the crack in the heavy velvet curtains. Gentle rays inched along the cold stone floor, up a mahogany bedpost, and dusted the sleep from the Prince's eyes. His brow wrinkled as he fought to stay with Iliana a little longer behind his closed lids. Reluctantly, Connor blinked his blue eyes open. Once. Twice. Then he sat upright.

It's Sunday, he thought. *Finally. Every good adventure starts on a Sunday.*

Stretching, he threw back the covers and cast his gaze around the room. Already, his mind whirled with preparations. He would need light clothes—nothing to weigh him down—and his compass. A list of items ran through his head, and he started moving about the room to retrieve them all. Although he tried his best to pack quietly, his excitement inspired slamming drawers and heavy footfalls.

He rummaged through pairs of leather boots. Buckles clinked together, and fabric murmured softly as he sifted through blacks, browns, and tans. He picked up a tall pair, frowned, then exchanged them for shorter ones, the leather well worn. He couldn't risk blisters today, and the tall ones rubbed his ankles.

Next, he dragged his knapsack from under his desk. The canvas was worn on a corner, a leather strap needed mending, and it had the faint aroma of wet dog; this was not something a prince would own. He had traded one of the serving boys for it, as all of his bags were much too fancy for expeditions.

He tightened one of the straps and his mind floated to the leather hilt of the sword in his dream. His sword. The sword of a knight. He paused and sighed as the thought struck him. To be a knight. Now that was the dream, but that was ridiculous. His mother had explained to him once that only women could become guards, and of them, only certain guards could become knights. The Knights of the Queendom carried the responsibility of taking another's life. Only those who could create life could be trusted with the burden of extinguishing it. Besides, at fourteen he wanted the glory, not the burden.

Indulging for a moment in the fantasy, he saw himself in the light armor of a knight, sword aloft, cape unfurling behind him, the wind blowing through his brown hair, commanding a battalion of strong and beautiful guards, all secretly in love with him, of course. He, the first male knight. Much more exciting than being one of a long line of princes. All princes got to do was learn how to be good advisors. Shaking the fantasy from his head, he turned back to his task.

He sighed. He couldn't be a knight, but he could be an explorer. He could be a conqueror of realms.

When he was younger, he used to pretend he was a bold adventurer: Connor the Conqueror. A man who bravely explored the herb gardens and discovered new tracks through the manicured hedge mazes. He chuckled at the memory. Since then, he had never felt quite comfortable as Cornelius; Connor was a better fit. Less stuffy, and most important, it was his. Something private. A rare possession for a prince.

His eyes scanned the bookshelf for his telescope. Not spying it there, he opened the large, studded trunk at the end of his bed. The hinges on the lid groaned weakly. He sifted through its contents, his fingertips brushing across an assortment of forgotten items at the bottom, until he located the desired object. A small brass spyglass. He tucked it in his belt in the same fashion as Amelia the Daring on the cover of *To The World's End*. He was almost ready.

Wincing at the thought of the commotion he had most definitely caused, Connor stepped back lightly to where his project of many evenings lay finished and gleaming on his desk by the window. In the new daylight, the hull shone a warm, rich red. It was a wooden boat and his ticket to adventure. The hull was about half the length of his forearm and was topped with a canvas sail. He picked it up carefully from where it had been propped up to dry and surveyed his handiwork. Not a splinter in sight (they had tended to prefer ending up in his thumbs).

He gently opened a small hidden compartment in the center of the ship's deck to reveal a rectangular recess. Then, placing the boat back on the desk, he opened the top drawer, withdrew the letter he had written the night before while the paint was drying, and rolled it up into a tight tube.

He slid his signet ring off his pinkie finger and held it up to the morning sunlight. Tilting it between his fingers, he admired as the light danced off the engraved Griffin. It pranced with wings unfurled and talons flaring as if to grasp the clouds it rose above. A design of his own request. It marked his first attempt at his own coat of arms.

Every fourteen-year-old should have their own coat of arms, even boys. He had debated what creature to choose for days. His mother had the lion on hers, his father had the eagle, but he had wanted something entirely his own. He had seen their likeness in paintings and tapestries throughout the palace, and twice in person when the Griffins had overseen an important audience in the throne room. They were magnificent. He had never been more in awe of another living creature in his life. When he one day became the Queen's advisor, he wanted to inspire that same awe. So, the Griffin he chose.

Master Aestos, the court goldsmith, had been delighted when Connor described the desired ring. Master Aestos, who insisted that Connor call him Heph (even though any person who was a master of their craft must be referred to as Master), would be far less delighted to find out where his intricate work was headed. Connor shook his head and pushed that thought out of his mind.

Placing the scroll inside the ring, he fished a small glass vial out of the top drawer and slotted the bundle into the vial. He stoppered it with a cork and took some time to seal the top with melted wax. That done, he delicately placed the sealed vial into the hull, slid the lid shut, and grinned. Now, he was ready.

Connor glanced out the window. The sun shone brightly on the horizon and sent tiny rainbows through the crystalline pattern around the edges of his large bay windows. It was shaping up to be a fine day. He wrapped the boat in a kerchief and placed it carefully in his knapsack. Swinging the pack onto his back, he shrugged his shoulders, letting it settle. With one last sweeping glance around his room, he crossed to the door.

Listening for any noise out on the landing, hand hovering over the pommel of a sword that was not there, Connor eased the door open a crack, an inch, then all the way. He looked up and down the empty carpeted hallway. Surely, not all adventures began so casually. He was almost disappointed not to be intercepted.

It wasn't until he descended the servants' stairwell that he encountered his first challenge. The decadent smells from the kitchen wafted up the stairwell and caressed his nose, making his mouth water. He had forgotten to pack food, and, as his days as Connor the Conqueror had taught him, he would need to maintain his strength for the long journey ahead.

Quietly, he snuck into the kitchen and ducked behind a large barrel of potatoes. The kitchen was alive with smells and sounds. Master Marmalade—no, Master Marmaduke, the head cook, was firing off instructions to her minions and sending them scuttling to and fro. Flour flew, pans clanged, and spoons were held out on demand for a taste.

The Prince could see the morning's breakfast coming together like a well-choreographed dance. He watched them for a minute before his stomach growled in protest and forced him into action. Crouching and hiding his face, he sidled casually along a sturdy counter until he reached the spot where an assortment of muffins and scones were laid out on cooling racks.

Using sleight of hand he and his friend Hector had practiced together, he swiped three muffins into the knapsack he had nonchalantly placed open on the floor. Careful not to draw any attention, he forced himself to slow his actions. He took a moment to lick his fingers clean of the crumbs and berry juice from where he had squashed a raspberry.

With that same practiced calm, he picked up his knapsack and sidled toward the door.

He was almost free when Master Marmaduke's loud, booming voice silenced the clatter of the kitchen.

"Wait!" Her voice cut cleaner than the knife she was using to slice a still-steaming loaf of bread.

The Prince froze and tried to look innocent despite his raspberry-stained fingers.

She surveyed him with her hands on her hips, her lips thin, and her eyes narrow. The flour clinging to her hair made her look older than her true years, and the premature gray streaked through her naturally brown locks spoke of a life not leisurely spent. Master Marmaduke had worked for the royal family for the past eight years, but the stress and responsibility of running the royal kitchens had aged her double that. Despite this, her hazel eyes still held a twinkle that sparkled brightest when regarding the Prince, as they did now.

"Prince Cornelius, that is not a proper lunch for a growing boy," she said and walked toward him, picking up a linen bundle filled to bursting with what she considered a "proper lunch" from one of the few unused counters as she spoke. "It always pays to be prepared." She winked as she placed the lumpy package of treats in his hands.

The Prince smiled. "Thanks, Master Marmalade," he said, using the nickname he had given her when he was a child.

The cook chuckled fondly. "So where are you headed so early? Will I need to send the search parties today?"

"That was one time, Master Marmalade, and I would have been fine if given another hour," the Prince said indignantly. Shrugging off his knapsack, he gently placed the packed lunch inside. Master Marmaduke cleared her throat meaningfully and held out her hand. Connor sighed and pulled two stolen muffins from his sack and placed them in her hand. She accepted them and clicked her fingers, her hand still outstretched. Grinning, Connor handed over the last muffin, squashed raspberry and all, and bowed, conceding, before turning toward the door.

Master Marmaduke laughed again. "All right, you just be kind to this heart of mine." With that, she picked up her knife and turned back to her chopping board. Connor grinned and let the door close behind him. He settled his now much heavier knapsack on his back. Shoulders back, he strode toward the gardens. He had a ship to sail.

Once Connor was out on the castle lawns, he took out his compass. He already knew where he was going, but he had been practicing using it with Master Boreas and thought he was getting the hang of how it worked. The needle spun and bobbed. Connor twisted it this way and that and pointed it first toward the sun, then toward the ground. Trying to remember his lessons, he frowned at the tiny, twitchy piece of metal. He studied it fruitlessly for a few more minutes before nodding decisively to himself and setting off in a westerly manner, or . . . maybe it was a northern stroll he was embarking upon . . . No, considering the angle of the sun, it was definitely an eastern expedition, he decided.

He headed in the direction of the South Tower and passed the Southern Rose Garden. Their many-hued heads nodded lazily in the slight morning breeze. The sound of bees flitting between flower beds rose and fell on the air.

Grass clung to the soles of Connor's boots as he walked across the expansive palace lawn. *A lesser man could get lost in grounds like these*, he thought. *But I am a fearless conqueror.* Remembering how Iliana had looked at him in his dream, he emboldened his stride and began to swing his arms slightly. It was another twenty minutes before he reached the forest and found himself on the banks of the river that his compass had pointed him toward.

The water gurgled and giggled in and around the time-worn pebbles and stones that lined the riverbed. The trees were less manicured here and hung low and irregularly along the banks, sometimes dipping their leaves in the fresh water, sometimes grouping together so tightly as to bar others from enjoying that particular stretch of riverbank.

Heading downstream, he felt the forest deepening, the river widening. Any sounds from the castle were now far behind him and his ears filled instead with the sound of rushing water. Every now and then he heard the groan of two trees colliding in the breeze. The jarring sound of trunk on trunk made the hair stand up on the back of his neck. He was deeply aware that he was an intruder in these parts. His games with the Lords' and Genteels' sons never took him this far. The Lords always worried too much about their sons venturing too far from the castle. Connor supposed that was just what mothers did, and their husbands or wives—the Genteels—tended to agree with whatever their Lord said.

A twig snapped, and he spun around.

"Who's there?" he asked, his voice thin and feeble to his ears. The moss and lichen absorbed any edge his tone may have held. A gentle breeze played with his hair in reply, and he smelled the damp rot of the forest floor. Heart aflutter, he swallowed and pressed on.

If Amelia the Daring had turned back every time a branch snapped, she wouldn't have left her grounds, he thought fiercely. The thought of Amelia staring defiantly into the void spurred him on. He may not be a brave woman, but he was not a boy anymore, he was almost a man, and Prince at that. Shoulders back and head high, he lengthened his stride and quickened his pace. *It's just a bunch of trees and some water*, he told himself. Briefly his mind flitted to Master Marmaduke, and he tried to deny the wave of relief that came with knowing someone would come to look for him.

Twig torn and grass stained, he followed the river for the better part of the morning. Suddenly, the trees thinned, the sun shone down on him, the earth disappeared a few feet in front of him, and he was there. He had made it.

The Edge of the World.

The Cliff.

The separation between the Upper and Lower Realms.

He had seen portraits and tapestries decorated with images of the Cliff. He had skirted the edge with his mother many times on horseback. He had even climbed halfway up Court's Mountain with his friend Hector to see the drop more clearly. But never had he been this close. The dense forest bordering almost the entire edge was enough of a deterrent for most Upperite citizens.

If not the forest, then the possibility of the dizzying fall itself deterred the rest. Connor had never been explicitly forbidden to venture this close; it was just assumed he would not entertain the risk.

His palms tingling, Connor paused several yards from the edge. The river tumbled over the Cliff in a wild and endless stream. The sound of the waterfall was swallowed hundreds of yards below. Steeling himself, Connor placed his pack at the base of the nearest tree. He dropped down on his hands and knees to crawl as close as he dared toward the abyss. Creeping forward and dropping to his stomach, he eased himself toward the large oak tree whose roots seemed to hold this section of the Cliff together. He peered over the lip, holding fast to the tree's rough bark. Some of the roots dangled free of the earth like veins outside of a body.

Whoa.

Connor's eyes flicked down—down, down, and down—the steep Cliff face. Too vast to comprehend, it seemed to curve at the periphery of his vision. He fought a wave of vertigo, closed his eyes for a moment, and opened them to inspect the world below. He saw the waterfall pool into a lake, then flow into a river that meandered its way to a small town. He shifted his gaze toward the line of mountains on the horizon and saw fields, villages, and small patches of forest plotted and pieced and stretched out like a patchwork quilt. A true pied beauty.

Whoa.

He often forgot the world was so big.

Living in the palace, it was easy to forget that the vastness of the Upper Realm was tiny compared to the rolling fields and hills of the Lower Realm. He followed the various roads that cut their way around and across the rivers and marshland with his eyes and marveled at the imposing border of mountains that cut the Lower Realm off from all that lay beyond. He could not believe his mother ruled such a large Queendom. There were still many parts of the Upper Realm he had not been to, and he had only been to the Lower Realm once as a baby.

All he knew about the Lower Realm he had heard from attending his mother's meetings with the Council of Four. Four stern women who advised his mother and had advised her mother before her. The Council never had nice things to say about Lowrians. Words like "simple," "dirty," and "greedy" were used often.

He stayed that way, frozen on the edge, for a long time, reminding himself to breathe, frequently closing his eyes, and focusing on the feel of grass and dirt under his palms when the height became too much.

But Connor had come here for a reason. Pushing down another wave of vertigo, he retreated a few yards from the edge and eventually made his way back to his knapsack. Once there, he felt the tightness in his chest release.

He pulled out the small boat and unwrapped it from the kerchief. Bending down, he plucked a few blades of grass, straightened up, and let them fall in the breeze. The wind was perfect for this vessel's maiden voyage.

He checked the ship over again, testing the sails, resealing the hatch, and inspecting the hull for any abnormalities. Once he had deemed the boat was seaworthy, and taking a moment to wonder if this was where the term *shipshape* had come from, he walked over to the water's edge.

I should say a few words, he thought.

Feeling silly for a moment but realizing there was no one around to care, he cleared his throat, stood solemnly on the banks of the river, and began.

"May your flags fly and your riggings hold true. May the wind always be at your back, and may the stars guide your journey. You are the first expedition to seek the land below and . . . er. . . good luck." He paused, then emended: "Goddess be with you all, brave women and men." He nodded, saluted the imaginary crew, then gently placed the small wooden boat in the water and nudged it toward the middle of the river.

For a moment, Connor thought the boat had sunk. He lost sight of the vessel as the water climbed over itself to get to the edge first, eager to leap into the void. Then he saw a flash of red in an eddy, and suddenly, the edge rushed up to meet the little boat. It hung for just a moment, suspended above the chasm, then toppled out of sight.

Connor grinned broadly. Carefully, he crawled over to the Cliff's edge again, trying to catch another glimpse of the boat as it fell. He watched the waterfall until long after any chance of spotting the boat had passed, and he rolled onto his back, his heart light and his mind following the ship as it embarked on its great adventure. He may be trapped in his palace, but somewhere far below, his boat ventured into the unknown.

2

WORK AND WATERFALLS

Wood splintered. Sails ripped and were torn free of their eyelets and rigging. The deck lurched as the ship was thrown violently to starboard. Water raced the little vessel through the air. Droplets hardened and glanced off the hull as it gained momentum. Thicker rivers of water threatened to tear the ship apart. It tumbled and spun through the void, crossing the chasm between the two realms, and landed with a soft splash barely audible above the waterfall's roar far, far below.

The force of the falling water pummeled it to the riverbed. It rose and was pushed back down, the tumultuous current buffeting the ship from above.

Further downstream stood a quaint farm. Hunched over her desk in her room near the light of a flickering candle, a young inventor was elbow deep in her latest project. Tongue out, brows furrowed in concentration, she tied off the final strand of flax, careful not to distort the shape of the basket. Mr. Grimsby had been very clear about that: if one strand was too tight or too loose, the whole basket lost its integrity.

"Jacqueline! Breakfast!" her mother called from the kitchen. Jacs blinked. How long had she been sitting there? She stretched and felt a series of pops ripple from neck to back.

Long enough to finish, she thought, a satisfied smirk tugging at the corners of her mouth. Clambering to her feet, she allowed a moment for her left leg to wake as she called out, "Coming!" and smoothed her skirts. Her split work skirts were a couple inches too short; she'd had another growth spurt since turning thirteen a few months ago.

Placing her completed flax basket carefully next to its twin, she picked up her candle and followed its light to the kitchen. The rooster had long since heralded the new day, but it would be another hour or so before the sun's rays were expected to light the Lower Realm. Her fingers brushed the scroll of her father's well-loved fiddle perched next to the doorway as she entered the main room.

Her mother stood with her back to Jacs. Long dark hair fell in waves to her mid back, just brushing the bow of her apron. Her faded blue skirts were cut above the calf and split down the middle like her daughter's, ripped leggings peeking through from underneath. She moved about the kitchen on callused bare feet. Turning, she beamed at her daughter. Tension suddenly left her features, and her shoulders relaxed. Jacs gave her mother a peck on the cheek and a swift hug, then set the table before sitting down.

"Good morning, Mum," she said brightly.

"Good morning, Plum—mind, it's hot, here you go—one egg or two? Chores straight after breakfast; we have a bit to do now the rain has stopped. Might as well make hay while the sun's out." Her mother slipped two eggs onto Jacs's plate and placed the third on her own. She dropped the pan in the wash basin and picked up her wooden chopping board. Placing a fresh loaf of bread on top, she carried it over to the table. Jacs stood up, fetched the small stone bowl of salt from near the stove, and settled in her chair again.

"Are we doing the beans today?" Jacs asked as she cut off a piece of bread.

Her mother nodded. "The beans, then we'll till the skirret carrot patch for the second planting, but remember to milk Brindle first; you know how she gets."

Jacs made a face but then sat forward as an idea hit her. "Mum," she asked, "can I go down the river when I'm done? I promise I'll be safe."

Her mother frowned slightly. "What do you want to go to the river for?" she asked.

"I want to test out my new traps," Jacs said through a mouthful of bread. She swallowed and explained, "I was talking to Mr. Grimsby. He showed me this trick to weave the flax to make a basket that the fish swim into, but how the opening is designed means the fish can't get out again. If it works, we can have fish for dinner." Her green eyes sparkled, and as she spoke she wound a strand of auburn hair around her finger.

Her mother's face softened, "Of course, as long as you make sure you get everything done before you go." Jacs nodded, finished the last of her breakfast, and then hurried to clear the plates. She had work to do.

Brindle was as grumpy as always. Jacs had to coax her to the middle of the barn with a handful of hay. She had made the mistake of milking her within hoof distance of the butter churn once and it now had a cloven dent to prove it. Talking softly, Jacs stroked Brindle's side for a minute before setting to work. Brindle snorted indignantly and stomped a rear hoof but was relatively well-behaved throughout.

The mangy gray cat whom Jacs had named Ranger slunk in through the open barn door at the sound of the milk hitting the metal pail. He casually wound himself around the legs of Jacs's stool, nuzzling her ankles.

Jacs half-heartedly shooed him away. "This isn't for you," she teased. Ranger mewed, making Brindle snort again and swish her tail in annoyance.

"Careful, Ranger," she warned. "Remember last week? Your tail still has a kink in it." Apparently, Ranger did not remember last week, nor did he pay any mind to his kinked tail. Instead, he mewed again and began to wind himself around Brindle's hooves. Brindle snorted a third time, flicked her tail, and kicked. Jacs was just in time to snatch the pail up before Brindle kicked again, right where it had been a moment before. Ranger yowled and raced out the barn door. Jacs staggered backward, placed the milk on the wooden workbench, and quickly tried to calm Brindle down.

"Whoa girl, there you go, that's it," she said in a low voice and hummed a fragment of a melody her father used to play. Stroking the stubborn cow's neck, she looked around to see where Ranger had run off to.

"Hey!" she yelled as she spotted him on the bench lapping up the fresh milk from the pail. He looked at her, froth stuck to his furry chin, and began to purr.

Jacs rolled her eyes and grinned before waving him away. "Mum would have kittens if she saw you." Ranger flicked his kinked tail triumphantly before jumping to the floor and trotting out of sight.

Picking and shelling the beans took much longer than expected. The rows of beanstalks nodded and bowed gaily in the breeze, leaf tendrils tugging them back into line if they strayed too far from their posts. Jacs's family had the best bean crop around, not that it was anything to brag about. Jacs would have much preferred to have the best strawberry crop around. There was only so much one could do with beans.

When Jacs was younger, she used to lie amongst the rows and look up at the plants as they crept up their training posts. She would imagine climbing one all the way up to the clouds, or even just to the Upper Realm. Now she was much more practical: a bean plant would not hold Ranger's weight, let alone hers. She had read once that clouds were just water and dust, so climbing onto them was not an option either. The Upper Realm though—Jacs sighed as her eyes flicked toward the steep Cliff a short distance from the edge of her family's farm—now that would be an adventure.

The Cliff rose like a smooth, impossibly high wall that spanned left and right as far as Jacs could see in either direction. If Jacs craned her neck and squinted her eyes, she could just make out the top, and could barely see the odd tree hanging over the edge.

Jacs's fingers worked deftly shelling the beans, throwing the pods in one barrel and the beans in another.

I wonder what it would be like up there, she thought as she picked a new bean pod from her basket and slit the seam with her fingernail.

There was a saying, "In the Lower Realm, the sun arrives late and leaves early." Which, while it was used to gripe, was more of an actual fact. As the sun made its way across the sky from east to west every day, it remained hidden by the surrounding mountains long after the workday had started, shone happily as it reached its zenith, then began to slowly slide behind the other side of the Upper Realm. The Cliff and the mountains caused an extended twilight and a premature sunset. But, if she lived in the Upper Realm, she would have hours of extra daylight. If she lived in the Upper Realm, she'd get to see a real sunrise.

She looked up at the Cliff again, streaked here and there with thin waterfalls that misted the space around it. *Too steep to climb up*, she mused and looked enviously at the swallow flying in the updrafts near the rim.

Discard the shell, save the bean, grab the next.

The Cliff's not the way to go anyway, but the Bridge is as far-fetched as my beanstalk idea, she thought as she popped a freshly shelled bean into her mouth.

The Bridge was less of an actual bridge one would use to cross a stream or river and more of a winding, heavily guarded ramp spanning the distance from the Lower Realm to the Upper Realm at a steady gradient to allow the braver wagons and carriages to make the descent. The expanses of ramp were suspended by elaborate cables and anchors in the rock. It looked like a child's marble track when seen from far away, marking a long zigzag up the Cliff face. To get from a zig to a zag, there was a lift at each edge, controlled by a guard in a toll booth.

Jacs's father used to always say that the toll guards had the easiest job in the Queendom, but that it was no surprise no one wanted it. The hours were long, and even though it was womanned all year long, the Bridge was only used once a year during Trade Week and very rarely by the royal family during Descension celebrations. It had not always been so rare for people to travel between Realms, but free movement between the Realms had stopped long before Jacs was born.

Trade Week was always exciting; everyone dressed in their best to watch the carriages filled with gold as they traveled the Lower Realm. As Bridgeport was adjacent to the Bridge, its residents always saw the procession at the height of its splendor. Even more lavish and exciting were the royal Descensions, the last of which had been almost fifteen years ago to celebrate the birth of the Prince. Jacs had not yet been born, but the townsfolk still told stories of the glittering jeweled carriages and the Queen whose hair shone like the sun.

Jacs popped another bean into her mouth; she had imagined countless scenarios that saw her up the Bridge. Some daydreams involved her tricking the guards to let her up each level, others involved her sneaking into the Trade Week procession, but none extended beyond the brink of the Cliff and into the Upper Realm itself. Her imagination could never get that far.

She chewed thoughtfully and looked from her somehow still full basket to the small piles of beans at the bottom of the barrel. Jacs always seemed to forget just how many beanstalks they had, and how many beans that meant she needed to shell, so it was well past noon before she threw the last bean in the barrel and discarded the pod. Her fingers were red, and she had bean bits under each of her nails.

Her mother had joined her some time ago and now looked up from her own pile. She smiled as her daughter looked over to the carrot patch.

Stretching, her mother glanced up at the beautiful blue sky and remarked, "You know, it is Sunday after all, and I would hate for you to miss out on this day. Go test your traps, we can save the carrots for tomorrow."

Jacs happily wiped her hands on her skirts and hugged her mother. "Thanks, Mum, I'll catch you some fish!" She beamed and rushed inside to get her things before her mother could change her mind.

Jacs hummed to herself, her two freshly woven traps tapping against her thighs as she made her way along the dirt path down to the river. There were a number of waterfall-fed rivers that led away from the Upper Realm. Jacs knew the best one for fish. It was a smaller waterfall, much wispier than some of the others, but considering how far the water had to fall, it was probably much more impressive at the top. In the dry season, the water sometimes did not reach the Lower Realm at all; instead, it disappeared and evaporated as mist halfway down. Luckily, the dry season was not for another three months.

The river was slow moving, wide, and deep; the perfect spot for fish to laze in the sun nibbling the mosquitoes and water striders that spent too long on the surface. Jacs could see their shadows darting here and there. She spent a few minutes watching them before she determined the best places to set her traps. The riverbank was dotted with numerous sizes of boulders that created caves and passageways for the fish to swim in and out of. If she were a fish, that's where she would hide. Considering that for a moment, she selected an area that already had two fish darting around in it.

She double-checked each trap separately, going over her knots and inspecting the narrow openings. Then she placed one in the spot in the shallows, nestled in the rocks along the bank, and tied the rope around a boulder a little higher up. The other one she tied to a tree stump first, then threw it out into the middle of the river. It bobbed and dipped in the water before sinking to the bottom. With her hands on her hips, Jacs grinned. It had been a while since she had had fresh fish for dinner.

Her work done, Jacs turned and walked along the riverbank toward the waterfall, carefully stepping from rock to rock until she reached a particularly flat one. She took off her shoes, rolled her socks up, and tucked them away, then dipped her feet into the cool water. The sun had warmed the rock and the water, so both felt pleasant.

Jacs lowered her still red hands into the river and half-heartedly tried to rid her nails of bean residue. She tried to see if any fish were taking an interest in her traps, but her hands had sent ripples across the water's surface and made it difficult to see the world below.

A small brown bird scratched at the dirt on the opposite bank. Jacs watched as the bird pulled an especially fat worm out of the ground and gulped it down. Her eyes shifted past the bird to scan the bank; she was sure she had seen something flicker. A flash of sunlight glinting off a rock, or maybe a trick of light off the water. She stood up and shaded her eyes. There was something caught on the other side of the river.

"Good afternoon, Jacqueline!" a voice puffed behind her. Jolted from her investigation, Jacs spun around to see Master Bruna Leschi, the town's inventor and head architect, carrying a large ceramic pot in her arms. Master Leschi's black hair was pulled back in a loose bun and streaked through with gray. Unruly wisps of hair poked out like wires around her head. Her cheeks were flushed, and she had a piece of chalk behind her ear. She wore cream and burgundy skirts split as though for riding, and each side panel had several deep pockets sewn into it. Jacs could see various tools and oddities poking out from within the folds. She recognized a protractor, the handle of a paintbrush, and a thick leather-bound notebook. The end of a tape measure hung like a ribbon down to her knee. As her skirts billowed around her ankles, Jacs noticed the solid and scuffed toes of Master Leschi's work boots.

"Hello, Master Leschi, do you need a hand with that?" Jacs asked. She used the title with reverence. To be considered a master of any craft or vocation was a deep honor, but to be considered a master of invention . . . one could only dream.

The older woman smiled. "Actually, if you don't mind, dear, only I seem to have overestimated my strength and underestimated the weight of this blasted thing."

Jacs put her shoes back on and made her way over the rocks that lined the riverbank.

"I usually send my son Phillip—you know Phillip? He'd be a few years older than you—to fetch the water, I mean, he's growing up so fast, I might as well put his muscles to good use, but I was in the middle of an equation," Master Leschi continued as Jacs took up half the weight of the pot. Master Leschi grunted as the weight shifted. "I'm designing the new clock tower, you see—and I thought to myself, I must have water from the Upper Realm. Elevate my thinking. And then when I thought that, I couldn't think of anything else, so here I am." She shrugged her shoulders slightly despite the weight of the pot.

Jacs inhaled sharply. "Wow, you're designing the new clock tower! What will it look like? When do you start building it? How long will it take you? What's the equation for?" As she rattled off her questions, she helped Master Leschi lift the ceramic pot higher, and together they walked over to the base of the waterfall. They set the pot on a large, flat outcrop and let the water flow into it.

Master Leschi cocked her head to the side to listen as Jacs finished speaking, then thought for a moment in the silence that followed. Jacs worried that she had annoyed her, but then Master Leschi's green eyes snapped into focus as a broad smile spread across her lips.

She took the chalk out from behind her ear, looked around at the rocks, and declared, "Wonderful questions, I'll show you, shall I?" Apparently satisfied with a flat rock to Jacs's left, she turned her back on the pot and began to draw a rough clock tower.

"The clock tower itself will not stand much taller than the old one, but it will be much more long-lasting, I assure you; I've designed a metal conductor on the top spire here," she pointed, "that will have a grounding cable running down the side of the tower here," she traced the line, "this way we won't have the gears of the clock frying and the whole thing burning down like the last one if lightning chooses to strike again. I know they say 'never in the same spot twice' but I never got a source on who 'they' claim to be. 'They' also said the sun revolved around the world at one point, so I won't take my chances."

Jacs grinned as Master Leschi continued.

"Of course, I've been given some artistic license, so I intend to add my own flare, you know." She smiled again, and Jacs noticed she seemed to buzz with excitement. "You see, the last tower was so wide across with such a sad excuse for a roof. I intend to top the entire structure with a dome."

She paused, her chalk suspended above the large arc she had just drawn on the top of the tower. Almost absentmindedly she started filling in the dimensions and sketching out the tiling pattern.

"As for when we start building, and how long it will take, I'm not sure. I hope to have the working drawings finalized by the end of the month." Master Leschi said.

"And the equation you were working on?" Jacs asked excitedly.

"Oh, yes, well I'm having a bit of trouble with the domed roof. I want to build it without the use of scaffolds because the tower itself is quite tall and wide across, but I am stuck with how to do it. I want the dome to be self-supporting. There also seems to be a lot of other little factors to consider that even had me thinking, well, thatch and canvas didn't look too bad, in the wee hours of the morning. Luckily, I slapped my own wrist for that thought. Hence the need to elevate my thinking with some Upperite water." She waved vaguely to the now overflowing pot. Jacs nodded in bewildered agreement, although unsure how Upperite water was supposed to help.

The sound of the waterfall filled the silence between them. Jacs studied the chalk outline of the clock with the high domed roof for a long while. She extended her pointer finger and started tracing the dome outline, not noticing that Master Leschi had stopped her detailing to watch her. As her finger completed the arc, she thought aloud, "What if you built two domes, one inside the other?"

Master Leschi's eyes snapped back to the rough sketch. "What did you say, dear?" She breathed.

Jacs hesitated. "Well, I just meant that you could build two domes, one inside that could be the structure and the scaffold that the construction workers could sit on to build the outer, stronger, and more weatherproof one." She hadn't realized that she had plucked the chalk out of Master Leschi's hands and started adding her idea to the blueprint as she spoke.

She looked up at Master Leschi, who appeared to have stopped breathing, her eyes wide. Jacs looked down at the chalk, at her additions, and quickly thrust the chalk back into Master Leschi's hands. White dust clung to her fingertips, and she scrubbed them quickly on her skirts.

Apologetically, Jacs began to mumble, "It was just a thought, but—"

"You brilliant, brilliant child! Of course!" Master Leschi cupped Jacs's face in her hands. "And the interior dome could be lightweight and easy to construct. Now, we still have the problem of how to build that first dome, and how to distribute the weight while we're building, especially when the mortar is drying. Oh, but I've been experimenting with a new design for bricklaying . . . and, my dear girl—oh, you marvelous girl—how old are you?"

Jacs was caught off guard by the sudden change of topic. "Uhm . . . Thirteen, ma'am," she replied.

"Thirteen, what an age, the cusp of womanhood! And with such potential! Maria Tabart's daughter, yes? Your father was Francis? Lovely man. Pity, that." Jacs blinked at the unexpected mention of her father, but Master Leschi continued, "Thirteen, hmm. . . thirteen years old, you'd be starting to funnel into careers at school about now wouldn't you? Do you enjoy school?"

Jacs nodded and added, "Yes, and Master Tremain has been bringing in people to talk to us about the things we can do, but everyone just assumes I'll keep working on Mum's farm." Jacs hurried to hide the disappointment she felt and continued, "I don't get to go to class all the time, especially when Mum needs extra help for the harvest, but I like to read, and Master Tremain gives me extra work so I can keep up."

Master Leschi nodded and tapped her chin with the piece of chalk absentmindedly, leaving a small white smudge behind. She clicked her tongue and declared, "Jacqueline, I think I will have a word with your mother, but first, I won't just assume so I'll ask: Are you interested in all this?" She gestured at the sketch.

Jacs looked first at the drawing and then at Master Leschi, unsure of what she meant. "You mean, clocks?" she asked.

Master Leschi smiled. "Clocks, yes, and learning how things work, how things are built, how to put things together."

"Oh, yes . . . yes I am, ma'am. Very much."

"Perfect."

Master Leschi walked over to her pot, attempted to lift it, tipped a little bit of water out, then tried again with little more success. Jacs hurried over to help her.

"Perfect," Master Leschi repeated. "Then I will have a word with your mother. You have given me a lot to think about Jacqueline, it appears my search for enlightenment via Upperite water was brought to me instead via conversing with you. Thank you!"

Jacs did not know what to say. She realized too late that she had been staring with her mouth hanging open and gave her head a quick shake, "Wha—um . . . you're welc—thank *you*!"

Together they carried the pot away from the waterfall and toward Master Leschi's small wheelbarrow that Jacs had not noticed before. Master Leschi made sure that the pot was secure, then moved to the back of the wheelbarrow and picked up the handles.

She smiled at Jacs. "I expect you'll hear from me shortly, but until then, it has been a pleasure talking with you this afternoon, Jacqueline." She gave the wheelbarrow an experimental first push, then set off down the path. "Goodbye! And keep reading!" She called over her shoulder as Jacs waved and bid her farewell.

Jacs watched her disappear toward the town. *Talk to my mother?* she mused. Could she really need my help with the clock? Jacs's grin widened, and she allowed herself a moment to imagine working alongside a woman like Master Leschi.

Sighing contentedly, she turned back to the river. The sun was inching lower toward the crest of the Upper Realm. Jacs checked each of her traps on the off chance that a fish awaited her—nothing yet. She threw them back in the water, made sure each trap was securely fastened to its respective anchor, and made her way back home, her steps light and her smile wide. Her mind buzzed with thoughts of what tomorrow would bring.

3

TWO TYPES OF SHIPS

Jacs was crouching on the rocks at the base of the waterfall again. It was midmorning; the rooster had long since heralded the new day, but the sun was not yet up and the grass was silver with dew. Jacs blew into her cupped hands to warm them. She had been so excited that she had taken a break from her chores to check the traps. Bending over, she pulled the rope of the first trap. She watched the water ripple as it began to surface and float toward her across the river.

Hoisting it up on the rock next to her, she peered inside. A satisfied smile spread across her face. Two fat fish were flipping their tails feebly; she could see the shine of their scales through the trap's opening. Eagerly, Jacs moved to where the second trap was tied and began to pull it in.

She had the trap almost to the bank when the sun broke over the horizon and lit up the river with a flash. Jacs, startled, lifted her arms up to cover her eyes and dropped the rope. She fumbled to catch it, throwing herself off balance with her eyes still blinded. Flailing to right herself, she stepped forward, slipped on the dew-covered rocks, and landed with a painful splash in the freezing water.

Jacs yelped and scrambled to get back on the rocks. The water was shallow, and it was not moving quickly, but the shock of the cold brought with it the memory of her father's voice, "Get to the bank, I'm right behind you." She panicked and hauled herself out of the stream, shaking. Her heart was in her throat and she screwed her eyes shut tight. Breathe.

She stayed curled up on the rock until her heart rate and her breathing returned to normal. Slowly she opened her eyes and looked around, her second trap had floated off and disappeared down the river in the commotion. The first trap was waiting for her farther up the bank. She took another couple of deep breaths and focused her mind on the traps. One gone, one full. Not a total loss. She gave her head a shake, struggling to push the memory's residue away.

The sun stretched its rays across the sky innocently. Jacs stood up to make her way to the remaining trap when a familiar glinting on the opposite bank caught her eye. Squinting, she tried to make out what it was. There was definitely something there, bobbing among the rocks. Curious, and eager to distract herself, she looked for a way across the river. The bridge was all the way in town and she did not fancy taking that detour.

Jacs walked over to the waterfall. She judged the distance between the water and the Cliff face to be just big enough to fit behind. Carefully, she pressed herself against the rock and slid behind the falling water; the world beyond looked distorted through the veil. Had she been taller or wider, she would have gotten even wetter than she already was. For a moment she existed safely in a world of rushing water. Her ears filled with the sound, and everything else faded away. She closed her eyes and smiled at the cold pinpricks of mist dancing across her cheeks and forehead.

When Jacs made it to the opposite bank, she walked over to where she remembered the object to be and searched among the rocks. It did not take her long to find it. She lifted it from the water. It was a small, red, very battered wooden boat. She turned it over in her hands, marveling at the intricate rigging of the sail and the delicate details on the hull.

Jacs sat cross-legged on the ground as she inspected it. Despite the damage, the boat still shone as the water beaded and slid off the hull. Her fingers traced the outline of the little door on the top deck. She gingerly opened the latch and slid the door open. A little glass vial lay inside.

Excitedly, she tipped the vial onto her palm. *What a find!* she thought. She could not believe her luck—where had it come from? Looking around, her eyes followed the waterfall up, up, up to the very top of the Cliff.

No . . . could it?

Her eyes widened at the thought. It's from the Upper Realm! She went to open the vial, when she noticed the sun had risen higher in the sky.

She frowned. She hadn't meant to stay this long, and she didn't want her mother to worry. There was still a lot to do today.

Hurriedly, she tucked the vial into her pocket, clutched the boat to her chest, and headed back behind the waterfall. Grabbing the trap, she set off on a jog home.

"Where have you been?" Ms. Tabart spun around as Jacs entered the house, her mouth falling open at the sight of her sopping-wet daughter. "You're soaking wet!" Her eyes shifted from the trap in Jacs's hands to the boat tucked under her arm. "What have you been doing?" she asked, more curious than angry this time.

Jacs laughed sheepishly. "I went to check my traps and I fell in and lost one—I'm fine, I'm fine." Noticing the look on her mother's face, she hurried to add, "I caught two fish in this one!" She brandished the trap triumphantly. "And I found this little boat washed up on the rocks and I," she paused and said reverentially, "I think it came from the Upper Realm." She was so excited she did not notice her mother's expression shift from joy to doubt, but when her mother frowned and said nothing, she asked, "What?"

Ms. Tabart bit her lip and said, "Well Plum, I'm just not sure about the boat—are you sure it's from the Upper Realm?"

Now it was Jacs's turn to frown. "I'm not one hundred percent sure, I guess it could have been left by someone playing in the stream, but . . ." She turned the boat over in her hands again, looking at its battered hull. "I mean, it's been through the works, so I just thought it came over the waterfall. Plus," she added as an afterthought, "It's a lot fancier than what the kids in Bridgeport would play with."

Her mother looked thoughtful. "Well," she began, "I suppose the chances of its owner coming all the way down here to look for it are slim."

Jacs grinned. "So I can keep it?"

Her mother hesitated. "Yes. But just be careful who you show it to."

"Why?"

"Because, well, if it is from the Upper Realm, we just need to be careful, that's all," Ms. Tabart said. Jacs looked again at the harmless little boat and raised her eyebrows at her mother.

Jacs's mother sighed, and her gaze shifted past Jacs's shoulder and out the window. "Oh look!" she exclaimed. "The sun's up and we still have a lot to do today! Let's put one fish in the cold box and I'll fry up the fatter one for lunch."

Jacs knew her mother was changing the subject on purpose, but her stomach growled loudly and interrupted her follow-up question. Resolving to ask later, she did what she was told and helped her mother descale, gut, and fillet the fish.

Later that afternoon, while Jacs was tilling the soft, loamy soil in the carrot patch, Master Leschi came to call. Jacs watched as her odd little horseless cart trundled up the dirt road to their house. Master Leschi was well known in the town for having the most unusual-looking (but very practical) inventions.

This cart was no exception. It was the size of a small wagon and seemed to be a four-wheeled bicycle. The cart could have fit four people in total; Master Leschi sat on the right-hand side puffing and pedaling. Jacs would hope that the three possible passengers would have pedals too as it seemed to be a lot of work for just one person. Jacs's mother had been spreading fertilizer on the cabbage patch.

She stood up and shaded her eyes when she heard Master Leschi approach.

"Good afternoon, Ms. Tabart!" Master Leschi called as she approached. She pulled the cart up near the front of the house and stepped out. Jacs's mother had made her way over and held out a grubby hand for Master Leschi to shake; she took it unflinchingly.

"Good afternoon, Master Leschi, to what do we owe the pleasure?"

Jacs wiped her hands on her skirts and came to join the two older women at the front of the house.

"Hello, Master Leschi." She greeted her shyly. "It's nice to see you again."

"Likewise, Jacqueline," Master Leschi replied, then turned to Jacs's mother. "Ms. Tabart, I was hoping to have a word with you, if you're not too busy, about Jacqueline."

Ms. Tabart looked concerned. "I hope everything is okay?" Her eyes met Jacs's. "Have you been bothering Master Leschi?"

"No, no, no, dear, oh my, I believe I should have started this differently." Master Leschi intervened as Jacs opened her mouth to reply. "No, Jacqueline has done nothing to be concerned about. In fact, you must be proud of the fine young woman she is." Ms. Tabart beamed as Master Leschi continued. "No, I was hoping to discuss Jacqueline's future, or at least, an opportunity I would like to share with her."

Jacs's cheeks flushed with excitement as she looked eagerly from her mother to Master Leschi.

"Oh," her mother replied. "Well, of course. Would you like a cup of tea? We can sit outside. Plum, why don't you finish with the carrot patch while we talk?"

Indignation colored Jacs's cheeks. She opened her mouth to protest, but Master Leschi beat her to it. "Actually, Ms. Tabart, if you don't mind, I would like Jacqueline to join us. A girl must be on her own jury when her future is being discussed. I'll help you with the tea."

With that, she motioned for Ms. Tabart to lead the way and followed her into the house. The two older women chatted idly about the weather and the harvest. When the kettle boiled, Jacs helped carry the tea tray out to the yard.

The sun shone brightly overhead. Cicadas chirped lazily in the midday heat. The trio sat beneath an old, weathered apple tree on stools fashioned from stumps by Jacs's father. The tray was perched on a larger stump in the middle.

Ms. Tabart busied herself with the pouring and serving while Master Leschi tucked a strand of hair back into her bun and began with a businesslike tone. "Now, Ms. Tabart—may I call you Maria? I will insist you call me Bruna, so it's only fair." Ms. Tabart smiled and nodded as she handed a brimming cup to Master Leschi and settled on her stool with her own. Master Leschi continued. "Jacqueline may or may not have mentioned it, but we ran into each other yesterday, and she helped me reach an epiphany. Without her, I daresay, I would have resorted to drowning myself in that water-fall to—oh dear, no, I didn't mean, Maria, I—I do apologize."

At Master Leschi's words, Ms. Tabart had flinched and spilled tea down her front. She hastily waved away Master Leschi's horrified expression, and Jacs pushed a cloth from her pocket into her mother's hand. Ms. Tabart mopped the tea up hastily with a shaky laugh, which did not quite dispel the sadness in her eyes.

"Oh, Bruna, don't be silly, of course you—well—what were you saying about your epiphany?"

"Ah . . . yes . . . if you're—I mean . . . yes," Master Leschi stammered. Her brows furrowed, then softened at an encouraging nod from Ms. Tabart. Haltingly, she pressed on, despite not quite knowing what to do with her hands. "Like I was saying, your girl Jacqueline here really helped me out of a mental bind." As she gained momentum, the businesslike tone returned to her voice as she described her problem with the clock tower and Jacs's idea to make two domes to support the roof structure.

Ms. Tabart, eyes shining with pride at these words, listened and glanced back and forth between Master Leschi and Jacs. Finally she asked, "That does sound impressive. So then, what does this mean for Jacqueline?"

Master Leschi nodded. "Well, Jacqueline's contribution got me thinking. I do understand that she has a number of duties that I would not dream of pulling her away from here. However, if you'll allow, I would like to take Jacqueline on as my apprentice." Master Leschi let the words reverberate under the apple tree's canopy. Jacs's jaw dropped.

Ms. Tabart looked from her to Master Leschi again.

"But— she is only thirteen! Surely that's too young to—"

"Definitely not, thirteen is the perfect age. Most women her age are being filtered into occupations, trades, or the military already, and while her role here on the farm is a given, it's important our girls have options!" Master Leschi's eyes sparkled.

"And you'd take her on for, what? A few afternoons a week?"

"Well, that would be up to her schedule here, and her level of interest."

"So, she would be working with you on the clock?"

"Yes, mostly. I also have some side projects that we could work on together." Master Leschi turned to Jacs, who was following the conversation with rapt attention. "Jacqueline, you have been very quiet through all of this, I am not only asking your mother's permission, but also your opinion. Is this a path you would be interested in traveling?"

Jacs nodded her head vigorously. "Oh yes! Most definitely!" She turned to her mother. "I have some time in the afternoons, especially if I get my chores done in the morning, or if it rains." She twirled a strand of hair around her finger excitedly.

Master Leschi chuckled. "Perfect. What do you say, Maria? We can always try a month and see how it goes?"

Ms. Tabart looked thoughtful and bit her lip, torn between pride and worry. "This work, this apprenticeship . . . will it be dangerous at all?"

"Well, at the beginning at least, most of the work would be purely theoretical." Master Leschi said.

"And after the theory?"

Master Leschi smiled knowingly, "Maria, while I cannot protect Jacqueline from paper cuts and minor bruising, you have my word that any practical work will be as safe as I can make it, or not attempted at all."

Ms. Tabart still looked uncertain. Master Leschi took her hand and assured, "No harm will come to her that is within my power to prevent."

Ms. Tabart's next words were soft and seemed to follow each other hesitantly into the air. "Well, as long as she's safe, and it isn't affecting Jacqueline's chores, and she isn't too tired, I guess . . . I don't see why not. At least . . . a month's trial at first . . ."

Jacs jumped up and hugged her mother, almost knocking her backward off her stool. "Oh, thank you!" she breathed excitedly, then turned to Master Leschi. "When do I start?"

"When you have an afternoon free, come visit my workshop in town and we can work until suppertime." Master Leschi smoothed her apron and tucked another strand of unruly hair back into her bun. "Oh, this is a very exciting day, indeed it is!" She stood and shook Jacs's and Ms. Tabart's hands enthusiastically. "Now, before I go, we should discuss the subject of payment."

Jacs's eyes lit up and she asked, "I'll get paid?" Both older women laughed at the look of astonishment on her face. Suddenly the day seemed brighter, and she began to hope for a future beyond tilling carrot patches.

⚜

For the rest of the afternoon, Jacs felt lit up from the inside out. Her feet barely touched the ground as she skipped about the yard, floating like a sparrow in an updraft. The rest of her chores passed by in a golden whirl. Her hands were left to their own devices as her mind soared miles away to a world of clocks, domes, and machines that clicked and buzzed.

Her mother had hugged her tightly after Master Leschi had left and mused. "My girl, an apprentice!"

The word kept flitting around between Jacs's ears, becoming more and more impressive until she imagined it had left an imprint on her forehead.

It was not until Jacs had changed for bed and tossed her clothes from the day in the wash basket that she remembered the boat and the message in the bottle. Hungrily, she retrieved both items and lit a candle. Careful not to drip wax on herself or her bedsheets, she slowly eased herself into bed.

Pulling her bedcovers around her, she brought the candle closer and looked at each item. She looked at the boat first; the sail was the worse for wear. It was ripped almost in half, and the water had damaged most of it. She could see the care taken in its construction despite the damage. Little eyelets had been hammered into the boom at intervals and the sail had been threaded through each one and pulled tight. The details on the hull were equally intricate. Candlelight danced and flickered to caress each brush stroke as she admired the little ship. Her eyes shifted to the small bottle, and she placed the boat to float in the folds of her blankets.

Jacs turned the vial over in her hands, the tightly rolled note shifting slightly with the movement, and heard a faint clink against the glass. A gold ring held the note. The top of the vial was stoppered in a rich, red wax. Her heart fluttered with excitement. She suddenly felt shy, as if she had stumbled upon someone's diary.

Tentatively, she ran her finger around the top of the bottle to break the wax seal. It flaked off in a large chunk that she gently set on her bedside table. Slowly tilting the vial, she gave it a little shake, and the roll of parchment fell into her outstretched palm.

Setting the vial on her bedside next to the circle of wax, she carefully slid the ring off the tightly rolled note. She tested the ring on each of her fingers until it slid snugly on her pointer finger. Smiling and angling it so the gold caught the candlelight, she studied the engraving. It was magnificent. A coat of arms unlike one she had ever seen at school: a Griffin proudly prancing in the wind.

She had never seen a Griffin except in books. Most Lowrians agreed that they lived in the highest peaks of the Upper Realm's mountains, well above anywhere Jacs could ever reach. Her heartbeat quickened, maybe it was from a Dame in the Upper Realm.

She must be important to have a Griffin on her coat of arms. She had a brief vision of climbing the Bridge and presenting the boat to a distressed young noble while the noble's mother, Lord of somewhere, pushed bulging velvet coin purses into Jacs's arms in gratitude.

Jacs picked up the parchment. Licking her lips, she slowly unfurled the little roll of paper. It crinkled softly in the still night. Angling the letter under the light of the candle, she read:

To the Great Unknown,

If you are reading this, it means my first scouting voyage was successful. I wish I could be talking to you in person, but as Amelia the Daring always says, never leap into the void until you are sure of a safe landing. I live in the palace, and I want to know everything about the land below the clouds. What do you do for work? What do you do for fun? Where do you live? Are your houses like ours? Do you know what our houses look like? Do you even live in houses? How much do you know about us? Mother says you are just like us, but then why restrict Descension and Ascension? Most Upperites, even my teachers, don't talk about the Lower Realm much, and you can only learn so much from books.

I hope to find the answers one day, and when I do, I hope to have a friend to help me find what I am looking for. I have included a token of my friendship and hope that you wear this always so that I may know you when I find you.

Until that day, I am,

Your friend,
Connor
Voyage 1

Jacs looked at the ring again. It shone in the candlelight. She turned it this way and that, watching it glitter, then frowned as she noticed the contrast of the immaculate gold ring and her dirt-encrusted nails. *Wear this always so that I may know you when I find you*; it would not last two minutes during the strain and stain from her chores, let alone however long it took for Connor to find her.

Jacs glanced around the room and spotted an unused length of leather cord from one of her earlier fish trap prototypes hanging from a hook near her desk. Leather, she had discovered, stretched and was not a very effective fish prison when wet, whereas woven flax had proven to be much stronger underwater. Rising from the bed, she measured out a length, found her knife among her other tools and projects, cut the cord, and threaded the ring onto it.

Satisfied, Jacs tied the end and looped the necklace over her head. The ring fell to rest on her breastbone and was easily tucked under her shirt collar. It felt warm where it touched her skin. She settled back into bed and examined the engraving again as her mind whirled. A boy from the Upper Realm who lived in the palace, and she was his point of contact. She was his friend. She looked at the boat, beautifully crafted; she looked at the message. She thought of the boy sitting at the top of the Cliff, looking far below, desperate for answers. The candlelight danced in her eyes as an idea began to form. She would not let him down.

4

A TREAT OF A LESSON

"Cornelius!"

Connor froze as a voice boomed down the hall, heralding his father's arrival. He had just finished helping Hector into one of the suits of antique armor that flanked either side of the passage and had been in the process of deciding which one he wanted to occupy. He jumped back guiltily with a nervous glance at the suit that held Hector.

The visor squeaked slightly as the other boy slid it open a crack. Connor shook his head vigorously and made a shushing gesture with his finger before spinning around. He heard the visor squeak shut as his father rounded the corner.

Although Connor thought he had assumed a "natural" pose, his father smiled broadly upon seeing him. "At ease, soldier. Good grief, my boy, you look like a cornered hare." The hall rang with the boom of his laugh and Connor exhaled; smiling sheepishly, he looked at his father. King Aren. The man cut an imposing figure. Tall and broad shouldered, he towered over most occupants of Queen Ariel's council chamber. His brown hair was flecked with gray and the creases around his eyes mapped the life of one accustomed to laughter and pain in equal shares. He was a man who knew what it was to toast a friend's engagement in the morning and speak at her funeral that evening.

Today he wore his leather riding boots and a deep blue cloak. His gray-and-navy tunic, gray pants, and soft leather gloves were simple, yet Connor knew that his father could make a curtain look like a vestment of state. As always, he had the Royal Advisor's seal pinned over his heart. A silver ring encircling a crossed sword and feather.

"Good afternoon, Father," Connor said. "Have you been looking for me?"

His father clasped his gloved hands together and bounced on the balls of his feet. "Not for too long, no, but I'm glad I found you with your nose out of trouble today. A Prince must lead by example."

Connor sighed inwardly but his face remained impassive. For the past two years, his father had taken to lecturing Connor about the roles and responsibilities of a Prince. No doubt at the urging of his mother, but at least her lessons always slipped in naturally. His heart sank. Which lecture would it be today?

His father had taken to reprimanding unprincely behavior and then spinning a life lesson out of it. So far this week, his father had not considered it princely behavior to use pumpkins in the vegetable garden as target practice and had made him apologize to Master Borage, the head gardener, as well as retrieve and mend all the arrows he had used.

His father had also not considered it princely behavior to spend time "bothering the cooks" or "gossiping with the serving women," and had made Connor sit in on boring Council meetings and take notes on the discourse he observed.

Connor thought about the little boat he had sent out on its voyage earlier that week . . . but his father couldn't know about that.

King Aren continued, "I hoped to find you before you disappeared. Walk with me." He motioned for Connor to fall into step beside him and set off down the corridor. Connor glanced at the suit of armor again, thinking of poor Hector. No doubt his friend would be stuck there until he could return.

Quickly he began, "Father, may I catch up with you in a moment, only . . ."

"Don't fret, m'boy, I'll send Alastor along to help the poor lad out. Is it Lordson Hector or Brutus in there today?" His father had not paused or looked back as he spoke, and Connor jogged to catch up with him.

"It's Hector."

"I should have guessed; Brutus would have learned his lesson from the last time. His mother, Lord Lemmington, was very displeased to have him come home late and in such a tattered state. He missed his cousin's arrival from Bregend you know," King Aren said mildly.

Connor did not reply; he had heard this story twice already. Instead he changed the subject. "Where are we going, Father?"

"We're meeting with your mother and going for a ride," King Aren replied.

They had turned toward the dining room, where Alastor had just emerged with a pair of candlesticks. Upon seeing his King, Alastor took up a position next to the doorway with his head bowed. "Good morning, Majesty."

King Aren eyed the candlesticks and beamed. "Good morning, Alastor. It's illuminating to see you!" King Aren boomed a laugh and the corners of Alastor's mouth twitched slightly. "Ah, Alastor, the day I make you laugh will be a very jolly day indeed." He chortled and scratched his cheek. "You're just the man I had hoped to find. In the Fallstaff corridor, you'll find Lord Barnaby's boy in a suit of armor. See to it that he is extracted and given some refreshments. I'm afraid I have whisked away his playmate and his helper today so whatever you can do to make him comfortable and help him find his way home . . ."

Alastor bobbed his understanding. "Of course, Your Majesty," and went to relieve himself of his candlesticks.

King Aren turned and set off down the hall. Connor walked beside him without being asked again. The King looked down at him thoughtfully and said, "You commissioned a signet ring from Master Aestos." It was not a question. "He was very impressed by your initiative and praised your design for your own coat of arms."

Connor felt panic flood into his chest like ice water. He had a vision of the little boat disappearing over the Clifftop.

His father noted the pallor creep across Connor's visage and the proud grin that had begun to spread across his own face hesitated and faltered. "I had hoped to see it for myself," King Aren continued, puzzled. "A prince should have his own coat of arms but . . . it appears to be causing you some anxiety."

Connor gulped and stole a glance at his father, though he could not meet his eyes for long. They had stopped and King Aren waited expectantly.

Connor did not know what to tell him, but he did know he could not tell him he had knowingly sent the ring off the Cliff.

"Well . . ." Connor began in a croak. He cleared his throat and continued, "um . . . it was beautiful and I . . . I couldn't have thought of a better picture . . . but . . . I . . . er . . . I lost it." He studied a spot on the floor in front of him while he waited for a reply.

There was a cold silence that spread like an ocean between them. King Aren shook his head sadly. "You lost it?"

"Yes."

"Son, to my knowledge, you would have had that ring in your possession for at most three days. It is an incredible act of disrespect to a man who loves you and who is proud to serve you to so callously misplace his work of considerable effort and skill." King Aren sighed and pinched the bridge of his nose. "You will go to him this afternoon and apologize, and you will not be so careless in the future. Are we clear?"

Connor hung his head even lower and felt the blood rush to his cheeks at the thought of telling Master Aestos the fate of his work. "Yes, Father," he mumbled. They walked the rest of the way to the stables in stony silence.

Queen Ariel was waiting for them. She was standing beside her palomino mare, feeding it slices of apple from her gloved hand. Her hair hung in a long intricate plait down her back and shone gold in the sunlight. Even feeding her mare, she held herself with the easy grace and assurance of one used to commanding a Queendom. It was often said of the Queen that she was radiant like the sun's rays and quick to incinerate any who threatened her people.

The Queen turned at the sound of King Aren's and Connor's footfalls across the gravel yard and her face lit up. Her blue eyes sparkled and put the sky blue of her riding habit to shame. She wore soft leather boots to match her gloves; she raised one of the latter in greeting as they approached.

"My Queen, you are a vision." King Aren brightened immediately and swept her into his arms. She laughed and batted him away half-heartedly while reciprocating his kiss. Connor looked away and winked at Edith, his valet who was waiting off to the side with a change of clothes for him. She grinned, dimples deepening in her cheeks, and eyed the royal couple wistfully.

"Good morning, you two," his mother laughed. "Cornelius, hurry and change and we can be off."

Connor followed Edith toward the dressing room at the rear of the stables. The stables were alive today; he spotted three stable hands bustling about with bridles and saddles, two mucking out the stalls, and two laboring under large oat sacks to replenish the empty troughs. He breathed in deeply as the smell of hay, horse, and the sharp scent of ammonia filled his nostrils.

It was a perfect day for a ride. The Queendom had been blessed for several weeks with perfect weather, odd for this time of year, but Connor did not mind. He turned to Edith. She was one of the attendants he got on with best; she was closer to him in age and always feigned ignorance when he snuck out for an adventure.

He muttered quietly, "Father found out I lost the ring."

She whistled low. "No wonder he came across the yard like a thundercloud. How did you lose it?"

Connor hesitated. "It's a long story."

Edith shrugged. "It always is with you. Well, I hope you aren't in too much trouble?"

"Not as bad as the time with the pigpen." Edith stifled a laugh as he continued, "But I'll be hearing about it for longer than the time I dented the armor, I think." Connor sighed and eyed the bundle of clothes in her arms. They had arrived at the dressing room and she opened the door for him.

"Where are we going today, do you know?" Connor asked her as he stepped inside.

"I heard the Queen mention a ride along the Cliffside. You are to be followed by a small escort too, so this is not going to be a public trip."

Connor frowned thoughtfully, accepted the bundle of clothes and closed the door behind him to change. The room was simple—wooden floors, wooden walls, and a small vanity and chair with a brush, a wash basin and towel, and some bottles of different fragrances. He looked at his reflection in the mirror. His blue eyes, so like his mother's, scanned the freckles on his nose and his mess of brown hair. He used a bit of water to try and tidy his hair. A small escort usually meant only two guard pairs, which, if he was lucky, meant Iliana Dryft might be one of the women in armor today. Maybe this time he'd have the courage to say more than hello to her. Either way, he wanted to look mature, dignified, and not like he'd been goofing around like a child all morning.

He grimaced. *A prince always presents himself in a manner that puts others at once at ease and on their guard.* His father's recent lecture came to mind, unbidden. It seemed it was never a straightforward thing to be a prince. He shrugged and began to dress, pulling on his tan riding pants and deep blue riding tunic. The trim was gold and he marveled at the way the tailor had put such intricate detailing on an outfit that was made to appear simple. He wrapped and tied a brown leather belt around his waist, taking time to make sure the woven pattern faced the right way. Last, he pulled on his boots and gloves, flexing his fingers, and clasped a light cloak around his shoulders. Appraising himself again in the mirror, he ran the brush through his now damp hair and headed out to where Edith was waiting for him.

Her eyes caught his carefully belted tunic and styled hair, and she grinned.

"Hoping Iliana comes to save you today, Your Grace?" she teased, taking the bundle of clothes he thrust at her.

Connor glowered. "None of your business, Edith," he said.

She just laughed. "You know she's much too old for you, and I won't be the one to say I told you so when she breaks your heart."

Connor waved her away, not deigning to respond to her comment.

Edith called after him, laughter in her voice. "Have a lovely day, Your Grace."

He rolled his eyes, a smile crinkling their corners, and strode back to the yard where his father and mother were waiting next to their horses. His father stroked the neck of a large blue roan mare with black mane and tail.

At Connor's approach the Queen and King swept themselves up onto their mounts' backs.

Connor spotted his chestnut filly, Zenith. Her coat was freshly brushed and shone red in the sun. His saddle beckoned and Master Boreas, the Head Groom, crouched low and offered his clasped and cupped hands to help him up onto her back. Once Connor had settled into the saddle, he looked around, noting the four guards kitted and armored, waiting for orders. Each woman wore a uniform designed for mobility and speed: light armor, a glinting dagger, and leather strap at the belt. It was said the less a woman had to unsheathe her dagger, the better she was as a fighter. Masterchiv Cassida Rathbone, captain of the Queensguard, wore a sword at her belt that had only ever been unsheathed twice.

Connor eyed each of the guards casually. To his delight and horror, he noticed Iliana Dryft in the ranks of the four women accompanying them today, her long black hair tied in a simple tail down her back. He swallowed and quickly averted his gaze.

Their saddlebags were laden with gear and, Connor hoped, lunch. At a nod from the Queen, the party set off as one, a guard pair in front and a guard pair behind. Iliana nodded formally to Connor as she passed him to bring up the rear. Smiling weakly, Connor kicked his filly to follow slightly behind his parents' steeds.

The birds chirped lazily in the midmorning heat, Connor swatted the occasional fly away as it buzzed near his ear. His parents were talking quietly together. Connor hoped it was not about the ring, but the way his mother looked over her shoulder at him made his stomach sink to the saddle. The horses clip-clopped across the gravel of the stable yard and down a cobble road until they reached a dirt trail winding toward the gardens and beyond, toward the Cliff face.

The guards had obviously been briefed on the day's route, as they chose each path with purpose and without turning to verify with the Queen. They traced a similar route to the Cliff as Connor had followed earlier that week with his boat. As his heart rate began to increase, he scolded himself for being paranoid. There was no way anyone but he knew what had happened that day, and even if they did find out, it was not illegal to make contact with the Lower Realm. Or, at least, he had never been told it was.

Even so, Connor sighed in relief when they rode across the stream he had followed to the Cliff edge, and left it behind them as they continued through the trees. The King laughed raucously at a comment the Queen made and roused Connor from his musings.

"Mother," he called, "where are we going today?"

His mother allowed her mare to fall back so that she could ride abreast with Connor. "What, your father never told you?"

Ahead of them, the King simply shrugged. "He never asked."

She rested a gloved hand on the pommel of her saddle. "Well, Cornelius, you've been very patient waiting for this long. Today we have a bit of a treat for you."

"Treat or lesson?" Connor asked simply.

Queen Ariel laughed. "My sweet son, the sooner you learn that life is an endless lesson, the better." She tilted her head to the side and looked at Connor until he looked away. "How about we settle for a treat of a lesson? I promise that you will laugh at least twice today."

Connor grinned. "Deal. So, what's the treat-lesson?"

"I think it better if we show you. You know I'm one for dramatics." With that, she reared her horse and began galloping away, ahead of the guards and the King, who clamored to keep up. Connor laughed and spurred Zenith to follow. The Queen called over her shoulder, "There's one!"

Queen Ariel finally allowed her horse to slow once they emerged through the trees to a large clearing on the edge of the Cliff. "Easy, Quinn, that's my girl," she murmured into the mare's ear.

"Whoa, Aster!" The King's voice reverberated through the clearing, seeming to echo off the large boulders that outlined its perimeter. Aster and her rider came to a jolting halt; she flicked her head and nickered. Connor's filly had begun to slow to a trot as they cleared the trees and he pulled gently on her reins, walking her to stand beside his mother.

They all dismounted and handed their reins to the awaiting guards, two of whom collected them and set about tying them up to graze while the other two began laying a blanket and setting out a picnic lunch.

There was a selection of fruits, meats, cheeses, and some crusty bread, all of which made Connor's stomach growl in anticipation. He was glad to see Master Marmaduke had included extra fruit tarts for him.

Once the guards had finished preparing the lunch for the royal family, Connor saw his mother retrieve four parcels from her saddlebags. He walked over to join her and she handed him two to give to the guard pair. He felt butterflies twitching in his stomach as he approached Iliana and the other woman who had tied up the horses. Iliana thanked him with a radiant smile. For a moment, Connor just stared until he realized he was staring and tried to say something impressive, only to find his mind had gone completely blank. Suddenly too shy to look her in the eye, he fought for a response. Not able to settle between "you're welcome" and "my pleasure," he stuttered, "You're pleasure—my welcome."

Mortified, he handed the second woman her parcel without a word and retreated. He felt his cheeks burn and noticed the guards share a look with each other, but they were kind enough to keep their thoughts to themselves.

The guards then walked to the edge of the meadow and positioned themselves at evenly spaced points in a half circle where the trees met the clearing. Connor continued to watch Iliana from the corner of his eye. She sat with her back to the clearing under a large oak tree and opened the parcel she had received. It was a packed lunch.

That was definitely more words than just hello, he thought glumly.

"Cornelius?" his father beckoned from where he sat on the blanket. "I can't be responsible for you missing the fruit tarts if you aren't here to defend them, m'boy," and he licked the remnants of custard off his thumb.

"Hey!" Connor called indignantly and hurried to join his parents.

They ate, for the most part, in silence that spoke to how delicious the meal was more than any remaining tension between father and son. For this Connor was grateful. He helped himself to another roll and began filling it with cheese and slices of meat, when his mother leaned back, dusted crumbs from her hands, and asked, "How much do you know about the Upper and the Lower Realms?"

Connor paused, laden roll halfway to his open mouth, and struggled to organize a coherent answer. She waited patiently and he knew from experience she could wait all day for a response. "Er . . ." he began. "Well, I know what Master Clio has told me in my lessons. I know that the Bridge is our only connection to the Lower Realm." *And the waterfalls*, he mused before continuing. "I know that the last time there was a Grand Descension was when I was born, and the last time there was an Ascension was . . . er . . . well, actually I don't know that. But even longer ago. And I know that the Upper Realm is where we live and where other noble families and . . . and there are cities and towns and farms in the Upper Realm. . . and I assume there are cities in the Lower Realm. And . . . er . . . sometimes it rains in the Lower but not in the Upper because I see the tops of the clouds, but they don't make it here . . ."

His mother let him ramble himself into silence and he finished somewhat lamely under her steady gaze. The truth was, he really knew nothing about the Lower Realm. He did not even know if it was part of their Queendom or if it had a different set of royalty.

"Well, it appears most of your information is based on observation rather than teachings— a fact that I will have to talk to Master Clio about. It appears her history lessons could do with some padding," Queen Ariel remarked dryly.

"No—no, mother, her lessons are . . . I know lots of history . . . I know about the Centennial Feud and how Queen Frea the third helped bring peace to the Upper Realm." He tried to list the Queens backward in his head, sticking his tongue out in concentration. "I think Queen Frea the third was Queen two Queens before you."

"You're right. Do you know how long the Centennial Feud lasted?" his mother asked.

Connor smiled, "One hundred years."

She nodded and smoothed out a wrinkle in the blanket. "And do you know how Queen Frea the third ended the Centennial Feud?" she asked.

Connor thought for a moment, then answered, "Was it something to do with the bridges?"

Again the Queen nodded, then explained, "During the Centennial Feud, there were five bridges between the Upper and Lower Realms. Trade between the two lands was frequent, and hostility between the two lands was constant. The Lowrians viewed those who lived in the Upper Realm to be arrogant, spoiled, and exploitative. The Upperites viewed those who lived in the Lower Realm as dishonest, greedy, and lazy."

"Rooted in truth, that one," the King said under his breath. Queen Ariel shot him a look and he busied himself with a piece of cheese.

"Many deaths occurred on the bridges," she continued, "and many fights resolved outside of the law created unrest in villages and towns throughout both lands. Guards kept making mistakes, citizens were wrongfully imprisoned, or worse, and the people were losing faith in their authority. The body count kept increasing and no one knew who to blame."

"So, it was a war?" Connor asked.

"No. There was never an outright battle. The bridges made it impractical to send troops up or down as the toll keepers could destroy the bridge at any point. The toll keepers, or toll guards, as they're known now, were employed from both Upper and Lower Realms to ensure that no one land had sole control of a bridge. They were also trained to destroy the bridge if any threat arose to either of the two lands," Queen Ariel explained.

Connor thought about this and shuddered. That was a long way to fall. He thought about the one remaining bridge. "Wait, then what happened to the four other bridges?"

"All destroyed," his mother replied, "and access to the one remaining bridge is severely restricted. There is now no toll to collect. Only express permission given by the Queen allows Ascension or Descension."

"Why?" Connor asked.

"Queen Frea the third believed that it was the 'tasting of greener pastures' that was the reason such animosity grew between the two lands." At the look of confusion on Connor's face, the Queen picked up two fruit tarts. "Say you have this fruit tart," she said, handed the tart to Connor, and held the other in her own hand. "You like fruit tarts." she stated.

"Yes," he said.

"Are you happy with your tart?" she asked.

". . . Yes?" He hesitated, his eyes darting to his mother's.

"But you're looking at my fruit tart," she pointed out simply.

"Yes."

"So even though you have a fruit tart, you are looking at mine—why?"

Connor understood; he answered honestly. "I was counting the strawberries. I wanted to make sure yours didn't have more."

Queen Ariel smiled, his father chuckled from where he had been watching the exchange and shook his head.

"You were envying my strawberries. Upperites envied the sprawling space and simplicity of the Lowrian villages; Lowrians envied the affluence of the Upperite cities. Whatever it was, the frequent visits apparently only made their avarice grow."

Connor began to nod, paused, then asked, "Avarice?"

"Envy, like jealousy."

"Oh . . . so then, by taking away the ability to visit, people didn't know what they were missing out on, and everyone was happy again?" Connor asked.

His mother smiled and brushed his hair away from his face. "For the most part, yes," she said.

"You're Queen of the Lower Realm too, how do you rule the Lower Realm if you barely ever go there?"

"Good question! Yes. I rule the Upper and the Lower Realms, however, the villages and towns in the Lower Realm are ruled by their own mayors and governors. They are a part of the Queendom but are free to make their own policies and laws that are relevant to their people. As long as they do not contradict the ruling values that were outlined by Queen Frea the third during the Great Divide—when the two lands were officially separated and the four bridges destroyed," she clarified.

"And you rule all of it by yourself?" Connor asked in a soft, awed voice.

Queen Ariel took a delicate bite out of her fruit tart before replying, "Not all by myself. I have your father to advise me, and of course the Council of Four."

Connor thought of the four stern women he often saw seated below his mother in the throne room, or on either side of her in the council chambers. "If father advises you, what does the Council do?" he asked.

"Well, they advise me too. It's always important to draw information from a variety of sources. Otherwise your knowledge and practices become rigid and stale. The Council of Four specialize in the traditions, policy, and cultural heritage of the Queendom. They advise me in a way that helps me maintain the integrity of our Queendom and ensures our ways continue on. They are also in charge of the Queendom's finances and have roles in the military."

Connor nodded, thinking. He asked, "So if you barely go to the Lower Realm, what's to stop them from finding their own Queen?"

At Connor's words, his father stiffened, and his mother blinked as though she had been slapped.

She put a hand on his father's knee as he opened his mouth to reply, and he closed it again. Connor felt the back of his neck grow hot; he had not realized the treason of his words until they fluttered boastfully around the clearing.

His mother smiled again, although sadly this time. "Gold," she replied simply. "There are no gold sources in the Lower Realm at all. We have it all, and they need it. So we have a situation where, as long as we rule fairly and do not presume to meddle in their ways of life, they do not appear to mind falling under our banners and attending our ceremonial processions. Once yearly, a shipment of gold is distributed to the various cities and villages in exchange for a percentage of their harvest, livestock, and minerals, like salt."

Connor could sense that there was more to the situation than she was letting on, but he liked the tidy bundle of information she had presented him with.

"No gold sources at all?" He racked his brain: surely Master Clio had mentioned where Griffins live. He couldn't remember her saying they had homes in the Lower Realm. Scratching his chin absently, he commented, "I didn't know we were the only ones with Griffins, but I guess that makes sense, I mean Lowrians could just fly on up if they had a . . . flock? . . . a herd? . . . a . . . pride? . . . What's a group of Griffins called?"

"A Court," his father answered automatically.

"A Court— oh, like *the* Court. Well, if they could just fly up on a Court of Griffins, the Bridge restriction wouldn't matter," Connor said.

"You're right," replied his mother. "And that's assuming a Griffin would ever let a human on its back. That feat has only happened a handful of times in recorded history. It's enough that they deign to share their golden eggshells with us, and that is only because they have no use for them," Queen Ariel paused, then changed the subject. "But we've steered very far off course," she said. "Come with me."

As she spoke, she stood up and held out her hand to help Connor to his feet. His father did not appear to need to follow and contented himself with eating the untouched roll Connor had prepared earlier. Mother and son walked over to the edge of the Cliff and stopped at the point where the updraft coming from the Cliff face began to ruffle their cloaks.

His mother stood for a time surveying the expanse of land laid out below, taking in the rolling hills, the viridian forests, and noting the sprawling villages dotted around the lakes, rivers, and bogs.

From up here, with the enclosing mountains, the Lower Realm looked like a big basin. She closed her eyes, inhaled deeply, and opened them again upon her exhale. Connor did not know why but he did the same.

Without looking at him, Queen Ariel affirmed, "I know you have noticed your father and I have increased our interest in your education."

Connor nodded. "Yes, I noticed," he said.

His mother chose to ignore the tone of his voice and continued, "You need to understand that these lessons are to prepare you for the life you are destined to lead. You also need to understand that we will not always be around to teach them."

Connor looked up at his mother sharply, but her face betrayed nothing.

"Our land and our people are our most important priority, sometimes at the sacrifice of our own lives, and certainly at the sacrifice of our own wants and desires. We must rule with strength and have the wisdom to understand when we need to be gentle. We must rule with intelligence, even in the face of peril. We cannot afford to indulge in a base flight or fight response because this response is rooted solely in self-preservation. We must always respond consciously and with the fate of our people at the forefront of our minds.

"You know more than anyone that, as I did not have a daughter who could have taken my place on the throne, you play an important role in the selection of our next Queen. I was born and raised to be Queen, I bested the Contest of Daughter-Heirs designed by the Council to prove my worth as future ruler, and I was lucky to find in your father my second half. If you are fortunate, in the next selection you will also find your match. A woman whose heart beats with yours and one who you will support to rule as an extension of her own thoughts. If not, you will be expected to serve as chief advisor to the Queen and she will be free to marry whichever woman or man she deems worthy. Either way, you will be her partner and will help her carry the burden of ruling.

"When the Contest of Queens reveals my successor, you will be expected to stand beside her as your father now stands beside me. Your training and experience under my teachings make you an invaluable asset to whomever takes my place.

"So, my sweet Prince——" she turned to him then and smiled "——spread out before you and stretching out behind you is your future. Both the Lower and Upper Realms will be your Queendom. If this thought does not terrify you, it will. And if it does, good. It is a responsibility that will consume you if you let it. You have a difficult task ahead of you, but I can promise you it is worth every moment." She turned to look again across the Realm.

Connor looked as well, now through her eyes, and the sun illuminated the far reaches of the Queendom as though the land were made of light, each hill a glistening emerald, each lake a sapphire. The jewels of his inheritance nestled in the impenetrable walls of the surrounding mountains.

A treasure trove so precious, it took his breath away. He bowed his head, humbled.

How could he be worthy of such riches?

His mother, as though guessing his thoughts, continued, "It will take time, and you may never stop doubting yourself. But beware, self-doubt does nothing for the people you are sworn to serve. You must believe in yourself, and others will too. And remember——" she drew him into a hug, her chin just resting on the top of his head "——you are only fourteen. You will learn much of this in time."

He laughed with a relief he could not hide from her and she grinned mischievously. "And there's the second. I told you you'd laugh at least twice today."

5

FIGHT OR FLIGHT

Jacs dragged her feet slightly as she walked the dirt road toward the schoolhouse. She was engrossed in *The Rise of the Fallen*, a novel about Icara Daidala, a Lowrian orphan girl who discovers she is the daughter of an Upperite noble and ventures up the Bridge to find her family. She had read the book twice before and knew that Icara never completed her journey. She is injured near the top of the Bridge and rescued by a Lowrian couple who adopt her into their simple life in the Lower Realm. The book served as a warning to anyone foolhardy enough to try breaching the Upper, but each time she read it, she could not help rooting for her futile endeavors. Maybe there was a sequel she had not heard about.

Carefully, she ducked under an overhanging branch and stepped around a larger rock in the road, all the while never taking her eyes from the page. She absentmindedly played with the ring hanging from her neck, brushing the pad of her thumb across the engraving and slipping it on and off her finger. The road became steeper under her feet and she followed them up the rise. The schoolhouse was at the bottom of the hill on the other side. She had just reached the part of her book where the girl talks with the first toll guard when a brutish voice cut into her concentration.

"Oi! Bookhead!"

Quickly, Jacs stuffed the necklace into her shirt, and reluctantly turned to see Mallard Wetler, son of the town baker, jogging to catch up to her. He was two years older than Jacs. Although he was shorter than her, he made up for it in width, and had the arrogance of a boy twice his height. Standing in front of her, he barred her path, folded his arms, and looked at her smugly, as though proud of the wit demonstrated through such a cutting remark.

"What, Mal?" she said, deftly marking her place and moving to shove her book into her shoulder bag.

"What? No, 'hello?' Manners, farmgirl." He made a tsking sound and shook his head. Suddenly, his arm shot out and he caught the book before she could stop him.

"Hey!"

"*Rise of the Fallen,* eh? I didn't pick you for an Upper sympathizer! What? Think 'cause you got all them brains you're higher than the rest of us?"

Jacs rolled her eyes. "It's nice to see you expanding your vocabulary. *Sympathizer,* that's a mouthful, even for your big gob." She crossed her arms to mirror Mallard and glared at him. "What do you want?" she repeated.

Mallard glared at the book and thrust it back at her. Surprised, Jacs took it from him and returned it to her bag.

Mallard explained gruffly. "Just thought we could walk to the schoolhouse together is all. Felt bad about last week, didn't I? Didn't think the pepper powder would be that bad." He paused, smiled, and then continued. "And I didn't know about Casey's trick with the inkwell. Honest."

Jacs felt her face grow hot at the memory of Mallard's prank, and she balled her hands into fists. "No thank you," she growled and tried to push past him.

He stepped back and blocked her path. "But I'm going that way too. Let me say sorry."

Jacs tried to sidestep him and he quickly blocked her again.

"You said sorry. I don't want to walk with you. Now move, Mal."

"Or what?" He grinned. A fire flickered behind his eyes, and she was suddenly aware of how empty the road was.

"Or I'll . . ." She was cut short by the clanging of a bell. Mallard's head swiveled toward the sound and she took her opening, ducking around him and sprinting up the hill. That was the five-minute bell, and Master Tremain did not like tardiness.

She heard Mallard yell, "Hey!" behind her, then the sound of heavy footfalls and heavier panting as he followed her up the incline.

Jacs had cleared the top, clutching a stitch in her side, and started down the other side of the hill when a sharp pain shot through the calf of her left leg and she felt it buckle underneath her. She heard a short, sharp, derisive laugh before her world began to slide from under her. Tripping, she tried to regain her balance, but her momentum and gravity carried her faster than her feet could gain ground under her. She felt herself flying very briefly and then she was crashing, tumbling, bumping, and blundering down the rest of the hill. Her bag collided with her hip and jaw, then was ripped from her shoulder. The dirt from the road marked territory in her teeth and in the broken skin that striped her limbs. She rolled to a stop near the schoolhouse steps and lay with her eyes closed a moment longer while the world stopped spinning. She was faintly aware of her classmates' voices above her head.

"It's Jacqueline!"

"What a tumble."

"Is she dead?"

"Course not, she's breathing . . . Is she?"

"Yeah, look, she moved."

"She looks awful."

Then a brisk voice cut across the chatter. "Step back, children, inside at once. Take out your workbooks, write the date, and wait quietly. Now!"

There was a flurry of activity as Jacs's classmates hurried to obey. Jacs still had not moved but she opened her eyes. Master Tremain was leaning over her, a look of deep concern on her face.

"Jacqueline?" she ventured, her tone much softer than it had been a moment before. Jacs moaned and made to sit up, but oddly enough, she did not feel anything. Master Tremain pushed her back down gently and murmured, "Easy now, take your time. Try wiggling your toes for me."

Jacs did as she was asked, marveling at the lack of sensation.

"Now wiggle your fingers, there we go."

She obliged in a daze. Then all at once, the pain hit her. It was as though pain had followed her down the hill and had needed a few seconds to catch up. Her eyes widened in shock, every muscle tensed, and she gasped for air. Her skin was on fire. Her breathing came in short ragged bursts and she felt hot tears prickle the corners of her eyes. To her horror, with her classmates still nearby, the tears began to spill down her cheeks. Everything felt bruised and raw. She was vaguely aware of Mallard as he slipped behind Master Tremain and into the classroom.

Her teacher began speaking in a soft, low voice, "That's the girl, it's all right. You had a bit of a spill. Take a few deep breaths, there you go. We'll have you cleaned up in no time." Master Tremain helped Jacs to her feet, Jacs inhaling sharply as she felt her raw skin stretch. Master Tremain said over her head, "Terra, I'm going to clean Jacqueline up. While I'm gone, you're in charge. Take attendance, and start the class on the work I put up on the board. I'll be in the next room so I will hear any misbehavior."

"Yes, Master Tremain," an older girl replied.

"And Casey," Master Tremain continued, "Gather Jacqueline's bag and set it at her desk."

Master Tremain headed to a smaller room at the back of the schoolhouse with Jacs limping along beside her. Stepping into the room, Jacs sat on the small white bench that took up one wall and her teacher crouched down in front of her. Master Tremain cupped her chin in her bony fingers and turned her head left and right, apparently surveying the damage. Then she looked over Jacs's limbs, instructing Jacs to move an arm, make a fist, and asking if certain points hurt when touched. When she was finished with the inspection, she exhaled slowly and clicked her tongue.

"You're lucky nothing's broken, I don't know how you managed such a fall."

Jacs sniffed and wiped at her eyes, looking about the room. The walls were painted white like the rest of the schoolhouse. There was a medicine cabinet in the corner of the wall opposite where Jacs sat on the bench, and a small basin with a pitcher of water and some fresh rags in the other corner. Master Tremain poured some of the water into the basin, dipped a clean rag into it, and began dabbing at Jacs's cuts and grazes. Jacs bit her lip as hot tears continued rolling down her cheeks. She could hear the muffled voice of Terra through the thin dividing wall between the two rooms, and did not want her classmates to hear her cry.

Once her cuts were clean, Master Tremain put an ointment on the worst of them and wrapped a bandage around a particularly painful one on her knee. The ointment burned worse than the water had and Jacs scrunched her eyes up tight.

"Almost done, there's a brave girl. There you go, that's the last of it. How do you feel?" Master Tremain said.

Jacs looked at the bandage on her leg and gingerly touched her chin. She pulled back her fingers sharply as a twinge of pain shot along her jaw.

"Um . . ." she began shakily, "I've been better . . ." Then, remembering her manners, "Thank you, Master Tremain."

Her teacher put the bandages and ointment back into the medicine cabinet and asked, "Do you feel up to joining the class this morning?"

Jacs slowly flexed her fingers, the pain was much less now. While she wanted nothing more than to curl up in bed and avoid talking to anyone, she had not had a chance to go to school all week and was conscious of falling behind. She looked up at her teacher and asserted, "I think I'm okay now, I can join the class."

"All right, then I'll give you a few moments to collect yourself, and I will see you in class. I must get back." Master Tremain shot a nervous look toward the classroom. The noise level had risen and Jacs could hear Terra attempting to rein in a few of the more rambunctious students.

Master Tremain patted Jacs gently on an unhurt spot on her arm, her brown eyes crinkled with worry. Then, she straightened up, tucked her dusty blonde hair behind her ears, settled her dress, and left the room.

She called above the chattering students, "Now, any student out of their seat by the time I get to the chalkboard will stay behind after class to clean it." A series of scuffles and the scraping of chairs followed her words. "Ah, thank you, Mr. Wetler, for volunteering."

A satisfied smile spread across Jacs's face briefly before turning into a grimace. She felt her left calf and winced as her fingers probed the already blossoming bruise. It was about the size of an apple. Jacs thought about the laugh she had heard just before she fell. Lately, Mallard's laugh often came before her own pain or humiliation.

"But a theory is only as good as its proof," she whispered to herself. She still did not understand why the older boy had picked her for his punching bag, but she hated having to explain each new bruise, cut, or pepper rash to her mother.

Panic gripped her as her hand flew to her neck. Fingers grazed the leather cord and followed it until she breathed a sigh of relief to feel the ring on the end. Carefully, she tucked it back under her shirt and patted it twice.

She got unsteadily to her feet and attempted to dab water from the pitcher on her face. Her eyes felt hot. Taking one of the remaining clean rags, she dipped it into the pitcher and pressed the cold cloth into her closed eyelids.

When she was finished, she dried her face, opened the door, and limped to her seat.

Every head turned in her direction as she made her way down the rows of desks. The walk seemed to take a century, and she tried not to make eye contact with anyone.

Several whispers followed her.

It was going to be a long day.

At least I'll get to see Master Leschi this afternoon, she thought grimly.

Sitting down at her desk, she met Master Tremain's eyes. Her teacher smiled at her and nodded before turning her back on the class and continuing to write on the board.

"As I was saying, our Queendom is nestled between the Queendom of Nysa and the Kingdom of Auster along the Azulon Sea. The sea and two mountain ranges act as natural borders, and hopefully, a big enough barrier to invasion. But we have another natural border within our Queendom. The Cliff. Once, it was lined with five bridges connecting the two Realms. That was until Queen Frea the third decreed to sever all connections between Upper and Lower Realms save the one bridge you see today. Who remembers why?"

Several voices rang out at once.

"Because they're a bunch of snobs."

"Rich pigs!"

"Da said it's 'cause they don't like the dirt."

"Enough!" Master Tremain's voice rang out.

The classroom fell silent. Master Tremain looked furious, and Jacs noticed, suddenly frightened. Her teacher's eyes darted to the soft glow of the large purple crystal on the wall above her desk and lingered there for several heartbeats.

Slowly, Master Tremain released the breath she had been holding. She turned to the class and said quietly, "While I try to make this schoolhouse a safe space to learn, consider, words can be treasonous, children. Your youth will not protect you in the eyes of those whose beliefs blind them."

A few of the students looked around nervously. Many shot furtive looks toward the crystal.

Master Tremain continued in a shaky voice, "The reason Queen Frea the third cut all but one bridge . . ."

Jacs's shoulder bag was hanging off the back of her chair. She flipped open the flap and pulled out her books. Setting them on her desk, she froze. They were all sopping wet. Her novel, her class workbook, and the notebook she had brought for the afternoon's lesson with Master Leschi. She hurriedly searched in her bag for her water skin. It was stoppered and full. Turning back to her books, she peeled the sodden pages apart and heard a stifled giggle coming from behind her. She felt the blood rushing in her ears as, almost disbelieving, she inspected each book. Willing at least one of them to be dry. She saw her carefully copied notes blurred and smudged on pages glued together. She saw her bookmark hanging out of *The Rise of the Fallen* limply, the words *Upper Dog* scrawled across the cover.

It was too much. She quietly closed each book, gathered them carefully in her arms, placed her bag on her shoulder, and stood up.

"Master Tremain?" Her voice came out calmly, but she felt a lump in her throat building and knew she needed to leave soon. Her teacher turned around, her sharp eyes taking in Jacs's red face, packed bag, and dripping stationery. The latter of which was causing a wet spot to spread across her front.

"Jacqueline, what—"

"Thank you for your help earlier, but I think I'll go home." She managed before turning and walking, head high, back down the row of students and out the door.

Once clear of the schoolhouse, she allowed herself to cry. Hot, angry tears spilled down her face. Twice in one morning, she chided, a new record. Not wanting to go home, and knowing that her mother did not expect her back until the evening, she decided to see if Master Leschi could start their lesson early. Dashing her tears away, she took a deep breath and headed into town.

She found Master Leschi's house easily. It was a story higher than the rest of the houses in town and seemed to lean at an odd angle. There was a small garden in front filled with more metal contraptions and whirring machines than plants; although, Jacs noticed, there was an abundance of rosemary. The enticing spicy scent made her nose tingle.

She watched a weathervane in the shape of a sparrow swing lazily in the light breeze. There was a small wind turbine that appeared to be powering a slowly rotating clothesline. A telescope hung like a soldier at ease in a corner of the garden, and Jacs's eyes widened as she counted six large clocks in varying states of repair. One appeared to be working, one was clunking sporadically, another chimed suddenly in an off-key splutter, making her jump. The other three, missing cogs and hands, were silent and still. Carefully, Jacs opened the low gate and stepped into the garden. She walked through the tangle of rosemary and machinery up to the front door, hesitated, and pulled the cord she supposed was the doorbell.

A beautiful melody rippled through the slanted house and she heard, "Coming! Oof . . . Hold a minute . . ." Then the door opened smoothly. Master Leschi, hair high in a bun filled with pens, quills, and what looked like a protractor, ink smudged down her right cheek, and an odd pair of glasses swinging from a chain around her neck, came into view. "Ah! Jacqueline! What a lovely— my goodness, what happened to you?!"

Jacs's smile faltered as Master Leschi looked her over in horror. She became aware of the still-wet books clutched in her arms, the dirt in her hair, the bandage on her leg, the scrapes down her arms, and the still oozing wound on her chin. "Oh . . ." she did not quite know where to start.

"Come in, dear, my gracious what a state you're in! Come, come. Come sit down and I'll make us some tea, shall I? Yes, tea always has a way of brightening a day, I say!"

She led Jacs into a well-lit sitting room and made her sit in an overstuffed armchair while she pottered about in the kitchen, fetching a teapot, cups, and setting a kettle over a potbellied stove to boil. Jacs looked about her in wonder. The room was full of books. Any wall that was not a window had a bookshelf on it. The small table in the middle of the room had a bookshelf underneath it, and books were stacked in piles beside each of the chairs.

"Whoa," she breathed.

Master Leschi came back in with a tea tray and a plate of biscuits. Setting them on the table, she poured Jacs a cup, took the wet books out of her hands, and replaced them with the hot beverage and a treat. Satisfied, she turned her attention to Jacs's damaged books and flipped them over in her hands. Her hand hovered and trembled slightly over the defaced cover.

She shook her head sadly and quietly repeated, "What happened, dear?"

Jacs took a deep breath and told her everything. Master Leschi let her talk and handed her a clean kerchief when needed without judgment. When Jacs had finished, she hid her face in her teacup in embarrassment.

This was not how she expected her first day as an apprentice to go.

Master Leschi gave her a few moments to collect herself again, then simply said, "Often the ignorant punish those who seek to broaden their minds. They are scared of the heights some dream to rise to and strive to pull them down." She set Jacs's teacup on the table and took both of her hands in hers. "You must remember, Jacqueline, you did nothing wrong. I commend you for your bravery and grace in such an unjust and cruel situation."

Jacs thought back on the blubbering spectacle she made of herself in front of everyone and blushed.

As if reading her thoughts, Master Leschi reiterated, "Yes, brave. Tears do not mean you are weak. Tears mean you feel. Nothing is gained from suppressing them."

Jacs nodded numbly.

"I can have a word with Master Tremain about your education. A hostile learning environment is toxic, and it sounds like this is not the first time your studies have been interrupted by a peer's maliciousness. Maybe we can reach an agreement . . ." Master Leschi trailed off as her thoughts took over her words.

Jacs took another biscuit while Master Leschi mulled some finer details over. She felt much better having told her.

Suddenly, Master Leschi's eyes snapped back into focus and she smiled broadly. "But! You're here! And we have more of this glorious day to spend together, so there's that silver lining to such an awful episode."

Jacs felt herself smile too. "What are we doing today?"

"Already, your questioning mind is at work! Brilliant! Today, being the first, I thought I'd show you around my workshop and introduce you to the clock project officially, then we can talk about what interests you." She beamed.

"Me?"

"Yes! It's important I know what you want to get out of this apprenticeship. No use in me teaching a fish how to fly . . . unless of course you are a fish who wants to fly. . . then I shall teach you how to make wings." Excitedly, Master Leschi jumped up. "First things first," she chimed brightly, seizing the three waterlogged books from the table and inspecting them thoughtfully, "I think. . ." her eyes darted to the still hot stove and the wire drying rack above it. "Let's try this, shall we? We just need to dry out the pages—sure they will be a little wrinkled, but at least they will be usable. Here, hold these." Together, master and apprentice walked into the kitchen. Master Leschi hung the books by their covers with the pages hanging through the drying rack over the stove. "I guess time will tell," she mused, then turned back to Jacs. "Right! Upstairs we go. I'll show you my—our—workshop."

Jacs felt excitement tingling through her like a current as they made their way up the stairs. Each step, she noticed, had a small pile of books at each end making the stairwell narrower. Once at the top, Jacs looked around and felt her jaw drop to the floor. The entire upper story of the house was a workshop.

Worktables littered with notes and books lined the walls; large prototypes and models of structures perched on tabletops, hung from the rafters, and sat neatly in corners. Every available wall space (not occupied by a bookshelf) was plastered with blueprints, schematics, and labeled diagrams. A large birdcage with a chicken-sized mechanical bird inside stood on a stand in one corner, it *quorked* and spun its head intermittently. Three clocks labeled YESTERDAY, TODAY, and TOMORROW were stacked on top of one another at odd angles and showed different times. Jacs noticed that the hand on Yesterday's clock spun much faster than the other two, as though time was speeding by more quickly. An abacus with white and blue beads was perched on a stool and a set of copper scales had a lemon on one side and a drawing of a lemon with its scientific name written out on parchment on the other. A porthole filled with a mirror reflected images upside down, and a clock small enough to fit around a person's wrist sat on a velvet pillow. Near the window, a spherical contraption with an open top and four handles or cranks held an enormous rosemary plant that filled the room with its fragrance.

An odd assortment of tools littered the room, and Jacs saw twice as many different writing utensils. It appeared Master Leschi was determined to have a pen at hand at any given moment. Feather quills, reed pens, charcoal, chalk, and what looked like sharpened sticks filled with a gray core littered the workbenches. The stairs emerged in the center of the room, and directly opposite was a large-scale model of the clock tower, only with aspects of the sketch she had seen that day at the waterfall added in. She was amazed to see that Master Leschi had already begun experimenting with a two-layered dome design.

"This is amazing!" Jacs exclaimed. "This is, look at . . . and here you've got a . . . wow!"

Master Leschi laughed. "That's not the first time a thought was left unfinished in this workshop. Let me show you around."

The Master spent the better part of the morning showing Jacs the different projects she was working on and talked at greater length about the clock tower. She went over drawings and pages of her personal notebooks, finally standing in front of the scale model and pointing out the various features she had described. They discussed the logistics of the two domes, and the older woman pulled out small replicas of the roof she had built in a variety of different ways, each later model improving upon the flaws of its predecessor.

Master Leschi listened as Jacs voiced ideas and talked them through with her, sometimes helping her see a flaw in her plan, other times helping her push a good idea further.

Jacs did not even notice the time slipping by until she heard the front door open and shut with a bang, and Master Leschi, wincing, said, "That'll be Phillip home for lunch. Bull in a glass blower's shop, that one. Let's join him, shall we? I'm a bit peckish myself."

They settled with some sandwiches outside on three chairs made of mead barrels. Phillip was both tall and broad, standing a head taller than his mother and much taller than Jacs. "Bull" seemed an apt descriptor. His hair was dark and wavy like his mother's, he had kind eyes and an easy smile.

At seventeen he was already working as an apprentice at Ms. Severin's smithy. Jacs smiled shyly when he introduced himself, but he shook her hand with such warmth, her shyness evaporated in an instant.

The smell of rosemary wafted in the heat of the day, and Master Leschi took a deep breath in. "Stimulates the mind, you know? Rosemary does. Rosemary for remembrance, they say, but that has entirely morbid connotations. To be more accurate they should say rosemary for memory."

Jacs took a bite of her sandwich and watched a hummingbird hover around a small feeder, darting in and out quicker than she could blink. She felt the weight of the ring around her neck and thought again of the little boat falling down the waterfall. *Gravity makes everything so easy*, she mused. Out loud she asked, "How could you make something fly?"

Master Leschi looked at her thoughtfully. "What kind of something? It would depend on the size and weight and where you wanted it to go."

Jacs chose her words carefully, still watching the hummingbird. Something willed her to keep the boat and the message a secret. "Well," she began, "say, something light; nothing more than a folded piece of paper."

"Like a kite, or a paper dart?" Phillip supplied with a mouth full of sandwich.

Jacs thought for a moment, then shook her head. "No, they just glide and don't go up very high," she said.

"You'd need something to propel the contraption upward in that case," Master Leschi reasoned.

"And that would give you more control," added Jacs.

"Right," Master Leschi did not seem as interested in where or why the question came about. She furrowed her brow to work out the thought experiment. "You need something that creates its own lift. How high would you want it to go?" she asked.

Jacs looked over at the towering Cliff face. "As high as possible, maybe even . . . above the clouds?"

Phillip smiled at her, making her blush, then stood up and dusted his hands free of crumbs. "I know when it's time to leave the minds at work," he said, kissing his mother lightly on the cheek. "I'm off to finish up at Severin's. Nice meeting you, Jacqueline."

Jacs smiled and replied in kind.

"Don't be late!" Master Leschi called as he set off down the path and waved over his shoulder.

Master Leschi watched him go for a moment, then snapped her attention back to Jacs. "You want it to go up . . . Hmm, well, if it only has to go up, then we don't have to worry about a steering mechanism or an engine, really . . ." Master Leschi said as she scratched her chin thoughtfully.

Jacs was thinking back to what she had heard in Master Tremain's class the week before. "Master Tremain taught us that hot air rises. That's why you have to lie on the ground when there's a fire because it's safer."

"So you're thinking of somehow harnessing hot air?" Her teacher seemed to know the answer already but was waiting for Jacs to figure it out for herself.

Jacs nodded, unsure. "Is that possible?"

Master Leschi grinned. "Of course," she said encouragingly, "but how would you do it?"

Jacs began twisting a strand of hair around her finger as she voiced her thoughts. "How to harness hot air . . . how do you contain air . . . maybe something like a fire bellows—they can trap air."

"Good, but remember, we want it to be as light as possible."

"Right, so an airtight sack, something lightweight, maybe waxed canvas, or a pigskin," Jacs said.

"Better," Master Leschi conceded, "and where does the hot air come from?"

Jacs twirled her hair faster. "Fire, a burning stick? No, too heavy and hard to control. A candle?"

Master Leschi was smiling. "Very good, now put them together and how do you make it work?"

Jacs scrambled to pull out the notebook Master Leschi had lent her to replace the wet one. Wordlessly, Master Leschi handed her a piece of charcoal from one of her many pockets, which Jacs accepted with a nod of thanks. "What if we put the canvas on top like an upside-down sack, and put the candle to hang at the bottom, maybe from cords, the hot air will fill the sack and lift the whole thing up!"

Master Leschi smiled. "You, my girl, have just created your own hot-air balloon." Jacs laughed with excitement as her mentor continued. "It looks like we have a new afternoon project."

They spent the rest of the day perfecting Jacs's hot-air balloon. When it was time for Jacs to go, she had a notebook full of pictures, revisions, and a workbench full of prototypes, candles, and string. The final product was clutched in her arms like a baby, and she could not stop smiling.

"Beautiful," Master Leschi commented.

"Thank you so much! I can't wait to test it out," Jacs said happily.

"And be sure to make note of your field trials," Master Leschi advised. "We may make mistakes, but the least we can do is learn from them. Keep moving forward, I say!" Master Leschi gestured toward the stairs and followed closely behind Jacs. "It's getting late, and I don't want your mother to be upset any more than those bandages are sure to make her. Let's get your things—hopefully those books are dry." When they reached the kitchen, Master Leschi plucked a book from where it hung from the drying rack and leafed through the water-warped pages. "Ah, well," Master Leschi said with resignation. "Not good as new, but slightly more useful than they were wet."

Not as bothered about the books anymore, Jacs happily put them in her shoulder bag, next to her new notebook. "Thank you," Jacs repeated as she hoisted the bag onto her shoulder and held on to the hot-air balloon carefully.

"And thank *you*, dear Jacqueline. I think this arrangement will work out wonderfully. Now, I'm not sure how busy you are with work at home, so I will not hold you to a set day, but come when you can. As I mentioned before, I will talk with Master Tremain. There are things I am able to teach you here to make up for any missed lessons at the schoolhouse. Most women start funneling into more specialized occupations and studies around your age anyway. While I'm at it, I can sort something out about that Wetler boy."

Jacs began to protest, her face reddening at the thought of what Mallard and his friends would make of her running to the teacher, but Master Leschi cut her off and assured, "Not to worry, dear, it will be done with the utmost discretion."

Not quite convinced, but not sure what to do about it, Jacs bid her farewell and began the walk home, cradling the hot-air balloon in her arms. Her thoughts shifted to her mission: how to send a letter to Connor. She just hoped that tomorrow was a still day, that the balloon would catch in a tree or snag in a place where he would see it, that the candle stayed lit the whole way up, and that . . . *oh goodness*—her mind reeled at all of the factors against her.

Then, her mouth set in a determined line, she resolved to make Trial 1, Flight of the Fallen, commence the next day.

6

FULL OF HOT AIR

Several weeks had passed since Connor and Queen Ariel had looked out over the expanse of the Queendom. As promised, his lessons had intensified even more. Master Clio had taken it as a personal insult to have her teachings questioned and had seen to it that the Prince's nose only left the grindstone to sleep, eat, and sneeze occasionally.

He somehow managed to escape her lectures for an entire afternoon and had a feeling Edith had something to do with it. When a small flood had "accidentally" plagued his study, she had been ready with a fresh pair of socks, his knapsack filled with lunch, and his exploring gear.

"Go," she whispered with a wink.

He would have to find a way to thank her. For the moment, Connor was making the most of his unexpected freedom on the Cliff's edge. He leaned his head back and bit into a fresh-baked cookie. Sitting against one of the larger trees next to the waterfall he had sent his little boat over some weeks before, he looked out across the Queendom. His view was slightly obscured by the large oak tree at the mouth of the river, but he did not need to get that close to the edge again. He watched a tiny wagon trundling its way around one of the larger hills, its rider too small to make out from so far away.

Dusting off the crumbs that had fallen on his tunic, he reached for a second cookie, when a sudden breeze whipped up and movement in the branches above him caught his eye. His hand froze midway to his mouth, cookie forgotten.

"What on earth?" he muttered to himself.

Craning his neck and shielding his eyes, he saw a white canvas balloon hanging in the oak tree at the edge of the Cliff. It appeared to have a small candle, still lit, hanging underneath it that swayed in the air. Slowly, he crept toward the Cliff edge. Holding fast to the oak, he reached up, standing on tiptoe, to where the balloon hung just beyond his fingertips. Gripping a lower branch tightly, he leaned forward, out into the void. His fingertips barely brushed the canvas.

He used a word he had heard Master Luppolo, the brewmaster, use when she cut her hand on a broken glass. Looking around, he saw a long, forked branch on the ground. Carefully, he grabbed it and, still holding on to the oak, wrapped it in the strings hanging from the little balloon. Still not daring to look down, he worked the balloon free so that it now dangled from his branch. Once he had it, he ran backward, away from the edge to where his pack lay, breathing hard.

"Ow!" he yelped and quickly blew out the candle. A small metal shield had protected the flame from the wind, and it, Connor found out, was extremely hot. Settling back down and sucking his forefinger, he looked at the contraption in his hands. He had never seen anything like it. He inspected the canvas of the balloon, looked at the little basket and shield—carefully—that had housed the candle, and tested the strength of the strings holding it all together. He lifted the basket up to inspect the bottom and, to his delight and increasing wonder, saw a little scroll of parchment tied to it.

His hands shook with excitement as he untied the scroll, placed the balloon carefully on the ground beside him, and began to unroll it. Eagerly, he read

To Connor,

This is my seventh attempt to get a message back to you, so if you are reading this, I am pleased to finally make your acquaintance. I'm Jacs, I'm thirteen and I am an inventor's apprentice. I'm so excited that this should reach you as it means I did it! I got your ship, The Endeavor, *eight weeks ago and have been trying to reply once a week ever since.*

In your letter, you had a lot of questions. I'll try to answer them all. For work we do a lot of things. The men usually stick to the heavy lifting and manual labor they're good at, while us women are able to do a lot of different things.

For fun I like to build things, read, play with my cat, go fishing, things like that. I live on my farm in a small house, but most people live in town, in Bridgeport. It's a nice town, it's got a beautiful clock tower I'm helping to redesign.

I'm not sure what your houses are like, but mine's definitely not a palace. What's it like living in the palace? What do you do there?

We really aren't told much about what Upperite life is like. I only really know about the bridges, and I can see the Bridge from my house. We don't even have books that talk about what it's like up there. I know that the Queen and King visited when the Prince was born—but I wasn't around for that—and we only see people from the Upper Realm during trade week. All those beautiful gold carriages almost don't seem real. Is there really that much gold up there?

I hope to be your friend, and I always wear your ring. I've had trouble losing the hot-air balloons so will wait until I have a better model before I can send something up for you.

I have some questions for you too. What's it like living in the Upper Realm? Have you met the Queen? Tell me more about yourself. How old are you? What do you and other Upperites like to do for fun?

Please note down in your reply (if you reply) what flight number you got so I know which hot-air balloon worked.

I hope to hear from you.

Your friend,
Jacs Tabart
Flight Test #7

Connor read the letter over twice more and felt his heart lift. It worked! *The Endeavor* made it! And he was lucky enough that an inventor found it. He had not considered how hard it would be for a Lowrian to get a message back to him. Carefully, he placed the hot-air balloon in his knapsack and gathered the rest of his things. He needed to reply as soon as possible. And she was wearing his ring! It had made it all the way down in one piece! He needed another boat . . . maybe a less elaborate one to save time. He did not want his new friend to waste more trials considering he had only just received number seven. A message from the Lower Realm! This must be a first in history!

Connor flew on feet that barely touched the grass all the way to the castle. Sneaking up the servants' entrance, he made his way back to his room, locked himself in, and started writing a reply. He made up his mind not to tell her he was the Prince. He liked that she thought he was an ordinary person. *When people know you're royalty, they act different,* he thought. Loading his pen with ink, he pulled a piece of parchment toward him.

Dear Jacs . . . he began.

7

THE TOS AND FROMS

Tell me more about the clock tower you're building. Connor had asked in his reply.

Jacs, working in the extended twilight under the glow of two candles, scratched away at her letter furiously.

> *It's an amazing opportunity and I'm so thankful to Master Leschi. Not that I don't love being able to help Mum on the farm—but a lot of that work is boywork which I'm not really built for . . . and I love that I get to use my hands* and *my brain with the work I'm doing for Master Leschi.*

And hopefully this means I won't be working on the farm all my life.

The clock tower is so interesting! I get to work on the building plans and also the plans of the clock's mechanisms . . .

Jacs skimmed over the next two pages of detailed outlines of the clock tower project excitedly. She had included a simplified diagram to show her new friend how she was helping with the domed roof's design, and a quick sketch of what the completed building would look like. Finishing, she wrote,

Your friend,
Jacs
Flight 2

Folding the letter into a tight parcel, she slipped it into the little slot built into the base of the candle's basket. The basket hung from cords attached to the balloon, and a small metal screen shielded the flame from the wind. She finished squeezing the letter into place and realized it was almost too thick to fit. *I'll have to adapt the design if these letters keep getting longer,* she thought.

Connor's next boat, a blue one, got caught in a swirling eddy within the makeshift harbor of rocks Jacs had built on one side of the river near the base of the waterfall. It contained an equally excited reply:

Your clock tower looks incredible! We have a clock tower like yours in the city, it is bigger, although I think yours will have more personality than ours once it's done. Ours is very white and the clock has big gold numbers. But there is a bookshop nearby that is my favorite. It has a

secret room behind a bookshelf with all the Queedom's maps in it. Not many people are allowed in it, but I'm one of the Prince's servants so when he goes, I get to go too. It's incredible to me that we feel so important in our lives, but when you look at a map, a whole city can be reduced to a dot on a page.

I can't fit a lot of pages in my boats, but here's a rough drawing of the map of the Queendom. I couldn't fit many place names . . . but I marked the palace and your town. I was speaking with Master Clio—the Prince's tutor—and she said that part of Queen Frea the third's laws meant that the Lower Realm was stripped of all information about the Upper Realm. That doesn't seem fair, everyone should know what their Queendom looks like. So you might not want to show anyone in case it gets you into trouble, but here it is.

Your friend,
Connor
Voyage 3

It wasn't long before Jacs was finding any excuse to sneak off to the waterfall to look for little boats caught in the reeds, or to the Cliff with a hot-air balloon wrapped in her arms to send up. Much of her wages from working with Master Leschi went toward canvas, candles, and parchment every month. Her mentor assumed her apprentice was simply perfecting an already perfect design.

"I see so much of myself in you, Jacqueline," she would say warmly when Jacs brought another set of drawings to life.

Although there was still no accounting for sudden changes in weather, Jacs eventually was able to account for most of the other factors working against her little balloons' flights. She found a crevice within the cliff face that ran just about the entire length to the top, almost directly below a large tree with branches and roots hanging out over the edge of the Cliff. This little three-sided chimney helped guide the balloons three-quarters of the way up the rock with very little interference. Once free of the fissure, there was only a short distance to the tangled limbs of that great tree. While it wasn't a perfect solution, it did significantly increase the chance of a successful flight.

To make sure she retrieved Connor's boats (and to reduce her time spent fishing for them), Jacs had spent several months weaving a net that spanned the entire river from bank to bank a short distance from the base of the waterfall. Then, all she had to do was reel the net in to collect the little vessels. The added benefit was that sometimes she also caught dinner.

Through Connor's eyes her life had taken on a shimmer, an almost glamorous sheen. He found even the most mundane of things, like milking Brindle, to be worthy of her one or two paragraphs of explanation.

She hadn't realized how many of her daily activities or interactions she took for granted until she began explaining them to a Prince's servant, who, obviously, never really left the palace.

His world was equally mysterious. Considering he served the Prince, Connor spent very little time talking about him or the royal family. Unless asked specifically, he tended to want to talk about other things. That was fine by Jacs; the day-to-day palace life was interesting enough to fill tomes.

One letter appeared in early spring and had Jacs's imagination spinning:

We had a gala for the Queen last night. A troupe of entertainers came to the palace and performed for everyone. These men were incredible! Throwing each other into the air and catching one another without even flinching, and they weren't little mice either. Everyone was having a wonderful time, until one of the dancers brought Lord Sybil Claustrom into the middle of the room to join their dance. Lord Claustrom is one of the most influential Lords in the Queendom. Now, they may or may not have known who they were dealing with, but they most certainly did not know that her Genteel, Brovnen Claustrom, is notoriously jealous.

So Lord Claustrom is twirling with the head troupe member, and Brovnen is getting redder and redder in the face, but he's not going to defy his Lord. So finally, he cuts in and begins dancing with the troupe member himself! The dancer, with a sly grin on his face, dips Brovnen low then throws him into the air as he had done the other men in his troupe before. Brovnen panics, and what should have been a graceful landing ended up more like a tangled mess on the floor. Anger's fire took him then and he began yelling at the dancers. Lord Claustrom, deeply embarrassed, ordered her guard pair to escort her Genteel out while he calmed down, then followed shortly after. To make matters worse, the troupe thought the whole thing was hilarious and reenacted it as a farce later that evening.

Do you have galas or balls in Bridgeport? I imagine they look quite different from ours. Do you like to dance?

Your friend,
Connor
Voyage 17

Months passed, and Jacs found herself feeling closer to this boy living miles above her than she did any of her peers in town. They shared their secrets, their hopes, and their ideas to make the

Queendom a better place. After an early frost spoiled the season's last harvest of tomatoes, Jacs reasoned:

> *If the Queen was required to visit the Lower Realm at least once a year, she could check in on us farmers and make sure our taxes were lowered on years when the crops are bad because of frost or drought or flood. Farmers shouldn't be punished for something they have no control over.*

To which Connor replied:

> *Since we don't have any farms in the Upper Realm (outside of little vegetable gardens I think), I doubt the Queen or the Council of Four really even think about stuff like that. It's crazy that their decisions affect people who lead such different lives.*

They didn't always agree:

The best cup of tea is made by steeping the leaves first, then adding milk and honey, Jacs wrote one bitterly cold winter morning.

His response was so infuriating that it was enough to warm her without the need of a fire. *No, you add the milk first so that you know how much milk is going into it, then you add the leaves and the hot water,* he replied.

That's disgusting! She wrote. *Then you're partially steeping your tea leaves in milk and that just seems . . . I don't know, but it's gross.*

What's the difference? He scribbled back. *It ends up the same anyway, this way you have more control over the amount of milk you're using.*

But despite who was right or wrong in their matters of debate, they always found ways to be there for each other when it counted.

A few months after their tea-making disagreement, Jacs found the contents of her letter about a particularly stubborn cog in the clock's mechanism shift to her worry about her mother.

The cog just won't move. That seems to be a theme around here, unfortunately. Mum hasn't been able to leave her bed the last two days. It happens every year, usually it only lasts the few days before and after the anniversary of when I lost Dad. I don't know what it is about this year, but she won't get up unless I make her. I think the cog's an easier fix.

His reply had been just the right assortment of words:

Jacs, that sounds awful. I doubt that the strategy you use with the cog will be effective with your mother. Matters of the heart rarely have blueprints. I can't imagine what it's like to have lost someone so important, and I know you are trying to be strong for the both of you. Something my mother does every year on the anniversary of her brother's death is take my father and I to her favorite spot with a bottle of champagne. We sit as the sun sets, toasting his life and sharing our favorite memories of him. I was young when he left us, but I still remember him showing me how to bridle my own horse. As the sun sinks behind the distant mountains, it feels like he's sitting on the lawn with us. That seems to bring my mother peace.

That evening, she bundled her mother in a warm shawl and settled her in her father's seat beneath the weathered old apple tree. They clutched hot mugs of peppermint tea, one with a splash of something stronger; her mother's eyes were distant. Jacs had brought her father's fiddle out with her. They sat for a while in silence. Tuning the fiddle in the extended twilight, Jacs felt the instrument come alive in her hands, and she began to play.

Her mother sat quietly through the first song. Through the second song, silent tears rolled down her cheeks.

Fingers blundering through one of her father's favorites, Jacs watched as her mother's brow cleared, then the corners of her mouth lifted. In a soft, wavering voice that grew stronger with each syllable, her mother began to sing. It was the first time Jacs had heard her sing since her father's death. The melody soared, lilting and weaving between the overhead branches and dancing in the evening breeze. Jacs heard her father's laugh as a harmonic within each chord, saw his smile in each sweeping bow stroke. In the dying light, they were a family again. Whole and happy.

Connor's gifts were not only written. On her fourteenth birthday, he sent her a single Griffin feather. It was as white as snow and edged in golden dust.

A short note read: *Happy Birthday, Jacs. One day I will take you to meet the Court. If I could be Queen for a day, I would choose today and make it a law that everyone on their fourteenth birthday got the chance to ride with the Griffins.*

Jacs had smiled at that and held the feather before her reverentially. The next day she asked for Master Leschi's help to fashion it into a feather quill, then wrote her thanks with her new stardust pen.

It was sometime after receiving the Griffin feather that she noticed her feelings toward Connor start to change. The changes were small at first: a spring in her step would accompany her to the pool beneath the waterfall; a tiny frown would appear and then quickly vanish at the mention of his latest twitterpation. In one letter he wrote about how amazing a guard named Iliana was at fighting, then in another about how prettily Dame Claustrom danced at a recent gala, and in another about his nerves at the prospect of riding with a young guard who was fast becoming a candidate for knighthood and even the Soterian medal. When this happened, she assured herself she wasn't jealous, that she was just concerned for him as he tended to give his heart to those who were reckless with it. However, she couldn't deny that her spirits would inevitably lift to hear when he had moved on.

Then the changes grew: her heart would beat faster to see a little boat caught in her nets; a smile would make her cheeks ache as she read his letter through once, then twice to make sure she hadn't missed anything important.

On a crisp spring morning, Brindle gave birth to a calf with a perfect heart shaped marking on her forehead and she found herself wanting nothing more than to tell Connor about this little miracle.

With every balloon she sent skyward, a part of her would ache to follow its course. She began fantasizing about one day standing beside him on the same ground. Would he be taller than her? How would his hand feel in hers? And when her heart felt like it might burst, a little voice inside whispered cautiously, *Did he feel the same?* She tried to look for clues of his feelings in his words, then in the spaces between them.

Once, when she was sick, she mentioned that Phillip had brought a bouquet of daisies to cheer her up. Connor's reply had been curiously prickly. He included an elaborately detailed sketch of an exotic flower she had not seen before.

Who is Phillip? Master Leschi's Phillip? Isn't he a bit older than you? I guess you spend a fair bit of time together. He sounds great. If I were there, I'd get you a bouquet of these. The royal greenhouse is one of the few places that can grow them properly. I guess daisies are good too though.

The next few letters afterwards had included an iteration of the question, *So how's Flower Phil?* until she clarified he was more of a brother to her. After that, he didn't mention Phillip again, and his tone brightened significantly—or was that just her imagination?

On her fifteenth birthday, after hearing that she wore his ring on a cord around her neck to keep it safe, he sent her a finely wrought gold chain.

The last lines of his letter read,

You deserve the world today, but because it won't quite fit in my boats, this will have to do. A chain of gold to match your heart. Happy Birthday, Jacs.

Yours,
Connor
Voyage 86

Jacs had blushed so deeply that, when she returned from the river with the boat clutched to her chest and his words ringing in her ears, her mother had checked her forehead for a fever.

A gold chain was a precious gift indeed. She supposed an Upperite palace servant was paid much more handsomely than a Lowrian inventor's apprentice. Despite her modest income, she did her best to reciprocate. For his sixteenth birthday, she saved her wages to buy cords of leather and a delicate silver clasp formed to look like a Griffin's head. She wove the cords into a band long enough to circle a boy's wrist and attached the clasps. When worn, the Griffin looked like it was holding the bracelet together with its beak, the opposite clasp in its mouth. She had used Phillip's wrist for measurements, and he had spent the next week pestering her for information about her mysterious sweetheart.

Now I have something to recognize you *by*, she wrote.

The next lines had been practiced on a different sheet, crossed out, rewritten, and scribbled over, until finally she copied the result into the letter.

> *I can't wait for the day that I get to meet you in person. I still can't believe how lucky I am to know you. You have my heart, Connor. It seems so wild to say since I only know you from your words, but I am,*
>
> *Yours,*
> *Jacs*
> *Flight 175*

8

LONG LIVE THE QUEEN

Jacs, now sixteen, was finishing up her most recent letter. She had wound her long auburn hair in a bun, like Master Leschi always did, with two pencils holding it in place. She was a foot taller since she'd written her first letter and moved with a confidence that had grown steadily while working with Master Leschi.

Spring was finally upon them, and the sun shone through the open windows. A cool breeze fluttered the papers in front of her.

She scratched away at her letter, her battered Griffin-feather quill running across the page as quickly as she could translate thought. Today she was describing her most recent project with Master Leschi—a flock of starlings had perched on the hands of the town clock and set it back five minutes. *You wouldn't think five minutes was enough to make or break people, but there you go,* she wrote. They had decided to simply reset the clock, strengthen the mechanism that became damaged in the stall, and if such a freak occurrence should happen again, possibly find a way to cover the large clock face. She also wrote of her excitement to see the royal family that afternoon.

> *Of course, I'm not likely to meet them personally, but I will get to see them as they walk through the town, and even just to watch the royal procession as it comes down the Bridge will be so incredible!*

She paused thoughtfully and added,

> *Fifty years since the Great Divide. If I'm honest, a part of me is very excited, and a part of me is terrified. I won't say too much because I'm not one to spread gossip, but the whole town feels like a powder keg. Street fights have increased since preparations for the Diversary began. People seem to be rallying into two camps and I don't really know if it's worse being called an Upper Dog or being praised as a True Lowrian. I don't know if I'm just being paranoid, but the amount of guard-pair patrols has definitely increased in the last month. Regardless, it will be a treat to finally see royalty! But above all, I can't believe we finally get to meet!*

Jacs could barely contain her excitement at the thought. As a servant in the palace, Connor had mentioned that he would be joining the royal procession. She knew to look for him, and that he would be wearing the bracelet she had made him. She had told him in her last letter that she would be standing below the clock tower dressed in yellow and wearing his ring.

She hoped it would be enough for them to find each other.

Smiling, she touched the ring where it hung in its usual place around her neck. It felt warm against her fingertips. Shrugging her shoulders to stretch them, she felt a small pop and sighed with relief. She had been hunched over her letter for about an hour without moving. Skimming over her words again, she finished:

I hope you are well, until our next.

Yours,
Jacs
Flight 213

"Jacqueline! I hope you're getting ready! The Descension is set to start at noon and we want to get a good spot!" her mother called from halfway across the yard. Jacs could see her through the window; she had just finished hanging the laundry and had the basket on her hip. Quickly, Jacs hid the letter safely between the pages of the nearest book. Standing, she stretched her back and hurriedly pulled the pencils out of her hair to braid it in a style her mother preferred. She pulled on a dress she had mended specifically for the occasion. It was yellow ochre with a white underskirt and a deep sienna bodice.

Last, she made sure Connor's ring on its gold chain had pride of place around her neck. Holding the ring between her fingers, she shifted it this way and that, admiring the way it caught the sunlight. Her mother came into her room and beamed.

"You look lovely, Plum. My, how much you've grown! Your father . . ." She paused delicately. "He would be very proud to see you now."

Jacs blushed and gave her mother a tight hug. "Thanks, Mum."

"But, please let me fix your hair! It looks like a bird has made its nest on the top!"

Jacs, containing the urge to roll her eyes, poked her tongue out playfully instead, and sat down. Her mother happily picked up her brush and set to work, chattering all the while. Jacs was only half listening. A part of her mind was still on the letter she had just finished, and the other part of her mind was occupied with thoughts of seeing the Queen.

". . . And Brindle is getting on in her years, she's starting to show her age and I'm not sure we'll get many more years of milk from her. Her last calf was quite sickly and . . ."

"Ow!" Jacs jerked her head away from her mother's rough brushing.

"Sorry, Plum, hold still. Almost done . . . there." She took a step back to admire her work. "No bird in there, I should think not!"

Jacs felt the intricate plait and took her mother's word for it. "Thanks, Mum," she said again.

"All right, you're set, I'm set, let's go!" Her mother clapped her hands and started for the door.

The two women made their way out the front gate and along the dirt road heading into the town. Her mother tried to persuade Jacs that the best place to watch the Descension was on the hill before the schoolhouse, but Jacs, thinking of her promise to meet Connor, insisted that if they waited there, they would miss getting a good spot by the clock tower to see the parade.

"Plum, we would see the parade from the roadside on the hill anyway," she reasoned.

"But it's better to be in the middle of it all, Mum!" Jacs insisted, then compromised. "Why don't we watch them come halfway down the Bridge from the hill, then we can head into town and wait while they finish the Descension. I'm going to bet the second half will be the same as the first half, just lower down." She grinned.

Her mother relented. "Oh, all right."

They found a spot at the top of the hill, and they were not the only ones with the same idea. Jacs waved to Ms. and Mr. Grimsby. "Good morning!" she called happily as she and her mother joined them.

"Good morning, Jacqueline, good morning, Maria," Mr. Grimsby replied, flashing a brilliant smile, his teeth a stark contrast against his dark skin. "Going to be quite the show! This will be my third Descension and I tell you, each time is better than the last!"

From their vantage point, they could see the Bridge clearly in the distance where it zigzagged its way up the Cliff face. Ms. Tabart spread out a shawl on the ground and she and Jacs sat down to wait. The Grimsbys sat nearby and exchanged pleasantries with Ms. Tabart. Jacs was too excited to listen; her eyes were glued to the Bridge. Watching. Waiting. She heard the town clock begin to strike noon. *Five minutes slow*, she thought. *They should have started by now.*

"Do you hear that?" her mother asked, cutting into Ms. Grimsby's comment about lavender. The party of four listened. There was a distinct sound of drums echoing down the valley, steady as a beating heart. Jacs narrowed her eyes and squinted at the top of the Cliff.

"There they are!" she cried. Impossibly tiny in the distance, the royal carts and carriages were at the top of the Bridge and making their way steadily down. The Descension had started. Jacs counted ten bright carriages and tried, but failed, to count the smaller carts and people on foot. She did not envy those foot soldiers. *Hopefully none of them get vertigo*, she thought. Everyone watched in silence as the procession marched to the end of the first length, then one at a time each carriage was lowered by the elevator to the second length.

"How long does a Descension usually take?" she asked.

"Hmm, quite a while, depending on how big the parade is, if there're any hiccups, and if all the lifts run smoothly," Ms. Grimsby answered, her husband looking slightly put out that she had answered as an authority on the matter. He had seen three in his lifetime, after all.

"And then what happens, they march the procession into the town? I heard there was going to be dancing!"

Mr. Grimsby jumped in. "Dancing, yes of course! They make their way into the town, everyone gawks and gapes, they stay at the inns and some of the servants set up camp in the surrounding fields. Then, when night falls, we all gather for a feast, music, and dancing. Merope and I danced for the first time at the last Descension." His eyes became misty as he looked at his wife.

Ms. Grimsby giggled and swatted his hand playfully. "I remember, you were the most handsome man in the square. I was so delighted when you asked me to dance that I didn't even notice you had two left feet until I took my shoes off later that night! Worse bruises you have never seen."

Even Mr. Grimsby laughed at that.

Their smiles died quickly as snatches of conversation darted up the hill behind them.

". . . Yeah, but it still stings like a brick to the face. The nerve of these Uppers, waltzing down the bridge, rubbing our noses in their finery, then toddling back up. Bunch of pricks."

Jacs's head turned to see a large group of people climbing up the hill. She saw Mallard Wetler and his mother, Patricia; Benjamin

Sternwall—but no sign of his daughter Casey—and four other families from town: the Bankses, the Orions, the Vaultlys, and the Severins.

Mallard had shot up and out over the years, Jacs noticed. She rarely saw him anymore. Since her education had been taken over by Master Leschi, there was no reason for them to cross paths, except accidentally.

Ms. Tabart eyed the newcomers warily. Then her eyes darted back to the Bridge and she exclaimed, "Jacqueline, that looks like halfway down to me, let's go into town and get a good spot for the parade." She attempted to keep her voice light, but it was edged with warning.

The Grimsbys took their cue. "Ah, yes, now that's a marvelous idea, Maria. Why don't we accompany you?"

Before the two groups had a chance to interact, Jacs was being whisked down the hill toward town.

When they were safely out of earshot, Jacs asked, "Mum, I have to check something with Master Leschi, can I meet you in the square?"

Ms. Tabart glanced behind her. "Okay, we'll be by the fountain—don't be too long." Her mother kissed her on the cheek. Jacs gave her a quick squeeze and darted off to Master Leschi's house. Ms. Tabart watched her run into the crowd and disappear down a side street.

Jacs bounded up to the front door and pulled the doorbell.

"Just a moment! Coming, coming!" came a slightly strangled response.

Jacs waited patiently as she heard her mentor thumping down the stairs. Phillip beat her to the door. "Hello, Jacqueline, you look nice today," he said happily.

"Hi Phillip, thanks! I just came to see if you and Master Leschi were coming to watch the parade. They are just about finished with the Descension."

Master Leschi came into view behind her son. "Hello, Jacqueline, lovely dress. What's this?"

Jacs repeated her inquiry and Master Leschi slapped a hand to her forehead.

"Phillip! I knew I was forgetting something, of course that's today! I've been so wrapped up in . . . well, come have a look, we still have time! Phillip, go put on a colorful tunic, it's the fiftieth Diversary. Today! How I let that slip my . . . oh never mind, follow me, follow me." She led a bewildered Jacs up the staircase into the workshop while Phillip dashed into another room to change.

"I've been working on that escapement to keep the town clock on time since you left yesterday afternoon. As you remember, the biggest problem with our town clock is its size. Hand weight variability, wind, rain, and flocks of starlings can affect the wheel train, which sets the clock back and brings the whole town down on our heads." Jacs nodded as Master Leschi pulled out a notebook and continued. "So that got me thinking, why don't we extend these arms within the mechanism itself like so, and use a small weight here—" she indicated the respective points on her diagram "—and let gravity and the swing of the pendulum reset the weights rather than the wheel train. That way, the escapement itself—"

"—is not affected by variations in the drive force," Jacs finished excitedly.

"Precisely," Master Leschi beamed.

"Incredible! That sounds . . ." A blast from a trumpet cut through their discourse. "The procession!" she squeaked. "Quick, Master Leschi or we'll miss it!"

"Right you are, let's find Phillip." Master Leschi grabbed a blue-gray cloak off of a nearby model of a pedal powered boat, threw it around her shoulders, and they both hurried down the stairs. Phillip was waiting by the door, his round face beaming above the collar of a green tunic. He had even run a wet comb through his hair so that it tucked neatly behind his ears. Master Leschi patted his cheek affectionately at the sight of him.

He opened the door.

"My mother said she would wait by the clock tower in front of the fountain," Jacs said, anxiously looking toward the sounds of the procession.

"Lead the way!" said Master Leschi as she fished in her large pockets for a key to lock the front door.

With the sound of the trumpets and drumbeats getting steadily louder, they raced to the town square to find Ms. Tabart and to catch a glimpse of the royal family.

The town square was packed with people dressed in a myriad of colors. Ms. Tabart was standing on tiptoe looking out over the crowd, and waved to Jacs, Master Leschi, and Phillip when she spotted them. The three latecomers squeezed and pushed their way over to her.

"Just in time," she breathed. "Look!" Ms. Tabart indicated the cleared main road. Two trumpeters flanked a lone drummer. They were dressed in bright yellow livery edged with gold-and-blue embroidery. The heralding trio urged the townspeople on the side of the road to step back. People jostled and ripples formed in the crowd as they attempted to clear the way.

Jacs held her breath, noting that she was not the only one who did so. The town square itself seemed to draw a deep, collective breath in as the first carriage rounded the corner at the end of the street and came into view. The carriage glittered like a star and made some people shield their eyes. Golden carriages glided down the street, putting even the town goldsmith's display window to shame. The horses were a motley crew, some brown, others beige, some with black manes and tails, others shining a deep auburn in the sunlight. All proud and noble-looking beasts, and all with golden bridles studded with sapphires.

Guard pairs flanked each carriage and were spaced evenly down the line, the only ones relatively unadorned and unsmiling, their eyes darting around the crowd, small decorative gold-gilt shields held at the chest on their left arms, daggers sheathed at their hips. Their leather armor was light and simple, though oiled to a shine for the occasion, and each woman had her hair tied in a tail down her back or in a twist at the nape of her neck.

Eyes moving from the guard pairs and back to the carriages, Jacs squeezed her mother's arm. She had never in her life seen such splendor before, and the carriages, carts, and musicians seemed to just keep coming down the road. Smaller carts filled to the brim with rose petals were interspersed between the larger carriages, their drivers tossing handfuls of the fragrant petals into the crowd. Musicians with instruments Jacs had never seen before played perfectly in time despite the absence of a conductor and being spread out along the line.

The music was beautiful and Jacs felt a warm bubble of euphoric laughter build in her chest until it burst from her, unbridled. Her mother was laughing too and clapping along with the intricate melody.

Several carriages passed by where Jacs stood with her friends and family, her hair now full of petals, when an excited hush spread down the length of the street.

"The Queen!" people whispered down the line.

Jacs craned her neck even more to see over the heads of those in front of her. She stood on the edge of the fountain for a better view. Suddenly, she saw them. The Queen, flanked by the King and the Prince, rode on horseback between the last two carriages. The Queen rode on a palomino, the King on a blue roan, and the Prince on a chestnut. They wore navy-blue velvet edged with gold trim and had gold capes draped across their shoulders.

The Queen's riding gown was embellished with gold studs that made her look as though she were wearing a night sky filled with stars. Her hair flowed behind her in a luxurious ribbon and glistened like spun sunbeams. A golden crown glittered above her temples. Two banner bearers followed her, holding the Queen's coat of arms; a roaring lion under a large oak tree.

Jacs was struck by how close the royal family was to the adoring masses. She could reach out and almost touch them, yet somehow, they were an entire world away. Her eyes fell on the Prince and her breath caught in her throat. He sat confidently in his saddle, his cape much shorter than even his father's, as was befitting a prince, and tied from one shoulder under the opposite arm. A simple gold circlet nestled in his windswept hair, and a flash of silver glinted at his wrist. His eyes searched the crowd and for the briefest of moments, their eyes met, and he smiled at her. She felt the blood rush to her cheeks.

"He's quite handsome, isn't he?" her mother teased in her ear.

"Mum!" Jacs giggled and unconsciously twisted a strand of hair around her finger.

The procession made its way around the fountain in the middle of the square and passed under the town clock. Jacs stretched up on tiptoe, her hand resting lightly on her mother's shoulder to keep balanced. She noticed the procession stop and craned her neck to see two figures in purple hooded cloaks standing in its path.

There was a guttural chorus of, "Level the Upper!" Jacs craned her neck toward the sound and saw several more hooded figures step out onto the scaffolding around the large clock face. The music faltered, then stopped. The Upperites and Lowrians looked around nervously.

In the sudden silence, Jacs saw the cloaks on the scaffolding part and a lone figure with a bow step forward. Her eyes darted back to the Queen; she heard a bowstring tighten and release. A sickening thud strangled a scream. The King, the Prince, and the Queensguard sprang into action too late. Already her body was arcing around the arrow, red blooming like a rose around a fletched stem. Jacs's eyes widened in shock as the Queen fell. She heard the Prince's cry of anguish, a single broken note, and everyone started screaming.

The crowd thrashed and writhed like an angry snake. Jacs was jostled, pushed from the edge of the fountain, and almost thrown to the ground. Pain shot up from her foot as someone shoved past her. She reached for her mother and grasped a stranger's elbow. Taking a hasty step back, she collided with someone, then was slammed forward. Bodies rushed past and were pressed against her from all sides. Panicking, she looked around frantically. "Mum!" she called with dozens of other voices, some calling for loved ones, but many repeating iterations of the unbelievable truth: "The Queen is dead."

"Jacqueline! Here!" Phillip's large form filled her vision, and he grabbed her arm in a vise-like grip. Relief flooded through her, and she clung to him. Acting as a human plow, he swept her toward a side street where her mother and Master Leschi were waiting, pressed against a wall. Jacs could not see the Grimsbys.

"Jacqueline! Thank the Goddess!" her mother sobbed, pulling her close in a tight embrace.

"We need to get out of here." Master Leschi articulated everyone's thoughts. "Back to my place. Although I'd like nothing better than to be as far from here as possible."

They all nodded in bewildered agreement and set off after her. Jacs held tight to her mother's hand and Phillip's tunic as they were borne along with the tide of people.

Her mind had stalled. *The Queen, dead!* As the small group was jostled further and further from the town center, the thought reverberated inside Jacs's skull. Her mind kept replaying the images of the red rose blooming from the Queen's chest with a still quivering arrow at its center. The look of horror on the faces of King and Prince as they turned too late to protect her. The Golden shields that rose and enclosed the family like an oyster protecting its pearl.

It was not until they were all huddled in Master Leschi's living room—Phillip standing at the door next to a pile of "just-in-case" backpacks, cradling cups of tasteless tea, all listening to the chaos that was beyond the barricaded door—that Jacs asked the first question her mentor ever failed to answer.

"What does this mean for us?"

No one slept that night. The sounds of chaos rang out through the streets. Shouts from Upperite guards and yells from Lowrian citizens blurred together, neither side distinguishable from the other. The cacophony left much to the imagination. Jacs winced with every clang of steel on steel, and her stomach rolled when the sounds of steel on something much softer filtered into the still room. Women and men shrieked in pain and fear as the guards swept through the streets, determined to quash any residual rebellion, but blinded as to what form it would take. Three times the group huddled in the living room ready to flee before Phillip assured them it was a false alarm.

"Better in here than out there," he kept muttering to himself.

Master Leschi wrung her hands until they turned red and attempted to pace a rut in the floorboards. Ms. Tabart sat with her head in her hands. Jacs would have said she was sleeping if she had not been so unnaturally still.

She busied herself by making tea when it was needed and looking out from each of the windows in rotation. The mantel clock ticked sluggishly, and each chimed hour made Master Leschi wring her hands harder.

Once she muttered, "It was our clock, our clock they used. Those bastards! Ignorant, foolish . . ."

Jacs shuddered and moved to the windows in the kitchen.

Morning seemed reluctant to shed light on the night's activity. Finally the sun peeked over the hills to the east, streaking through the windows and illuminating the new lines and dark shadows around the eyes of those within the quiet house. Nobody moved. The streets were silent.

The day hardly dared to breathe.

The full extent of the damage done that night was revealed over the following days. The fountain in the town square was destroyed, trampled and broken bodies lying like discarded toys around its base. Upper and Lower citizens seemed equal only in death, their bodies lying side by side.

The royal procession had become a fortress overnight in a field on the edge of town. Carriages surrounded by wagons that in turn were surrounded by an ever-vigilant guard pair rotation meant that no Lowrian could get within arrow range of the royal family. Not that anyone would have dared. As the riot raged, guard pairs took to the streets. With cold contempt guiding their attacks, they cut down anyone wearing a hooded cloak. Anyone who got in their way was swiftly detained.

On the second evening, Jacs and Master Leschi stood, hands clasped, at the window of the upstairs workshop and watched in horror as their clock tower went up in flames. The dark sky glowed red above the rooftops and filled with plumes of smoke. With wild eyes, Master Leschi watched as the flames consumed her pride and joy. Hand to her mouth, she folded in on herself, sobs raking her narrow frame. Jacs, silent tears streaking her cheeks, held tight to her mentor. Phillip and Maria hovered nearby, unsure how best to help. They watched until the flames died and darkness swallowed the wreckage.

The King, anger's flames burning him from within, had ordered that the clock tower be burned to the ground. The still smoldering remains served as a warning to any rebel sympathizers. Three bodies were found in the wreckage, all too badly burned to be identified. Families most likely too frightened to claim them.

A number of heralds summoned the townspeople to attend the King's address the next morning. The sun hid behind a thick blanket of low-lying clouds, flat light making the world look two dimensional. Marching to the forlorn tolling of a bell, Jacs, Ms.

Tabart, Master Leschi, and Phillip joined the wary stream of citizens to meet once more in the town square. Mind numb as she looked at the ruin of the clock tower, Jacs marveled at the difference a few days could make. The memory of vibrant colors and lilting music seemed a lifetime ago in this gray town of mourning.

Eyes bloodshot, the King, heavily guarded, surveyed the crowd with a cold gaze. He stood in front of the broken fountain, bodies laid out in rows at his feet. The Prince stood to his right, hands clasped behind his back and head lowered. Four older women stood one pace behind the King, one speaking softly into his ear until he nodded and stepped forward to address the crowd.

"Lowrians," the King's voice echoed through the town, though he did not appear to raise it, "a faction among you have committed the highest treason. If any of you have information about their identities, step forward and be redeemed."

The crowd remained motionless.

The King's face hardened and he continued. "Your loyalty is misplaced. You cannot begin to imagine the grace, strength, and wisdom our Queen possessed." He paused. "In this time of great sorrow, we must stand firm under one banner. However, we cannot ignore the source of this tragedy. An act of such treason will have its consequences, and those responsible will be punished. The future of the relations between Upper and Lower Realms depends on the trust we are able to rebuild in the coming months. During this time, the Queendom will begin the designated period of mourning. In one year, we shall hold the Contest of Queens to determine our new ruler."

He was struggling to keep his face impassive as emotion threatened to break his composure. One of the women behind him cleared her throat and murmured a few words to him. He nodded, adjusted his coat, and continued. "We will also reconsider contact between the two lands. Our trade agreement will be revised to better protect the people of each land." Protests began to rise from the crowd. The King held up his hand for silence. "Details of this revision will be delivered once decisions have been finalized."

People were muttering angrily, and the crowd began to buzz like a hornets' nest. Seeing the volatile nature of the situation, the guard pairs tightened their ranks, and the King, the Prince, and the four women were guided off the makeshift podium to where their horses waited restlessly. The King's expression was like thunder, his eyes burned and shifted about the crowd. He glowered at any who dared meet his gaze. The four women strode near him, heads aloft, looking neither left nor right. One of the women, a pinched-face brunette with dark eyes, bent to speak in the King's ear. Finished, she straightened, and his expression darkened further.

Jacs's eyes moved to rest on the Prince. His expression was different from his father's, his manner different from the four circling women. He stared ahead blankly, hands clasped in front. Shoulders slumped, he seemed to fold into himself. One of the guards gently guided him toward his horse, her partner ready with a firm grip on the lead rope. While his body reacted to the touch automatically, his face registered the change in direction a few seconds later, like an echo after the initial scream has died away. He turned to the guard with that same lost look in his eyes and did what was instructed.

The ensemble gathered and moved at the command of a trumpet blast from the head of the line. Like an enormous beast lumbering to its feet, the procession lurched into motion. Jacs watched with a yearning she could not explain as the bright carriages were marched solemnly out of town.

9

PLANS AND INTERLUDES

The journey back up the Bridge was the longest Connor had ever experienced. His father rode beside him in silence. Pain and rage radiated from the King like a palpable force. Connor sat in shock, the breathtaking view and impossible closeness to the void that had enthralled him during the Descension barely registering with him now.

His mother. How could anyone want to hurt his mother? A woman who embodied kindness and care from the inside out. A woman who treated all of her people's needs before her own. The woman who taught him how to use a sword and spent just as much time teaching him when not to use it. His mother, now used for target practice in a Lowrian town square. In Jacs's town square. His eyes darkened. He saw the clock tower she had always raved about in her letters, saw the hooded figures step forward onto the scaffold, saw the archer aim true.

Murderers.

He gripped his reins tighter.

Lowrian cowards.

He shot an accusatory glare at the land that stretched out below him. The darkness in his eyes colored his view. The emerald green of the forests appeared gangrenous; the lakes and rivers, the color of bruises. Buildings speared the sky like rusty nails, striving but failing to reach the redemption of the Upper Realm.

And Jacs, his friend, his . . . no . . .

She designed the tower that supported those hooded traitors. His eyes fell to the woven band that encircled his wrist. The silver Griffin's-head clasp glinted in the sunlight. Jacs had sent it up for his sixteenth birthday once she had been sure the parcel would reach the top.

Seizing the dagger at his hip, he cut it off and let it fall into the void. It fluttered and twisted in the air. He spurred his mare onwards.

None of them should be trusted.

His father cleared his throat. "Son, I . . ."

Looking around, Connor fell into pace beside the King on the Bridge. His father's face was ashen, and his eyes held a faraway look, as if unable to focus. He groped for the right words and shook his head. "Son, I never thought I would be in this position. I do not . . . I cannot . . . but we must make plans."

"Father, isn't it too soon to—" Connor began.

"Too soon? No. To remain stagnant is to invite another attack."

Connor shivered under the intensity of his father's stare. There was no shred of the man he loved left in this stranger's eyes.

"We need to elect a new Queen. You need to take your place at her side. The Queendom will fall without her."

The words whipped around them in the wind. Connor looked to make sure they were not going to be overheard. He felt a conversation like this needed walls and locked doors. Instead they were suspended between the two realms, endless sky above, treacherous land below.

"Cornelius, we have one year to prepare for the Contest of Queens."

Connor's mouth fell open. "You were serious! I thought you said that to . . . to . . . I don't know, show the Lowrians we could not be so easily defeated."

The King looked at him. "Do you have a woman in mind to nominate as Queen; to challenge the Contest independently?"

Connor looked away, his face growing hot. He thought of the noblewomen in the Court—Hera Claustrom matched him in wits, but there was always something . . . off about her. Cynthia Doeboare made him laugh, but could she be serious when appropriate? Danielle Hart was gentle but too timid. Jacs . . . he shook his head angrily. Not even an option. To imagine choosing one of the other women for his Queen . . . "No," he mumbled. "I don't have a woman in mind."

"At seventeen, I should think there'd be at least a few women on your mind," the King said humorlessly. "None you would put forward as a nomination?"

Connor blinked the thought of Jacs away again. "Not to be Queen, Father."

The King studied his son thoughtfully and nodded, satisfied.

"Very well. Like I said, we have one year to prepare the three challenges. One year to put your mother's and my teachings into practice to help us find the woman who will rule the Queendom."

Connor hurried to recall what he had learned about the Contest of Queens from Master Clio.

"We will invite all eligible Upperite women of age to attend, and by the end of the third challenge, we will have found our Queen." His father spoke with a conviction Connor envied.

"Yes, Father," he said.

"Traditionally, each task has been based around the ability to demonstrate certain crucial traits a Queen must have to be an effective ruler. Your mother spent the better part of the last six years impressing upon you these traits and—" his voice faltered "—she should have been the one to assist you in creating these tasks, but . . . as it stands now, it will be your duty to determine what these traits are, and how you will test for them. Of course, you can peruse the historic records of past contests for inspiration, but keep in mind that this is to find the suitable Queen for this age. Not the age of Queen Hendrick or Queen Thea."

Mouth still hanging open, Connor reeled with the responsibility suddenly heaped on his shoulders. "Why me?" he spluttered.

His father pulled his horse up, causing a ripple down the procession that he did not appear to notice or care about.

"Son, you have been trained since birth in the ways of our people, our land, and our culture. You have studied the political system and have mastered the correct protocol for interacting with the Court. You were born to take the role of advisor to the Queen. You know the traits required in a Queen to ensure the best possible future for our Queendom better than you know yourself. It is your duty." His father pushed on, ignoring his son's stricken face. "Don't forget, you have the Council of Four to oversee your efforts and to go to for guidance. All plans will go through them."

Connor looked ahead to the large gold carriage the members of the Council were currently occupying and frowned as his father continued. "As for the guest list, the feasts, and the celebratory ceremony, I will handle those. Any questions, boy?"

Connor cleared his throat. "How long do I have to plan?"

The King paused thoughtfully. "If you have the tasks designed in six months, that leaves us six months to assess them and pull them from paper to reality."

Nodding, the Prince sat taller in his saddle. "Then I had better get started."

The funeral lasted three weeks in the Upper Realm. Connor passed through each ceremony, feast, and celebration of life as if in a trance. Despite his resolution on the Bridge, he had not thought about the tasks since first speaking of them with his father. He had not thought much about anything.

He was only aware of a dull throbbing in his brain and a sharp, jagged pain in his heart, as though he had been the one shot with an arrow.

He found himself waking in the middle of the night with a start, hand clutching at a fletched shaft that was not there. He had worn off the embroidery on the chest piece of his mourning attire. His perpetual rubbing of the area over his heart had become a habit, much to the seamstress's displeasure.

Noblewomen and men offered their condolences as frequently as they seemed to offer their daughters to his attention. He thanked them respectfully and talked with the daughter in question for a length of time that appeared to satisfy her parents before making his excuses and withdrawing, only to be met with another Lord and her daughter.

"Prince Cornelius, we are terribly sorry for your loss and for the loss of our Queendom. May I introduce my daughter, Dame Fawn Lupine . . ."

News of the contest had spread quickly.

While Connor felt as though a gear had stalled in his mind, his father had been seized by a violent passion to act. The fire, always ready to take control of any man who succumbs to his temper, had raged within the King as he had watched the Lowrians' clock tower fall to ash, and now he desperately fueled the flames with his grief. He did not appear to pause for sleep or meals. Instead he barked orders at distressed serving women and men at all hours of the day and night.

Making preparations for the funeral. Making preparations for the contest. Seeing to royal decrees and plans of action surrounding future trade with the Lower Realm.

Connor marveled at the man's stamina. He hesitated before entering his father's study; he could hear the staccato of his father's voice through the door. Edith hovered with a food tray near his elbow and nodded at him encouragingly.

"Send patrols into Nadir and Southgate. We need to increase our presence in the Lower Realm, and we need to send reinforcements into Bridgeport; the Levelists are gaining more and more confidence since . . ." the King barked.

Connor pushed open the door and his father cut off.

"What is it? What's happened?" the King demanded, his eyes bloodshot. He was standing behind his desk, a map of the two realms stretched out on its surface and weighted at the corners with books. Four people Connor recognized stood around the desk. One, Masterchiv Rathbone, the head of the royal guard, leaned over the map intently like his father, her golden cloak thrown back out of the way to reveal a worn but well-polished sword at her waist. Its hilt was delicately engraved with a roaring lion's head. Councilors Portia Stewart and Rosalind Perda stood on either side of the King. The former looked as though the slightest draft from the fireplace would sweep her off her feet, and the latter had a pinched look on her face that intensified with Connor's entrance. The fourth was the servant Perkins, who had ink stains on his nose and splattered on his writing hand from his haste to record his King's orders. Connor noticed that Cllr. Perda whispered to Perkins while the King was distracted by his entrance. Perkins crossed lines of writing out and wrote new lines in at her word. Connor frowned.

"Good afternoon, Father," Connor said loudly. "I brought you lunch." He nodded to Edith, who hurried to set the lunch tray on the least-papered area of the King's desk.

His father's eyes narrowed, and he looked at his son with a slow-dawning recognition. He turned back to the map and dismissed him curtly. "No. I've only just broken my fast."

Cllr. Perda cleared her throat and said crisply, "Your Majesty, it is well past noon. I'm sure we would all benefit from some refreshments." Her tone bordered on patronizing, and she shared a brief look with Cllr. Stewart.

A look of confusion flashed across the King's face as he glanced at the clock on his mantel. "Ah . . ." he faltered. "Too right, Cllr.

Perda. It appears time has flown by. Yes, let us break for now. We can reconvene—"

"Let us reconvene at three o'clock, Your Majesty," Cllr. Stewart almost whispered, her voice breathy but carrying an authority that allowed her to cut through the King's command. "You should meet with Lord Claustrom. She has sent a message about her concerns regarding the upcoming contest."

"Lord Claus . . . yes. Yes, of course." The King looked down at the tray of food, then at Connor, his eyes slightly out of focus. "Thank you, boy."

Connor bowed, recognizing the dismissal. He gestured for Edith to accompany him out. Cllr. Perda's voice followed them through the door. "And Your Majesty, after your meeting with Lord Claustrom, we need to discuss the implications of recent events on our upcoming Trade Week. It is the Councilors' opinion that we redu—"

The door clicked closed behind him.

Late afternoon found the Prince sitting on a bench in the gardens. He was surrounded by the fragrance of rosemary and lavender, the buzzing of bees, and his thoughts. How he had managed to evade the simpering nobles was beyond him. He could not decide which was worse to navigate, his father's ire or the nobles' weighted condolences.

At least his father was honest and could be honestly dealt with. He plucked absently at a lavender flower, spreading the little petals on the stones at his feet. He hated the layered conversations with the nobles. A chickadee chirped happily on a rosebush and flew over to land in a nearby birdbath. It hopped around the rim before jumping in with a ruffle of feathers. Really what he wanted was someone to talk to.

He had a letter scrunched up in his fist, the words

Heartsick, but still,

Yours,
Jacs
Flight 218

visible near his palm. He could not bring himself to reply. What would he say? Anytime he started a response he just ended up looking at an empty page, watching the scene from that day play out in his mind.

There had been so much blood. He did not want any reminder of his trip to the Lower Realm, and these letters kept showing up with infuriatingly precise regularity. Her words wrote themselves in circles around his head:

Connor, I'm worried. Were you hurt in the riots? We had a mass funeral service today. None of the . . . them matched your description, but I haven't heard from you since.

Connor, it's been weeks and I haven't had any letters from you. Why have I not heard from you?

The Queen's death has made everything here worse. Connor, I miss you. Please send a letter down. I need my friend back, I need to know you're okay.

He could no longer sit in his favorite spot by the Cliff's edge without seeing a balloon hanging from the branches of the oak tree. Written in angry scratches and smudged in places, today's letter had been the worst:

> *Connor, I know what Upperites think of us. We had a town meeting today and they're going to be installing scry crystals in more shops and even some along the main streets. It's supposedly for our protection, but I know it's so they can watch us more easily. They see us as criminals, even murderers. They treat us like we're already guilty. If that's how the Upperite guards see us, I think I can guess how you see us. How you see me.*
>
> *It's garbage, Connor. How dare you be like them? Don't you know me at all? We've known each other for over three years now and suddenly you've forgotten? I thought we were—or at least I thought you were better than them. Basemutts they call us, and worse. I can't even think of a name for you. What kind of friend abandons you when you need them the most?*

It went on. Angrily, he stuffed the letter into his pocket. His other hand massaged a spot on his chest. With each new letter, guilt crept around his heart.

He wanted to be angry.

It was so much easier if he just hated them all. *But . . . Jacs is one of them,* a little voice whispered in his mind. He found it much harder to hate her.

He heard stones crunch under slippered feet and turned his head toward the sound.

"Forgive me, Your Grace, I just . . . I thought you might be hungry." Dame Hera Claustrom stepped into view. She was a vision, her blonde hair swept up in a mourning veil. Her black dress was simple yet fell about her luxuriously. She wore an expression that Connor guessed she hoped was timid, but her blue eyes were proud.

She hovered for a moment before holding out a small basket. "I spoke to the kitchens and Master Marmaduke prepared this for you." Without waiting for his invitation, she approached his bench and sat down next to him.

Connor bit his tongue and smiled gratefully. "Thank you, that was very thoughtful of you, Dame Claustrom." He looked in the basket. "Fruit tarts. Master Marmaduke never fails." He offered her the first pick, insisting as she made to wave him away.

She smiled contentedly and obliged, biting into the delicate pastry and trying to salvage the crumbling disaster that ensued. "There's no graceful way to eat these, is there?" she mused.

"Definitely not," he agreed, as custard covered their fingers and spilled onto their laps. "That's why she will always pack . . ." He rummaged in the basket. "Ah! These!" He brandished a handful of napkins like a bouquet of flowers and they laughed, Hera's laugh like a chiming bell in the still garden. They both fumbled with fruit filling and mopped at the mess.

Brushing off his hands, he said, "Thank you, Dame Claustrom, I have not had occasion to laugh for some time now."

She looked down and made to touch his hand before thinking better of it.

"Your Grace, no words I can say can aptly describe the depths of my sorrow for your loss. Queen Ariel was a shining beacon of hope and a true ruler of light. She will be missed in all the breaking hearts around the Queendom. And—" she paused delicately and met his gaze "—I know it may sound selfish, but I thank the Goddess every day that you escaped those Lowrian creatures." She dabbed at nothing near her eye. The intensity of her words made the blue of her irises sparkle. Connor's gaze shifted unconsciously from the depths of her eyes to her lips.

Abruptly he rubbed his chest and looked away, intoning the same script he had used with every other well-wisher. "Thank you for your kind words; they are a source of solace in this time of sadness."

They sat in silence for a time. Hera attempted more than once to catch his gaze again, but he was absorbed in his own thoughts and did not notice. Almost to himself, he said, "A Queendom cannot function without its Queen. We will all have to be strong in the months to come."

"We are lucky to have your expertise in the creation of the contest. Have you any thoughts on what the tasks will entail?" she asked hesitantly.

"I . . ." He looked at her sharply, a knowing smile stealing across his face before he could stop it. "Well, if you are to be a contestant, I cannot give you any unfair advantage, now can I?" he said wryly, by now well used to women attempting to find out more about the upcoming contest. Annoyance flashed across her face and she hurriedly looked at her hands clasped on her lap. He paused, and when she did not reply, he asked, "Am I right in thinking you will be competing?"

She smiled coyly. "Perhaps."

"Then I had better guard my tongue," he said.

"And I had better guard my heart," she purred.

"S-some would say matters of the heart have no place in the Contest of Queens." Connor stumbled; her words had thrown him.

"Perhaps," she said in a low voice, "but they are not designing the tasks."

He was very aware of how close they were.

A chickadee chirped happily near the birdbath. He could count the moments passing, slipping through his fingers like sand. He was conscious that it was his turn to say something, but he could not remember what they were talking about. She was looking at him from beneath her lashes. A soft breeze caressed her hair, and he lifted his hand to do the same, when a sudden clatter made them both jump. The wind had knocked the now empty basket to the ground.

The moment shattered, Hera smiled at him and rose from the bench. Connor hurried to stand too. Taking the basket in her hand, she curtsied and stated, "But I have intruded upon your company for too long, Your Grace. I should return this to the kitchens." She indicated the basket. Moving closer, she said, "Again, I am so very sorry for what you must be feeling. Please let me know if there is anything I can do to help." She rested a hand briefly on his arm. "Anything at all."

Connor watched her go, his arm tingling where she had touched him. As though a fire had been lit beneath him, he hurried to the study. Pulling out all the books, scrolls, and tomes he could find on past contests, he snapped an order that he was not to be disturbed and set to work.

"What does it mean to be Queen?" he murmured to himself.

10

MALLARD AND MEMORIES

J acs read over the letter once more, brushing her fingers over her words, and hovered on the last paragraphs:

I won't apologize for my last, but I will say I sent it in haste. You'll think I'm exaggerating but . . . Connor, I'm really not doing okay without you. Mum's worried about the farm, Master Leschi has not left the house in weeks, Phillip is just . . . he's so angry right now, and we're not allowed to meet with people like we used to, so even if I wanted to visit some of my friends here, I can't. Being in town is dangerous. The guard pairs are everywhere and they're awful. I think the scry crystals are contagious, they multiply in number by the day.

Now they're in every shop and on every storefront.

Connor, I don't know why I haven't heard from you, but please just let me know you're okay. I understand if you're angry with what the assassins did to our Queen, but you have to believe it wasn't Master Leschi, and it certainly wasn't me. We lost our Queen too that day, and we're being punished for it still.

Please write back.

I just . . . I really miss you,

Yours,
Jacs
Flight 222

Hating how pathetic she sounded, but not knowing how else to share the pain his silence was causing her, she folded the letter, and slotted it into place at the base of the candle. With well-practiced hands, Jacs lit the little candle carefully, let it hang beneath, and held the balloon until it stretched taut and nudged gently for release. Smiling sadly to herself, she held it at arm's length and guided it up and out of her hands. She watched as it rose serenely up the fissure following the length of the Cliff. It was a perfect day for flying, and the balloon made its ascent with only the slightest of wobbles as the air pressure changed around it. Clutching Connor's ring where it hung around her neck, she watched as the balloon almost disappeared toward the top and willed it a safe landing in the large tree overhanging the Cliff edge.

The land must look so peaceful from up there, she mused, *but I suppose everything looks better from far away. I wonder what Connor sees when he looks down at us.* Jacs stared up at the waterfall, miserable. She still had a few hours before the newly instated curfew, so she threw herself down on the grass and picked at a stalk moodily. It had now been five weeks since she had last received word from Connor. Five weeks of perfect summer days to send her balloons up. Five weeks of no reply. There had never been such a severe break in their correspondence, especially during such good weather.

She understood that the whole Queendom was in mourning, but it just did not make sense that she would not have heard from him by now.

Maybe something had happened to him.

She shook her head at the thought. If anything, he was doing what the guards were doing: lumping all Lowrians in with the assassins. Likely, he would have decided not to keep the acquaintance of a basemutt like her. She had thought he was different.

But he knows me, a voice in the back of her mind whispered reassuringly.

But my people killed his Queen, another voice, harsher than the first, whispered back. She huffed angrily, tears prickling the corners of her eyes. Chin resting on her fist, she swept the other hand across the yellow grass. It was dry and crinkled like strips of paper under her palm.

In an effort to distract herself from the ache in her chest, she tried to remember when it had rained last. Craning her neck to look up at the waterfall, she noticed that it was more of a drizzle than a torrent. She rolled over on her back to look at the sky. Cloudless and perfect blue. The same as it had been for the last month or more. Their crops could only realistically take a few more weeks without rainfall. She studied the sluggish river for a while, imagining ways to divert it through her farm.

Her musings were interrupted by heavy footfalls on the dirt road. She slowly turned over onto her stomach and lay very still.

The Upperite guard pairs had not left Bridgeport with the rest of the royal procession and had taken to harassing anyone for information about the assassins.

Peering from her spot on the ground, she was surprised to see Mallard stomp along the riverbank, sit down heavily, and throw a stone into the water. Jacs was torn. She wanted to leave, but she did not want Mallard to notice she was there. As she lay undecided, she heard Mallard sniff and watched as he wiped something away from his eye.

He was crying.

Jacs did not know what to do. She could just stay where she was and hope he didn't notice her, but the thought of him finding out she had been there the whole time was not a pleasant one. Instead, her instincts screaming at her to stop, she stood up slowly, walked over to where he was sitting with his back to her, and put a hand on his shoulder as she sat beside him. He gave a start and pushed himself away from her.

"Who—? Jacqueline! How long have you . . ." He looked around wildly.

"Is everything okay, Mal?" she asked softly, stifling the urge to flinch.

"What? Yeah . . . yeah, of course . . . I was just . . . everything's fine." The silence stretched awkwardly between them. His eyes held a challenge.

"I was really sorry to hear about your dad," she said finally. Her voice was low as if she were soothing a wounded dog. After the dust had settled, the town held a service for all those who had died on the day the Queen was murdered. Gordon Wetler, Mallard's father, was one of the names among dozens now engraved on the memorial stone erected where the fountain had stood.

Mallard sniffed again and wiped his nose with the back of his hand angrily. "No you're not, not really," he spat. "No one is. You don't know what it's like. People think he was one of the killers, you know. Got guards harassing my Ma, 'Where was your husband? Who does he associate with?'" He threw another stone angrily into the water. "As if she needs all that. Harassing me: 'Did you know of any plans your father may have had?'. . . Like he would have told me even if he had any plans!" He looked at Jacs desperately. "He may have hated the Upperites, but my Da was no killer."

Jacs did not know what to say; she patted his arm and wished she had just stayed lying in the grass.

He scoffed. "See, you don't get it."

Jacs dropped her hand, hugged her arms around her knees, and stared at the water, the last of the ripples fading away.

"It sounds like it's been really hard for you," Jacs said quietly. "I guess I just don't really know what to say to help. Words often fail when you need them the most." Her brow furrowed and she continued. "It's not right you have to deal with grief while your Da's name is being slandered by people who didn't even know him."

Mallard nodded slowly and threw another stone into the river.

Jacs did the same, and they watched the ripples collide and blend together. "But I do know some of what you're feeling," she continued haltingly, "and I wouldn't wish that on anyone. I'm so sorry, Mal. When I lost my dad . . . It was . . . I mean . . . I'm so sorry for what you're feeling, and for what you and your Mum are going through."

Mallard looked at her sideways. "Thanks," he muttered finally.

They were silent for a long time, Jacs staring out over the water, thinking. The memory, so frequently shunted to the back of her mind, bloomed behind her eyes; the petals enveloped her and pulled her down to relive that day before she had a chance to stop it.

Eight years had passed since, and Jacs could still feel the soft weight of her new wool coat. It fell to her mid-thigh and made her feel like a Queen. Spring was just around the corner and they had decided to get one last skate on the ice in before it all melted. Jacs stepped out of the front door and swept her coat around her playfully as her father pulled up on the reins, stopping the cart in front of her. Pretending to lift up the hem of a long skirt with one hand, Jacs placed the fingers of her other hand delicately into her father's outstretched palm and he pulled her up to sit in the cab beside him. Francis expertly flicked the reins, asking as the wagon began to move, "Where to, miss?"

Jacs laughed, playing along. "The moon!"

Her father scratched his chin thoughtfully. "I'm not sure Clover has it in her. How about the river instead?" They both laughed, and he whistled Clover into motion. The wagon trundled off down the snowy lane.

Clover slowed to a stop at a soft call from Francis, and they pulled up by the bank of a wide stretch of the river. The snow was almost untouched, and Jacs felt as though she had stepped into a dream. The trees were laced with snow that floated down around her, cloaking her in the purest white when her father shook the branches. Tiny icicles hung from the tip of every pine needle and clinked together softly like a wind chime when the breeze rustled through them. The river rocks looked like holiday puddings, the thick layer of snow like icing.

Her dad retrieved an old broom from the wagon and cleared the snow from an area of the river, revealing the smooth frozen surface, while Jacs tied her skates on. Wobbling slightly, she walked onto the ice, her father close behind. They skated for most of the afternoon; Francis spun Jacs around in his arms, holding her tight in case she fell. Jacs looked up at him, her anchor, her world. He twirled her out and let go, sending her spinning away from him across the rink. She came to a stop beyond the boundary Francis had swept clear. She turned and grinned at him.

"Look!" she called. "No hands!" And she waved her arms above her head laughing.

That's when it happened.

Jacs lost her balance, and her skates slid out from under her. She fell on the ice. Hard. As she lay on her back, trying to draw breath into her lungs, she heard the sound that made her blood run cold as the water beneath. A deep booming crack that reverberated inside her heart.

"Stay where you are!" Francis yelled. "I'm coming to get you."

A ringing filled her ears as she felt the ice shift beneath her hand. Deep cracks ran around and away from her like a spider's web. She hardly dared to breathe. She shifted her head slightly to see her father lower himself to the ice and spread himself out, crawling toward Jacs on his stomach. The distance between them stretched out for miles, and he seemed to take forever to reach her, each movement sending a ripple through the ice. The web of cracks danced and shuddered. Finally he grasped her hand, an anchor.

"It's gonna be okay, we're okay," he murmured.

She squeezed his hand tight. The ice moved again. The vivid cracks spread like veins, separating them from the bank.

"I'm sorry," Jacs stammered. "I slipped, I'm so so . . ." She gasped as the piece of ice she was on tilted and freezing water rushed to meet her. Francis gripped her hand tighter and looked around him.

"It's okay, it wasn't your fault." He paused and seemed to nod his head as if agreeing to what he was about to do.

"Okay, honey," he said, "here's what I want you to do. No, look at me, not the ice, there's a good girl. Okay, we need to get back to the bank, so listen carefully." Jacs whimpered, but he continued. "I want you to shift onto your stomach, slowly, easy now."

She did as she was told, tears leaking out from under her closed eyelids.

He went on. "Now, see the wagon? I want you to slide over there carefully, take your time." She looked at him fearfully and whimpered again.

"You can do this sweetie, and I'll be right behind you." He tried to smile encouragingly. Slowly, she let go of his hand and began to slide along the ice on her belly. Francis stayed perfectly still. She had moved no more than a few yards when the ice beneath her vanished. Her wrist plunged into the water. The sudden cold sent a shock through her system and she scrambled backward in panic. Her weight shifted, the ice fractured beneath her and buckled. With a jolt, the solid became fluid and she went under, her scream freezing in her lungs as the icy depths claimed her.

"JACS!" her father's roar rang in her ears as she slipped under the ice.

Cold blackness engulfed her and seemed to pour through her veins. Jacs felt her arms move in slow motion, the freezing water sending daggers to her bones. She screamed again. Bubbles erupted from her mouth and rushed upward to escape the depths she was now sinking into. Her skates pulled at her feet, her coat dragged at her limbs, the current swept her sideways, and she no longer knew which way was up. She willed her legs to kick and her arms to stroke, but they would not listen.

She saw light filtering through the ice that had settled on top of her. The pieces were jagged and confusing like the fragments of a broken mirror. Her mind stalled. Her lungs burned. The river prepared to claim her for its own.

Then an arm was around her waist, and she was yanked upward. Ripped from the river's grasp. Her head broke the surface; she coughed and gulped in breaths of air. Jacs dipped beneath the water again, but her father forced her into the light. His grip broke through her numbness and she felt her limbs respond. Her legs kicked. Her hands scrambled as she clutched at the ice, fumbling for a hold on the smooth surface.

"Quick," Francis said, shivering, "get to the bank, I'm right behind you."

The current was strong. He fought to keep them both above water as it threatened to sweep them under and away. With one hand grasping at the fracturing ice, and the other wrapped tightly around Jacs, he struggled against the cold, the weight, and the will of the river. Letting go of the ice, he grasped Jacs's waist firmly with both hands, kicked hard, and launched her into the air. The effort shot Jacs out of the water and along the ice, away from the jagged hole.

His head sunk below the surface . . . and did not come up again.

Without looking back, Jacs scrambled across the ice. The jigsaw-like pieces tipped and pitched, threatening to send her under but she did not go in again. Reaching the wagon, she collapsed onto the ground, shivering uncontrollably.

After a few minutes, she noticed the silence. Wiping her eyes, she lifted her head and turned to where her father should have been. All she saw was the empty river. Panicking, she looked around her wildly.

"Dad?" she called.

"Dad!"

"DAD!" Tears were streaming down her face. Shaking off her skates, she stood and stumbled back to the bank, scanning the surface for any sign of him. Her heart stopped. "No," she whispered. She watched, not quite believing, as the ice serenely settled back into position.

He was gone.

Jacs scrunched up her face as the memory faded, leaving icy fingers in her mind. She looked away from Mal and hurriedly wiped her eyes.

Mal had not noticed, or if he did, he did not say anything. Instead, he hesitated, his mouth forming words well before he asked. "So . . . I mean . . . I know we're not . . . you know . . . but you . . . know . . . how long does it take to . . . to sink in . . . I mean . . ."

Jacs looked at him quizzically.

Mal gestured vaguely with his hands and explained. "I still can't believe he's gone. I keep setting him a plate at the table. Keep expecting him to come in with flour on his boots and have Ma tell him off. Some days I can't—" he gestured vaguely to his chest "—and other days I go to ask him where he put the bread knife." He looked at his hands and muttered, "I guess it sounds dumb." His cheeks were bright red, and he picked up another rock to throw into the water.

Jacs answered slowly. "I'm not sure it ever really does. Sink in, I mean. At least for me, I'm always half expecting to see him walking down the field." She wrestled with the lump in her throat for a moment. "But, I don't think that's a bad thing. Sometimes it feels like he's right here with me. I find strength in that."

Mallard nodded. It was his turn to awkwardly pat Jacs on the back. He looked at her as if for the first time and said hesitantly, "Listen . . . I, ah . . ." He cleared his throat. "I'm sorry I was such a prick to you at school . . . I'm sorry you stopped coming 'cause of me . . . And I know it doesn't make it better . . . but I'm sorry . . . I was a real . . ." His face was glowing red now.

Jacs cut him off. "You really were." Then softer: "Thanks, Mal."

A bell started tolling in the town. Jacs and Mallard looked toward it warily.

"That's the ten-minute warning," Jacs noted.

"Yeah," Mallard grumbled. "Still can't believe we're being told when to go to bed."

Jacs made a noise of agreement. "I heard it was so that people don't meet after dark. It just seems like they want to let us know they still have control."

Mallard stood up and stretched, a shy smile on his lips. "Hey, Bookhead, can I walk you home?"

Jacs rolled her eyes and smiled. "Only because we're going the same way."

Jacs arrived home to find her mother sitting at the kitchen table with notebooks and parchment spread out across its surface. She was muttering numbers to herself and flicking through different pages to check facts. The frown on her face deepened.

"Hi Mum," Jacs called when her mother did not look up at her entrance.

"Hi Plum, hold on one moment." She finished counting and wrote down the number on another sheet of parchment. She looked it over and sighed.

"What is it?" Jacs sat down next to her, looking over her mother's shoulder.

Shaking her head, Ms. Tabart put down her pen and turned to face Jacs. "I'm going over our budget. The King just announced the trade cutbacks, and what with how this drought is going . . ." She sighed heavily. "Sweetheart, we're in trouble."

Jacs looked down at the numbers, willing them to rearrange themselves.

"How much trouble?" she asked.

"Well, we're going to have to make some cutbacks of our own. We can sell Brindle and Delilah." Jacs groaned as her mother continued. "Brindle's old, and having a horse is a luxury we can't afford to feed right now. We will also have to tighten our purse strings a little—" Ms. Tabart corrected herself "—a lot. I think we should cut our losses and harvest what we can while we can. I just don't see how we will make it through the winter otherwise."

Jacs looked over the numbers and knew she was right, but it did not stop her from cursing under her breath.

The sun's final rays shone briefly off an object in the corner of the kitchen that Jacs had not noticed before. It was a large, pale purple crystal about the height of Jacs's hand. A scry crystal. It sat, glinting in the dying sunlight, as though it had always been there. Issued by order of Queen Ariel years ago, the crystals had adorned the corners of all schoolhouses, courthouses, and training barracks for as far back as Jacs could remember. No one was sure exactly how they worked; they had been told that they were for surveillance. But now it was in their kitchen.

"Mum?" Jacs ventured. "What's that doing in the house?"

Ms. Tabart looked up and followed Jac's gaze. She sighed. "Oh, that is our new, standard-issue scry crystal. The King decreed that every household have one installed in the largest room. That reminds me, go say your full name into it, Plum. It needs to register you."

"Register me?"

"Yes, the King's messenger came by this afternoon while you were out. He said that each member of the family needs to speak their name into the scry crystal to register themselves in it. That way, should the scryers have need to, they can locate anyone as long as they are within range of a crystal. Apparently, in the town they were just using the registered guards' names to see the streets and that was enough, but now that they're in the homes . . ." She shook her head. "I didn't quite understand the why of it, but now the scryers can keep an eye on us eating breakfast." Ms. Tabart rolled her eyes. "What else they're expecting to see, I don't know, but just be careful around it. Just the thought of it gives me the chills." She shuddered.

Jacs stared from her mother to the purple crystal in shock. "They can't—"

"They have, Plum. Careful." Ms. Tabart pressed the last word like a baker rolling out dough and looked at Jacs pointedly.

Jacs bit back her comment and instead walked over to the crystal.

"Jacs Tabart," she said clearly and felt a small electric shock run through her. The crystal shone brightly, then resumed its subdued glow.

"Your full name, Plum." Ms. Tabart sighed.

Jacs opened her mouth and stopped. She turned from the crystal defiantly and said, "No, they can bloody well ask for that if they need it."

Her mother bit her lip but said nothing. She returned to the numbers in front of her and sighed again. ". . . Big trouble," she whispered.

11

A VISIT WITH MASTER LESCHI

Ms. Tabart had not been wrong—they were in trouble, but so was the whole town. The trade revisions had affected everyone, and the stress of it was plain on every face. Scry crystals glimmered everywhere now. They sat, merciless sentries, silently watching and waiting for a Lowrian to incriminate themselves. A purple glow seemed to cling to the peripheries of each person's vision, until people started dreaming in shades of purple.

The guards' presence had doubled, but their inability to find out the identities of the remaining hooded traitors led them to double their efforts and shift to ever more brutal methods. They treated every Lowrian as a criminal or an accomplice. Their suspicion spread through the town like poison and caused the citizens to distrust their neighbors. Fights broke out more frequently as tightly wound individuals snapped at ever increasing intervals. If the skirmishes were not settled quickly, they were settled ruthlessly by the guards. Jacs found it harder and harder to see the guard pairs as women like her, their actions and words transforming them into cruel armored creatures of malice.

The guards always traveled in pairs. They carried daggers and leather straps to restrain their quarry, but from Jacs's observations, these tended to be more for show or for particularly harsh lessons than anything. The guards themselves were weapon enough. Each woman in a guard pair worked with her partner seamlessly and beautifully. Watching them work was like watching a well-choreographed and extremely violent dance. They had a way of completely overpowering and throwing their opponent off balance (regardless of size) that Jacs found both impressive and terrifying.

She experienced their force firsthand one morning while walking past the clock tower. One minute she was reaching into her satchel, and the next she was on the ground with her arm wrenched behind her back. Pain seared through wrist, elbow, cheek, and knee. Now, as much as possible, she avoided going into town. For the first time in her life, she was truly thankful to live on a farm. The guards did not patrol as rigorously outside the town boundary, so she and her mother escaped the brunt of their patrols.

Six months passed, and for Jacs they passed slowly. She still sent letters to Connor, but rarely, and was always careful to do it at dusk, for fear of discovery. She still had not received a reply, but she continued to check for his boats. If anything, the activity was a small source of hope, and was something to do that shone as a blatant act of defiance against the ever-increasing restrictions. Her latest one was full of treasonous ideas, and made her glad she had always written as "Jacs." A name only she and Connor used:

> *Remember when we used to talk about the changes we would make if we were Queen? Back then it was things like, "less chores," "everyone gets to ride a Griffin on their fourteenth birthday," "boys get to try out for guards if they want to," and other silly wishes like that. I was thinking this morning about what I'd do if I were Queen now, and my ideas were much less fanciful:*

> * *Give all citizens of both realms the right to a fair trial. No punishments or executions will be allowed unless a person is judged to deserve them by a group of their peers.*
> * *Remove scry crystals. No: Destroy scry crystals. These are an invasion of privacy and an act against our basic human rights.*
> * *Frequent travel between the realms is a must. When one group of people does not know of or identify with another group of people, it is dangerous and only breeds hate, prejudice, and violence. If travel is not possible, education is the next best thing.*

> *But this is a working list. I am sure I will think of more by this evening. I hope every day that I will check the nets and find one of your boats there. Until that day, I am and always will be,*

> *Yours,*
> *Jacs*
> *Flight 225*

Following a skirmish Jacs had had with a particularly spiteful pair of guards while purchasing jars in town, she now sat at the kitchen table shoving a number of very sad-looking cucumbers into jars of brine. She screwed a lid on savagely. *It's been more than six months since the Queen died, why can't they just leave?* The salt stung a fresh graze on her palm. She scrunched up her nose at the memory of her face pressed against the bricks of Ms. Orion's bookshop, a low warning whispered in her ear, and reached for another jar.

Jacs had kept busy as the summer heat continued to scorch their crops. A hot summer followed by a sweltering autumn gave them no respite. She had tried a different approach with the cucumbers, growing them inside and protecting the water in their soil from evaporating with sheets of waxed canvas. It did not work as well as she had hoped, but it was better than nothing.

The design needs tweaking, she mused to herself, and suddenly her thoughts shifted to Master Leschi.

Guilt twisted her stomach. Jacs had not been able to visit in a month. Screwing another lid closed, she looked out the window and decided. She would visit her that afternoon.

Master Leschi's doorbell clunked sadly when Jacs pulled the cord. She waited and listened for movement inside. Finally she heard, "I told you once, I'll tell you again, I built the clock to tell people the time, not to shoot people from!" A haggard Master Leschi pulled open the door, her eyes taking a moment to focus on Jacs.

"Ah!" She slumped against the door frame. "Jacqueline, it's you. Come in." She turned and walked back into the house, leaving Jacs to follow and close the door.

The sitting room was a mess. Books were strewn everywhere, plates of half-eaten and abandoned food scattered across available surfaces. Master Leschi threw herself into an armchair, draping an arm across her eyes, and did not react as her movement sent a small tower of papers skidding across the floor.

"Oh, how the mighty have fallen," she drawled sardonically.

Jacs looked around and could not locate the smug little purple crystal anywhere. Whispering, she asked, "Where's your crystal?"

Master Leschi laughed bitterly. "Why, in my largest room of course!" She gestured to a large pile of books arranged in a sort of fort and a small harp that had an odd, spindly attachment. "Which reminds me," she said suddenly, standing up and shuffling over to the instrument. She flicked a switch; a pendulum started to swing, a mechanism began to whirl, and the harp began to play. There was no particular melody, just constant sound. It was not unpleasant, but it was unexpected.

"Now, we can talk in privacy. They don't see, they don't hear, they don't get the satisfaction," Master Leschi explained as she sat back down.

"Can they really hear us too?" Jacs asked. "I thought they just watched us."

There had been a number of different opinions on what the crystals did circulating around the town. The guards tended to exaggerate their abilities or contradict the existing rumors when asked. As a result, many regarded the glowing gems as sinister, omniscient, uninvited house guests.

Master Leschi waved a hand vaguely above her head. "Who knows what they can actually do," she said dramatically. "Better to be careful though."

Master Leschi covered her eyes again.

Jacs felt a pang in her heart. Master Leschi never dismissed an unanswered question.

Jacs cleared a spot on another chair and sat down gingerly.

"How are you, Master Leschi?"

Her mentor waved a hand to take in the disheveled room. "Been better, dear. Definitely been better."

Jacs looked around helplessly. "I'll make tea," she offered and hurried into the kitchen. She returned a little while later to see that Master Leschi had not moved. Coaxing her upright, she pressed a full cup into her hands, and she sat back down to wait.

"It's those damn guards." Master Leschi sighed. "It's bad enough that my life's triumph was an assassin's perch, but then to have it burned to a crisp like that." She stifled a sob. "And those paired beasts won't leave me alone. Two-headed vipers. They took Phillip in for another bout of questioning this morning and I can't imagine what they're doing to him." She scrubbed angrily at the tears welling in her eyes.

Jacs's face creased with concern. "Did they say when he'd be let go?"

"No."

Jacs swore under her breath. "I'm so sorry, Master Leschi. I should have come to see you sooner."

Master Leschi shook her head. "You came when you could, I appreciate that. You've got your own fish to fry."

The two women sat in silence for a time.

"There must be something we can do," Jacs thought aloud.

Master Leschi laughed without humor. "With the guards? It's not their fault. Not really." She smiled bitterly at the confusion in Jacs's eyes. "Think about it, they're all Upperites. They were most likely brought up and trained with a preconceived notion of what kind of people live in the Lower Realm. They never meet us, so they have no evidence to the contrary, and they live in their elevated chunk of the Queendom with even nature telling them they are above us."

Master Leschi drew a breath and took a despondent sip of her tea. "Then they finally visit us, and we are what they expected: shabby, less affluent, a crowd of fawning simpletons, and boom!" She slopped tea onto her lap as she gesticulated wildly. "We kill their beloved Queen."

"Our beloved Queen," Jacs corrected.

Master Leschi raised an eyebrow. "Our Queen? In name, sure." She waved the comment away and looked at Jacs intensely. "Now they have years of prejudice validated and they feel justified spreading this image of Lowrians to include every Lower citizen they meet. They expect to see a town full of lying, scheming, unlawful threats to the Queendom, and so that's exactly what they see. Then they treat us accordingly. Ironically, how we react to their treatment tends to justify it. Contempt breeds contempt." Master Leschi finished with the satisfaction of one tying a bow on a present.

Jacs shook her head, thinking of Connor. "But we're not like that. That's not right."

Master Leschi nodded. "Just because it isn't right, doesn't mean it isn't true. They are doing only what they think is justified. That is not to say that it is. No one thinks of herself as the villain. There are no 'good women' and 'bad women.' There are just people trying to do what they think is the right thing to do."

Jacs heard the tremor in her voice and realized her mentor was trying to convince herself for the sake of her son just as much as she was trying to convince Jacs.

"Do you think it will get better, or worse?" Jacs asked.

Master Leschi sipped her tea and sighed. "I hope it will get better, but without anything to change the track we're on, how can it not get worse? I just hope our new Queen has some of the same mercy Queen Ariel possessed."

The two fell into a thoughtful silence. Jacs thought about the upcoming contest. She knew very little about it except that it was through this contest that a new ruler would be deemed worthy.

Whatever "worthy" means, she thought bitterly.

She tried to imagine the type of person this new Queen might be. Where would her sympathies lie? Would she visit the Lower Realm more than Queen Ariel had? Would she care about the Lower Realm at all? If only there was a way to make her care. To show her how the Upperite policies were affecting their way of life. A wheel in her head clicked into place and started turning. What if she knew their way of life?

"Master Leschi," Jacs began. "Who is qualified to enter the Contest of Queens?"

"Pardon?" Master Leschi said absently as she blew on her tea.

"The Contest of Queens. Is it just Upperites who can enter, or anyone?" Jacs asked.

Master Leschi looked thoughtful. "I . . ." She hesitated. "You know, I'm not sure. I would say only Upperites would qualify, but the last contest was decades ago."

Jacs bit her lip. "And given what happened, I doubt they would accept Lowrian contestants."

Master Leschi nodded. "Fair assumption."

"But what if we found a way to enter a Lowrian? Then, if she won, the Queen would know what it was to be from the Lower Realm and would rule with our well-being in her best interest," Jacs said.

Master Leschi nodded again, considering. "So, hypothetically, you're suggesting we find a candidate to somehow sneak up the Cliff, pass every toll guard, and blend in enough with the Upperites to enter the contest unnoticed. Compete in each task, making sure to never break her cover—no, not just compete in, win each task. Then win the contest itself that is designed with women from the Upper Realm in mind as the contestants, to become Queen?"

Jacs looked down glumly. "Well . . . when you put it that way—"

"First obstacle. How would we get you up there?" She now sat upright, her brows furrowed. She placed her teacup precariously on a pile of books and rested her chin on the tips of her steepled fingers.

Jacs spluttered, "What? Me? No—"

"Of course you. You've got the only head I trust for the crown. But it's the Cliff that is the biggest hurdle. The Bridge is simply out of the question; you can't hope to sneak past one, let alone all of the toll guards, unnoticed." The spark had returned to Master Leschi's eyes, and she scrambled for a pen, loaded it up with ink, and scoured the papers on the floor for a blank sheet.

"A project!" she exclaimed. "That's what we needed! And one with a purpose! You brilliant girl, the way your mind works, I could kiss you! Ah, here we go." She extracted and brandished an empty notebook. "Grab your cup, let's go upstairs. This is much bigger than a clock and we only have—" she paused to count "—five and a half months to pull it off!" She took the stairs two at a time, Jacs jogging to keep up.

Two hours later and they were still no closer to finding a way up the Cliff face without using the Bridge. Papers were piled and thrown about the large worktable they were sharing. Rough pictures of grappling hooks, spiked boots, rock-climbing equipment, and what appeared to be a design for attachable wings littered the surface. Jacs had been glad when they moved on from the rock-climbing idea. She was not sure five months was long enough to gain the skills to climb all that way. Plus, they would need an awfully long rope.

Master Leschi stood up, announced she needed another cup of tea, and headed down the stairs. Jacs was lying in the middle of the floor on her back, willing an idea to come to her. She let her eyes roam the odd contraptions hanging from the ceiling and spotted one of the earlier hot-air balloon models. She screamed in triumph.

"Master Leschi!" She shot up and ran down the stairs, almost knocking Master Leschi off her feet in the kitchen. Excitedly, she clasped her arms. "Master Leschi! What if we made one more hot-air balloon?"

Master Leschi's face shone with realization. "My dear," she beamed, "there will come a day when they sing songs about you!" She paused and added thoughtfully, "We are going to need a lot more canvas." Her eyes widened suddenly, and she seized Jacs's shoulders. Her voice was full of warning as she cautioned, "Jacqueline, you must understand. What we are doing is dangerous and could be considered treason. If we decide to do this, you must not tell anyone. Not even your mother. Not yet. If you are willing to go through with this endeavor, you need to realize that you are gambling your life for an outcome we can only pray for."

Jacs felt a stone form in the pit of her stomach. She had been so caught up in the plan that she had failed to consider the enormity of her role in it. Her mind began to race. Even if they could get her up there, even if she found her way to the castle, and even if she could get into the contest, could she win? She—Jacs—a poor Lowrian girl? Would there be any point in trying if she had even the slightest of doubts? She would be putting all of her eggs and all of her hopes in one very rickety basket.

Her musings were interrupted by the opening and closing of the front door.

"Phillip!" Master Leschi cried and rushed to meet him. Jacs followed slightly behind but ran to join them when she heard Master Leschi gasp. Rounding the corner to the entrance hallway, she stopped short.

"Oh, Phillip," Jacs moaned. "What did they do to you?"

Master Leschi had her hands over her mouth, eyes wide. Phillip was hunched over, clutching his side with what Jacs suspected was a bruised or broken rib. His face was a mess. One eye was swollen shut, the other had a deep purple bruise blossoming already. His lip was split and bleeding, and he had a muddy, bloodied graze along his jawline.

"Hi, Ma. Hiya, Jacqueline," he muttered. Master Leschi had seized him under his arm and began helping him into a chair in the living room. Jacs ran to the kitchen, collected a fresh towel and basin of water, and brought it to Phillip. Without a word, she began dabbing at his lip and jaw.

He winced but let her finish.

"Phillip, what happened?" Master Leschi breathed once he was settled. "What did they want? Information? Did they . . . torture you?" Her voice dropped to a hysterical whisper.

"No," he touched the skin under his bruised eye gingerly and pulled his hand away with a grimace. "They brought me in for questioning and they let me go after they were satisfied."

"Then what happened to your face?" Jacs asked.

"This was after. I saw a couple of guards threatening Mr. Severin outside his shop. His shop's two down from the clock tower. Those bloody she-wolves, picking on him like it was sport." He paused to adjust his seat, slumping further into the chair.

The women nodded and gestured for him to continue.

"You know George—bit gruff around the gills but loyal to a fault, especially when it comes to the royals," he said. "So I go over to see if I could help, but they didn't take to that. Evened the odds a bit much for their liking, I guess. Next thing I know, George is doubled over with his wrists strapped together, and I'm on the ground." He shook his head slowly. "It all happened so fast, I can't even remember what I said to finally make them stop." He sighed. "When it was over, they took George with them and left me on the ground. Couldn't move my arms at all. Don't know what they did to me. I must have passed out but came to, probably a few minutes later. They were gone by then. Ms. Kato found me and set me right. I'm okay, really. It looks worse than it is." He shifted his weight and pain flashed across his battered features.

"My boy." Master Leschi's hand fluttered nervously for a safe place to rest to provide comfort.

"But you did nothing wrong!" Jacs felt the blood rushing in her ears. Phillip, her bear-sized lamb—how could they? The damp cloth in her shaking hand dripped red streaks down her forearm.

Master Leschi's cheeks flushed and her voice trembled. "Protectors of the peace," she spat, "those brutes! Those good for noth—"

"Ma," Phillip interrupted sharply, "don't, they might . . . or someone might . . . just, be careful with what you say! I can't protect you . . . you know what they're like."

The room fell into an uncomfortable silence.

Phillip groaned. "I need to lie down." He stood slowly and his mother helped him limp off to his bedroom.

When she returned a while later, Master Leschi saw that a light had ignited in Jacs's eyes.

"Let's get started," she asserted, and almost dragged her mentor up to the workshop.

12

PREPARATIONS

Connor took a breath and rapped confidently on the door to his father's private study.

"Enter!" King Aren's voice called. Connor shifted the books and papers in his arms to turn the doorknob. Pushing the door open, he stepped into the room and let the door close behind him.

The room was in a state of organized chaos, as it always was of late. Maps covered the large desk, and papers covered the maps. A half-empty goblet of wine acted as a paperweight, and a cold cup of tea held a book open.

Bookshelves lined two of the walls, and a map of the realm hung on the empty space above the mantel. His father sat at his desk with his back to the window. He was reading from a large book and looked up as his son entered.

"Cornelius, good morning!" His father's voice cracked. He had aged ten years in the last six months.

"It's afternoon now, Father," Connor replied.

"Ah, so it is!" His father eyed a clock on the mantel and sighed. "Time sure does fly when you're immersed in trade law."

Connor smiled weakly. "I'll take your word for it. Father, do you have a moment?"

His father waved him into a chair opposite. "I finished the plans for each task," Connor said as he sat down.

His father leaned forward excitedly. "All three?" he asked.

"Yes." Connor spread out the papers with pictures and plans for each task outlined clearly. The six months since the Queen's death had been a whirlwind of planning for the Prince. It had been a cruel job to receive. He struggled to busy himself with work to avoid thinking about his mother, but was forced in every aspect of the contest's design to consider her. Finishing it well and quickly seemed to be the only way to escape this specific brand of torture.

In the end, he had based the three tasks on the teachings she had instilled in him. He began describing what was involved in each task, and which trait he expected to target. A Queen must rule with strength, and have the wisdom to know when a gentle approach is needed; a Queen must rule with intelligence, even under perilous circumstances; and a Queen must be the voice of her people, often at great personal sacrifice.

As he reached his description of this last trait, he felt a lump form in his throat. His father reached across the plans and patted the back of his hand.

"She would be proud, my boy," he said gruffly.

Connor nodded, cleared his throat, and pressed on with the rest of his plans. His father listened eagerly, asking some clarifying questions, but for the most part, letting his son speak uninterrupted. Finally, as Connor finished, King Aren sat back in his chair and surveyed the Prince carefully.

"My boy," he marveled, "I think you've done it. They're a little unorthodox, I'll admit, and we'll have to speak with the Court, but any woman who bests each of these tasks will no doubt make a fine Queen, and possibly a fine match."

Connor beamed and breathed an inward sigh of relief. The dark rings under his eyes spoke of the many sleepless nights he had endured designing each of these tasks.

"So," his father clapped his hands together, "now we have just under six months left. That will give us enough time to clear the plans with the Council, set up the tasks, and make all the necessary arrangements for the contestants. I will have Alastor send the invitations out to all the eligible Upperite women tomorrow."

Connor's mind flashed to his airborne correspondences. Without thinking he asked, "And what of the Lowrian women?"

His father looked stunned but recovered quickly, "Well, they will find out the identity of their new Upper-born Queen once the tasks are complete." He looked at his son with eyes of steel. "Why? What of them, boy?"

Connor shook his head, "Nothing, Father. Forgive me, I have not been sleeping well."

After a moment, King Aren nodded, then stood up pointedly. Connor scrambled to his feet and gathered up his papers.

"Leave them," his father commanded. "I'll send for Perkins to collect them for the Council. After they have reviewed it, he will oversee bringing your vision to life." By way of explanation he supplied, "He is loyal and he knows to hold his tongue so we won't run the risk of a well-connected Dame gaining the upper hand."

Connor nodded in agreement. Suddenly he felt lightheaded. It was really happening.

In the few months leading up to the contest, Connor thought of little else but the coming tasks. He was grateful for the distraction as it meant that he did not have to think too hard about that day in the Lower Realm, and it also meant that those he talked with had something else to talk with him about. He had taken to guarding his words so much around possible contestants that he felt as though he could only speak in riddles.

The court preparations were consuming the staff. Feasts were planned, courses perfected, and dishes endlessly created, sampled, critiqued, and altered. Various ingredients from all over the Upper Realm were brought to the castle in droves. At all hours of the day, Connor could expect various mouthwatering smells to waft through the castle hallways. Master Marmaduke might as well have grown an extra pair of arms to keep up with the workload.

In anticipation of the increased number of guests, every available room had been cleaned and furnished. It was decided that the rooms within the castle would be reserved for the chosen contestants and their families.

A small town's worth of large tents had been erected for unsuccessful contestants, serving staff, and any other spectators wishing to attend. He had heard that most Inns and boardinghouses in Basileia were completely booked for a month either side of the contest.

Connor did not envy Perkins in the slightest. Although the tasks he had designed did not require extensive construction, that did not mean the organization was easy. As the Prince was returning to his room one evening, he almost ran right into the poor man as he bustled around a corner.

"Apologies, Your Grace," Perkins yelped and bowed hurriedly, spilling a number of small purple crystals on the ground. He bent to pick them up. Connor retrieved one from near his heel and examined it. He recognized it as one of the scry crystals his father had begun installing in rebellious centers of the Lower Realm. The crystals Jacs kept complaining about in her letters. Looking at them up close, they were rather beautiful.

"What are you doing with these, Perkins?" he asked with wonder, watching as the candlelight danced across the faceted surfaces and seemed to absorb into the depths.

Perkins swelled proudly. "I have been working with the Court Scryers to find a way that would allow spectators to see what was happening during the tasks, especially the first two. While they are wonderful tasks, Your Grace, brilliantly thought through to be sure, they do not offer much in the way of—" he paused to search for the appropriate word "—viewability for those not directly involved. These crystals will be placed at various points around each course. Spectators will then be able to view the contestants using a mirror or water basin. It's quite simple, really. Just say the name of the contestant you want to observe into a mirror, and poof! Her image will appear on the surface, as long as she is in range of a crystal. Spectators will be able to watch what is happening on the course, without having to be on the course!"

Connor's mouth opened in awe as he turned the little crystal over in his hand. "Perkins, this is genius!" He watched his reflection flicker across one of the planes, then suddenly frowned. "I trust all crystals will be collected and accounted for at the end of each task?"

Perkins nodded, suddenly serious. "Oh yes, Your Grace. Yes, we have documented each one and will be sure they are well protected. Convenience will not endanger the Queendom, I give you my word." The Prince nodded and thanked Perkins for his hard work. The genial servant bowed again and departed.

Shortly after, Connor finally reached the quiet of his chamber. He closed the door softly behind him, crossed the room, and fell onto his bed with a sigh. A slight figure he had not noticed by his desk suddenly straightened with a squeak.

"Your Grace!"

It was Edith.

Connor propped himself up on his elbow warily. "Good evening, Edith." He took in her stricken face and asked slowly, "What were you doing?"

"I—I came to light the fire," she stammered.

"Ah . . ." He glanced at the empty fire grate. "Did you get lost?" He rose from the bed and moved to stand before her. She did not reply and would not meet his eyes. He noticed she had shifted a large object on the desk behind her back. "Edith," he said quietly, as she shifted uncomfortably under his gaze, "I will ask you again, what were you doing?" When she did not answer, he asked, "Edith, were you looking for information about the contest?"

Her head shot up sharply. "No! No, Your Grace, I would never!"

Connor's heart felt lighter but now he was even more confused. "Well then, what is it?"

She took a breath in and said, "I came in to light the fire, and the window was open, so I went over to close it and knocked a box off of your desk." Connor felt a weight form in his chest as she continued, "Paper went everywhere so I picked it all up but I didn't know what they were. I didn't realize they were letters until I read some and . . ." Her last words were barely audible. "I'm so sorry, Your Grace. It was not my place."

Connor had grown cold. Letters. Jacs's letters. Lowrian letters. The implications of Edith's discovery threatened to overwhelm him but he forced himself to remain calm. "You read some? How much is 'some'?"

"Not much at all, only enough to realize it was private and then I put them all away and that's when you came in."

Connor scrutinized her pleading eyes and blushing cheeks. He expected to feel betrayed but was surprised to find he felt relieved. He sighed and sat on the edge of his bed with his face in his hands.

Edith, shocked by his sudden change of demeanor, stammered, "Y-Your Grace, are you well? Shall I fetch someone?"

He waved away her concern, "No, no. Edith, sit, please."

She hovered, uncertain, wringing her hands before obliging. She sat awkwardly on the edge of his bed and reiterated, "I really am sorry, Your Grace. I didn't think."

Connor smiled and looked at her. "It's all right, they're just letters." He paused, and added, "That does not mean I want to catch you reading them again. They're still—" he groped for the right word "—personal."

She nodded and looked at her hands clasped in her lap. He stood and walked over to the box she had hurriedly returned to his desk. It was a rich mahogany so skillfully crafted that it did not appear to have seams, hinges, or joints.

He returned to the bed and carefully, reverentially, opened the box. There were hundreds of carefully folded letters inside.

He found the letter that had been opened and refolded it properly. Edith's face burned.

"These are from my . . ." He paused, unsure of how to continue, then ran his thumb along the words *Yours, Jacs* and finished, "an old friend. But I have not communicated with her since . . . in a long time." He had not told anyone about his correspondence with Jacs. Now, finally, here was an opportunity, and still he teetered on the edge of his decision. To tell Edith would be to make it all real. *And then what?* a voice chided.

Edith still did not look up, did not notice the struggle flashing across the Prince's face, but something drove her to ask, "Will she be competing?"

Connor shut the lid with a snap. "No," he replied curtly. The moment passed. "No, she will not. You may go, Edith. I will not need a fire tonight. I trust you will keep this box and our discussion to yourself?"

She quickly stood up and bowed, "Yes, of course, Your Grace. Thank you." Hurriedly she gathered her things and left. Connor heard but did not see the door close behind her. He stared at the box in his hands for a long time after. The candles burned low, spluttered, and went out.

13

FIRST FLIGHT

Dear Connor,
   You need to know that though I don't think I'll ever understand your silence, I forgive you for it. Now and forever, I will always be,

   Yours,
   Jacs
   Flight 227

It was three days before the contest and the weather was perfect. The clear spring day had eased into a cool, still night. Jacs and Master Leschi were in the Tabarts' barn, carefully folding an impossible amount of material. Jacs's mother stood in the corner of the barn, her arms crossed and her brow furrowed with worry. Once the design of the balloon had been perfected, it had been impossible to keep their plans from Ms. Tabart. And it was Ms. Tabart who had suggested the barn when they had needed a space big enough to hide their equipment.

"This is madness," Ms. Tabart muttered.

"It's funny how often madness and genius are confused," Master Leschi mused, causing Jacs to smile. She sobered at the look on her mother's face.

"Mum, you know I have to do this. We can't afford to have another winter like the last, and the guards . . . If all I do is tell those in charge about the damage the guards are causing, then at least I've done something. They can't ignore us then."

Her mother pulled the strand of hair Jacs had been twirling furiously out of her hands and brushed it behind her ear. "I know Plum." She sighed. "And you are very, very brave for what you are doing. But I'm your mother, and it is my right to worry about you."

Jacs grinned and hugged her. "Once I'm in the contest, you'll be able to see me through the scrying mirrors anyway, so I won't seem so . . . so . . . far away." She finished in a small voice.

The whole village had been called to a meeting by royal command the day before. A droning guard had shown them all how to use small basins of water and mirrors to view the contest. As it would have taken too long to send messengers with the contestants' names to each town and village in the Lower Realm once they were chosen, the Lowrians were given the name "Amanuensis" to use. When speaking this name, it would show the woman writing up the highlights at the end of each day of the contest for the Lowrians to read. Their viewing was severely restricted, but almost everything was at this point. It was from this meeting Jacs had discovered that the contestants were selected at the opening feast at the palace. So all she had to do was attend that feast and make sure she was chosen.

The setting sun shone through the high barn window and Master Leschi cleared her throat. "Okay," she asserted, "we have half an hour of light left so let's go over the rigging one more time." She unfurled a short roll of parchment and began checking items off while muttering under her breath. Satisfied, she walked over to where Jacs and Ms. Tabart were standing.

"I still can't believe you are doing this without a trial run!" Ms. Tabart suddenly exploded, all her months of worry boiling to a point.

"We have tested each aspect as best we could, Maria," Master Leschi soothed. "You know we can't risk being spotted! We're just lucky the guards don't seem to care about what goes on inside this barn."

Ms. Tabart bit her lip and Jacs felt her stomach twist painfully. She did not want to add to her mother's worry any more than needed, but she was terrified. She clasped her hands in front of her to hide their trembling.

"Besides, Mum—" she feigned levity "—I've been making these things for the past four years. This one is just a bit bigger. That's all."

Her mother raised her eyebrow and shot her a look but said nothing.

Jacs kissed her lightly on the cheek and went to collect her small bag from beside the door. The trick was to make sure the basket was as light as possible, so she was only taking what was necessary. A small packet of food, a skin of water, the clothes on her back, and Connor's ring on the chain around her neck. She had debated for a long time whether or not to take it, but in the end she realized that it was the best chance she had of finding him. A part of her hoped desperately to find him in the palace to see that he was okay. A larger part of her wanted to find him to throw his ring in his face. Maybe he'd respond to that.

She was wearing the dress she had worn during the Diversary and tried to ignore any notion of omens. The dress had required mending in places and she had altered it to accommodate how much she had grown in the last year. Despite the memories that hung from the garment like fog, it was still the nicest thing she owned. To compete to be Queen, she assumed she would need to look like one. She smoothed her skirts nervously, suddenly wishing she had asked Connor more, or any, questions about Upperite fashion. Her nicest dress may look like rags compared with their finery. Her mother, Master Leschi, and Jacs had all scrounged, sold, and borrowed as much as they could, given the circumstances, so that she now had a hefty weight of copper yoals, silver scyphs and even a gold faering in her bag to buy a new outfit if needed, but what if it wasn't enough?

"All right, Jacqueline," Master Leschi said, "Help me with this side. Maria, grab that corner; we are on a tight schedule, so let's hurry!"

Together, the three women packed and loaded the hot-air balloon on the back of a wagon. They waited until the sun had completely set and the moon hung low on the horizon before opening the barn door and slowly walking the wagon out into the night. Since selling Delilah, they no longer had a horse, so the women pulled and pushed the wagon out of the farm and toward the Cliff. Jacs pushed at the back while her mother and mentor pulled from the front.

She stifled a laugh at how absurd they all must look. They had scouted out a perfect location for launch weeks before, choosing a spot that was a safe distance from the Bridge, the town, and any major roads to avoid being spotted. It was quite a distance from the farm as a result. Soon, they were all sweating profusely and panting hard as they pushed the wagon across the scorched grassland. Dust filled their noses and made them sneeze. Jacs silently cursed the heavy folds of her skirts that tangled about her calves.

By the time they arrived at the desired spot, the moon had risen. The sliver of a crescent glowed softly as if careful not to reveal them by shining too brightly.

Master Leschi's eyes gleamed with excitement. "Right!" she whispered, "Let's set up."

They spread out the large balloon flat on the ground. During their many experiments, they had discovered a lightweight material used by the town florist and the town goldsmith. Getting enough of the fabric had been tricky, but little by little they were able to collect a sufficient amount. They then made the fabric airtight with a sealant similar to the wax Jacs had used on her smaller models. However, this sealant did not melt as it warmed up. The most difficult aspect had been how to stoke, stock, and contain the fire. As this problem had only been worked out theoretically, Jacs just hoped their calculations were correct.

Jacs was pleased to feel the chill of the night air on her skin. Colder external air would help her balloon lift more effectively, but on the other hand, it also meant that she would require more fuel to keep the temperature inside the balloon up. She studied the small pile of wood in the balloon's basket. She hoped it would be enough.

Jacs jittered almost visibly with nerves, and Master Leschi wordlessly took from her fumbling fingers a length of rope that she then finished tying. Jacs nodded gratefully and moved to help her mother set up the basket.

"Now remember," Ms. Tabart said quietly, "once you get to the top, get out and get rid of the balloon as quickly as possible. We will be well clear of the area, so push it over the Cliff and let us pick up the pieces. You cannot be discovered." Jacs nodded seriously, neither of them mentioning the fact that, without a way down, this was effectively a one-way trip.

"I love you so much, sweetheart, and I'm so very proud of you." Ms. Tabart squeezed her daughter tightly.

Jacs swallowed the lump in her throat, "I love you too, Mum. Thank you for helping me do this. I promise I won't let you down."

Ms. Tabart smiled sadly. "You never could. I know it sounds selfish, but right now I really wish you had taken up a milder inter-est . . . like fishing, or embroidery." They both attempted to laugh.

Master Leschi cleared her throat awkwardly. "Jacqueline?" she ventured as Jacs turned to face her: "It has been an honor watching you explore the possibilities of this world. I have enjoyed every moment being your mentor. I am—" her voice caught for a moment "—so very proud of you." Jacs hugged her and drew her mother in for a group embrace.

"Everything will work out—we've planned this down to the stitch," Jacs said with forced optimism. "Let's get the fire started or I won't get off the ground before dawn."

With the balloon laid out and the fire lit, Jacs, Ms. Tabart, and Master Leschi all sat on the wagon watching with unrestrained awe as the balloon began to fill with air. Like a giant beast slowly waking from slumber, it stretched and rose with feline grace. The anchor ropes extended from each corner of the basket, tethering it to the ground.

All too soon, Jacs was climbing into the wicker basket and making herself comfortable on the pile of wood on the floor. She felt ridiculous. Her mother had done her hair in a delicate plait and she was wearing a bright yellow dress. The juxtaposition of attire and situation brought a smile to her face.

Master Leschi and Ms. Tabart leaned over the lip of the basket to give her one last hug.

"Now, when we cut the lines, you'll start heading straight up. You can't steer, but it's a still night so you should be fine. I've included a grappling hook if you need to grab onto a tree or something at the top to pull yourself in," Master Leschi said quickly. She took a shaky breath before continuing, "You can always dampen the flame to slow your ascent, and stoke it higher to quicken it."

Jacs nodded. She had been over all of this a thousand times but it seemed to ease her mentor's nerves to remind her. "Mum, Master Leschi, I'll be fine. There's no wind, the night is cool, all I have to do is go up." She smiled with a confidence she did not entirely feel. "I love you both, and will come back either with a crown on my head or with an army of guards on my heels—kidding, Mum, only kidding," she hastened to add.

One last tight hug and a kiss for her mother, and the two older women moved to their places by the tethers. They had decided that they would cut the tethers diagonal to each other to avoid destabilizing the balloon.

"Three," announced Master Leschi.

"Two," forced Ms. Tabart. The first two lines were cut and the women hurried to the second set.

"One," Jacs whispered and closed her eyes. The basket tipped slightly, and nothing happened. She opened her eyes in disappointment but squealed when she saw the ground smoothly disappearing beneath her. She saw her mother with a hand to her mouth, clutching Master Leschi's arm, and Master Leschi waving excitedly with her free hand.

Jacs laughed, exhilaration and relief radiating from her in waves. She closed her eyes and felt the brisk night air caress her cheeks and hair.

With every flicker of flame in the burner, she rose higher and higher, until she could barely distinguish the two women far below and could only just make out the outline of the wagon.

The balloon rose up the Cliff face in eerie silence. Only the crackle of flames and the groaning of the fabric met her ears. She saw the dim lights of the town far in the distance and wondered where her farm was.

It was impossible to make out much in the faint light of the moon.

Scanning the ground beneath her, she thought she saw a small cluster of lights detach itself from the town and make its way in the direction of the Cliff. Squinting in the darkness, she could not make out what or whom the lights belonged to. Swallowing a wave of uneasiness that caused her stomach to clench, she shifted her gaze to the horizon.

The stars seemed to float down to meet her as she climbed ever higher in the balloon.

She allowed herself a moment to purely enjoy the flight. Just a moment to marvel at the grace of the giant balloon. A moment to take in the dim glowing line of the horizon far off in the distance, and to feel the air dance around her.

Then she forced herself to focus. In the dark she did not want to miss the top, get ensnared in outlying roots or branches, or have her balloon damaged on the Cliff face. Alert, she added more fuel to the fire, craning her neck to study the rock gliding past meters from her, wary for signs of change.

About an hour of steady ascension passed, with Jacs guiding the balloon up the side of the Cliff, pushing herself away at times with a long pole when the balloon floated too close to the sharp rocks and adjusting the fire as conditions changed, until she saw the Cliff edge. An outcrop of roots and tree branches came into view, and she fumbled around the basket for her bag and the grappling hook, placing the pole at her feet. She would likely have only one chance at a landing. She dampened the fire by reducing the airflow to the flame and felt the balloon slow down. Her breath came in short, sharp bursts and she forced herself to calm down. *It will be fine, just like you practiced . . . on the ground.* She swallowed.

The top of the basket was now level with the Cliff edge, although too far away. Jacs sent thanks to Master Leschi for the grappling hook. Balancing the hook in her palm, her other hand holding the length of rope it was attached to, she scanned the Clifftop for an anchor point. Spotting a large tree close to the edge, she swung the hook and let it fly. It fell short. Jacs swore. She licked her lips, pulled in the hook, and tried again. This time it caught briefly on a root before swinging free. The basket was climbing steadily higher and Jacs felt the beginnings of panic spreading across her heart. She shook herself and, focusing intensely on one of the tree's branches, she tossed the hook a third time.

"Yes!" Jacs hissed as the hook held and the rope pulled taut.

Quickly, she pulled the basket closer to the Cliff edge. Working fast, she turned and cut off all airflow to the fire, sealing it up and allowing it to die completely. She then turned back to the rope and—

"No . . ." The word broke from her.

In the time it took to kill the fire, the length of the rope tied to the hook had slipped over the side. She hadn't tied it to the hot air balloon. Cursing her oversight, Jacs looked around her; the balloon had started sinking. Soon the basket would be below the level of the Clifftop. She was sinking back into the void.

Although she had lost her anchor line, Jacs was only a short distance away from solid ground. If she stretched out her hands, she could touch it. Ignoring the dizzying nothingness below her and steeling herself for what she had to do, she gathered up her skirts, put one foot on the basket rim, and without looking down, sprang from the basket, pushing it away from her as she flew through the air. The Clifftop rushed to meet her and she scrambled to grab hold of anything as she felt the basket tip away from her. With a jolt and a tumble, she rolled onto the grass. Laughing close to tears, she hugged the ground, turned over, and watched as the balloon floated slowly down, the air inside the canvas cooling.

Sitting back from the edge, she hugged her knees to her chest and looked out to the Lower Realm. A golden glow lit the mountains to the East. Shielding her eyes, she gasped. The dawn broke. Her heart skipped a beat. She watched, with childlike wonder, the sunrise for the first time in her life. Lowrian sunrises were afterthoughts, the world already alight by the time the sun peaked its face over the mountains. But this . . . her breath caught in her throat as the world lit up before her. The sun spread its rays like arms outstretched in welcome, painting everything in a golden glow. Rolling onto her stomach, she shimmied to the very edge of the Cliff and looked down, her head resting on her hands. Still shrouded in shadow was a collection of houses far below. Was her town really that small? Jacs thought she spotted her farm but could not be sure. Looking straight down, she saw her balloon finishing its descent toward the matchbox wagon. They had done it!

Scanning the ground, Jacs looked for her accomplices. A rushing filled her ears and her mouth went dry. Where she expected to see two ant-sized women waiting for the balloon to land, she saw eight, six of whom moved in pairs, some carrying torches.

The realization left Jacs's stomach plummeting off the Cliff.

Jacs swore loudly. "No, no, no!" Tears stung her eyes and she watched, helpless, as the tiny scene unfolded below. Two of the six approached her mother and her mentor. Jacs squinted, desperately trying to make out what was happening a world away below her. The pinprick figures converged. Jacs cried out and felt icy fingers clench around her heart as the group moved toward the nearby horses.

Her imagination ran wild. She thought of Phillip's battered and bloodied face. She thought of the square filled with bodies lined up in neat rows before the King. She imagined the limp bodies of the two women she loved most in the world being dragged to . . . to . . . where? What would their punishment be?

The other four guards waited as the balloon finished its descent, then began loading it into the wagon.

Jacs shuffled backward away from the edge and stood up shaking. They had been caught. It was all her fault, and she had no way to help them. No way to get to them. No way of knowing what would happen to them.

Suddenly she was eight years old again. Her father slipping beyond her reach. The image of ice serenely settling into place floated into her mind's eye. Her mother and her mentor, her lifelines, now far below, and Jacs was just as powerless now as she was then. Just as helpless. Her protectors, gone.

Because of you, a cruel voice breathed from the back of her mind.

Stop that. Jacs shook herself, gripping her arms tightly as though to pull herself away from the abyss she had fallen into countless times before.

You survive and they pay the price, the quiet, familiar voice accused.

No. Tendrils of panic began to twist themselves into her mind.

Just like your dad, the cruel voice whispered.

STOP, a louder voice commanded.

Standing up, she paced back and forth angrily. She bit the skin around her thumbnail until she tasted blood. Fighting the ice, fighting the panic, Jacs fueled anger's fire. How could she have been so arrogant as to think they would get away with this? It was a giant balloon—how did they possibly imagine no one would notice it?

Her thoughts continued to race. She could not get down. She could not get help. She did not know if they knew she had been in the balloon, although, as Maria Tabart's daughter and Master Leschi's pupil, she could guess it would not take long for someone to notice her absence and connect the dots. *More like stars in Orion's belt,* she thought bitterly. It was all her fault. Taking a shaky breath, and another, she forced herself to calm down.

Jacs twisted a strand of hair around her finger as her thoughts settled. There was nothing she could do to help them, except what she had come here to do. Win the contest. She had to win the contest. She was not helpless. This she could do. Breathing heavily, she forced thoughts of the two women from her mind and focused on the next step.

Dusting herself off, Jacs took stock of her situation. First, she examined the state she was in. Her dress was ripped from the fall, dirt and grass stains streaking the yellow fabric. She had her draw-string bag, which she slung over one shoulder, and the grappling hook, which she retrieved from where the rope had fallen on the grass. She had scratches on her arms and legs and her hair had come loose of its plait. Definitely not Queen material, she determined with a sigh of resignation. Her gut unclenched slightly. She turned away from the Cliff edge toward the trees and looked around her. Despite her worry, a warm thought spread across her mind and filled her heart, coursing through her veins like an elixir.

She had made it; she was in the Upper Realm.

Jacs stood in a small grassy clearing surrounded by trees. It was much greener up here, she noticed. Too green. It appeared fake. A bird chirped too loudly in a discordant melody she did not recognize. Each shrub was similar but so very different from the ones they had in the Lower Realm. She suddenly shook herself. If she were to convince people she was Upperite-born, she needed to act it. Resolving to be more nonchalant, she took one last look at the Lower Realm, sent a silent prayer for her mother and another for Master Leschi to a goddess she was willing to start believing in, and entered the forest.

Walking through the dense bush on the edge of the Upper Realm was much more difficult than Jacs had anticipated. Ferns hid brambles that caught at her skirts and tore across her shins. Branches jutted out at odd angles and ducking to avoid one often meant colliding with another.

The forest became a malevolent entity around her. She felt it claw at her, ensnare her, bind her, and attempt to pull her down. She forced herself onward.

After traipsing through bushes and stumbling through creeks for what felt like most of the morning, Jacs finally found a cobbled road. She settled down on a large rock while she debated which direction would lead her to the castle.

Feeling despondent, she opened the small bag she had brought with her and pulled out an apple. Munching thoughtfully, she peered first one way and then the other. The road stretched out in either direction with minimal deviation before being swallowed by the trees. Too late she thought about the little compass sitting on Master Leschi's workbench. Although without a map of the Upper Realm a compass would have done little good.

Jacs looked left, then right again and scrubbed tiredly at her face. Head in her hands, she wondered what she should do. The cuts and scrapes had begun to sting, and a place on her side had started throbbing. Knowing that she couldn't stay where she was the whole day, she picked a stick up and tossed it into the air. It turned once, twice, then fell with a clatter on cobbles to the right of where she sat.

Well, any plan is better than no plan, Jacs thought glumly. Hesitantly, she slid from her perch, dusted off her skirt, and ventured to the right. The sun filtered through the trees on either side of the road. Too hot. Too bright. The cobbles were cracked and jagged from years of having carriages travel over them. She stumbled slightly over the uneven surface and cursed under her breath.

Jacs threw her apple core into the bushes and steadily made her way, hopefully, toward the palace. Rounding a bend, she noticed that a carriage farther down the road had stopped. She froze like a hare that caught a fox's scent. Her breath hovered in her throat. She squinted her eyes. The carriage was beautifully built, painted a powder blue with silver trim.

As she crept slowly closer, she noticed two individuals dithering around the front axle. A petite woman and a portly man. Two bay horses had been unhitched and tied to a nearby tree where they could graze.

The portly man's voice carried down the road toward Jacs. "Well, I'm sure it's not that bad."

"Westly, let me just see if we have something in the carriage, I'm sure there's a spare or something?" The woman disappeared inside. The door shut with a snap and dainty white lace curtains fluttered through the open windows.

The pair had not yet noticed Jacs and she hesitated to make herself known. These were the first Upperite citizens she had met, and the first she had seen since the Queen's assassination. Apart from Connor, they would be the first she will have spoken to. Painfully aware that she was well out of her depth but knowing she would need to talk to an Upperite citizen eventually, she walked closer.

"Excuse me, is everything all right?" Jacs called.

The portly man looked up and shielded his eyes against the morning sun. He was dressed in the livery of the same powder blue as the carriage with black trim and silver buttons. He had an air of one who took pride in every aspect of his uniform. His buttons gleamed, and his seams were ironed crisply. He had neatly combed, though sparse, gray hair around his temples, and a small bow tie peeked out from under his second chin.

"Oh! Yes, well no, actually, we've had a bit of a—" he seemed to have only just taken in Jacs's appearance and stopped midsentence to gape at her. "Good heavens, are you all right?"

Jacs looked down at herself, her tattered dress, scratched arms, and the hefty grappling hook dangling from her shoulder, and shrugged. "I've had a morning, but what's happened to your carriage?"

The man looked back at the state of his carriage and wiped the back of his hand across his forehead.

"Well, it's just the queenpin. It snapped. Who would have thought the whole contraption comes apart without the queenpin." He chuckled ironically.

"Westly! We have nothing! A dozen hats, and three belts. Why did I need so many hats? But nothing we can use." The voice of the young woman wafted out of the window. It was shortly followed by the appearance of the woman herself as she opened the carriage door and stepped down onto the road. She was about a head shorter than Jacs, with thick black hair tied up in an intricate knot. Her hazel eyes were outlined becomingly with thick black lashes, and the ghosts of freckles dotted her nose. She wore a travel outfit that took Jacs's breath away: lilac with white lace edging. She blinked prettily in the sunlight with a look about her that resembled a doe stepping into a glade.

Taking in Jacs's disheveled state, she gasped, "Oh my! Who are you? What's happened?" She turned to Westly for information, who opened his mouth to respond but did not appear to know how to answer her. He made a couple of noises before shutting his mouth and shrugging.

Jacs waved her question away, a puzzle before her and an idea forming in her mind far more interesting than thinking up an explanation.

She looked at the broken queenpin.

Then at the empty axle.

"If I may," Jacs began, "I might have a way to fix your carriage. How attached are you to one of those belts in there?" she inquired as she pointed to the carriage.

"Belts?" the woman asked, perplexed.

Jacs nodded, looking around her for something to use. *A stick would break,* she thought.

"Do you have, like, a rod or a—a—" She looked down at the grappling hook at her hip and laughed. "Oh, this might work. And your least favorite belt, please." She directed the last part to the woman.

The woman looked to Westly and then back to Jacs, still bewildered, and went to retrieve a belt. While she was gone, Jacs stepped forward and tested the width of the hook's shaft through the hole in the steering mechanism. The hook rattled against the sides, loose. "And some water!" Jacs called.

Westly peered over her shoulder. "Lucky you have one of those on you." He chuckled again, this time more warily. "Why, exactly—" he began but was cut off as the woman came back with a belt in one hand and a wineskin in the other.

"Is wine okay?" she asked, slightly breathless.

Jacs looked up and smiled. "Depends on the vintage."

The woman laughed uncertainly and handed her the belt. "I've heard it's a good year," she said, her forehead wrinkling.

Jacs took the belt and began wrapping it around the shaft of the grappling hook. "I'm sure it's fine if you don't mind that you won't be drinking it. Leather swells when it's wet. So if I wrap this hook up in your leather belt, douse it in wine, and put it through the hole. . . Ta-da, we have a makeshift queenpin that should hopefully get you where you need to go." She poured wine over the wrapped hook as she spoke, splattering her dress in the process. The woman winced and took a delicate step backward to protect her own attire.

"That should do it. Where are you going anyway?" Jacs asked. The pin fit snugly. Taking the length of rope still attached to the hook, she tied the whole thing more securely in place.

The two travelers looked at each other, to the now fixed carriage, and back to Jacs.

Westly took Jacs's hand and shook it heartily. "Thank you! How did you . . .? That was . . ." his cheeks turned red as he struggled to articulate exactly what that was.

The woman removed her gloves and held out a hand. Jacs hesitated a moment before shaking her hand too, a red wine bloom staining the woman's clean palm as she let go.

"I'm Dame Lena Glowra, daughter of Lord Ava and Genteel Kristoff Glowra. Heiress to the Glowra estate in Terrelle. You have done me a great service today. Thank you."

Jacs felt the extent of her disarray for the first time that day. "O-oh," she stammered, "Dame Lena Glowra, it is an . . . honor to meet you." She felt her cheeks rush to match Westly's hue and realized she did not know the first thing about what to do when one meets a Dame, or what a Dame really was, or where Terrelle was or . . .

Dame Glowra smiled. "What is your name?" she said kindly.

Jacs swallowed hard, her mind working furiously. She thought of the places Connor had mentioned in his letters: nothing came readily to her. Instead, the cover of *The Rise of the Fallen* floated in her mind's eye. Realizing she had to say something, she let words flow as confidently as she could muster, "I'm Jacqueline . . . Daidala, daughter of Maria and Francis Daidala. My mother is a goldsmith in one of the smaller towns about four days' ride from here."

Lena tilted her head to one side thoughtfully and interjected, "Wrenstrom? Newfrea? No . . . that would be Parima?"

Jacs nodded gratefully. "Yes," she blustered, "Parima, that's the one."

Lena smiled. "Lovely to meet you, Jacqueline of Parima." Her gaze slid over Jacs's dress and her brow creased with worry. "It seems you have had an adventure of your own this morning. Are you hurt?"

Jacs looked down at her arms and turned them over. "No, just a few scratches."

"What on earth happened to you?"

"To me? My ah—" Jacs looked over at the horses on the side of the road, "My horse got stung by a bee and threw me. I couldn't catch her so I've been making my way to the castle hoping I spot her along the way."

"You poor thing!" she exclaimed. Then her eyes lit up and she clapped her hands together. "But what luck you have found us then! We're going to the castle! Are you going for the contest?"

Jacs nodded and Lena squealed. "Oh, this is perfect!" she said, "I'm entering the contest also! We can escort you." She nodded to Jacs confidently and continued, "It's the least we can do as a thank you."

Jacs blinked. "Uh . . . that's fantastic. Thank *you*!"

Lena looked Jacs over again, a frown forming on her brow. "Although," she began, and Jacs's heart sank. "While your dress is, or most likely was, lovely, I'm afraid it will sully the cushions in our carriage." She turned briskly to Westly and commanded, "Westly, fetch one of my gowns for Ms. Daidala to wear."

Jacs raised an eyebrow, "Are you sure that's necess—" she began before Westly cut her off.

"May I suggest the green velvet? Ms. Daidala is slightly taller than you and the green is a little longer. With luck it may pass for an above-the-ankle length that is quite popular in Bregend."

Jacs felt panic rising as Dame Glowra nodded eagerly and Westly hurried to fetch the gown. "Please," she squeaked. "No, I have a dress. I—my dress is fine. Thank you."

"My dear, it's wine-soaked, war torn, and just cannot go near the upholstery," Lena said, waving away her protests. Her eyes slid past Jacs to a spot behind her. "Ah!" she beamed, "Westly, that's perfect. Thank you."

Still not believing her luck, Jacs allowed herself to be steered toward the carriage, where Westly was waiting with a luxurious, forest green gown in his arms.

"I really . . . this is so kind, but honestly I . . . couldn't accept."

"Jacqueline of Parima, you have fixed our carriage. In doing so, your garments got covered in wine." Jacs looked down at the few flecks of red on her skirts and raised her eyebrows as Lena continued, "I just so happen to have a dress that does not fit me. It seems the stars have aligned for you today. Please, put on the gown," she said sweetly. She smiled and gave Jacs a small but firm nudge to follow Westly.

He ushered her into the carriage to change. Jacs bit back a squeal of delight as she took in the beautiful interior of the carriage and set to work. She had never before held a dress this elaborate. Feeling like she was solving a complex puzzle, she decided to keep her underskirts on and attempted to place the yards of fabric over top. After several minutes of silent wrestling and squirming, she had managed to settle the gown as best she could. She heard a soft knock on the window.

"Ms. Daidala?" Lena's voice called. "Do you need some help?"

Jacs wriggled around in the folds of fabric for an exit, marveling that she could figure out how to fix a carriage with no problem, but putting on a dress was apparently beyond her. "Yes please, I think I'm a bit stuck," she said.

The carriage door opened, and Lena stepped inside. She began doing the stays on the back of the dress with deft fingers, all the while apologizing: "My serving women all went ahead to get my things settled yesterday, otherwise they would have been able to help you much more effectively, but I think we've done it. There you go!" She stood back slightly to admire her work. Jacs ran her fingers down the luscious folds of the gown. It was the finest thing she had ever felt.

"Ms. Daidala, I do think that green is your color."

Still too nervous to move lest she somehow ruin the lustrous fabric, she said absently, "Jacqueline, please."

"All right, Jacqueline." Lena smiled.

Jacs heard the sound of Westly hitching the horses to the carriage. She heard him clamber onto the driver's seat, tap twice on the window, and whistle to the horses. Jacs felt a slight clenching in her stomach as the horses slowly inched forward, picking up the weight of the carriage and setting the wheels in motion. After a few minutes, she breathed a sigh of relief. It held. She grinned and turned her attention to her new companion.

"Oh, and this works so well," Lena was saying. "Now I have someone to keep me company for the rest of the journey. Although—" she paused as a mischievous glint appeared in her eye and her smile turned into a smirk "—don't think that I've forgotten you are also competing in the contest. We may very well be rivals soon, so you will get no damning secrets from me!" She laughed.

Butterflies danced in Jacs's stomach as she saw the forest slide by her through the carriage window.

"So," Lena said conspiratorially, "what do you think Prince Cornelius is like?"

The two women spent the remainder of the trip discussing the Prince, the contest, and what they thought the upcoming tasks would be like. Using her newfound position as a goldsmith's daughter to explain her lack of knowledge of the royal family and the life of a noblewoman, Jacs let Lena do most of the talking.

She found her to be a wealth of knowledge on what etiquette to follow in the castle— "Because you're not a noble, you will always bow first and tuck your foot behind the other like so, then shake the person's hand and wait for them to introduce themselves before introducing yourself"—important possible contestants to look out for—"Dame Hera Claustrom, she is a piece of work, careful what you say around her and don't take anything she says at face value. Oh, I do hope Chivilra Amber Everstar is competing, I bet she is, I've always wanted to meet her. My mother and I have been following her career; youngest knight since Chivilra Strellen, and just awarded the Soterian Medal this year" —and a very vague idea of what to expect of the contest itself.

"You're smart to come early really," Lena acknowledged. "The days before, while not technically part of the contest, are said to be filled with celebrations and chances to mingle with the other contestants and even the Prince, if you're lucky. Since the last contest was well before I was born, it really is hard to say what will happen, but I heard from my mother that there will be a great feast and then, of the hundreds of possible contestants, only a handful will be chosen to compete."

Jacs gave a start and wrapped a strand of hair around her finger absentmindedly. "But what if you are not chosen?" she asked.

Lena tapped her chin thoughtfully. "Well, I suppose you just stay and watch the rest of the contest." Jacs's heart sank at the thought. Lena continued. "But my mother said that's why it is very important to make sure to talk with the Prince or the Council of Four during the first days of celebration. Give them a reason to want to keep you in the contest. Then when you're in, it's up to you and your skill to be best at whatever each task has in store." At the worried look on Jacs's face, Lena brightened. "But we mustn't worry about all that now, that's something that is out of our hands anyway. As my mother always said, Worry is like a rocking horse, it fills the time but does not get you anywhere. Can I fix your hair?" she diverted suddenly.

"My hair?"

"Yes, it's at odds with the dress in the state it's in now and we have the time," Lena said simply.

Jacs felt her hair and pulled a leaf from its tangles. She giggled and assented, much to Lena's delight.

14

BASILEIA

Feeling like a queen, her hair now neatly woven into a series of braids around her head, Jacs watched as the trees lining the road thinned and were replaced with manicured gardens and little stone houses.

Forgetting herself, she cut off mid-sentence and pressed her face to the window when the first house appeared.

"Look!" she cried excitedly, tapping Lena on the arm.

Lena looked at Jacs, puzzled, her eyebrows raised in question. "At . . . the house, Jacqueline?" she asked, unsure.

Hurriedly, Jacs dropped her hand and fumbled for an answer, "No, I uh . . . I thought I saw something but . . . it was only a bush."

"Oh," Lena replied awkwardly, then looked at Jacs with inquisitive eyes. "Jacqueline," she began, "have you never been to Basileia?"

Jacs weighed her options and replied truthfully, "No, we live so far away there never seemed to be a good enough reason to leave the uh . . . workshop for that length of time. This was to be my first time . . ." She trailed off.

Lena was still looking at Jacs thoughtfully. "Jacqueline," she said again as though nervous not to offend, "I should have asked this before, but I've only just realized . . . it's just you said you were thrown from your horse, but Parima is a four-day ride from here. Where were your things? Who else was with you? Should we think about finding them? You haven't mentioned anyone and I just think, well . . . were you traveling alone?" She said the last word tentatively, as though unable to believe that was the case.

Jacs felt her chest constrict. Keep it simple. She thought, Stick to the truth.

"I came alone," she said slowly. "My mother will only worry if I don't return after the contest."

Lena considered. "That's very brave of you," she said after a time. "I wouldn't dream of going off on my own like that, let alone know what to do if I lost my horse."

Jacs floundered for an answer. "Maybe you have just never had to. You never know what you're capable of unless tested," she replied finally.

The size of the houses slipping by the window steadily increased as they moved farther into the city. Jacs, not sure how grand the other Upper Realm towns were, saved her outward excitement for the most opulent structures and statues, but inside she was buzzing. She could not pick where to look first and wished the carriage would slow down so that she could spend more time staring at each building. They passed the clock tower Connor had mentioned in his letters. His description had not come close to capturing its magnificence. It was so beautiful, Jacs forgot to breathe. The clock face was three times the size of the one she had spent so many years working on. It was expertly crafted with large gold numbers around the outside and a smaller, separate dial superimposed on the first that appeared to depict a series of constellations. The tower itself rose into the sky as though attempting to pierce the clouds above.

Lena took to her role as tour guide eagerly and maintained a running commentary of the buildings and different areas of the city as they passed through.

". . . and there's a lovely little pastry shop that sells the most delicious cream puffs you will ever eat in your—Oh, and that's the bookshop the Prince supposedly frequents! Now we're coming up the main square, and that is the memorial statue for Queen Ariel. I see they've decorated it especially for the upcoming contest."

The statue was the height of one of the smaller buildings surrounding the square in which it stood. It depicted a woman standing proudly with her hand resting on the back of a large gold lioness. Both the woman and the lion looked out over the people with the alert and watchful gaze of mothers protecting their young. The likeness to the Queen when she had lived was uncanny, and the way the sun flickered and played across the golden surface of each statue made them appear almost alive. In celebration of the upcoming contest, people had laid bouquets of flowers at the base of the two figures and draped large wreaths around their necks. The different colors of the flowers stood out like so many jewels.

"She was beautiful," Jacs murmured.

Lena nodded in agreement.

They left the square with the Queen's statue and turned into another, smaller, courtyard. Westly rapped twice on the front window and Lena hurried to pull the velvet cords holding the curtains open. With the cords untied, the curtains settled into place to obscure the scene unfolding in the courtyard. Jacs had just time to glimpse several men and a couple of women shackled and tied to pillories of varying heights, or with their feet stuck in stocks. A small crowd gathered around the group and Jacs could hear their jeers and taunts as the carriage continued on.

Lena attempted a casual air but appeared to be unsure as to what to do with her hands, first resting them on her lap, then cupping her elbows, now tidying her hair.

"What's going on out there?" Jacs ventured, her curiosity quickly getting the better of her.

"Oh, that. Yes, quite unpleasant. Unfortunately, there isn't really a way to avoid it. The whole area is designed so that you more or less have to pass through this square. It makes for quite the jam in the busier months, but I suppose that's the point," Lena said.

"The point for?" Jacs asked.

"Public shaming. Surely you have one in Parima? For those accused, tried, and found guilty of sexual assault? Queen Diana's ruling . . ." Lena trailed off when she saw realization dawn on Jacs's face as she nodded in understanding.

Jacs knew about Queen Diana's law, of course. Everyone did. In order to combat what the Queen had deemed the private horror experienced by those who had fallen prey to the lowliest of predators, she had decreed that all sexual offenders be subject to a period of public shaming of a length as befitting the severity of their crime in addition to their prison sentence. This included any man who conceived a child against his partner's wishes by not taking his monthly dose of silphium resin. Connor told Jacs in one of his letters how horrid the resin was. It tasted foul, caused abdominal pains, and made him either despondent or more prone to anger's fire in the days after taking it. However, he took it religiously every full moon since his voice had changed at thirteen.

Jacs knew, depending on the town in the Lower Realm, the extent to which the public shaming varied. Some paraded the offenders through town, and some had pillories set up in a central location on a much smaller scale to the one they were passing by. Regardless of how it was done, the rules were the same. The offender was to be physically unharmed, and his or her name was to be heralded and written out clearly to identify them to the crowd.

As if to herself, Lena intoned, "May those who lurk in the shadow be brought to Justice's light."

"And Goddess preserve the survivors," the two women finished together.

They passed through the square in thoughtful silence. When they were clear of the spectacle, Westly tapped on the window again and Lena opened the curtains. The ritual seemed well rehearsed, but Jacs did not think it appropriate to ask why her new friend chose to close her blinds to the display. She supposed whatever reason it was would be a personal one.

"This must be it!" Lena clapped her hands excitedly. Westly had turned the carriage down a short, hedged driveway and drew to a halt in front of a two-story inn. A sign above the door read, THE GRIFFIN'S DEN.

Lena turned to Jacs, "I never asked, but where will you be staying? We can have the coach drop you off."

Jacs smiled and said, "Thank you very much for loaning me your dress and for the ride. I feel you have gone above and beyond to help me get here. I had nowhere specific in mind, so if your coachman could take me to the nearest inn, I would be most obliged."

Lena stared at her for a moment. "But Jacqueline," she said with concern, "the inns will be booked up this close to the contest."

Jacs felt her stomach clench and felt the blood rush to her cheeks. She hadn't even thought about finding accommodation as so much of her plan had focused on simply getting to the Upper Realm.

"Oh, that's fine, then would the carriage be able to drop me off near the statue of Queen Ariel?"

Lena studied her face, smiled, and shook her head. "Jacqueline, you have done me a great service today, and have been a delight to talk with on what would have been an otherwise tedious journey. If you have no other plans, would you join me for the rest of your stay here as my companion?"

Jacs felt a weight lifting from her heart and nodded. "It seems you're the one doing me a great service."

As soon as the carriage wheels crunched to a stop, two serving men rushed out to greet them. Lena explained, "Mother booked a suite for the days leading up to the contest. She and Father said they would arrive closer to the time but wanted to be sure I was well rested and had a chance to meet the competition." She winked at Jacs. "Apparently some of the other contestants will be staying here too!"

Jacs looked up at the building in awe. It was bigger than any of the houses in Bridgeport and twice as grand. The serving men opened the carriage doors and helped Lena down, hesitating only briefly before helping Jacs down shortly after. Westly gave orders for one of them to take the two traveling cases Lena had brought with her. A stable hand had emerged from the side of the building and begun tending to the horses.

Westly looked to Lena in question as Jacs stood awkwardly next to her. Lena pronounced: "Ms. Daidala is to stay with us as my companion. As her belongings were lost to her on her journey here, she will require a formal gown, a nightdress, two tunics, a pair of trousers, and anything else you think I've missed."

Jacs stood with her mouth open.

Turning to the serving man who had just let go of Jacs's hand, Westly ordered: "Fetch Master Moira; we will be needing a wardrobe for Ms. Daidala." He indicated her with his hand, and Jacs felt the blood rush to her cheeks.

"Dame Glowra, this is really truly too much."

Lena turned to her, "Nonsense, if you are a member of my household, even a temporary one, you must uphold my household's standards of dress. One torn and one ill-fitting dress does not an appropriate wardrobe make." She held her hand up to silence Jacs's further protests. "And if you are to be my companion, I insist you call me Lena, or else I'd struggle to feel at ease around you amongst all the formality."

Taking Jacs's moment of stunned silence as agreement, she turned to Westly and asserted, "It's settled. She is to stay with us for the duration of the contest as my companion."

Satisfied, he nodded and began detailing the wardrobe items Master Moira was to prepare for Jacs to the servant. As he spoke, a fourth, much more lavishly dressed, attendant strode over to Lena and bowed. He wore an immaculate white tunic with a thick black belt flecked with gold thread tightened around his slim frame. His face was long and thin, and his gray hair was slicked back.

Westly puffed his chest out and announced, "May I present the Dame Lena Glowra and her companion Ms. Jacqueline Daidala."

The man bowed and introduced himself. "Good journey, Dame Glowra. We have been expecting you. My name is Galvene, and I am humbled to serve you in my establishment for the duration of your stay. Your serving staff arrived yesterday and your rooms have been set up." His sharp eyes took in Jacs and he raised his eyebrows slightly. "Although it appears we were mistaken with regard to how many guests we would be accommodating. I am deeply sorry." He clapped his hands twice and another serving man appeared. Turning to him, Galvene said, "Ensure Ms. Daidala is provided for in Dame Glowra's suites."

That settled, Galvene led the two women up the front steps and into the inn, with Westly following a short distance behind. Jacs followed in a daze, unsure which blessing to count first.

They were met with an affluence of which Jacs had only read about. In the entrance hall, a chandelier made of gold-tipped antlers hung from the high ceiling. Jacs could see, through an open door opposite the entry, a large common area with a number of luxurious chairs arranged around carved wooden tables. She watched a pair of guests playing chess pause their game as a serving woman approached them with a tray of cold beverages. Stretching away from the common-room door were two enormous stairways that led to the upper suites.

Galvene led them up the staircase on the right, and along the upper landing past elaborate tapestries depicting scenes of hunting, celebration, and battle. One caught Jacs's eye—it showed a golden warrior, hair streaming behind her as she stood on the edge of the

Upper Cliff, holding back a horde of demonic figures climbing up from the Lower Realm. Jacs shuddered and looked away.

A short way down the corridor, Galvene stopped, bowed, and opened a door. Lena, Jacs, and Westly stepped through and it was all Jacs could do to resist gasping in wonder. The suite was elegantly furnished with gold-trimmed white velvet settees, a white marble fireplace, and a chandelier of entwined golden roses hovering above their heads. Following Lena as if in a trance, she saw that the suite contained three rooms as well as the sitting room they had just entered.

Galvene gave them a quick tour. "You may have your meals here if you wish or join the rest of the guests in the dining hall downstairs. A bell will sound for mealtimes but if there is anything our kitchens can make for you outside of those times, please do not hesitate to pull this bell cord—" he indicated a thick pull cord by the door they had entered through "—and someone will be up to fulfill your request. Here is your chamber, Dame Glowra. I trust your companion will be lodging with you?" Galvene inquired. Lena confirmed.

Jacs only had a brief moment to take in the four-poster bed with thick green velvet hangings and the sunlight streaming through the bay windows before he moved past her and continued. "Here is the washing room; we are always ready with water downstairs to draw you a bath should you so choose. I expect you will want one after such a long journey?"

Lena assented.

"I shall arrange to have one prepared as soon as possible," he said in a clipped voice.

Jacs saw a bathtub big enough to comfortably fit two people in the center of a white stone room. Fluffy towels sat on a delicately carved wooden bench in the corner next to a basin with a round gilt mirror above it.

Galvene moved back into the sitting room and gestured to the remaining room. "This room is another bedchamber—your mother requested a west-facing window." He opened the door briefly to show the two girls that the window did, indeed, face west and closed it again. Jacs supposed Westly and the other serving staff Galvene mentioned would stay elsewhere in the inn.

Bowing again, Galvene said, "If there is anything else you need, do not hesitate to ask. I will see that your bath is filled promptly." With a flourish, he left and closed the door behind him.

Lena removed her travel cloak and handed it to Westly. Jacs hurried to do the same, but hesitated to have Westly wait on her. Westly did not appear to mind, and took hers happily.

Marveling at the room, her thoughts were cut short as a sharp knock made everyone turn. Westly carefully hung up the two cloaks on a stand by the door and opened it.

"Master Moira for Dame Glowra!" announced a small voice at the door.

"Ah! Yes, splendid, come in, come in!" Westly said.

The woman who entered moved with the grace of a swan and was the size of a bear. She wore a gray gown expertly tailored to her form. As she moved, flashes of brilliant color peaked through slashes and pleats in skirts and bodice, creating an appealing kaleidoscope effect. Jacs felt with each spied glint of color that she was being let in on a secret. She noticed that Master Moira had a small pillow full of pins attached to her wrist, and a number of leather pouches around her waist.

A slim woman in a far less flamboyant gray gown who carried a notebook and pencil followed in her wake.

Master Moira fixed her eyes on Lena and beamed. "Darling Lena," she said warmly as she clasped the young woman's small hands in her large ones, "how wonderful it is to see you again. You look marvelous as usual—of course, I dress you, so of course you do!" She laughed in short, sharp bursts that filled the room. Her eyes slid over to Jacs and she frowned, "My dear, that dress was not made with you in mind. I should know, I designed it. It cuts you off horribly at the calf." As she spoke, she waved her arms in a delicate, seemingly choreographed dance. The pins at her wrist flashed in the candlelight. "No, no," she continued, a hand at her breast, "no, this will not do. Westly!" she snapped, "This is the young Daidala I've been sent to wardrobe, is it?"

"Yes, Master Moira, the very same," Westly hastened to clarify.

"Thank heavens, I would have insisted if not." Before Jacs knew what was happening, Master Moira had her standing on a stool, arms out, and was stretching a measuring tape around and across different sections of Jacs's anatomy. Her hands arranged the tape and froze rapidly. At each pause, she dictated a number that the other woman hurried to write down. All the while she spoke to the room at large about the merits and pitfalls of different cuts. ". . . with your shoulders dear, thirty-six bust, you really need a scooped neckline, and with your height, twenty-eight waist, don't sell yourself short." She laughed explosively again, the creases around her eyes deepening. "Long lines darling, looong lines." She looked pointedly at Jacs's shorter dress and made a tsking sound before continuing. Jacs grinned and let the waves of Master Moira's commentary flitter around her.

Just as suddenly as the seamstress had begun, she tucked the tape into a pouch and informed the room, "You can expect the first gown and a nightdress this evening and the rest will follow in the next few days. Darling Lena, it was wonderful to see you again. I daresay you will be needing new bodices at the rate you're growing, so I will be working with you soon. Ms. Daidala, I'm glad to have met you, and know that your calves will never again suffer under my watch. Good afternoon!" And with that, she and the other woman left with a snap of the door.

Standing on the stool, Jacs looked at Lena in bewilderment. "Is she usually like that?" she asked.

Lena giggled. "Always." She helped her friend settle back onto solid ground.

Once the enormous bathtub had been filled, Lena and Jacs took turns scrubbing off the journey's grime. The two women wrapped themselves in the thick blanket-sized towels and jumped onto the velvet cushions of the large four-poster bed. The soft feather-stuffed mattress was a relief on bones jostled by the wagon's journey.

Outside in the entry area Westly hid a smile at the eruption of giggles issuing from the room and arranged a dignified expression on his face as he hastened to answer another knock at the door.

It was the first of Jacs's gowns and a nightdress, as promised. As the door swung closed behind the delivery boy, the two women entered the sitting room. Lena clapped her hands happily and demanded Jacs try the gown on.

Her mouth hanging slightly open, Jacs lifted the first garment from the paper wrapping. Reverentially, she let the material flow across her palm. The nightdress was a light wool with a corded neckline. She ran her hand across it and turned to the gown nestled beneath. It was a simple linen gown befitting of her station, but it was finer than anything she had ever owned. It was the same green as the gown she had borrowed earlier that day, with a half circle skirt to fall to her ankles and a scooped neck. The sleeves were slashed to reveal white fabric lining. A brown leather belt came with the dress.

At Lena's repeated urging, she placed the nightdress back in the box and gathered the gown in her arms. Holding it before her like an offering, Jacs slipped into the bedchamber to change. She placed her new gown on the edge of the bed, spreading it out gingerly. Savoring the process, she stepped into her underskirt, and tucked her necklace with the Griffin ring into the neckline of her undershirt. Then, as if in a dream, she let the green fabric fall over her head and settle around her. It fit perfectly. She smiled shyly as she emerged from the bedchamber and turned to Lena. "One day I will be able to repay all you are doing for me."

Lena waved her comment away and prompted her to twirl. "Oh, Jacqueline," she exclaimed, "it's gorgeous, you're gorgeous!"

Jacs performed another twirl, her heart light. Suddenly it all seemed possible. She had made it to the Upper Realm, she had found an ally, she was only moments away from meeting the Prince and tackling the contest. Twisting a strand of hair around her forefinger excitedly, she gestured to her friend's post-bath towel-attire and said, "Your turn. Put something on and let's find out if there are any other contestants here!"

Lena emerged from the bed chamber moments later in a deep purple gown with silver trim and embroidery along the sleeves. She performed a twirl of her own as Jacs clapped and, finally ready, they met Westly and headed for the common room.

15

CARDS AND CONFESSIONS

The fire in the large stone fireplace warmed the common area with a soft glow. Candles dripped wax that pooled at their bases like molten pearls. At the doorway, Westly informed Lena and Jacs that he had sent both women's names to the castle to enlist them in the contest and dismissed himself to arrange the next day's trip to the palace with the stable hands. Jacs thanked him before he left, and saw his eyes crinkle in a smile as he bowed and departed.

There were three other patrons in the common room; two women were in the middle of a game of cards, and the third, a boy, was reading a book in an armchair by the fire. They all looked up as Jacs and Lena entered. Jacs heard Lena say quietly, "Oh," as one of the card players beckoned her over excitedly. The woman who seemed to recognize Lena stood and rushed to greet them as they approached the table. She was taller than Jacs—therefore much taller than Lena. She had a square jaw and thick curly hair pulled back and restrained at the base of her neck.

Bending to sweep Lena into a hug, she exclaimed, "Lena! I've missed you! It's been months. What luck we're both staying at the Griffin's Den! Of course you'd be competing. You look great." As the two broke apart, Jacs noticed both women's faces were flushed. The tall one appeared to just notice Jacs standing slightly behind Lena. She frowned and looked at Lena questioningly.

"Oh!" Lena squeaked again. "This is Jacqueline Daidala, a friend, we met . . . she helped fix my carriage . . . Jacqueline, this is my—this is Ms. Anya Bishop." Lena's face flushed a deeper hue as she stammered through the introductions. Jacs looked at her, mildly perplexed, before holding her hand out for Anya to shake. Anya eyed it suspiciously before taking it and squeezing rather harder than Jacs thought necessary.

Resisting the urge to wince, Jacs supplied, "My horse threw me and ran off while I was on the road here. Luckily for me, Le— Dame Glowra needed a new queenpin, and I had a grappling hook. She was nice enough to take me in after that."

"A queenpin and a what?" Anya looked at Lena, incredulous, unsure if Jacs was joking. "That sounds just like Lena though— always picking up strays."

Not knowing how to respond, Jacs turned her attention to Anya's companion and held out her hand to her. "Jacqueline," she offered.

The other woman's green eyes glittered in the firelight. "Dame Shane Adella," she replied, not taking Jacs's hand. Jacs sighed inwardly, realizing too late that she was probably supposed to curtsy.

A heavy silence fell among the four women. Lena's gaze darted around the room and fell to rest on the cards that had been abandoned.

"May we join your game?" she asked, a slight plea in her voice.

"Sure. I'll deal," Anya said warily. As she and Lena turned, Jacs noticed Lena's hand twitch toward Anya's before she quickly caught herself, her hand settling into her skirts instead. A blush stole across Lena's cheeks for a moment but disappeared before Jacs could question what she had seen. They all settled into the soft suede chairs set around the card table.

Shane seemed to glide to her chair, her curtain of black hair sweeping behind her like a painter's brushstroke. Jacs brought up the rear. She hoped Upperite games were not too different from those played in the Lower Realm.

The cards were dealt, and the players picked up their hands. Jacs looked over the various symbols and felt her heart sink. It was definitely different from the card games she had played with her mother. The sudden rush of a memory sitting around her small kitchen table with her mother while Ranger purred on her lap collided with the image of the woman falling from the blow of a guard's baton.

Jacs tucked a strand of hair behind her ear with shaking fingers and glanced around the table. To her left, Anya had set a pile of cards in the middle with one facing up. Lena placed a card on top, Shane followed suit, and three pairs of eyes turned to Jacs expectantly. Jacs studied her cards again, looked at the two cards with stars on the corners that had been played before, and placed a card with crescent moons in the corners on top.

Her three opponents looked at each other, then looked at her. Jacs felt her face grow hot.

Sighing, she said bluntly, "I'm sorry, I have no idea what we're playing."

Lena gaped at her, Shane raised a sharp eyebrow, and Anya was the first to laugh. It escaped her like a shock. The sound cut through the room and shattered the tension at the table so suddenly that the other three women joined in with a mixture of relief and alarm. Jacs laughed sheepishly and felt a weight lift from her chest ever so slightly.

Wiping her eyes, Anya clapped Jacs on the back. "We're playing Pantheon," she said and set to teaching the rules between residual giggles.

Once Jacs was appropriately placing stars on stars and moons on silver arrows, she was free to engage in the conversation that flitted about the table.

"So, Jacqueline, you were thrown from your horse, you say? That must have been exciting. Do tell," Shane said, her disinterested tone a sharp contrast to her words.

"Oh, well, yes, I suppose you could call it that," Jacs faltered.

"And you saved a Dame, so I suppose that gives you additional training for the contest," Shane continued dryly.

"I guess if the tasks involve axles and wine, I'm golden. But I've had to fix a few wagons in my life, and no one has ever wanted to crown me for it," Jacs replied, earning a weak smile from Shane. Jacs continued. "Although, if it weren't for Dame Glowra, I would still be wandering along the road. So, she's the real hero of the day." Lena hid a shy smile. Anya noticed and looked away quickly, her face impassive. Jacs continued. "Does anyone know what the tasks are?"

Anya looked thoughtful and placed an owl card on top of a spider card. "No one does, really. This generation's tasks for our

Contest of Queens . . . well, they have been set by the Prince, and I doubt the young Queen—Goddess rest her—had thought she would need to make such preparations."

"Contest of Queens . . . as opposed to?" Jacs ventured. Her Lowrian education had only ever dealt with the contest in general terms, and Master Leschi had only known a little about the policies behind it.

"The Contest of Daughter-heirs, which is set by the Council, and the Contest of the . . ." Anya snapped her fingers, searching her brain for the word.

"Elect," Lena supplied as she played the tapestry card and took the stack into her own hand. Shane groaned and picked up.

"And what are those?" Jacs asked. At the shocked look on their faces, she hurried to add, "My mother never imagined I would enter any of these so she never talked about it at home."

Shane looked at her with a touch of pity and said, "It is a hard thing to defy one's mother; that would have taken courage." As before, her voice betrayed not a shred of emotion or interest. Shuffling her cards around in her hand, she continued, "The three types of contests are all based on where the future queen is coming from, but they all do the same thing, which is to say, they all test the character of a person to determine if they are worthy to be queen.

"If the current queen has one or more daughters, the daughters must complete the Contest of Daughter-heirs. This contest is set out by the Council, and the winner becomes queen, or the lone daughter must complete the contest lest her failure invoke a Contest of Queens that is open to any eligible female. This is the contest we have now, and ours was created by the Prince. Unusual, but most likely the Council had enough on their plate so they gave him something to do. The third is the Contest of the Elect, and that one rarely happens. It occurs when the queen does not have any female heirs and a member of the royal family elects an individual to compete alone. Again, if she fails, then the Contest of Queens occurs."

Jacs placed a golden-apple card on the empty space Lena's stack had left. Anya quickly placed the owl card on top, and Lena, her tongue sticking out of the corner of her mouth in concentration as she shuffled through her larger hand, brandished a dove card.

"So, the tasks in the contests are completely different every time?" Jacs asked.

"Supposedly. It has to be different or else you could prepare for them too easily, or most likely the task wouldn't suit the type of queen needed for the time," Anya answered. "My mother told me that, no matter what, each task needs to meet certain criteria, but only those with access to the royal archives know exactly what the criteria are. I guess we will all find out soon enough anyway."

"Just think," added Lena, "we have tomorrow, which will be all feasting and festivities, then we're in the contest." She could barely conceal the excitement in her voice.

Shane begrudgingly closed the fan of her cards with a snap and picked up another card from the pile. Lena grinned, and Jacs noticed Anya smiling at the look of contentment on Lena's face. Jacs plucked a peacock card from her hand and finished the set, claiming the pile.

"That's assuming we all get picked," said Jacs, remembering her discussion with Lena in the carriage. The others became pensive at her words, and Jacs almost wished she had kept the comment to herself. "What do you hope will be in the tasks?" she asked in an effort to lighten the mood again.

"Swimming," Lena said quickly.

Shane's eyes shone mischievously. "I'm hoping I get to use these," she answered, and before anyone realized what she was doing, she produced a small knife from somewhere in her thick sleeve and flicked it over Anya's shoulder. It shot past her ear—Jacs could have sworn it trimmed a few of Anya's flyaway hairs—before landing with a soft *thunk* halfway up one of the white candles on the table next to theirs.

"Whoa," Jacs breathed as Lena clapped, and Anya felt her hair gingerly.

Shane retrieved the knife and returned to her seat with a smirk.

"What about you, Anya?" Jacs asked.

Anya let her hand rest on the table and drummed her fingers. "Honestly," she began, "I am amazing at two things: horseback riding and flower arranging. The first might come in handy, the second . . . I'm not so sure."

Lena smiled and patted her hand affectionately. "You're selling yourself short," she said warmly. Turning to the others, she added, "Anya and her family have been doing the flowers for my family's manor for as long as I can remember, and some of the things they can do within a bouquet will take your breath away."

Anya visibly bristled as Lena finished, and pulled her hand away. Lena looked at her, and the smile slid from her face.

"Yes, and we are always so thankful for your patronage," Anya replied in a cold voice before stretching and yawning elaborately, "but it's time for this flower girl to get her beauty sleep. Dame Adella, Jacqueline, it was lovely to meet you both. Dame Glowra." She stood and took her leave, ignoring the confused and slightly hurt look on Lena's face.

Shane bid them both good night shortly after, leaving Lena and Jacs at the table. The boy in the chair by the fire turned a page. The shuffle of fingers on parchment disturbed only the sound of the fire crackling softly.

"It is getting late," Lena said quietly. "Shall we go to bed too?"

Jacs nodded and helped her pack up the cards. They made their way back to the rooms in silence, both deep in thought.

Jacs knew better than to pry, but her curiosity got the better of her once they had taken turns washing at the basin and had changed into their nightdresses. Settling into the large bed, Jacs propped herself up on her elbow and asked, "So . . . what was all that with Anya?"

In the dim light of the bedchamber, Jacs saw several emotions dance across her friend's face. Lena rolled over to face her and said softly, "Can I tell you something I can't tell anyone?"

Curious, Jacs said, "Of course."

"Because it means going against my mother's plan for me and she's had this plan for as long as I can remember and I am trying, and I do want to . . . but I also don't want to and it's so silly but then it's all about station and class and nothing to do with love. We have to follow all these rules that aren't even written down anywhere . . . and then there's the problem of heirs and I don't have any siblings, so naturally there's that pressure . . ." Jacs's mouth fell open as Lena began working herself up, speaking faster and faster the more she said. ". . . And I hadn't seen her in months and didn't dream she would be here of all places but I suppose of course she would try out too—"

"Lena, hold on, what are you talking about?" Jacs interrupted.

Taking a deep breath, Lena rolled onto her back and looked up at the canopy of the four-poster bed without truly seeing it. "Jacqueline, I tell you this in the strictest of confidence. I know I only met you this morning, but you don't have any connection to my world, so really, what's the harm in telling you? I feel like I can trust you." She paused as if not sure how to proceed. "Because of her family's business, Anya has worked for my family for as long as I can remember." Lena paused again and then finished in a small voice: "And I swear I've loved her longer."

There was a pause as the words settled in around them, huddling within the cocoon of the heavy bed curtains. Then Jacs squealed. Lena jumped, startled, and Jacs covered her mouth with her hand, removing it to whisper, "Of course! Oh, that makes so much sense!"

"What do you mean?"

"Just. . . the way you were acting with each other," Jacs replied, waving her hand vaguely.

"Oh."

"Do you know if she loves you too?" Jacs asked.

Lena sighed, "I'm not sure, it's a complicated thing."

"What's so complicated? Have you asked her? Have you told her how you feel?" Jacs twirled a strand of hair excitedly around her finger as she spoke.

Lena took a moment to respond, "My mother has the expectation that I will marry someone of either the same class or higher. She just wants what's best for me, I guess. Anya is the daughter of a florist. Not that I care, but my mother does.

"When I mentioned it to her, she sent me to my aunt's for the months leading up to the contest. She lives one town over." A smile touched the corners of her mouth and colored her tone. "Mother would have a fit if she knew Anya was staying here too." Lena rubbed her face with her hands. "So how can I tell Anya the truth? It wouldn't be fair if I can't promise anything will come from it. She's as conscious of her station as I am—maybe more so, as it only seems to be a sore point for her. She's so proud."

Jacs did not know what to say. She realized that she had never had to consider such differences in class before. Not among the Lowrians at least. It all seemed so arbitrary.

"But . . . if Anya makes you happy, I'm sure your mother would come around. What does your father think?" Jacs ventured.

"Oh, he and my mother are of the same mind. Further the family status and fortune, ensure future stability. I think he would come around first though . . . but that's only because he married below his station." She giggled. "Mother never talks about that."

The two women listened as a slight breeze caused a tree branch to tap lightly on a windowpane. The sounds of the Griffin's Den were winding down as servants and patrons alike settled in for the night.

"But," Lena began, so quietly Jacs almost did not hear her, "if I become Queen, I will be able to choose whomever I want to rule by my side. If Anya would have me, of course," she hastened to add.

"She would be lucky to have you," Jacs replied, "and while, of course, your secret is safe with me, I just wonder if it needs to be secret from Anya. I mean, what if she's just waiting for you to say something first? Especially if she is as proud and aware of her status as you say. You will never know how she feels about you if you don't at least try."

Jacs rolled onto her back, her thoughts flitting to Connor before she could stop them.

Would an Upperite palace servant consider himself above the station of a Lowrian inventor's apprentice?

What's the hierarchy here? She swallowed.

The letters leading up to his silence had filled her with a longing she had not felt before. The shift had happened so gradually that it was not until the letters stopped that she realized how much she looked forward to his replies, and how much his letters meant to her. Jacs felt a familiar tightness in her chest and a prickling at the corners of her eyes. Well, obviously she hadn't meant as much to him. She bit her lip, and her fingers found the ring around her neck. She traced the engraving with the pad of her thumb though she knew it by heart.

"Thanks, Jacqueline," Lena said, stifling a yawn. "Maybe you're right. During those months with my aunt, I spent hours imagining finally confessing my feelings for her with a crown on my head and the world to offer. But it's not that easy, even with a crown. And I would hate to ruin our friendship. What if she says no? And my mother . . ." Doubt filled her voice as she trailed off. Lena turned to plump her pillow. "Regardless, it's something I will have to address after the contest. The time I had to spend without her . . ." She shook her head in the moonlight and lay back down.

Jacs found her hand and gave it a quick squeeze. "These things have a way of working themselves out, but usually it's not by doing nothing," she said, stifling a yawn of her own. "But neither of us can win a contest tired. Good night, Lena."

"Good night, Jacqueline."

While sleep claimed Lena as soon as she closed her eyes, it got lost on its way to Jacs. She lay awake, listening as Lena's breathing slowed and deepened. Tomorrow. The day she had been preparing for this past year. She would see the castle, she would talk with the Prince, she would make sure she was chosen to compete, she would become Queen and save her people. Not too difficult.

And maybe I'll find Connor. The thought sent a pang through Jacs's chest. She rolled onto her side and frowned. She did not need any distractions. Not now. It would be best if she focused on the task at hand. She chewed her lower lip. But a part of her yearned to know what had happened all those months ago. To know why he had stopped replying. To know how he could so easily cut her out.

Jacs rolled back over and stared at the velvet canopy. No. She had to stick to her mission. He could be anywhere in the Upper Realm anyway. But surely it couldn't hurt to find the river where it all began? To stand where he stood. To see what he saw. And maybe, just maybe, if not to find answers to at least obtain some closure. Resolving to seek out the river the next day, her last thought carried her away to a fitful sleep.

16

FIREWORKS

The guests had been arriving steadily since early that morning, not that Connor had been able to sleep at all that night. He had dressed three times before the first horse and carriage made its way down the long expanse of driveway. The household had been prepared for the early arrivals and Connor knew a breakfast banquet had been laid in the entrance hall. His presence was not expected until later that afternoon so he was free to see to final preparations and to do his best to avoid the crowds until then.

Sitting at his desk, he pulled the side drawer open and retrieved, as he had done many times before, a small wooden boat from its depths. It had been over a year since he had sent his last message, but he remembered the ritual well. His boats were far less elaborate than the first one had been. They served only to protect the glass vial from the rocks on the way down. He smiled at the thought of how their means of communication had become more efficient as the years passed.

Jacs once described to him the series of nets she had installed below the waterfall to ensure his boats did not float too far downstream. She delighted in telling him about the fish she would catch as a result.

It was bigger than my head! And another one, I thought it was dead, but when I laid it out on the bank it jumped and flip-flopped its way back into the water.

He read over his letter again and brushed his thumb across the now-dry ink.

Dear Jacs,

I know my last was well over a year ago, and I hope you have found happiness in that time. I could not bring myself to respond because, if I'm honest, I just didn't know what to say. I have been to the Lower Realm. I have seen what your kind are capable of. While our Queendom lost its Queen that day, I also lost my mother. All of what that statement implies is true. My mother was Queen Ariel. I am Prince Cornelius Frean.

I'm sorry I never told you. Any reason I try to write sounds silly and childish, but that's beside the point now. Because now, on the precipice of our new Queen's reign, I can't help but think that I may have lost you. The last part I didn't realize would hurt so much. I guess I just want to say that I'm sorry. I'm so sorry if I have caused you pain. I look back to your letters often and I am so ashamed to think that I so completely turned my back on you.

After today, everything will be different, but I don't know how to face it without knowing I will have you to talk to. I hope you can forgive me, and I pray for the day I see a balloon hanging from the branches of our tree. In your last, you said you forgive me for leaving you like I did, and I am going to do all I can to deserve that forgiveness. Know that, no matter what happens, I will always be,

Yours,
Connor
Voyage 113

He still did not feel as though it did justice to the time that had passed, to all he had not told her, and to all the worry and pain his silence had caused her. Her last letters had been difficult to read and he knew she was not telling him the half of it all. He still did not know exactly how he felt toward her, but he knew there had to be a reason why he could not stop his thoughts from landing on her. There had to be a reason why he kept the box of her letters, and why he would look through them now and again. He folded and rolled the note carefully, slipping it into the small glass vial.

The wind danced in the leaves of the large oak on the edge of the Cliff. Connor stood at the base of its gnarled trunk and marveled, as he had done so many times before, at the basin of the Lower Realm stretched out before him. Realizing that he did not have much time to waste and that it would not be long before he was missed, he checked over the boat again. He smiled as he remembered the first voyage and the blessing he gave the little vessel. Placing the boat in the lazy current—the lack of rain had continued to affect all water sources—he watched it bob and dip as it found its bearings. A rapid caused it to spin in a circle before gaining speed and rushing toward the edge of the land. He saw it teeter on the brink for a moment and topple over, disappearing from view.

". . . Whoa!" The sound of a woman's voice followed by a loud splash made him turn around sharply. "Great, just fantastic, you get a new dress, and you end up swim—Oh, hello, I'm so sorry to uh . . . I really didn't expect to see . . . I've probably just disturbed your solitude, haven't I?"

Without a second thought, Connor ran to help the woman to her feet and out of the river. "I'm . . . Oh thank you, that's very kind of you," she said.

Connor took her by the hand and was surprised to feel the calluses on her palm. He had expected the familiar soft hands of a Dame. As he helped her to the bank, their eyes met and he felt the moments slow and reflect in the shades of green in her eyes. She smiled, her cheeks pink—from the fall or from embarrassment, he was not sure.

Her auburn hair was woven in a delicate braid around her head but had come loose in places and had a leaf nestled in its strands. She wore a simple dress of deep green. The dress itself fit her slim figure well and hung limply at the hem halfway up her shin, where it had been drenched in the river. Connor caught himself staring and his gaze flicked down to the ground. He noticed that her soft brown leather slippers were completely waterlogged.

"Are you all right?" he asked, meeting her eyes again.

"Yes, thank you, just lost my footing. Lucky the water's warm!" She laughed. The sound was a dancing melody above the river's instrumental.

He smiled back, then looked around, puzzled. "What are you doing all the way out here? Are you lost?"

She laughed again, realized she was still holding his hand, dropped it, and began settling her skirts. "No! No, I'm here for the uh . . . for the contest and, it's a long story, but I was following along the river to find the Cliff. It's going to sound silly, but I came out here to find a particular oak tree—" She cut off with wide eyes, as if suddenly taking in his finery and the crest on his tunic that marked him as nobility. "Oh dear, and now I've forgotten the—" She sank into the clumsy hybrid between a bow and a curtsy of someone who was still not sure of where each limb should go. Offering her hand, she waited with her head bowed.

Connor had to bite the inside of his cheek to keep a straight face. He did not think he had ever been offered a hand to shake, as it was customary for his subjects to kneel. He took her hand respectfully, and bowed his head in return.

"Well met, my lady, may I ask your name?" he inquired somberly.

"Jacqueline Daidala, daughter of Maria and Francis Daidala of Parima," she replied, her tongue fumbling over the last word.

"You have come quite a distance to be here today," he commented, impressed.

"You have no idea," she said, her eyes sparkling, then ducked her head again and added, "And, what is your name, sir?"

Bracing himself, he replied, "Cornelius Frean."

The color drained from her face and a hand flew to her mouth. Connor grimaced inwardly and waited. To his surprise, she started giggling.

"I'm . . . Oh, I can't . . . and of course of all the people . . . and I didn't . . . It's not funny . . . I'm so sorry. It's just . . . well . . . I should have recogn—I mean . . ." she managed before cutting off sharply.

Suddenly serious, Jacqueline arranged her features to an expression of dignified solemnity and offered, "Please, let's start over." Clearing her throat, she dropped to one knee. "Your High-ness—"

"Grace," he said quickly.

"Pardon?"

"The Prince is Your Grace, the Queen and King are Your Highness . . . or Majesty." He clarified and saw her cheeks redden further.

"Right, so sorry. Let's start over *over*. Your Grace, it is the greatest honor to meet you. Please forgive my intrusion. I thank you most humbly for your much-needed assistance and for your compassion toward my severe ignorance," she said, a smile in her voice.

Connor assumed the stance his father took when meeting with subjects in the throne room and replied, "Rise, Jacqueline Daidala. Given the circumstances, I would say there was no intended breach of decorum, and I hope I may escort you safely to the palace?"

Jacqueline looked briefly over Connor's shoulder to where the river disappeared into nothing. A mixed emotion, somewhere between longing and resolve, flitted across her features. Then as if deciding, her eyes rested on his as she smiled again. "I would be honored, Your Grace."

He held out his arm for her and she took it shyly, although the forest did not allow them to walk casually side by side for long. As Connor helped Jacqueline over a particularly large fallen tree, she ventured, "What brought you all the way out here, if you don't mind my asking?"

Connor thought of the little vessel plummeting to a different land and replied, "I had some time before everything gets started and I thought I'd go for a walk. It's one of my favorite spots on the grounds and I know I won't be able to visit it much in the coming days."

"It's a beautiful spot; you can see so much of the Lower Realm from up there." Jacqueline pulled her skirts up slightly to avoid a bramble.

"Yes, but many things look beautiful given enough distance." Disdain edged his words and she looked up sharply.

"This is true, but you would never get to the heart of a place, never understand a place completely if you spent your life looking at it from so far away as to not see its flaws."

"Are you suggesting that I don't understand my own Queendom?"

Connor had stopped walking. Jacqueline turned and stopped too. Her head was cocked to the side as she studied him. His voice had held no anger, he was simply taken aback by her blunt critique.

"Well," she began slowly, "do you?"

"I . . . uh . . ." He cleared his throat. "No, I suppose I don't. Not completely at least."

She grinned. "And I don't think anyone would expect you to, either. It's a very large Queendom, and it's not customary for royalty to visit most of it except on special occasions."

The absurd truth of her statement struck him. Jacqueline turned to continue through the trees and he hastened to follow.

She was quiet for a moment, then said, "My father always said, 'A wise woman—or in this case, a wise man—admits three things readily: when he's wrong, when he doesn't know, and when he's sorry. And when he's wrong, he'll learn, when he doesn't know, he'll find out, and when he's sorry, he won't do it again.'" She laughed, "But then again, he used to say that about how he managed to keep Mum happy. I guess it's transferable advice."

"He sounds like a wise man," Connor said.

She smiled sadly. "He really was." A silence fell between them and Connor waited for her to continue. Finally she explained, "He died when I was young."

"Oh, I'm so sorry, Jacqueline."

Their eyes met. "Thank you," she said simply and added, "What is your father like?"

Connor smiled at the innocence of such a loaded question. "Well, you will see him tonight at the banquet, so I will allow you to judge for yourself." He paused, unsure, then added, "He is a great man who is doing all he can to honor his Queen's legacy and ensure an appropriate heir is found."

Jacqueline nodded and they fell into a comfortable silence as they reached the edge of the forest and made their way toward the castle across the lush lawn.

"What are you most looking forward to tonight?" Jacqueline asked before clarifying, "I mean, politics and purpose aside. I spent the morning with my companion talking about what tonight's festivities would include, and you would not believe the rumors she's heard. Some even said the Court would make an appearance!" She glanced sidelong at him for a reaction, "But I don't know . . . Is there something specific that you are really looking forward to seeing or experiencing tonight?"

Connor laughed. "Well, I don't want to give too much away, and to quash the imagination of those rumors takes the fun out of it." He thought for a moment. "Hmm, but I really have always loved fireworks, and I heard the display is going to be spectacular."

Jacqueline clapped her hands together excitedly. "Oh I can't wait. If I'm honest every moment I've been here has been spectacular. I suppose I'll reach my saturation point, but I can't see that happening anytime soon. The architecture alone!"

Connor looked at her fondly, his hand floating to her lower back to steer her around a sizable gopher hole, and he hid a smile as he saw a blush steal across her cheeks.

"If you are interested in architecture, and if you have a moment, possibly after the contest—" he laughed "—you should most definitely go and see the palace library; the patterns in the vaulted ceilings are mesmerizing."

"That sounds beautiful. Is it open to the public?" Jacqueline asked excitedly, her eyes shining.

"Only at certain times . . . but in the company of a prince there are few doors that remain closed." He said with mock seriousness. Hearing the words ring in his own ears he could have kicked himself. *She's going to think you're a pretentious prick*, he thought with disdain.

Jacqueline bumped her shoulder against his playfully, "So now I just need to find one of these princes you speak of."

Connor shrugged and grinned. "And then the world is your oyster. Although where you will find one of those, I just don't know." Still smiling, he asked, "And what are you most looking forward to over these next few days?"

She looked at him knowingly, "Well, as much of the specifics are new and very mysterious, it's all very exciting. But I guess what I'm most looking forward to is proving myself a worthy queen to all our people."

Connor did not quite know how to respond to that; he admired the simple conviction in her voice. Her eyes shone as she looked at him and he found himself wanting to believe she could.

"Well, Ms. Daidala, I wish you luck in the days to come."

"Thank you, Your Grace." She bowed her head formally.

They walked the rest of the way to the castle talking comfortably. Jacqueline described how she had met Dame Glowra on her way to Basileia, and Connor shared a memory of his mother defying and subsequently befriending a band of highwaywomen while in the Lower Realm that had attempted to steal their pack horses. They found their common ground in discussing past adventures. Jacqueline was eager to learn of his travels throughout the realm, and Connor was happy to oblige. Connor marveled at how easy it was to talk to her. He felt as if they were old friends. He racked his brain to think of the last time he was in Parima and decided that, even if he had been recently, they could not have crossed paths. He would have remembered a smile like hers.

Reaching the edge of the lawn, the two ducked under an overgrown archway and entered onto the palace gardens together. The flower beds were alive with color and bumblebees wafted lazily between the petals. The scents of lavender and rosemary filled the air. Jacqueline smiled and plucked a sprig of the latter from a nearby bush, rubbed it between her fingers, and breathed in the aroma.

"Rosemary for memory," she said, more to herself than to Connor.

"A scholar's best friend," Connor agreed. "You know," he said, "you are the first contestant I have talked with for any length of time who has not even tried to get information about the upcoming tasks."

Jacqueline tucked a strand of hair behind her ear and looked at him mischievously. "Would you have told me if I had asked?"

"No," Connor conceded.

"Then what would be the point? Plus, it's far more interesting to win of my own mettle." She twirled the sprig of rosemary between her fingers idly.

Connor laughed, "I suppose, but you know, not all contestants think like you."

"True. But they won't all become Queen," Jacqueline said simply.

Again, Connor felt the certainty radiate from her words. There was a ferocity beneath their cadence that he had not expected. They passed rows of thyme and oregano, and as they entered the lily garden, he saw Dame Claustrom and the heiress of Luxlow— what was her name? He ran several different iterations beginning with *D* through his head as they approached.

"Your Grace!" Hera beamed. "What a surprise! Devon—"

Devon Witbron, that's the one.

"—and I were just admiring the—Oh, you have company." The radiant smile froze on her cheeks, letting the last words squeeze their way through still lips. Connor smiled and indicated Jacqueline. "Dame Claustrom, this is Ms. Jacqueline Daidala of Parima. She will also be competing in the contest. Jacqueline, this is Dame Hera Claustrom of Hesperida, and Dame Devon Witbron of Luxlow."

Jacqueline attempted a more polished version of the bow-curtsy-handshake maneuver she had used with him earlier. Hera raised a thin eyebrow and reluctantly offered a gloved hand to shake. Devon shook Jacqueline's hand more warmly. She was petite and stood at least a head shorter than the other two girls. Her hair was a mousy brown and hung in loose ringlets around her pointed face. "Lovely to meet you, Ms. Daidala," she said in a high voice.

"And you," Jacqueline returned, obviously not perturbed by Hera's chilly reception. "It seems you two have found quite the perfect sun spot."

"And it seems you have had quite the spill—what on earth has happened to your gown?" Hera asked as she recoiled delicately.

Jacqueline looked down at the water-stained fabric and Connor was surprised to see her chuckle to herself and twirl in a circle. "Oh this? Don't you love it? I'm going for a new look. It was inspired by Nature herself."

Connor and Devon both laughed. Hera however, delicately tapped her forefinger to her chin and said, "But surely that's no way to meet royalty. With all due respect, Your Grace, I feel I must apologize on this woman's behalf for presenting herself to you in such disarray. One would think her a Lowrian with such manners."

The laughter died on Connor's lips and he frowned as he looked at Jacqueline, who had become quite still and appeared to deflate. A flush flared in her cheeks and an emotion that looked almost like fear flashed in her eyes. The corners of Hera's mouth struggled to hide a satisfied smirk, and Devon began studying her cuticles.

Connor opened his mouth, ready to defend Jacqueline, but she had already taken a step toward Hera. For a moment she seemed to draw herself up.

She met Hera's eyes and in a steady voice said, "Thank you for your consideration, Dame Claustrom, however, I do not require you to apologize on my behalf." She turned to Connor, "Nor will I apologize on my own behalf, respectfully, Your Grace. I think it pointless to apologize for an event that was neither my fault nor intended to preface an encounter with a member of the royal family. I think the only apology I will need to make will be to my companion for keeping her waiting for me so long. If you will all excuse me, I should return to her before the festivities begin." She bowed to Devon and Hera in turn and said politely, "I hope to see you both at the feast." She then turned to Connor and met his gaze. "Your Grace, thank you. . . for everything. I look forward to the fireworks."

Looking as if she wanted to say more, she searched his face for a moment. He felt a mild panic erupt in his chest.

He did not want her to leave yet, especially not on the tails of Hera's comment.

Not knowing what to do, he simply swept her hand up in his and kissed it lightly. "Well said. Thank you for the pleasure of your company this afternoon, Ms. Daidala. I would not dream of stealing you from your companion a moment longer if it would cause her distress. I urge you and your companion to find seats at my table tonight. I feel our conversation deserves a proper closure."

He dropped her hand. Jacqueline bowed again and made her exit. He watched her make her way along the path, lilies brushing the folds of her skirt as she ducked through another overgrown archway and out of sight. He turned back to Hera and Devon.

"Oh dear," Hera simpered, "it does appear we have frightened the girl off. It does not bode well for her ability in the upcoming tasks."

Connor feigned a polite smile. "On the contrary, Dame Claustrom, it may be that Ms. Daidala knows which battles are worth her energy. I will be interested to see how she fares against a true adversary. But I too am reminded of the time. I look forward to seeing you both at the feast this evening. Good afternoon." He inclined his head as the two women hurried to make their curtsies, and left the garden.

The voices from the hall clamored over each other to escape the room's windows and doors. Connor and his father were waiting in a small room off to the side of the great hall, waiting for all the guests to find their seats before making their entrance. Connor felt his palms prickle with sweat. This was it. He had been imagining this night and the days to come for a year, his life's purpose had been building up to this moment, and he still did not feel ready for it. This contest would determine the fate of the entire Queendom. This contest that was largely created by him. He took two large gulps of air and pulled at the collar of his tunic.

He was adorned as befitted his station in navy blue and gold. Edith had draped and smoothed the embroidered cape over his shoulders with tears in her eyes. "Your mother would be so proud," she whispered before hiding her face and moving to straighten his collar.

His father was dressed in similar colors. His brow was decorated with a thin, simple gold-wrought crown. It held one jewel in the center of his forehead. A deep blue sapphire. Connor's crown was a plain gold band. The last time he had worn it had been for his mother's funeral. It weighed heavily on his temples and he tried to ignore the dull pain in his chest. He rubbed the spot absentmindedly and looked about the antechamber for a distraction.

There was very little in the room to hold his attention long. A velvet sofa, a small end table with a bottle of wine and the glass he had not touched, and a large oil painting of an ancestor he did not know the name of.

"Nervous, boy?" His father's gruff voice cut through his musings.

"Yes," he said simply.

"Good."

There was a pause in which Connor took in his father's rugged appearance. Despite the finery and the two glasses of wine he had quaffed while they waited, his father looked like the ghost of the man he had been a year ago. The creases around his eyes ran deep, his cheeks were sallow behind the wine's blush, and his eyes were dim. It was as though Connor were looking at his father's reflection in a darkened window.

"What was it like? I mean, when mother competed?" Connor asked hesitantly.

His father paused, his wine glass halfway to his lips. A spark ignited briefly in his eyes with the memory and he almost smiled. "It was like watching a dove take to the air, like a painter to a canvas. We all knew we were watching a queen do what she was born to do."

The door opened and Perkins, dressed in light blue and gold livery, bowed as he entered the small chamber. "Your Majesty, it is time," he said.

The King handed Perkins his glass and clapped Connor on the back. "Here we go. Just remember to keep breathing."

Connor nodded and took his place a step behind his father. Perkins placed the empty glass on the end table, approached the door, squared his shoulders, and pushed it open.

Light and noise buffeted them as they emerged into the hall only to be snuffed out as if by magic when the guests caught sight of the royal family. Trumpets blared from the upper balcony, which stretched around three walls of the room. The banister of this balcony displayed the coats of arms of previous Queens in chronological order. Queen Ariel's coat of arms hung above the head table beside the fourth wall.

The fourth wall did not have a balcony nor banisters running its length. It was dominated by a two-story waterfall. Water cascaded over polished marble, was caught in a large domed pool on the second floor, and flowed down the wall with gold inlay, which caught the candlelight in a mesmerizing dance. The guests held their breath as Connor and his father made their way to the head table stretched in front of the waterfall's base facing the hall. The four members of the Council flanked the two center chairs set aside for him and his father. Two women on each side. Connor noted that each Councilor looked tired, tense, or both. Of course he understood why Councilors Beatrice Fengar and Gretchen Dilmont appeared to be fighting off yawns; they had been up all night reviewing the list of women who had signed up to compete. However, seeing Councilors Rosalind Perda and Portia Stewart so tightly wound, with such dark circles under their eyes, was unusual. He supposed they were all nervous about the upcoming tasks.

Connor was glad to see Jaqueline, without leaves in her hair this time, next to Dame Glowra. Jacqueline caught his eye and smiled at him, her fingers playing with a gold pendant on a chain around her neck. He noticed Dame Claustrom and her mother three seats down from them.

Connor and his father reached their seats and remained standing. His father surveyed the room with the authority of a man who was used to having others wait for him. Connor took in the room in a way he hoped was similar. He looked out on the sea of color. Every eligible woman and her mother or father had turned up in their best. Merchants beside Dames, knights next to bakers. The leveling of class for the sole purpose of finding the individual best suited to lead them all.

His father cleared his throat and began to speak, his voice echoing throughout the hall. "Welcome! Welcome and good luck to you all. We are all brought together on this day to embark on the course of our future. The late Queen Ariel, as you all know, was a beacon of hope and ruled with justice and compassion. It is not an easy role to fill, and it may be that, for one of you, today is the last day that you are able to consider your life your own.

"Today marks the day we find our Queen. The Queen who will give her life and love to the Queendom. It is an honor to share this moment with you all. To share this moment with my son, the Prince." There was a smattering of applause throughout the hall as the King paused and gestured to Connor.

Connor looked around the room, caught Jacqueline's eye for a brief moment and smiled.

Many eager faces looked up at him.

The King continued: "There will be time enough over the next few days for speeches and toast making. As you know, tonight we are here to enjoy ourselves. Eat and be merry! We will have a glorious fireworks display in celebration, and then tomorrow, those chosen to participate in the contest will be announced, and the first task will commence." Another burst of applause followed his words.

The King held up his hand and the sound died away, "But now, in this moment, on this night, I will take in a moment of silence for our late Queen Ariel. May her memory live on in all those she served. May her kindness be carried in the hearts of all, and may we never forget her legacy. Tonight marks the turning of a new page in our history's book. May all contestants sacrifice any personal desire for power and remember what it means to be the Queen our Queendom deserves." He raised his goblet. Connor and the rest of the room followed suit.

"To Queen Ariel!" he cried.

"To the Queen," echoed an ensemble of voices.

"May we never forget," he finished.

"May we always remember," called the voices in return.

King Aren took his seat and the hall was filled with the cacophony of benches scraping and skirts rustling as the guests hurried to follow suit.

Connor accepted the wine offered by the serving boy and reached for his fork when a sound like thunder and a force like a hurricane ripped through the corner of the room to his left. The air rippled as hundreds of fireworks exploded in unison. The blasts reverberated inside his skull. Screams filled the air as rock and debris blew into the hall. Dust billowed, catching in his throat and stinging his eyes. Connor was knocked to the floor. Chairs and benches toppled.

He felt the heat before he saw the flames licking at the tapestries on the walls, dancing into the open room; an uninvited guest intent on making its host pay for the slight.

17

THE UNEXPECTED TASK

Jacs scrambled to pick herself up off the floor and hurriedly scanned the room. The hall was in chaos. Women were running for the exits, rushing to get through the few doors on the far side of the hall. Those closest to the explosions were struggling to regain their feet. The air was quickly becoming thick with smoke. Flames greedily snatched at tables and benches closest to them.

Turning, her eyes darting around the room, Jacs saw the Prince being helped to his feet and ushered away from the flames. The King, dust and debris turning his graying hair white, was surrounded by guards who had appeared as if from nowhere. His leg had been injured in the blast. He was leaning heavily on the two guards flanking him as they too headed toward the door at the other end of the hall.

The shouts, the dust, the crackling of the flames—Jacs was transported back to the riot that had changed everything one year ago. Only this time there was no Phillip, no Master Leschi, no mother to protect her. Her mother, crumpling under a guard's baton . . .

"Jacqueline!" Lena's voice cut through the screams. She gripped her arm tightly, her eyes wide. "We have to go!"

Jacs snapped to the present. "Right! We have to . . ." she looked to the door at the far end of the room. Women were fighting each other to get through and away from the fire. *There are too many of us.* She saw a number of women injured by the blast, lying prone under tables and benches. Her eyes flew to the two-story waterfall, took in the collecting pool on the second floor, the cracked stone basin, the angles of the fallen pillars, and she made a decision.

Anya had run over and taken Lena's hand to pull her toward the exit.

"Wait!" Jacs said, catching them both, "There are too many women injured, and we won't have time to get everyone out— especially with that one exit."

"Jacqueline, hurry, Lena—we have to move." Anya finished with a cough and pulled Lena toward the door.

"Anya, listen!" Jacs ran and cut her off from the exit. "I have a plan."

"A plan for what? We have to go!"

"Jacqueline, get out of the way!" Lena had tears in her eyes, from the smoke or something else, Jacs was not sure.

"Trust me! We won't all get out if we just leave now." Jacs was fighting the panic in her chest. The smoke was getting thicker. They were running out of time. Her last words had caught the attention of not only Anya—who turned to look back at Jacs, her eyes flickering around at the number of bodies on the floor—but also three women nearby. The first, a short brunette woman who was half carrying, half dragging a friend across the hall. The second, a tall blonde woman who had just put out the flames of the third woman's velvet gown. Seeing her chance, Jacs hurriedly began to delegate.

"Okay, Lena, you, and you," she pointed to the brunette and the scorched redhead in turn, "go round up more women to help carry the injured to the door. We need more hands and we can't do it without help." Three heads nodded, determined, and the women sprinted across the room, the brunette helping her friend a short distance behind them. Lena squeezed Anya's hand briefly as she left.

Jacs turned to the blonde woman. "Okay, who are you?"

"Cynthia, Cynthia Doeboare," the woman replied, bobbing a curtsy and appearing confused as to why she had done so. Jacs nodded and addressed Anya and Cynthia together. "We need to divert the water from the waterfall's pool toward the flames." They looked at her with wide eyes as she continued. "The way the wall has fallen gives us a way up, but we'll need to shift that pillar and open the side of the pool, there." She indicated with her finger. "Got it?"

Two heads nodded. Jacs coughed through the haze, looked down at the table and grabbed three cloth napkins, dipped them in a water jug and handed them to the other women.

"For the smoke."

Anya and Cynthia took the napkins and covered their mouths and noses.

The King was being helped toward the exit. The Prince was carrying an unconscious Hera and yelling for his attendants to help two other fallen women. Jacs could just make out Cornelius's features through the smoke. Their eyes locked for a moment. His brow furrowed, and he motioned to the exit. She shook her head, painfully aware there was no time for explanation, and turned back to her impromptu team. She beckoned for them to follow.

The three women made their way toward the flames. Anya called out, "Stay low! Smoke rises!" And as one, they crouched and hurried forward.

The heat rolled into the room in waves as the flames billowed. Everything seemed to slow until Jacs could only focus on the sound of her breath in her ears, and the hazy shapes of the wall and the debris that shifted in front of her.

They reached the jagged remainder of the wall and used the ruins as steps. They pulled themselves up to the second floor, hands fumbling and eyes streaming. Jacs saw blood on her palms from cuts she did not feel.

Her heartbeat spurred her on like a war drum. She motioned to the other women to take their positions and began to try and shift the remains of a pillar to create a diagonal trough from the pool to the hole where the flames kept pouring in. Heaving and sweating, inch by inch, they moved the pillar into place.

Coughing and spluttering, they climbed the rest of the way over the rubble toward the pool. The crack in its basin was smaller than Jacs had hoped, and the basin itself had much thicker walls than expected. Jacs looked around desperately for a solution. Anya grabbed her elbow and pointed to the remains of another pillar nearby. This one was smaller than the first, and appeared to be for decoration rather than support. It had almost fallen into the chasm created by the blast and stood now precariously close to changing its mind.

Anya reached it first, with Jacs close behind. The smoke was thicker on the second floor and she was beginning to feel lightheaded. Ignoring the panic fluttering in her chest, she joined the two women and braced herself with her palms flat against the pillar. Jacs's hand rested next to Anya's with Cynthia on the other side of her. As one, they threw their bodies against it, all purposefully avoiding looking at the drop into the inferno inches from their slippered feet. The pillar crunched and shifted on the stone base. It teetered for a moment, then fell with a crash against the side of the basin. The pool burst open like a popped soap bubble. A flood of water followed the path created by the larger pillar and swallowed the flames at its base. Smoke erupted from where the two opposing forces met and the fire hissed its dissent.

"It's not out!" Cynthia cried, disappointed, her voice hoarse. Jacs saw she was right. Though the flames that had entered the hall had been extinguished, Jacs could see that the room they had come from was still alight.

"No, but we bought more time. Come on, let's help the others," Jacs croaked through her now dry napkin, her throat raw from the heat and the smoke.

They made their way back down the dripping wall, trying not to slip and forcing themselves to move slowly despite their instincts.

Jacs landed next to Anya, and Cynthia followed close behind. She saw that Lena and the others had enlisted more women to help carry those in need from the room. Hunched and hobbling figures struggled through the gloom, panicked screams now replaced with shouts of orders and directions.

"I need a hand over here, a table's pinning her legs!"

"Cover your mouth and nose!"

"Faya, thank the Goddess, grab her arms, will you?"

"Clear a path!"

"I found two over here!"

"Stay low! Come back if it's too much, we don't wanna have to come looking for you!"

Jacs turned back to her partners and said, "Okay, grab who you can and head for the door."

It was not until the hall had been evacuated and everyone had made it to the safety of the palace lawn—not until she stood in the cool night air after helping a tall, dark-eyed woman she had been supporting—that Jacs collapsed. Her world was reduced to the feel of the damp grass on her cheek and the rasping of her own breath. Far away voices called her name and to Jacs it was a moment before her vision returned and she saw Lena, Anya, the dark-eyed woman, and Cynthia leaning over her.

"Goddess be praised, she's back!" Cynthia's voice verged on hysteria.

"Jacqueline, are you all right?" Lena cooed.

"She was out for an age. She needs a medic." Anya craned her neck to locate one.

"I'm fine," Jacs began, but she was interrupted by a fit of coughing and tasted blood. She wrestled with a wave of nausea.

"That's cute," the dark-eyed woman retorted, not unkindly, and placed a hand on Jacs's chest to stop her from rising. "Rest," she instructed. Her tone was of one used to delivering orders, and Jacs noticed her long ash-blonde hair hung down her back in a military grade tail.

A line of guards and castle staff had formed to pass pails of water from a large fountain on the grounds up to the fire still smoldering in the great hall. Jacs lay on her side with her eyes closed, listening to the bucket brigade calling to one another above the sounds of the hall occupants searching for friends and family. Lena sat worriedly beside her, rubbing her back every time she coughed.

"Your Grace," the dark-eyed woman sunk to a one-kneed salute. There was a commotion above Jacs as the women hurried to make their appropriate bows.

"Rise, please, now is not the time for formality. Is everyone— Jacqueline!" The Prince had evidently spotted Jacs on the ground.

She felt Cornelius land on his knees beside her and blinked her eyes open as his fingers felt for a pulse on her wrist. He saw her stir, shifted backward to lean on his hand, and ran the other hand across his face and through his hair. "Thank the Goddess, I thought . . ."

Four voices attempted to assure him that she was fine and trailed off as the Prince regained his composure.

"I'm all right, Your Grace, I just need a few moments to catch my breath." The words scraped like knives through Jacs's windpipe. She attempted to sit up but the world began spinning in protest and she lay back down.

Cornelius laughed shakily. "And now it seems I need to do the same."

The dark-eyed woman spoke up, "Your Grace, Chivilra Andromeda Turner, Knight of the Brinora division. This woman not only pulled me from the hall, but one other, and led Ms. Anya Bishop and Ms. Cynthia Doeboare to put out the majority of the fire with the waterfall. I insist she be seen by a medic at once; she's inhaled far too much smoke."

Jacs began to object, but the Prince cut her off, addressing first the knight and then her in turn. "Thank you, Chivilra Turner. Ms. Daidala—" he paused, grasping for the right words "—many on

this lawn owe you their lives. Myself and my father among them."
He stood and called to a nearby attendant, "Brandon, send for
some water and for Master Epione. She should be finishing up with
Dame Claustrom by now." The attendant voiced his understanding
and hurried off.

The Prince then removed his cloak, folded it into a bundle and
offered it to Lena. "For her head," he said. Lena lifted Jac's head
gently and slid the bundle beneath it. Jacs squeezed her eyes shut
against the wave of nausea that rolled through her body.

"Thank you, Your Grace," Lena supplied, in Jacs's stead.

"Make sure Master Epione tends to all of you when she
arrives," he pressed. "I must find the King, but know that you have
all acted with honor and bravery this evening."

The standing women sunk low as he departed. No one said
anything until Cornelius was well out of earshot.

Finally Lena blurted out, "Jacqueline, since when are you on a
first-name basis with the Prince?"

Jacs smiled and cracked one eye open. "Let's just say it has been
a very bizarre day."

Master Epione arrived shortly after the Prince left and saw
to each woman in turn. She was light haired and dark skinned,
although, on closer inspection Jacs noticed her gray hair implied
an age that her face did not admit. She could not have been older
than thirty-five.

She busied herself applying salves and ointments to various
lacerations. Anya and Cynthia had cuts and scrapes similar to Jacs's
on hands, knees, and arms.

Lena had also inhaled a substantial amount of smoke, so she
and Jacs were given a small glass vial each and told to inhale the
contents. Jacs did so warily and immediately felt a cooling relief

fill her lungs. Chiv. Turner had a nasty bump on her head and appeared to have sprained her ankle. Master Epione worked meticulously with her medicines and after a few minutes, the knight was standing and gingerly testing her weight on her ankle, which was already less swollen.

"You'll be right as rain come the morning," Master Epione remarked. "I'd like to tell you to take it easy over the next few days but as the contest has begun, all I ask is you get as much rest as you can." Shaking her head, she bustled off to help others, her vials and bottles clinking slightly as she made her way across the lawn.

Hours later, once the fire was successfully extinguished and the guests had been attended to, the King positioned himself on a balcony overlooking the lawn. Silence fell among the crowd below as he held up his hand.

"True adversity has the power to draw people together. When the Lowrian assassins—" There was a general outcry of disgust from the crowd. The King raised his hand again for silence and continued "—took our beloved Queen from us before her time, the strength the Upperite citizens showed in their support for one another made us stronger as a Realm. Now, on the eve of the sacred Contest of Queens, we were threatened again, and again we showed our strength united."

Jacs frowned, leaned over to Lena and whispered, "Did he just suggest the explosion was planned?"

Lena shook her head. "He can't have meant that. I thought it was just the fireworks gone wrong."

Chiv. Turner growled, "Lowrian lovers, this reeks of Levelists."

The King continued. "Traditionally the contestants are chosen based on observed merit in the days leading up to the contest. The Council has decided to consider the actions displayed tonight as representative of each woman's ability to respond with honor, integrity, and bravery in a threatening situation. Therefore, any woman who was observed to flee onto the lawn without any regard for their companions will be disqualified from the competition. Those who stayed to help will remain in the competition."

Uneasy murmurs filled the still night air, and again the King waited for silence before continuing. "Each registered contestant has been reviewed by a panel of witnesses and myself. Ten women will be competing in the Contest of Queens as a result of their selfless bravery. However, many contestants were, unfortunately, injured. As those who were injured were in a reduced position to demonstrate their virtue, their qualification in the contest will be based on an interview, should they still be willing and able to compete. We expect to have final numbers decided before the first task tomorrow afternoon."

"Ten!" Jacs whispered. Her voice barely audible over the other whispers spreading through the crowd.

The King finished his speech. "Please, allow me to congratulate the following contestants:

Dame Shane Adella
Dame Lena Glowra
Dame Fawn Lupine
Dame Devon Witbron
Dame Danielle Hart
Chiv. Amber Everstar
Ms. Anya Bishop

Ms. Jacqueline Daidala
Ms. Cynthia Doeboare
Ms. Faya Goldenrod"

The rest of the King's speech was drowned out by the rushing in Jacs's ears and the squeals and disappointed outbursts from the crowd. She had done it.

She had made it. She had qualified. Her thoughts were cut short as Lena pulled Jacs to her feet and hugged her tightly around the middle.

"We did it!" she squealed, then she turned and embraced Anya.

Jacs felt a tap on her shoulder and saw Cynthia offer a formal bow, then clasp her hand warmly. "Thank you," she said solemnly, "and congratulations."

"And to you," Jacs said, fumbling.

The brunette and the redhead who had helped Lena get women to safety found the group in the crowd and offered their congratulations. The brunette introduced herself as a knight "— Chivilra Amber Everstar—" and punched Jacs playfully on the arm, smirking. "Just because I took orders from you in there, doesn't mean I'm gonna fall in line in the tasks! Watch yourself, Daidala, we're rivals now."

Fawn, the redhead, adjusted her singed skirts and attempted the same bravado but fell short. "Yeah, and maybe you'll be the one on fire next time . . . I mean, if it's a fire-related task, but I don't want you burned of course . . ."

Chiv. Turner shared a knight's salute with Chiv. Everstar— crossed wrists tapped together twice, fists closed, palms up—and, after thanking Jacs again, bid farewell and hobbled toward the castle for her interview.

The castle sat smoldering, yet the extensive damage was brushed aside as a minor inconvenience. It appeared the King was determined to push on with the contest according to schedule regardless of catastrophe or disaster. Already the firefighters were meeting with a team of decorators to discuss the level of damage and the salvageable structures.

The King's voice could be heard booming across the expansive lawn as he demanded flower arrangements be brought in to mask the "blasted smoky smell."

Staff were overheard gossiping about the explosion. While Jacs heard several confident firefighters mention the "poor fireworks storage" and "careless lamp placement," it did not seem to quash the murmurs that were spreading through the crowd.

"Lowrian filth, here to finish what they started a year ago."

"Trying to send a message."

"Biding their time until—"

"Treason."

Jacs tried to shut her ears to it, or at the very least not respond in a way that might be suspicious.

The contestants, gathered together after their names were called, began to make their way to their sleeping quarters for the duration of the contest. The servant entrusted with the task of leading them was quite young and extremely nervous. He attempted to point out interesting landmarks and features within the castle as they walked until he tripped on the corner of a rug and appeared incapable of speaking past the lump in his throat.

Lena asked, "What if it was a part of a Lowrian plot?" as they walked.

Jacs was bent slightly so that Lena could more easily whisper in her ear. "What was?" she whispered back, her throat dry.

"The explosion! I mean, it's quite clever to mask it as a fireworks accident. Plus, it'd be just the kind of stunt they'd pull . . . We know what they're like."

Jacs frowned and straightened up. Careful not to lose her cover, she remarked, "No. We don't know what they're like, and feeding the conspiracy beast is a waste of breath."

Lena shot Jacs a bewildered look, "But it makes sense, with all their little sabotages leading up to the contest too. Ever since the Queen passed—Goddess rest her—they've been finding ways to derail plans and all the rest. It fits."

"Like what?" Jacs felt as though an ice shard had slid its way into her belly. Somehow she had not expected this of Lena. Guilt and apprehension writhed inside her at the thought of how Lena would react to find out her companion was Lowrian.

Lena opened her mouth to continue, but the group suddenly halted and she whispered, "I'll tell you later."

The servant had stopped beside a corridor that split off to the left of the hallway. He cleared his throat and, in a voice that broke and shifted from blustering staccato to rehearsed eloquence, informed the group, "We have arrived at the contestants' wing. You may notice it has been recently refurbished for the occasion. Although you come to this hall with different titles and rank, may you enter these rooms as equals. There are four beds per room. Your households or companions or other . . . ah . . . company, have been informed of your contestant status and castle staff will be sent to collect your things from the inn later this evening.

"May I—er, I mean, if you, ah, look at the portraits lining the walls, you will see the faces of past Queens who, like you, participated in the contest. Although, these are the winners, and only one of you—er, that is to say, I . . . best of luck to you all, and to all a good night." He made to leave, then realized he had forgotten a piece of information and stammered, "There are pull cords in every room should you need me . . . or anyone . . . not just me. Thank you." He bobbed a hurried bow and backed away down the hallway.

Amber remarked dryly, "Silver tongue, that one. Guard your hearts, ladies."

Several contestants stifled giggles and the group slowly dispersed down the corridor and into the various spaces. Jacs followed Lena and Anya into a vacant room.

"Wow," muttered Anya.

The room was simply furnished yet stunning. The stone floor was covered in a lush white rug and four four-poster beds lined the walls, each with a nightstand to the right, and a trunk at its foot. A small fireplace warmed the room and bathed the scene in a cheerful glow.

Anya had thrown herself onto a bed close to the window. "What a night," she exclaimed, her face full of pillow.

Lena shot Jacs a smile and settled onto the bed opposite Anya's, also close to the window. She smoothed the folds in her dress and looked about her happily. "And I imagine it's about to get even more challenging," she said.

Jacs made her way to the bed next to Lena's and touched a tassel on the hangings.

"Room for one more?" a voice at the door said. Jacs turned and saw Amber grin and make her way to the last vacant bed. "Seems the smartest idea to stick with the fire quenchers, especially since they've given us all our own." She laughed and pointed to the domestic flame. Noticing Anya, she approached and held out her hand, "I've met the others, but I'm Amber, Amber Everstar. Chiv.

Amber Everstar of the Royal Forces, Springbank Division if you want to throw in titles, but apparently we're to leave those at the door."

"Anya Bishop, pleasure."

"All mine, I'm sure. I saw what you and Jacqueline did with the waterfall. That takes guts. I respect anyone willing to get their hands that dirty."

"Thanks, I'm sure there will be plenty of opportunities to do that in the next few days."

Amber grinned again and sprawled on the edge of her bed. "You said it."

"So, Amber, where are you from?" Jacs ventured.

"Springbank originally, but moved to Basileia when I was fifteen to become a knight. Been here ever since. You?"

"Bri— Parima. My mother's a goldsmith there."

"Huh, I've never been out that far myself. How about you?" Amber asked Lena.

"I'm from Terrelle. My parents are Lord Ava and Genteel Kristoff Glowra."

Amber nodded. "Apologies, Dame Glowra, I meant no disrespect."

"No! Please, it's like you said, titles at the door. Call me Lena. And I . . ." Lena hesitated and suddenly looked nervous. "Congratulations on your recent medals, Amber. The Soterian Medal . . . that's such a feat, and youngest knight since Chiv. Strellen, even more so. My mother and I have been following your career and it's . . . you've done some truly remarkable things." Her cheeks flushed, and Jacs noticed Amber inflate to stand to her full five foot five. Amber accepted the praise gracefully and, with a bemused smile on her face, agreed to sign a kerchief for Lena's mother.

The conversation fell to a lull while Jacs stood beside her bed. She looked from the delicate brocade of the bedspread down at her torn, stained, and singed gown. The smell of smoke clung to her garments and rose from her hair when she moved her head. She could not bear the thought of sullying such riches and looked around the room for a water basin. She caught Lena's eye and said, "Does anyone else fancy a bathe?"

Three soot-covered faces nodded in agreement and they all rose to find the bathhouse.

Hours later, now sufficiently scrubbed and wrapped in yards of soft, fluffy towels, Jacs lowered herself onto her bed with a contented sigh. Lena stood next to Anya speaking softly and gazing out the window at the grounds. Amber stoked the fire back to life.

There was a knock at the door and an accompanying voice inquired, "Dame Lena Glowra?"

"Here!" Lena said, stepping toward the door. A number of staff members brought in various-sized bundles and packages. Jacs heard Westly's voice before she saw him round the corner.

"And there she is! Congratulations, my dear! Your parents are so proud, they arrived this evening and have taken to bed early— long day of travel, you understand—but they wanted me to tell you how very happy they were to hear the news!" He performed a formal bow, then embraced Lena warmly.

Lena's eyes darted to the other women in the room, and her cheeks turned a delicate shade of pink, her embarrassment was endearing. "Thank you for coming, Westly. Will you be staying in the castle too?" she said softly.

"No, dear me, no. I will be nearby though, at the Griffin's Den, so if there is anything you need, the staff here knows where to find me. And Jacqueline—" he turned and grasped Jacs's hands in his own "—congratulations to you as we— Ms. Bishop!" he exclaimed, only just noticing Anya at the other end of the room.

"Good evening, Westly. You look well," Anya said warmly.

"Ah . . . yes, good evening, Ms. Bishop. I daresay I have not seen you since . . . well . . . most unfortunate. And you're to be sharing this room. Well . . . yes . . . too right . . . and why shouldn't you? Of course what Mistress does not know . . . congratulations to you, my dear. Very well done indeed." Westly turned a hue to match Lena's. Jacs raised an eyebrow at Amber, who shrugged.

"Oh Westly, Mother has much more pressing matters to worry about than who I share a room with," Lena cut in hurriedly. "Thank you very much for seeing my things got here all right."

"Of course," he said tentatively, glancing back at Anya.

"It is truly wonderful to see you after the evening we've had," Lena continued.

Westly cupped Lena's cheek in his palm and in a much gentler voice said again, "Of course. We're all . . . and I'm just . . . so relieved you are all right."

A young woman dressed in a pale blue split dress with the Queen's crest embroidered on her cap sleeves knocked softly on the door frame. She stood in the doorway holding a wrapped bundle and inquired to the room, "Ms. Jacqueline Daidala?"

"That's me," Jacs replied.

The woman settled Jacs's belongings on the trunk at the end of her bed, next to where Jacs had placed the Prince's cloak. "Your things, ma'am. Please let us know should you need anything further."

"Thank you," Jacs said as the woman bowed and left. Anya and Amber responded in kind as more serving staff came in with their belongings.

Westly, composed now, gave Lena another hug and, once he was satisfied all of her things had been put away neatly, said his good-byes and left. There was a sudden silence as the door shut behind him and the room began to settle again.

"That was . . . odd," Anya ventured, looking at Lena. "What was all that about?"

Lena's color deepened and she busied herself in her trunk, apparently looking for something. Her voice was higher than usual as she spun around, brandishing a number of hair supplies. "What was *what* about? Oh, Westly brought two hairbrushes, I guess that is a little strange but maybe he thought I—"

"No, not the hairbrushes, he got all blustery when he noticed I was here," Anya pressed.

"Oh, I'm sure he just didn't expect to see you here. That's all. I don't think he knew you were competing. Plus with all else that's happened tonight, maybe he was just surprised."

"But I stayed at the *Griffin's Den*. Surely you mentioned—"

"Must have slipped my mind with all that was going on—"

"Slipped your mind?" Anya bristled.

"Well . . . yes, with the contest and—" Lena faltered.

"And why would your mother care if we shared a—"

"You know what, you're right. He did seem a bit funny, didn't he? Not sure what he meant by most of it. Maybe he was upset because of the fire. He is so sensitive sometimes. I'm sure he meant nothing by it," Lena babbled, her voice rising to cut off Anya's.

Jacs groaned inwardly, not sure how to help her drowning companion. As Lena continued to dig herself into a hole, Jacs interjected loudly, changing the subject, "Well, we really did have our trial by fire. I wonder if the tasks are going to be that extreme."

"It definitely saved them the hassle of choosing who gets to compete," Amber agreed, "although you'd think there'd be a more efficient way to go about it. Maybe one that saved the tapestries. Sorry, I shouldn't joke, it's just . . . it's all a bit bizarre, really."

Jacs perched on the edge of her bed with a pillow in her lap. She ran a tassel through her fingers absentmindedly and smiled. "Extremely bizarre."

Anya, still looking perturbed, sat on the edge of her bed with a wide-toothed comb, unwound her thick, wet, curly hair from the bun at the nape of her neck, and began combing out the tangles. "And for it to happen tonight of all nights . . ." she mused.

Jacs glanced at Lena, who was bent over her trunk again but no longer rifling through it.

"Well, if rumors are to be believed, it wasn't chance at all," Amber supplied. She was lying diagonally across her bed on her stomach, her wet hair fanned out across her shoulders. Her eyes glittered with intrigue.

"What do you mean?" Jacs asked.

"Haven't you heard? The Lowrians are coming!" Amber wiggled her fingers as her voice took on a warbling tone. "Load of rubbish," she added, dropping her hands to the covers with a resolute *thump*. Jacs kept her expression neutral.

"You think so?" Lena commented.

"You don't?" Amber replied, her eyebrow raised.

"Well, I think they've shown us the lengths they would go to sabotage our way of life. Ungrateful dogs. It's as if they forget they need us far more than we need them."

Jacs's eyes widened.

She couldn't believe the contempt in Lena's voice.

"That's your mother talking, Lena," Anya scoffed, not unkindly. "You don't know—"

"It is not! It's the truth. Without us, they'd have no economy, no culture, no structure, no . . . no morality!"

"Hang on—" Jacs began. She felt a stone forming in the pit of her stomach. Her guilt now twisted with fear. If this is what Lena thought of all Lowrians, how would she react when she found out Jacs was one of them? Worse, that Jacs had lied to her. Quickly, she pushed that thought away.

She couldn't worry about that now.

"Regardless, there's no way they were behind the fire. That kind of stunt requires brains and planning. They've got beans and pigs. Hardly the toolbox of criminal masterminds," Amber asserted.

"I think you're both forgetting the fact that they'd have to make it up the Bridge first. There's no way that would have gone unnoticed," Anya said.

"What if they stowed away after the last Descension?" Lena fired back.

"You think there would be even the slightest relaxation of security after the Queen died? Goddess rest her," Anya replied. "I refuse to believe that anyone could have come anywhere near the royal procession without an alarm being raised."

Jacs shut her eyes to the image of the red rose of blood blossoming on blue and gold. "Has anyone—" her voice cracked. She cleared her throat and tried again. "Has anyone ever actually met a *person*—" she paused delicately "—from the Lower Realm?"

The three women looked at Jacs and then at one another. Each muttered a no.

"Why?" Amber asked, propping her chin up on her hand.

"I just find it interesting how you each have such strong opinions of people you have never met. I only wonder what their opinions of you—us—must be."

The soft crackling of the fire followed Jacs's words. A contestant could be heard berating a staff member farther down the hall, "No, the *lace*. Honestly! *Highly recommended* my big toe! Wait until Mother hears how you've ruined my silks!"

Jacs yawned extravagantly. "Well," she declared, "it has been a wild night. I'm sure we could stay up talking, but I have a crown to win." She grinned mischievously. "So, I might get ready for bed."

The others agreed and very soon they were all settling under their covers. Jacs noticed Anya looking thoughtful as she prepared her things for the next day and attempted several times to catch Lena's eye. Lena was staring determinedly into the fire, plaiting a ribbon into her dark hair. The fire flickered and danced benignly. Silence settled around them like a blanket, each woman thinking about what tomorrow would bring, all perched on the edge of their next chapter.

18

LATE NIGHT, EARLY MORNING

It was an hour that, depending on the person experiencing it, could be considered either very late, or very early. For Connor, it was very, very late. He was sitting across from his father in the study. Perkins hovered timidly to the King's left, Masterchiv Rathbone stood at attention by the door, and two members of the Council sat around the large desk.

The first, Cllr. Gretchen Dilmont, a tall, thin woman with short, spiky hair, held a magnifying glass to better read the neat scrawl written across one of the many pieces of parchment that adorned the desk. To her right stood Cllr. Beatrice Fengar; a number of different writing tools were worked into the mass of brown hair on top of her head, giving her the appearance of a pin cushion. Her fingers flitted and sifted through the stacks of paper. Every so often she would straighten a paper in her hand and quickly scan its contents.

Connor rubbed at his eyes and made a mark on his parchment. The clock on the mantel ticked sluggishly toward the next hour. Finally the King put down his paper and sighed.

"Upon third revision," he said wearily, "I do think we have come up with the final additions to our list of contestants."

Cllr. Dilmont put down the magnifying glass and plucked a short stack of papers from the mess. Clearing her throat, she stated, "So then we are all agreed that the following five women will be joining the others to compete in the Contest of Queens: Dame Hera Claustrom, Chiv. Andromeda Turner, Ms. Christina Bergamot, Ms. Hanlen Mar, and Ms. Verona Julliard. This brings our total number up to fifteen."

Connor turned to Perkins and began, "Perkins, I will task you to alert the Court and make sure the necessary preparations are made. Ensure they have provided the appropriate number of eggs for the first task." Connor saw some of the color drain from Perkin's already very pale face at his words and he added firmly, "The Court is expecting our report, Perkins. Do not make them wait any longer than they already have."

Bobbing his understanding, Perkins put down his notes and bustled out of the room. Cllr. Fengar stretched and remarked, "I do not envy that boy's job. The Court has been especially ill-tempered of late."

"It's always a waltz with them, Councilor," the King said, stifling a yawn. "We're pushing our luck as it is, changing the qualifying ceremony like we did. They've always been a stickler for tradition and, unfortunately, they have far better memories for it than we do." He scratched his cheek roughly.

"Fifteen out of hundreds . . ." Connor mused. "How can we be sure our future Queen is among them?"

"What's that, boy?" the King demanded. His eyes were bloodshot and dark rings shadowed his lined face.

"Well . . . I was just thinking, how much of this is fate and how much of this is merit? How can we be sure these tasks will reveal the rightful ruler? What if the true Queen is out there without the means to attend? What if she had a bad case of the flu that kept her in bed? What if she's a Lowrian?" Connor felt his face flush with the doubt and emotion he had not realized he had been ignoring until now.

The King looked as though he had been slapped. The Councilors became very still, surveying Connor warily. Masterchiv Rathbone cleared her throat roughly, her hand hovering near her hilt.

"A Lowrian? A Lowrian be Queen? Have you lost your mind?!" his father roared. He brought his knuckles down on the table hard and took a few deep breaths before continuing. "This contest has been selecting rightful Queens for centuries. Our Council has been selecting the rightful Queens for centuries. I will not have its validity questioned by anyone—let alone one of the key people who helped create this generation's tasks! How. Dare. You," he breathed vehemently.

The two men glared at each other. The King's gaze held fire beneath bushy gray brows. Connor could hear the blood rushing in his ears. Two stags clashing crowns, locked for a moment, suspended.

The clock ticked.

Then Connor dropped his gaze and unclenched his fist.

He sat down, dimly aware that he must have stood up. "Forgive me, Father. I have not slept. My doubts speak to my personal anxiety rather than any distrust in the Contest," he intoned dully.

"Trust in the Contest, trust in the Council. The Queendom has prospered under that way of thinking for decades," Cllr. Dilmont said lightly. Her gaze, however, was steel.

"Cornelius, you think too hard on matters that do not require your attention. Focus on the tasks you have designed. That is where your efforts are best placed," Cllr. Fengar simpered.

The King pushed up and away from the desk and straightened his tunic. "Too right," he said gruffly. He took a moment to compose himself. "I suppose it is past time we all get some sleep. Tomorrow is a very important day. We wouldn't want any more delirium taking away our wits. Cllr. Fengar, Cllr. Dilmont, as always, your dedication to our Queendom is greatly appreciated. I will see you on the morrow." He dismissed them with a wave of his hand. Connor noticed a flash of irritation in Cllr. Dilmont's eyes but she blinked and stepped forward to incline her head to the King before marching from the room. Cllr. Fengar, hands still full of papers that she hurriedly placed on an already precarious stack, bowed lower than Cllr. Dilmont and left.

Masterchiv Rathbone closed the door behind them and stood ready. Connor looked at his father, but the King had moved to stand by the fireplace and was staring into the ashes.

"Father I—"

"You best watch your tongue, boy," his father all but whispered. "Now is not the time to appear weak, unsure, or in any way sympathetic to those Lowrian mutts. Especially in front of the Councilors."

"But Father—"

"No!" The King whirled around. "No more. Bed. Now. I will see you at breakfast."

"Of course, Father." Connor inclined his head and left without another word. As he passed Masterchiv Rathbone, she stepped toward the King, pulling a piece of folded parchment out of a pouch at her waist. "Your Highness, now may not be the time, but we need to discuss the two Lowrian rebels. General Hawkins apprehended them mere days before the contest with what appeared to be a giant—"

Masterchiv Rathbone's message was cut short by the slamming of the door.

The palace thrummed with life despite the hour. Connor's nose told him the cooks were busy with preparations well before he rounded the corner by the kitchens. Master Marmaduke was directing workflow with rapid-fire directions that made Connor's head spin.

"Stir the sauce, don't whip it. Watch it, hot behind. No, Milly, the other pot, you'll not have room in that one. Claire, what are you blubbering about? Run it under some cold water. Darrel, take over for Claire. Light and fluffy! Don't be scared of it, it's already dead! Now get slicing!"

Connor smiled and continued on down the corridor. Lost in his thoughts he almost ran right into Edith as she came out of the laundry with her arms full of linens.

"Oh! Your Grace," Edith yelped, "I'm so sorry, I did not see you—nor expect you so early. Is everything all right?"

Connor helped her balance the now teetering pile and replied, "Forgive me, Edith, I was not paying attention to where my feet were taking me." He righted the pile. "There you go."

Edith studied his face as he looked up, and she frowned. "Sire, is everything all right?" she repeated, this time more gently.

Connor had a ready reply on his lips, but her tone caught him off guard. He felt like a boy again. A boy who had been dismissed by a disappointed father. He took a breath to loosen the tightness in his chest and said quietly, "Actually, after you finish with that, could you bring some tea to my chambers? And a second cup. I could really use a friend."

She smiled knowingly. "Of course, Your Grace."

He made up his mind as he walked back to his rooms. Crossing to his desk, he pulled the mahogany box out from the depths of one of the drawers and brought it over to a small table by the fire. He then pulled two armchairs up to the table and sat down in the one facing the door. He stood up almost instantly and paced the length of the mantel before sitting back down again. Repeating this action twice more, he opened the box. Closed it again. Opened it and carefully unfolded the last letter. Refolded it and placed it back in the box.

He had removed his boots and was moving his chair closer to the fire when he heard a soft knock at the door. He crossed the room in three long strides and stood back to allow Edith in. In her arms was a tea tray laden with a simple silver teapot, two cups, and a plate of sugared biscuits. A thin trail of steam rose from the spout of the teapot.

Edith hesitated when she recognized the box on the table and looked up at Connor questioningly. He gestured and she placed the tray next to the box before pouring them each a cup. He sat and she followed suit.

They both sat in silence for a moment. Connor picked up, then put down, his teacup. Finally he leaned forward with his elbows on his knees and said simply, "Edith, I need to tell you about the letters."

"The letters? Surely there's no—they're yours. Your private letters," Edith stammered.

"Yes. I need to tell someone. With the contest, with the explosion, with all that's about to change, not to mention all that has changed already . . . I need to know I've done the right thing. I need someone else to know. To not be the only person who knows about Jacs. You have always been a faithful and loyal friend to me. You must promise me that this stays between us."

She hesitated for only a moment. "Of course."

So he told her.

It felt as though a floodgate had opened. He told her everything: he told her about the first voyage and his pen name, Connor. He told her about the hot-air balloons and the ring, about Jacs's bracelet that he had cut off and thrown from the Cliff, and the years' worth of letters. Mostly, he told her about Jacs. About her inventions and the conversations that would often send him to the library late at night to discover what she had been talking about. How, despite not knowing what he was, she was able to understand him on a level that no one else ever really had. About all the time they had spent solving the Queendom's problems as though they were particularly tricky thought experiments. How he had spent his entire life learning about the traits and requirements the future Queen must have and how, on the eve of the contest he helped design, the only woman he could possibly see worthy of the crown was a whole world away.

"I know I was wrong to ignore her like I did this past year. I know she may never forgive me for that. I also know that she may not even want to be ruler at all, given the chance. But how can I serve whoever comes out as Queen when I know who should be wearing that crown?" He hid his head in his hands.

"Wearing the crown, or wearing your ring?" Edith asked quietly.

"What?" His head shot up to look at her.

"They are different, sire. I want to be sure you understand them to be so."

"Different? Of course I know they're different. I know it's not expected—" Connor began.

"Forgive me, sire, but it sounds like your personal guilt and desires are clouding your public duty. You are not finding *your* Queen through this contest, we are finding *our* Queen. This is not about you or what you want. It's about what is right for the Queendom."

Connor ran a hand through his hair and threw a biscuit into the fire, "I know! I know . . . but she is what's right for the Queendom."

Edith set her cup down. "I'm not sure . . . I honestly don't know. I'm sorry I can't be of more comfort but . . . I think that, feelings aside, all you can do is trust in the contest."

He pressed his thumb and knuckles into a spot to the left of his breastbone. "Feelings aside?" he asked.

Edith shifted in her chair. "Well, you obviously feel something for this woman. It's only natural that you would see her as your Queen."

"What? I . . . no it's not like that at all!"

"You don't have feelings for her?" Edith raised an eyebrow.

"No! I mean, maybe. I don't know!" Connor stood up and began pacing.

"Your Grace, I meant no disrespect," Edith started slowly, "It's just that I know you, I've known you for years. I've watched you fall in and out of love. I am concerned that you're letting your emotions mar your judgment. You can't let your feelings for Jacs get in the way of your duty to help the Queendom find its next Queen. Forgive me if I speak out of turn, but if you had not wanted my opinion, you would not have asked me here this morning." Her words came out in a rush and hung between them heavily.

He scratched the back of his head and sat back down. Finally he sighed. "You may be right." He picked up another biscuit and crumbled small fragments onto his plate. "The contest will tell."

Edith patted his hand affectionately, "And even though she will not be your Queen, that does not mean she will not be your friend, or who knows—maybe more. It may take time, but any woman with any sense would give you a second chance. You'll see."

"Thanks, Edith."

"The world for you, you know this." She smiled and began putting their cups back on the tray. "She is a very lucky woman to have caught your heart, Your Grace. I do hope I get to meet her one day."

Connor laughed dryly. "Me too."

19

WELCOME TO COURT

The sun rose over the already bustling Queendom. As if apologizing for keeping so many waiting, it shone brilliantly across a sky of clear blue. Servants who had the fortune of sleeping at all had been up for hours, and many had the red-rimmed eyes and peaked complexion that spoke of a busy, sleepless night. Rested or not, each sported impeccable livery of pale blue and gold, pressed and freshly laundered for the occasion.

Many hands were directing and pointing guests throughout the palace. The forced smiles and pained eyes were a credit to their training. One such servant could be heard speaking with an older gentleman, "No sir. Yes, I understand you wish to walk the grounds.

All the way from Newfrea? My word, what a journey. If you would follow me, sir. I assure you that you will have time to admire the crocuses after the first task. Yes, they will still be there. You have my word. No . . . no, sir, this way."

Those who had been invited to the palace to watch the first task unfold were gradually being shepherded to the various tables surrounded by chairs and benches that were scattered across the open lawn and in several of the halls and larger rooms. A scryglass was perched on top of each table in the form of either a shallow basin of water or a mirror. The guests had been given a tutorial for viewing the contestants at breakfast in case they had missed the numerous instructional meetings each town and city were required to hold during the weeks leading up to the contest. Each contestant had sat before the palace scryers earlier that morning and spoken their full names while holding a crystal to ensure they could be located on the course. A small note card sat on each table with the list of contestants' names written out neatly for the crowds' reference.

The servant in charge of producing each note card sat in a corner of the wine cellar with her hand resting in a pail of ice water. Ink splotches stood out like freckles on her cheeks and nose.

The guests consisted mostly of nobility from neighboring towns and villages, with a handful of merchants trying their best to blend into the splendor around them. They appeared as geese among swans.

A bell began to toll and the guests took their seats. Slow, even tones stretched out across the still morning. Some guests had trialed the scryglasses already and were running through the list of contestant names to choose their favorites and get a sense of the competition. Some voices could be heard boasting of acquaintances.

"See Fawn, Fawn Lupine? Taught her how to ride her first pony!"

"My gardener's wife used to care for Ms. Goldenrod when her mother was away. Said she was a sweet kid: liked strawberries."

"Well, Chiv. Everstar once courted my son's friend. It didn't last, but she came round for dinner once and complimented my quiche."

Various faces could be seen in each scryglass, each looking flushed and nervous. Some looked eager to begin, others fidgeted with their clothing. The fifteen women stood spread out in a line at the base of a mountain, each dressed in a variation of trousers, a light tunic, and boots. Some had their hair tied back in intricate woven braids and bands, others sported more practical styles with tails pulled back tightly to fall freely down their backs. Each one of them looked like a potential Queen.

The King and Prince stood facing them with their backs to the steep, craggy slope. One step behind them stood the Council of Four. Guard pairs were stationed in a half circle around the King, and Masterchiv Rathbone stood just to his right, her hand resting on the pommel of her sword. Her facial expression was one of almost boredom, but her sharp gray eyes never stopped moving.

There was a long, low table stretched out between King and contestants. This table was covered with a velvet cloth that concealed the fifteen bundles evenly spaced across it. As the last chime died away, the King cleared his throat and addressed the contestants.

"Good morning. I hope you all slept well, despite last night's ordeal. Last night, through acts of courage and bravery, ten contestants were chosen to compete in the Contest of Queens. Following the night's events, five more were identified who, through no fault of their own, were unable to prove themselves through action on that particular occasion. These women were chosen to have the opportunity to compete as well, to show us in their actions what they vowed to possess in words. Those of you who were identified through the interview process as contestants, please step forward."

Five women stepped forward at his command.

"I have the honor of introducing Dame Hera Claustrom." Hera stood proudly, honey-blonde curls shining in the sunlight, a smile flashing across her lips.

"Chivilra Andromeda Turner." The knight stood at ease with her chin jutting forward. Her height and straight, dusty blonde hair were in stark contrast to Hera's short stature and bright curls.

"Ms. Christina Bergamot." Christina grinned and waved at the surrounding crystals. She bore a cut from ear to collarbone that was an angry red but appeared to be healing (no doubt thanks to Master Epione's ministrations).

"Ms. Hanlen Mar." Hanlen nodded stoically, her brown hair pulled back into a sharp knot at the base of her skull.

"Ms. Verona Julliard." Verona blushed nervously, pink splotches peppering her round cheeks, and tentatively tucked her short dark hair behind her ears.

The King paused, then nodded. The women fell back in line with the remaining contestants.

"Before me are fifteen women, each with their own skills, ambitions, and values. Only one of you will prove to your Queendom that you are worthy to serve as our Queen. Today, your numbers will be reduced by half. Know that this does not make your presence here any less important, or any less momentous."

Jacs looked down the line at the competition. She was placed between Amber and Lena. Amber winked at her as she caught her eye, while Lena stared determinedly at the King. Only Jacs noticed the tinge of green to her cheeks, as it had been Jacs who had held Lena's hair back as she relived her breakfast earlier that morning.

The King continued, "My son, Prince Cornelius, will now outline the first task. I wish you luck." He inclined his head and stepped back for his son to take his place.

Prince Cornelius stepped forward and cleared his throat. Jacs stood straighter.

"To be Queen. What does this mean?" Connor began, pausing for a moment to allow his question to hang heavily in the air. "Well, I can never know firsthand, but what I do know, I learned from one of the strongest Queens our Queendom has had since the Great Divide. Goddess rest her." He paused again while this sentiment was repeated in unison by all present. "She taught me much about strength, and what it means to be truly strong. She taught me that true strength was much more than a physical feat. And that strength, in the absence of that which is gentle—compassion, kindness—is often brutish and cruel. As Queen she demonstrated this balance and it is this balance that we will be watching for as you complete your first task. A Queen who does not temper her blade with the understanding of when it is better sheathed is simply a soldier without a commanding officer."

Chiv. Andromeda Turner and Chiv. Amber Everstar appeared to perk up at these words. Jacs noticed that Amber at least seemed eager to demonstrate the difference between an unguided soldier and a knight. The Prince moved to the edge of the table. He gathered the fabric in his hands and gently pulled it to reveal the bundles beneath. There was a collective intake of breath as the contestants saw fifteen perfect golden eggs, each three times the size of a chicken's, perched on small cushions.

"Many of you may have heard of the Court of Griffins, yet I doubt any would have had the honor of meeting them," the Prince said. "The Court supplies us with the gold that enriches our Queendom. The eggshells, useless to their kind once the fledglings emerge, are given to a select few who have been accepted to receive such treasures.

"For this task, the Court has been magnanimous enough to entrust us with fifteen of their eggs. I will allow a moment for the weight of this honor to fully register." He looked at each contestant in turn. Jacs forced herself to meet his gaze steadily.

"The Court expects each egg to be returned safely. A member of the Court awaits you at the top—" he swept his hand and gestured above and behind him "—of this peak. Failure to return your egg by nightfall will result in elimination; purposeful tampering with another contestant's egg will result in elimination; failure to demonstrate the aforementioned qualities in your completion of this task will result in elimination; and any damage to your egg will result in much worse. If any of you do not feel able to complete this task, there is no shame in standing down now."

Again, he paused and surveyed the contestants. There was a suspended moment broken by Faya Goldenrod, a petite blonde with dark rings beneath her eyes and a birthmark stretching from elbow to wrist. Her hands were squeezed into tight fists and her eyes shone with unshed tears. Stepping forward, she said with measured deliberation, "These are the offspring of the Alti." She shook her head and continued, "This task is too great for one such as myself and I must insist on withdrawing my name from the contest." She sank to one knee.

The minutes expanded, and the silence fell about them louder than any bell toll.

The Prince walked over and stood before her. Gently, he prompted her to rise and said, "I trust you know your mind above all others, however, I will give you one chance to reconsider." Their eyes met and she shook her head. "Very well," he concluded, "I thank you for your honesty and I congratulate you for the courage it takes to recognize and identify your limitations. You will be accompanied back to the castle and we encourage you to remain for the rest of the contest as our honored guest."

He signaled for one of the guards to escort Faya, and they left quietly together after she briefly grasped the hands of each contestant in turn. Jacs shot Faya a small smile when their hands touched and the latter whispered a quick, "Good luck," before moving down the line.

Jacs reached out and squeezed Lena's hand. She felt a reassuring squeeze in response.

Prince Cornelius resumed his post and finished. "I expect each of you to show the appropriate respect to the Griffin awaiting you. Please approach and collect your egg."

Each contestant moved forward and stood in front of her egg. Faya's charge was delicately swept away by another guard who then followed the retreating backs of the former contestant and her escort.

Jacs looked down at the little orb of gold. What she had previously assumed was the sun's reflection off its polished surface now appeared to be a faint glow coming from the object itself. Instinctively, she reached out to touch it. It was warm and seemed to pulse with life. Her breath caught as she lifted it from its cushion; how fragile it felt! It was heavier than she expected and fit in her two cupped palms. She tore her eyes from the sphere and glanced up at the mountain. The terrain was rough, and she could already see she would need to climb over and scramble through some sections. She glanced again at the egg. Too large to fit in any pocket and too smooth to comfortably hold in one hand without risking it slipping.

Aware of the other contestants looking around at how others were planning on carrying their precious cargo up the climb, she forced her face to remain neutral and waited for the Prince to continue. All the while, her mind raced with possibilities and designs.

"Good luck to each of you," the Prince said. "Begin!"

Three contestants raced off with their eggs at his word. Jacs recognized Shane, Verona, and Fawn as they jogged toward the base of the first rise. Hera, Devon, Danielle, and Hanlen followed shortly after. Jacs forced herself to take a breath and placed her egg back on its cushion.

"Jacqueline! Come on!" Lena urged as she and Anya set off.

"Right behind you!" she said to their backs.

Working quickly, she tore a sleeve off her tunic. She could almost hear Master Moira's gasp. She tied a knot halfway down the sleeve and slipped first the cushion then the egg into the open end. Looking at all the abandoned cushions left on the table, she picked up another and slipped it in on top of the egg. She then tied another knot above the egg and, conscious of the time she was using up, fashioned a sling that she looped around her neck and pushed one arm through. It fell diagonally across her body with the egg nestled safely on her front. She tested the contraption's durability and stability as she bent forward, shifted from side to side, and jumped a couple times on the spot, purposefully ignoring the eyes of the remaining guards as she did.

Satisfied, she nodded briefly to the King, smiled at the Prince, and headed toward the base of the mountain. Two women,

Andromeda and Christina, remained behind fashioning forms of slings or small bags to carry their eggs, but the rest of the contestants had gone on ahead.

Some had bundled them in the front of their tunics; one woman had simply hoisted it under her arm, and a few others had decided to carry their eggs with two hands.

It's not a race, Jacs reminded herself, her strides lengthening regardless. The egg was nestled beneath her heart and Jacs would have sworn it to be beating with a pulse of its own.

Just as Jacs had predicted, the terrain was rough. She was glad for the use of both her hands as she scrambled and pulled herself up the first rocky outcrop. Dusting her hands on her trousers, she looked up straight into the soft purple glow of a crystal. She felt something cold settle into her stomach before she remembered their role in broadcasting the task. Looking up the course, she noticed soft purple pin pricks dotted all along the course. Feeling uneasy, the back of her neck prickling, she forced herself to ignore them and pressed on.

She came across Fawn, who was struggling to climb one-handed. She was at the base of a small rise of rock that was not exactly vertical but close to it. The woman had sweat beading her freckled forehead and was cursing a foothold just beyond her reach. Jacs saw Fawn's egg slip slightly in her damp palms.

"Fawn!" Jacs called as she came within earshot. The woman turned around, Jacs pointed to the patterned headscarf that was holding her red hair out of her eyes, "Use your scarf, make a pouch or something. It'll be a lot easier."

Frustration flared in Fawn's eyes, and her face flushed beyond the hue brought on by the exertion. "That's Dame to you, goldsmith. If I had wanted your advice, I'd have asked," she hissed.

Jacs, panting slightly as she began her climb, raised her eyebrows in surprise. Without slowing, she picked a route up the rocks that avoided Fawn's and simply said, "Suit yourself, Dame," as she pulled herself past the red-faced noblewoman and cleared the top.

The sun beat down on the back of Jacs's neck and it was not long before she was wishing they had been allowed a waterskin for the journey. She passed Verona and Hanlen, who had found a shady patch beneath an overhanging ledge to catch their breath. Nodding to the two women, she continued on. *One foot in front of the other*, she thought.

The women inched their way up the mountain as the day wore on. Those who overtook were soon overtaken and vice versa. Some women had made alliances and were helping each other where they could, but each understood this to be a cliffside full of rivals. Most contestants had not slept much, if at all, the night before, and tiredness, the heat, and the exertion wore even the most patient individual thin. The mountain seemed endless. False peaks promised success only to reveal another height to strive for. Jacs's pace had slowed but she forced herself to keep walking, even if her gait was nothing more than a shuffle. The egg hung like an anchor around her neck and her shoulder blades burned.

Around noon, Jacs came across a mossy clearing. The shrubbery had thinned the farther she climbed but her heart felt lighter at the sight of the glistening green carpet. *Moss! Moss means water.* She stumbled forward and placed her palms on a particularly spongy patch. She felt cool dampness on her skin and laughed out loud. She touched her fingertips to her face and neck, delighting in the cooling sensation. She looked around for the water source. A stream, a spring, there had to be something.

Looking up at the cliff face that rose from the other side of the clearing, Jacs saw that what at first she had thought was dark stone was a wall of trickling, dribbling water channels. The entire wall was covered in mossy tendrils and water ran down them like moving icicles. Liquid stalactites.

Jacs stood up and ran over to the wall of water. She stood beneath a small overhang and smiled as the water fell like soft rain on her cheeks and eyelids. As best she could manage, she took a few grateful sips and felt the water like a balm in her parched throat. The shadows of the wall enclosed her and she felt light for the first time that day.

Raised voices echoed across the clearing. She opened her eyes and saw Hera and Devon. They were so focused on their discussion they did not appear to notice the moss, or Jacs. She slowly lowered herself to a crouch and shifted further into the shadows. She heard Hera hiss, "Of course they're both the same! But that one was rightfully mine, when we lined up, I was opposite it—remember? The order got muddled when that drip Faya eliminated herself."

"If they're both the same, why does it matter who has which one?" Devon asserted stubbornly.

"I don't know, I don't make the rules, but what if they have . . . marks . . . or trackers on them? You don't want to take credit for my trip and I certainly wouldn't want to take credit for your feats."

"You're being ridiculous; an egg is an egg, and I'm not giving you mine. You heard the rules, tampering with another contestant's egg will result in elimination. I'm not risking that so you can have the satisfaction of getting your way." Devon made to stride off, but Hera caught her arm.

"That's what I'm saying! Don't you see? You technically have my egg. Please, just do this for me? It really probably doesn't even matter, but if it does and we get disqualified for having the wrong eggs, we would both lose." Hera had a look of concern on her face but her eyes glittered the way Jacs remembered from their encounter in the garden.

Devon hesitated, and Hera pounced. "We need to stick together, you and I! There are far too few Dames in this contest, and I would hate to see the crown go to a mere commoner, or a knight!"

Devon bit her lip. She looked down at the egg in her hands and then to the bulge in Hera's tied-up pouch that hung from her hip. "Well . . ." Devon began. Hera stood motionless. Jacs felt like she was watching a spider observe a fly buzzing closer and closer to its web.

Finally Devon took a deep breath and said, "Fine, but I get to keep that pouch thing too."

"Of course," Hera said quickly and began untying it from her belt.

The exchange was made, Hera looked pleased, Devon looked resigned, and Jacs felt an uneasy tightness in her stomach. She watched as Hera darted ahead of Devon, wishing her a cheery "good luck!" and Devon made her way more slowly behind.

When the clearing was empty again, Jacs emerged. She walked over to a thick patch of moss and began peeling a section off the rock. Deep in thought, she brought the moss to the water dripping down the wall and soaked it until it was saturated. She ripped her other sleeve off her tunic and soaked that too, then placed the moss inside and tied it loosely around her neck. *That's better*, she thought, cool water trickling down her back and soothing her burning shoulders. The glee in Hera's face when Devon handed over her egg still tugged at her mind. Her logic made no sense—they weren't even standing by Faya's egg.

Jacs sighed and pushed on. She would think about it later.

Jacs passed Devon soon after. She was struggling to tie Hera's pouch to her belt. "Need a hand, Devon?" Jacs offered as she came within earshot.

Devon looked up, startled, then smiled nervously, "Oh, hello, Jacqueline, um . . . sure. I just can't seem to get it hanging right."

Jacs smiled kindly and looked over the rigging Devon was attempting. Tentatively, she said, "Would you mind if I make a suggestion?"

Devon cocked her head and replied, "Uh . . . sure?"

"Only if you have it on your hip, you're more likely to knock it on the rocks and things . . . but if you hang it around your neck like this, and you can pinch the corners and loop them through the sides of your tunic here so it doesn't flop forward and . . . there you go! As safe as it can be, I guess." Jacs stood back and looked over her handiwork. Devon bounced a little on the spot to test the stability.

A broad smile broke across her angular face. "This is perfect. Thank you, Jacqueline!"

"No problem. See you at the top!"

Jacs shook her head at her actions as she continued on past Devon, who was taking a few more moments to try out the new setup.

I shouldn't be helping the competition, she scolded herself.

The afternoon wore on. Jacs was thankful for the wet cloth on her neck as the sun blazed overhead. She could see what she hoped was the final peak in the distance. The image of it filled her mind and kept her moving. Pulling herself up a boulder with rough footholds cut into it, she sat for a moment. The view was spectacular.

She had not spent much time with her eyes off her feet or the peak and had almost forgotten that all the climbing would mean an incredible view.

"Wow," she breathed.

"Lena!" Jacs recognized Anya's voice as it echoed around the cliffs and ledges. Jacs scrambled to her feet and ran in the direction of the voice. It was coming from farther on up the trail. She bounded over small rocks and ledges before rounding a curve in the trail and—

"Lena!" Jacs cried.

Anya was kneeling with Lena's head on her lap. Lena had her eyes closed, and her chest rose and fell in rapid and shallow movements.

"Anya! What happened?" Jacs darted over and knelt beside them.

"Jacqueline! Thank the Goddess! I don't know, one minute we were walking, the next she just collapsed. Said she was dizzy, and now she won't wake up." Anya sounded hysterical and swatted angrily at tears on her cheeks.

"Okay, we're gonna be okay, she's going to be okay," Jacs murmured and felt Lena's cheek.

Unbidden, her father's voice filled her mind. *It's gonna be okay, we're okay.*

She forced it away.

Jacs felt her heart hammer and willed it to slow so she could think. Her eyes grew wide and she hurried to untie the wet cloth from around her neck. "Here! Here, let's put this on her forehead, she's probably dehydrated. We need, we need . . ." Jacs looked around them at the barren, dry surroundings, "We need more water. We need to get her into the shade."

Anya nodded as Jacs continued to babble. She pressed the wet, moss-filled cloth onto Lena's pale forehead and touched her fingertips tenderly to her cheek.

Gently, Anya lifted Lena's head off her lap, and together, Jacs and Anya lifted their friend up and made their way to a shady spot beneath an overhanging slab of granite.

Anya was cooing softly to Lena, "You're going to be all right, Lee, we're here."

Jacs started untying Lena's boots. Anya looked over at her, puzzled, "What are you doing?"

Jacs's fingers shook as she pulled the first boot off, "I don't know. But she's hot, we have to cool her down. If she keeps sweating, she keeps losing water. We don't have any to give back to her. Not here."

Anya nodded again. Their eyes met. Anya was as pale as Lena.

Lena's breathing began to slow as the two other women appeared to hold theirs.

"She's going to be okay." Jacs attempted a shaky smile. "She's very lucky you were with her."

Anya looked away.

Jacs busied herself with removing Lena's socks. She looked up when Anya did not respond and asked, "Anya, are you okay?"

Anya nodded, bit her lip, and looked up at Jacs. Tears streamed anew down her cheeks. "It was just . . . She went down, and she didn't respond, and I thought I . . . I thought I lost her. I just . . . I can't . . . thank you." She cleared her throat and tried again, "Probably being dramatic, it's been a long day." Her bravado was returning with the color in her cheeks.

Jacs laughed, "Definitely not a walk in the glade."

They sat in silence for a few more moments and watched Lena's impassive face for any signs of change.

"Shouldn't she . . . I don't know, is it normal for her to not be awake?" Anya brushed some stray hairs from Lena's forehead.

"I don't know . . ." Jacs bit her lip and looked back the way they had come and then to the peak. "Anya," she began, "We should get her some help. She can't stay here."

Anya looked about them, back in the direction they had come. "We could try to carry her?"

They both studied the treacherous terrain they had spent all day struggling over. They both shook their heads at the same time. Jacs said, "We can't go back down. I had a hard enough time getting up, and that was with the use of both my hands."

Anya scratched her cheek and looked again at Lena's unconscious form.

"That leaves either staying here or going to the top." She rubbed her eyes.

Jacs thought for a moment, "Wait. You're right! Maybe the Court will be able to help. There's supposed to be a Griffin at the top, right?"

"Yeah?"

"Well there's probably someone who can help at the top too! I don't know, maybe a person to welcome those who made it, or even an interpreter." Jacs nodded her head curtly, "That's it, that's what we do. We could probably carry her the last little bit of the way, right?"

Anya looked past Jacs to the peak that had looked so close a moment before, but now seemed to stretch away above them.

"Are you sure we can make it?" Anya sounded doubtful.

"Not even a little bit, but worse comes to worse, we get her closer to someone who can help and one of us can go on ahead to alert whoever is up there."

"What about the eggs?" Anya asked.

Jacs looked down at her own and then at the two bulges tied up in the other two women's tunics. "We can do this, Anya. We'll keep the eggs safe, we'll get Lena to the top, and we'll even manage a bit of grace for a fraction of it."

Anya laughed despite herself.

Lena's dead weight was awkward to carry. They tried a few different arrangements—one person lifting her legs and the other her arms, one person carrying her while the other carried the three eggs—but the technique that seemed most effective involved strapping each of Lena's legs to one of their own, as though they were competing in an odd four-legged race. With this arrangement, they were both able to support Lena's arms, her feet weren't dragging on the ground, and they could each strap an egg to their fronts. Regardless, their journey was slow going. Very slow. Shane and Hanlen passed by and, although they shared their comments of sympathy, neither offered to help. Anya cursed their retreating forms, but half-heartedly. She and Jacs were both so tired. Finally, after a particularly steep section of the trail, Anya called for a break. They placed Lena gently on the ground in the most shade they could find.

Jacs straightened and stretched her back. Anya worked a kink out of her neck. They looked at each other, then back down at Lena. Worry was etched in every inch of Anya's face.

"Listen, Jacqueline," she began, "we're not helping her by taking all day to get there. We need to get her help soon."

Jacs agreed: Lena needed water and definitely was not benefiting from being tugged and jostled the way she had been.

"One of us needs to stay with her, and the other can go on ahead and get help," Jacs said solemnly.

Anya did not miss a beat. "I'll stay with her."

Jacs hesitated, "Are you sure?"

"Of course."

"All right." Jacs looked at Lena again and clasped Anya's hand. "I'll bring help as soon as I can, I promise."

Anya's lips were a thin line as she attempted a smile. "Goddess guide you."

"Take care," Jacs replied before standing up and starting the final stretch of the mountain.

The image of Lena in Anya's arms fueled Jacs the last span of the journey. She did not register the terrain she passed by, only taking note of where to put her feet and hands and forcing herself to ignore the pains in her body. Nearing the top, she slipped. One hand grabbed for the egg while the other reached out to break her fall. She landed heavily on her wrist, and the rest of her body twisted to protect the egg. Her bracing hand rolled off the loose rock. She heard a crack and felt something snap. A sharp burst of pain shot from wrist to elbow, and she let out a cry. On her knees, she cradled her injured arm, fighting the tears that welled in her eyes. Breathing heavily through her mouth, she turned her arm over and inspected the damage. She had definitely sprained, maybe broken, something. Blood slipped warmly through her fingers from a deep gash spanning the base of her thumb. She could already see her wrist beginning to swell.

Gritting her teeth, she ripped the hem of her tunic off and wrapped it roughly around her now useless hand. She took two more deep breaths to center herself and stood up. The world swayed around her. Groaning, she pressed on.

Finally the trail leveled and the mouth of a large cavern loomed above her. Jacs's jaw dropped. The entire top peak of the mountain was a roughly hewn cathedral-like structure. It looked at once naturally formed and purposefully crafted. The doorway was big enough to fit ten people standing shoulder to shoulder through and just as high. Hands fluttering to the warm egg by her chest, she stepped slowly through the entrance.

The interior was breathtaking. Gold glittered everywhere. Torches hung at even intervals around the circular chamber; the ceiling stretched high above her. The flames shimmered and danced in reflections around the room. It appeared as though the entire room was alight. In the center was an expansive nest constructed of twigs, hay, velvet, and feathers. There was a clutch of golden eggs nestled within.

Beside the nest stood a Griffin.

It had not yet noticed Jacs, and was instead studying the reflection in a shallow pool of water at its feet. Jacs noticed that the pool reflected the image of a contestant she could not make out from where she stood. As she watched, the Griffin bowed its head and touched the pool with its beak. The pool rippled, the image shimmered, and as the ripples subsided, a different scene with a different contestant appeared. This time Jacs recognized herself. The Griffin lifted its sleek head slowly and appraised her.

It was the most beautiful being Jacs had ever seen. She touched the ring hanging from her neck. The image engraved on its surface that she had memorized and grown up with now appeared a grave insult to the majesty that stood before her.

She took two steps forward.

The Griffin leaped over the pool and landed in front of her, head high, eyes flashing. It moved through the air as a fish swims in water, the air whirled around the room and caused the flames to flicker.

The creature was pure white and shone subtly with a golden light. Its head and shoulders were that of a great eagle, and its back legs and tail were that of a lion. The feathers on its back smoothly transitioned to glossy luxurious fur past its wing joints. Its wings unfurled and folded back up along the length of its body as it took a step toward her.

Jacs sunk to her knee as she would for a Queen. Injured arm tucked around the egg, head bowed, she felt rather than saw the Griffin approach. It paused, its tail whipping back and forth. After what seemed like a lifetime, it bowed its head toward Jacs's and Jacs felt its razor-sharp beak on the back of her head. It worked its beak slowly and carefully through her hair as Jacs held her breath. It was a few moments before she realized, *It's preening me.* Finally the Griffin straightened and took a step back. Jacs looked up. It looked at her expectantly and flicked its head upward in a short jerking motion.

Jacs understood and rose. The Griffin bid her follow and walked to the nest. Jacs followed as if in a trance and stopped short of the edge. She slowly unfastened the sling from around her neck and awkwardly untied the knot at the top of the egg with one hand, removed the cushion, then carefully pulled the egg out and held it out, offering it to the Griffin. The creature stepped aside and motioned with its beak to the nest. Jacs approached cautiously and gently settled the egg next to the others. Each pulsed with a life of its own. Jacs noticed one separated from the group, it had a deep crack down the length of the shell. She gasped and looked quickly at the Griffin, who shook its head from side to side and stamped its taloned front foot.

"I'm so sorry," she breathed. "Will it be all right?"

The Griffin walked to the edge of the nest and shifted it gently with its beak. The gentleness of the action brought back the image of Anya brushing Lena's hair from her forehead. She searched the room for another person. She was alone with the Griffin.

The Griffin was beckoning for her to follow it toward the back of the chamber. Jacs saw a smaller archway she supposed led to a way back down the mountain. She took a step backward and shook her head.

"Please, it's my friend. She needs help. I need help." She was not sure how much the Griffin could understand, but there was an intelligence in the way its eyes glinted and she tried anyway. Using one-handed gestures, she began again, "Please, um, esteemed member of the Court, Your Excellency, I'm so sorry I'm not better versed in the correct protocol but I need your help. She's not well and needs to get off this mountain immediately."

The Griffin regarded her silently. It cocked its head, first to one side and then the other. Jacs felt the intensity of its gaze and tried to meet it evenly. After a long moment, the Griffin stepped forward. It was close enough that Jacs could feel its breath rush past her like a wave. It bent its neck and placed the blade of its beak against her chest. Jacs could feel the slight pressure in the spot above her heart. She held her breath. The Griffin closed its eyes. She could count the smaller feathers that edged the top of its beak. They stayed like that for an eternal second.

Suddenly, Jacs felt a jolt pass through her, spreading from her heart outward to her fingertips and toes. An explosion of emotions hit her all at once, and hundreds of her memories rushed through her mind. They climbed over each other to make themselves felt and seen. Images and feelings blended and twisted into each other. Faces merging, scenes shifting. Her life became an instantaneous kaleidoscope. The deepest secrets of her heart burst from her, unrestrained.

She felt herself falling inward. Her mind was pulling her down into an internal landscape until her psyche landed in a dark room looking into a deep, black pool. Tentatively, she moved her mind's eye out over the inky depths. Where her reflection should have been, she saw her father's face.

Unable to move, unable to scramble backward, she stared with lidless eyes. His face had a shimmering quality, his features not quite certain. Blurred by memory, he smiled in a way that was both familiar and unrecognizable to her. His face, so full of life, began to change. The color slowly faded from his cheeks. He wilted before her eyes, his life draining away. Cheeks became hollow and gaunt. His eyes bulged. Pink lips turned purple and cracked, black blood trickling down his ashen chin. The pool began to freeze over top of him, obscuring him from view.

She tried to scream, but a maddening silence pressed down on her.

The pool thawed and her mother and Master Leschi beamed up at her. Pride shone in their gaze. In a moment, their faces transformed in horror, and they plummeted into the shadowy depths. Ripped from her anew.

As suddenly as it had begun, it ended. The Griffin stepped back, and Jacs fell to her knees, gasping. Tears flowed freely down her cheeks.

She felt raw and exposed, as though the Griffin had laid her life's deepest pains bare to watch old wounds bleed. The Griffin waited silently as she composed herself, its sharp eye watching as she put her pieces back together. It looked for a display of weakness, expected her to remain curled on the floor. A part of her wanted to sink back to the black pool, but the thought of Lena forced her to lift her chin. She met the Griffin's eye as it studied her. Something flickered within its iris and she knew, somehow, that she had passed its test. The Griffin had deemed her worthy.

It inclined its head slightly to her and opened its beak. The sound that emanated from its maw was both an eagle call and a lion's roar. It sounded like a crash of thunder. The Griffin called in this way for four short sharp bursts and tossed its head. Jacs remained on her knees, frozen in place.

Moments later, a clatter of talons on stone echoed behind her. Dashing her tears away, she spun around to see another Griffin, this one larger than the first—its feathers gray and haunches ashen rather than white. This Griffin towered over Jacs. She bowed her head again and felt its beak nip her ear. Rougher and more business-like than the first had been. The white Griffin called again, the gray lowered itself to its knees and motioned for Jacs to get on.

Jacs hesitated, still shaken and trying to understand what had passed through her. The gray Griffin growled and she hurried to do as she was beckoned. She kept her injured arm close to her center and clumsily climbed onto the Griffin's back. She grimaced as blood flecked its flawless flank. Her mind had gone blank, and she only half felt the feathers beneath her as she settled in front of its great wings. The implications of getting on a winged creature's back only registered as it made its way out the entrance and into the open air.

The moment caught up with her as the Griffin launched itself into the air and she felt the world shift away from them.

She screamed, then squealed, then laughed as the wind rushed through her hair. The Queendom stretched out far below. She was flying. Basileia unfolded beneath them, gardens, streets, and edifices scattering the landscape like an elaborate maze. Jacs couldn't wait to tell Connor about this in her next letter, before remembering all that had changed between them. Pushing the thought out of her mind, she embraced the freedom of the moment.

The Griffin rose higher and higher; soon she could see almost the entirety of the Upper Realm.

Above the towering mountain of the Court they soared, smaller towns dotting the plateau until the ground disappeared. The Cliff stretched jaggedly along the border as though cut with a knife, the Lower Realm a deep, vast basin enclosed by the distant mountains. Shifting to look north, she scanned the horizon. Jacs's breath caught in her throat as she saw, for the first time in her life, the Azulon Sea. Blue and unbelievably vast, it spanned the northern border of the Upper Realm and disappeared into the horizon.

After growing up in the safe embrace of the Cliff and mountains, Jacs suddenly felt incredibly exposed in the open sky. More than anything else, she felt free.

She clutched at the Griffin with her knees and whooped in the brisk air. Her heart felt lighter than it had in months. The Griffin roared in return.

The sound snapped Jacs back to her task.

Focusing on the mountainside, she began scanning the ground for the place she had left Lena and Anya. She called out, "We need to get closer!" and the Griffin obliged, bringing the world beneath into clearer focus. She saw the mountain terrain below and leaned forward over the Griffin's shoulder to search the ground for signs of— "There they are!" she cried and pointed to two figures, one waving her arms frantically, the other lying very still.

The Griffin roared, its cry echoing around the mountain, and angled toward them. It circled the ground a few times, creating tighter and tighter circles as it flew and slowed itself to land lightly, meters from where Anya sat with her mouth open.

"Jacqueline, how did you . . .? Oh!" Hurriedly, Anya bowed awkwardly with Lena in her lap. "Thank you, great Griffin of the Court."

The Griffin bent down again for Jacs to get off, and Jacs ran to Anya. The two women embraced carefully so as not to disturb Lena

"Sorry I took so long," Jacs said.

The Griffin clicked its beak impatiently. Jacs turned back to it and said, "Your Excellence, how many can you fit on your back? Only, Lena cannot fly by herself in the state she's in."

The Griffin stamped its talon twice on the stone beneath it.

"Thank you, thank you so much, that's perfect." Jacs turned back to Anya. She looked at their two eggs nestled in scraps of fabric on the rocks. She considered the time it would take to fly up to the nest and then back to the palace, the time they had already wasted with Lena in the state she was in, the ever-blanching pallor of Lena's complexion, and said quickly, "Okay, give me your egg and pass me Lena's, I can take them back up to the top and you can take Lena down to the bottom where she can get help."

Anya began to protest, but Jacs cut her off, "Anya, Lena needs you right now! Besides, I can't hold her with one arm." She gestured to the blood-stained wrappings. Anya's eyes grew wide and Jacs cut her off again as she opened her mouth, "I'm fine, I'll be fine. But these have to get to the top regardless." She gestured to the eggs. Anya closed her mouth and looked at Lena.

Jacs continued, "This way, you both get your eggs to the top. They can't disqualify you. This is too important. I'm sure they'll understand." Jacs just desperately wanted this day to be over. She wanted the pain in her wrist to stop, she wanted the aches in her body to vanish. She wanted a long drink of water and a big bowl of stew. Pushing these thoughts aside, she said to Anya, "I will need your help to tie those in a sling around my neck, then I can help you settle onto the Griffin."

Anya simply nodded and they quickly set to work placing the eggs around Jac's neck and strapped the bundle to her body so as not to jostle them. Then Jacs helped Anya carry Lena over to the Griffin and together, with the help of the patient creature, they settled her in front of Anya on the Griffin's back. Anya had gone very pale and very quiet.

Jacs patted her knee, "It's a piece of cake, just like riding a horse—only higher up! You said you were a good rider, right?"

Anya barked a nervous laugh and the Griffin tossed its head. "Okay, ready," she said in a small voice.

Jacs bowed before the Griffin again and said, "I cannot thank you enough. You have saved the life of a very dear friend. Thank you. I hope we meet again." Then to Anya she called, "Good luck! Safe flight! Keep breathing, and hold on tight!"

The women exchanged tired and terrified smiles. Jacs watched as the Griffin crouched slightly, then sprang into the air like a cat to a window ledge. Anya squealed but Jacs was relieved to see both bodies stay on the back of the Griffin. She waved until they were far below before turning to walk back up the rest of the mountain.

If the white Griffin was surprised to see Jacs again, it did not show it. As the Griffin drew closer, Jacs bowed deeply and braced for the onslaught of memories that did not come. Instead, the Griffin simply ran its beak through her hair again. Jacs noted that it was much more gentle than the first time. As before, she nestled the two eggs with the rest of the clutch and this time followed the Griffin to the back of the chamber. There awaited six mountain ponies tied to a long fence that Jacs noticed had space for fifteen, the empty spaces denoting those who had finished already. She was surprised to see as many as six left. She attempted some quick math in her head.

Three for Anya, Lena, and I, one for Faya . . . there are two left on the course.

Jacs looked out toward the horizon. The sun was getting low. It would already be twilight in the Lower Realm. No wonder the day felt so long. A part of her felt a twinge of concern for the two left on the mountain, but her exhaustion got the better of her. She bowed again to the white Griffin, chose the most docile-looking mare, and pulled herself painfully onto her back.

And we'll even manage a bit of grace for a fraction of it, she scoffed. Still waiting on that grace.

The little bay mare perked its ears forward and set off at a relaxed pace down the mountainside. Jacs rested the reins around the pommel and strapped her legs to the saddle. Fighting sleep, she bobbed in and out of consciousness and trusted the little mare to find her way home.

Home, she thought wearily, *I'm a very long way from it.*

20

CHESS

Connor and his father were seated at a small table at the base of the mountain path where the returning ponies had been filtering through all afternoon. They each had a mirror with which to view the contestants. A game of chess was set up between them and had been interrupted so frequently that they had both lost interest in the outcome.

The four members of the Council were seated in pairs at similar tables. Councilors Beatrice Fengar and Gretchen Dilmont whispered together with reams of paper between them, taking notes in between viewings of various contestants. Connor noted that Cllr. Fengar appeared to have even more utensils protruding from her brown bun. Cllr. Portia Stewart, her wispy white hair floating wildly around her head, had a cup of tea halfway to her mouth, while her partner, Cllr. Rosalind Perda, talked through the merits of a contestant's specific action.

A tent had been erected with simple refreshments set up inside for the tired contestants. Fresh water carafes and sandwiches had been replenished throughout the day. A handful of guard pairs were doing their best to look engaged, but the day had been hot, hands settled lazily on dagger hilts, and eyes roamed wearily.

"Check," Connor said, sitting back in his chair.

His father leaned forward and counted spaces with his fingers. "Blast . . . aha!" His queen took Connor's knight with a satisfying clink of marble on marble.

"Your Highness! Is that . . .?" A guard exclaimed, shock cutting off her words as she shielded her eyes with one hand and pointed toward the mountain with the other. Both Connor and King Aren looked up from their game, and Connor understood why the guard did not finish her sentence.

The gathering watched in stunned awe and confusion as a great gray Griffin flew toward them. Wings outstretched, it blocked most of the mountain from view as it came closer. Sunlight radiated from its feathers and surrounded the figure in a golden halo. All present dropped to their knees in respect, King Aren and Prince Cornelius dropping to one knee and bowing their heads. The Griffin landed softly, its wings beating with quick broad strokes to slow its descent. It walked toward the King, who smoothly removed his crown before bowing his head lower as the Griffin began to preen him.

"Well met, Altus Hermes," King Aren said. "To what do we owe this hon—" the rest of the King's sentence died on his lips. "In all my years . . ." he whispered.

Connor looked up from the ground and saw Anya Bishop and Dame Glowra perched on the Griffin. Time appeared to stop. The incongruity of the two worn women on the back of such an exalted creature jarred his brain.

"Please, Your Highness, we need your help. Dame Glowra's been unconscious for over an hour now and needs water." Ms. Bishop seemed unaffected by the spell that had settled over the group on the ground and was hurrying to dismount the now kneeling Altus Hermes.

At her words, something clicked back into place and everyone sprang into action. A guard pair rushed forward and helped Ms. Bishop find her feet on the earth again, while another two steadied and lowered Dame Glowra off Altus Hermes's back, carrying her carefully into the tent. Ms. Bishop bowed low to the Griffin before rushing forward and gripping it tight around the neck. Tears colored her words of thanks.

Altus Hermes did not appear to mind the familiarity of the embrace and clicked its beak reassuringly. Bowing again, Ms. Bishop straightened and rushed to follow the guards who had removed Dame Glowra.

Connor realized his mouth had fallen open. He hurried to close it and regain his composure. He ducked his head as Altus Hermes stepped in front of him, its beak running lightly through his hair. Formalities restored, it tossed its head and whickered before it stepped back two paces, crouched slightly, unfurled its wings and shot up into the air. In moments, it was gone. The guards looked at each other in bewilderment, still not quite sure what they had just witnessed.

Connor and his father exchanged a look before they followed Ms. Bishop into the tent. The King headed toward the corner where Dame Glowra lay prone. Already, Ms. Bishop had put a wet cloth on her head, and the order had been given to fetch Master Epione and some smelling salts. Connor made his way to where Ms. Bishop stood at the refreshment table.

She was filling a cup with shaking hands; water speckled the surface of the table. Connor gently took the water carafe from her, finished pouring, and handed the cup to a nearby guard. The guard rushed to Dame Glowra's side and Connor indicated to Ms. Bishop to wait a minute before joining them.

"Thank you, Your Grace," she said as she watched one guard prop Dame Glowra up and another begin to wet her lips with the water.

Connor poured another for Ms. Bishop and handed it to her. Then he set the jug down and put a hand on her shoulder. "Ms. Bishop, what happened?" he asked.

The touch seemed to break something in her and fresh tears trickled down her cheeks. Connor quickly found a chair and helped her into it. She took a few gulps of water and fought to regain her composure. He settled next to her and waited patiently.

Finally she took one shaky breath, then another and told him. Her sentences were short and succinct and her eyes kept darting over to the corner where Dame Glowra lay.

". . . and then Jacqueline came back with the Griffin," she finished.

"Jacqueline?" the King barked from the other side of the tent.

"Wait, Jacqueline brought Altus Hermes? But then, where is she? Why isn't she with you?" Connor asked.

"It could only carry two people. Jacqueline hurt her arm pretty bad. She couldn't hold Le—Dame Glowra. She insisted I take her. She took our eggs to the top instead. She insisted on that too—said we might still be in the contest that way." Ms. Bishop glanced over at Dame Glowra again. "Is she going to be okay?"

At that moment, Master Epione came through the entrance pulling a vial from inside one of her pouches and unstoppering it in a fluid motion. "Where is she? Where—ah! Oh my, how long has she been like this? When was the last time she had anything to drink?" Her voice filled the tiny tent.

Ms. Bishop stood up and stepped forward. "She was sick this morning and hasn't had a drink all day and she's been unconscious for over an hour. Will she be okay? What's going to happen to her?" she said shakily, her knuckles stood out white around her cup.

Master Epione shooed one of the guards aside to get closer to Dame Glowra and knelt beside her. She put a hand to her forehead, her cheek, and felt a pulse at her wrist. She took the vial she had opened upon entering and wafted it under her nose. Dame Glowra's eyes fluttered open and patches of color appeared on her cheeks.

Ms. Bishop let out a sob of relief and her hands flew to her mouth. The cup fell to the ground, forgotten. She darted to Dame Glowra's side and clasped her hand.

The Dame's eyes slowly began to focus on her surroundings, light returning.

She saw Ms. Bishop and smiled weakly.

"Hello, flower girl," she said, her voice raspy.

Ms. Bishop pressed Dame Glowra's hand to her cheek. "Lee, thank the Goddess," she said.

With the feeling that they were intruding on a private moment, Connor tapped his father's shoulder and motioned for him to follow him outside. Once they were a short distance from the tent, he said, "Father, no one has been judged to be worthy to ride a Griffin in years . . . decades! Now three women have done so in the span of an hour. What does this mean?"

King Aren scratched his jaw thoughtfully. "Well, for one thing, we know that they are all appropriate candidates for the contest," he said.

Connor almost rolled his eyes in exasperation but refrained as his father continued.

"We will speak with the Council of Four but most likely they will each be granted additional points toward their final score. Their names, of course, will be recorded and included in our historical records. From what Ms. Bishop has said, technically, it was at Jacqueline's urging that the other two be granted the honor to ride with Altus Hermes, but I feel that technicality is trivial. These women have been anointed by the Court and will receive the appropriate honors." King Aren paused. "Of course, we will consult the Council. But I imagine this is what will be done."

Connor's eyes darted to the approaching figure beyond his father's shoulder. King Aren noticed the distraction and turned around to take in the slightly out of breath page who had evidently run from the palace. "Your Highness," she panted, "I have . . . a message . . . update . . ."

The King held up his hand, "My dear child, go get yourself a drink and come back when you have air in those lungs again."

She bobbed low in thanks and rushed to do as she was bid. The King winked at his son and stood waiting for her to return. "There now, all settled? What was it you had to tell me?" he asked as the girl returned.

"News from the scryers. Ms. Cynthia Doeboare has failed to return her egg to the Court and has begun her descent the way she came," she reported.

"Pity, make sure there are two attendants waiting for her at the starting point with refreshments and possibly some first aid. We will take her egg up with Ms. Goldenrod's this evening," he replied.

"Yes, Your Highness. Also, Dame Hera Claustrom is requesting an audience with the Council of Four. She has concerns for the integrity of the contest, as she put it," she added.

The King raised one eyebrow but kept the rest of his face impassive as he said, "I see." He glanced over to where the Councilors were working with heads together, deep in conversation. He considered for a moment, then said, "Tell her she can speak with the Prince and I. The Council is busy with matters of import. As Prince Cornelius and I must remain to ensure the last two contestants return safely, you may tell her she can attend an audience here, or she will have to wait for tomorrow."

"Very good, right away, Your Majesty. One more thing, the scryers report that Chivilra Andromeda Turner has just deposited her egg and is on her way down now, and Ms. Jacqueline Daidala is injured, but she too is on her way down and will be returning soon."

Connor started forward and asked, "How badly injured?"

The page's eyes grew round as she looked at Connor. She blushed, looked at her toes, and mumbled, "They didn't give me much detail, but mentioned her arm had been injured, Your Grace."

Connor strode over to the scryglass that was sitting beside the chess set. He held the mirror in both hands and said clearly into the glass, "Jacqueline Daidala."

The glass fogged over as if from his breath then cleared to show . . . nothing. The King, who had followed him after dismissing the page, peered over his shoulder.

"She must be on the route down. We did not put scry crystals along that path, did we?" the King asked.

"No," said Connor. Disappointed, he put the mirror back. The King studied him with an expression caught between amusement and pity on his face.

Much sooner than they had anticipated, Dame Hera Claustrom came striding across the lawn with the page skipping to keep pace. Dame Claustrom's expression was thunderous, but as she approached the Prince and his father, the storm appeared to dissipate. Her brow softened and furrowed in a pained concern that did not reach her eyes. Connor and his father had settled once more at the table to continue their chess game. She stopped in front of the King.

"Good afternoon, Dame Claustrom," the King said.

"Good afternoon, Your Highness, Your Grace," she replied and took to one knee, bowing to each of them in turn.

"Rise. You sought an audience? What are your concerns?" King Aren placed his pawn back on the chessboard and surveyed Dame Claustrom with a steady gaze.

"Your Highness, I understand that it will be the Council who will ultimately judge those competing in the contest, but I just witnessed a most egregious act that clearly violates the rules we were expected to abide by. I could not stand by without making sure it would be appropriately looked into," Dame Claustrom said. She stood with her shoulders back and chin jutting forward defiantly.

Connor raised an eyebrow and looked to see his father's reaction.

The King looked intrigued. He clasped his fingers together, rested his chin on his knuckles, and asked in a low tone, "That is a very serious accusation. And what, Dame Claustrom, is this egregious act?"

She cleared her throat and said, "Your Highness, this morning, his Grace informed all of the contestants that it would mean immediate disqualification if a contestant attempted to tamper with another contestant's egg." King Aren nodded and bade her to continue. "Well, while I was consoling Dame Witbron—she has been quite beside herself after the dreadful business with her egg—"

The King held up his hand to interrupt, "Ah yes, we've been informed. Were you a witness to the event?"

Dame Claustrom faltered for a moment before tossing her hair behind her shoulder and replying, "Oh, it was awful, I was right behind her going into that . . . cave. The poor beast looked as though it were heartbroken. It started screeching and flapping its wings when it saw the cracked shell. Devon almost fainted, poor dear. She really should have been more careful with that egg. She cried all the way down and I haven't been able to cheer her up since."

"Did you or she know she had cracked her egg before it was presented?" Connor asked.

Dame Claustrom's eyes darted toward him and the corner of her mouth twitched. She fixed a look of concern on her features, "I had no idea, and Dame Witbron had apparently not checked in on her charge or else she would have been mortified. It was cracked from top to bottom. She must have knocked it against a rock or something on her way up without realizing."

Connor scratched the back of his neck and felt heat rise in his face. He could not help but feel responsible for the damaged egg. It was his task that had put the eggs in danger. He had not dreamed any contestant would be so careless with such precious cargo.

"Which brings me to my point of concern," Dame Claustrom continued. "I observed Ms. Daidala interfering with not one, but two contestants' eggs. She carried both Dame Glowra's and Ms. Bishop's eggs to the summit. If my actions today show anything, it's that I am invested in retaining the integrity of this contest and I wish to ensure appropriate action is taken against a contestant with such little regard for the rules."

The King straightened slowly and looked at Connor to respond.

Connor cleared his throat. He looked over at the Councilors, three of whom were currently engrossed in conversation, papers, and their mirrors. Cllr. Stewart had drifted over as Dame Claustrom spoke and was nodding her head. Before Connor could respond, she said, "Thank you for your concern, Dame Claustrom. It is a true act of integrity to bring your concerns to our attention."

Connor opened his mouth to speak, but Cllr. Stewart held up her hand and continued. "We are well aware of the actions Ms. Daidala took with regards to the eggs of Dame Glowra and Ms. Bishop, the latter contestant having presented a firsthand account. We will, of course, be speaking with Ms. Daidala once she returns. The matter will be addressed in accordance with the rules. You are to be commended in your determination to put the Queendom's interests before your own." Cllr. Stewart smiled down at Dame Claustrom, who blushed with pleasure and bowed.

"And," Connor interjected, "taking into consideration the nature of the act as well as the circumstances by which the tampering was deemed necessary by the contestant." He finished.

Cllr. Stewart glanced at him as though he were a small child vying for attention. He fought to keep any emotion from his face, and did his best to ignore the tickle of irritation that threatened to break his composure.

The King stood up and added, "Thank you for your . . . diligence, Dame Claustrom."

The Dame understood she was being dismissed and bowed again to each of them. Cllr. Stewart smiled sweetly and drifted back to her table.

As both women departed, the King turned to his son and simply said, "I'd watch that one," with a knowing smile, before settling back into his chair and retrieving his pawn. Connor could not be sure who he meant.

Connor felt like a tightly wound spring. He tried to pay attention to the chess game but found himself glancing up so frequently from the board that his father eventually dozed off waiting for his turn. Every shift in the wind sounded like horse hooves as his ears strained to hear.

Finally Jacqueline's silhouette could be seen slumped over the neck of the little bay mare who held her own head high, proud to have found her own way down the mountain.

"Someone call Master Epione! Ms. Daidala has returned," Connor barked to a guard who had been picking dirt from beneath her nails. The King awoke with a start and sat up straighter.

"Ah, here she comes. That just leaves Chivilra Turner on the— boy, get back here." His father's mild comment turned into a hiss. "If she made it up to the top twice, rode with a Griffin, and came all the way down to this point, she does not need assistance for the last stretch. Do not reduce her triumph with coddling." Connor looked at his father sharply, a retort on his tongue, but his father held up a hand and continued. "We must receive her as we have all the other contestants and show her the proper respect. Let her complete this task alone."

Connor returned to stand beside his father and waited with his hands clasped behind his back. He drummed his fingers of one hand against the back of his other wrist to keep from fidgeting. He knew his father was right, but his face still burned from the rebuke.

Jacqueline and the little mare came closer and closer. He watched as she struggled to sit up straighter in her saddle as she approached. The mare slowed to a halt in front of the King and Prince, and waited patiently while Jacqueline dismounted. Cradling a bloodied arm, Jacqueline carefully knelt before the two men. Pain flashed across her weary features.

"Congratulations, Ms. Daidala. You have completed the first task," Connor repeated the words as he had for every other contestant that day, but could not keep the relief from his voice, or the smile from his face.

"Thank you," Jacqueline nodded to each of them and fixed Connor with a steady gaze. "Have Dame Glowra and Ms. Bishop returned? Are they okay?" she asked. She looked at him in earnest. Instinctively he reached for her and bid her rise.

Wincing slightly, she placed her free hand in his and he helped her to her feet. An answer hovered on his lips as he stood transfixed. The sun at her back set her hair alight; the last rays flickered around her like glowing embers before being extinguished beyond the horizon. Cloaked in the sunset, she was, for a moment, a being of golden light.

21

MOONLIT CONVERSATIONS

"I could definitely get used to this," Amber sighed as she ran her hand through the petals floating on the surface of the water. They dipped and swirled in the little eddies evoked by her fingertips. Jacs smiled and gently lowered herself into the pool next to the muscular brunette, careful to hold her splinted arm above the water. The nine remaining contestants were in various states of relaxation in the open-air hot springs, interspersed between the three pools of varying sizes in a walled courtyard. Reading alcoves and daybeds were spaced around the perimeter. The pools were connected by small waterfalls and sparkled like opals in the center of the room under a layer of steam that rose from the surface.

Jacs could not think of a time she had ever felt more bruised, or more relaxed. The air hung heavy with essential oils. "I don't know if I'd do it all again, but this does beat that pony ride down," she said.

"I don't even remember the pony ride," Andromeda said from the other side of the largest pool. "I spent so long on that mountain; I swear I've blocked the last part out."

"What happened up there?" Amber asked, not unkindly. "It's just . . . you took so long—we were all getting worried about you."

Andromeda shrugged, "I took a false route up thinking it was a shortcut. Ended up having to double back a fair way. Plus, I'm still not right from the fire."

Verona nodded knowingly, her chestnut bob nodding with her. "Tell me about it—you'd think they would have factored in that we were all recovering from smoke inhalation, or worse. Well, the most important part is you made it at all. I can't believe six contestants have already been eliminated."

"Wait, what? In a contest designed to choose one winner of fifteen, there are eliminations? Good gracious, what a plot twist," Shane drawled from a daybed. She had not opened her eyes but delicately laid the back of her hand against her forehead in mockery.

Several of the women giggled, and Verona frowned. "You know what I meant," she mumbled.

"I'm shocked only six were eliminated considering the gross misconduct that went on today," Hera piped up. She was receiving a massage from a servingman and waved him away disdainfully. Pulling a towel around herself, she began massaging lotion into her legs. "Honestly, what a joke. Why even have rules?"

Jacs rolled her eyes at Anya, who hid a smirk. "Why Hera, what could you be referring to?" Jacs said sweetly.

Hera shot her a glare and tossed her head, "Jacqueline, you know exactly what I'm referring to; you and your beast-loving posse might as well have spat on—"

"Hera, come on," Anya spoke over Hera with exasperation.

"—the rules quite clearly laid out by the Prince hims—"

"The Prince and the Council reviewed her actions and saw no violation!" Lena's still-raspy voice rose as she spoke over both women, her tone one of a patient parent explaining a simple concept to a stubborn child.

"—self. Oh sure, of course you two would defend the Griffin-wrangler. A northern Dame and a nobody, you're both lucky to still be in this. Riding on the skirts of—" Hera's voice rose above Lena and Anya's.

Jacs interrupted her. "Hera, are you really mad about what you perceive to be a rule violation, or are you just upset you couldn't get us disqualified the way you got Devon?" The sweetness evaporated from her voice.

"What? How dare you—"

"I saw you. I saw you make Devon switch eggs with you." Jacs's implication rang out around the chamber and the others fell silent to watch. "I couldn't figure out why it even mattered to you, but that's because your egg was damaged, wasn't it? And you needed a new one, so why not force someone to switch with you? Devon probably didn't even think to check it or take it out of the pouch you gave her."

"I would never! This is ridiculous! We needed to switch because of a mix-up," Hera said through gritted teeth.

Jacs shook her head. "It doesn't matter, it's not as if anyone can prove it. But if you think for a second I'm going to sit and listen to you moan about rule violations when your actions got another contestant eliminated, you're more of an entitled plip than I thought."

Hera looked as though she had been slapped. "You forget your place, Daidala," she said vehemently, her voice low. A warning.

"Give it a rest, Hera. She rode with a Griffin today, her place is far loftier than I think you realize," Amber said with a laugh that almost eased the tension. The other contestants eyed Hera and Jacs warily, and it was a while before conversation dared to start up again.

Fawn shot Jacs a withering look and made her way over to Hera, who had turned away sulkily. Jacs watched Fawn put her arm around Hera's shoulders as the two began talking in low tones. She did not need to use much of her imagination to guess what they were talking about.

After a time, Jacs retired to one of the alcoves set around the walls. She had told Lena and Anya the heat was making her dizzy, but the truth was, she desperately needed a place to think. Plus, she was so tired. So, so tired. It was a wonder she could keep her head above water. She rested on a number of plush pillows, a cool cloth scented with lavender over her eyes.

Listening to the others, as well as to a short debrief while she was getting patched up by Master Epione, she had learned that, apart from Devon and Faya, Danielle, Hanlen, Cynthia and Christina had all been eliminated. Of the six, Faya and Danielle had been the only two to actually fail to deposit their eggs. The other four had been disqualified by the Council for failure to demonstrate the necessary qualities of the task: to show strength and to understand when a gentle approach is needed. Devon hadn't demonstrated enough gentleness as evidenced by her damaged egg. Cynthia and Christina had been disqualified for bickering about who got to deposit their egg first and endangering their eggs in the subsequent scuffle. Hanlen had been disqualified for begging Shane to carry her egg for the last quarter of the journey; this was deemed an embarrassing display and classified as lacking strength of character.

Jacs had been lucky her actions had been deemed honorable and in line with the task's expectations. Anya and Lena had been lucky to have demonstrated enough strength and compassion throughout the task so as to have been made an exception. Jacs thought of Shane walking past them as they struggled to move Lena's limp form up the mountain. Shane had been lucky too, it seemed. We can't all be lucky. The image of the broken egg floated behind her eyes.

Andromeda and Amber had moved to an alcove nearby and were discussing difficulties with the recent recruitments. Jacs caught a segment of their conversation.

"Guard training is hard enough," Amber was saying, "The pair selection process itself takes months. Then the additional training it takes to be a knight . . . It's no wonder we're having trouble finding new recruits."

"I heard they were toying with the idea of letting men apply," Andromeda said in a low voice, as though nervous of who might hear.

"You're not serious?"

"Argument is they've got the physical strength for it."

"So does an ox," scoffed Amber, "but if it was down to brute strength, I'd be out of work. Plus, they don't have the mumma-bear instinct. You can't teach that."

"Exactly," agreed Andromeda.

"They need to stick with what they're good at. Simple manual labor. They don't have the biological instincts, the mental and physical finesse, the blood bonds, the . . ." Amber paused. "Men becoming guards, honestly."

"Not just guards, but they're thinking they could eventually become knights."

There was a longer pause. "That's just stupid," Amber supplied finally.

"Nothing will come of it," Andromeda said calmly. "But you know how it is, these fancies come and go. The bottom line is, if you can't create life, you can't be trusted to take it."

Jacs frowned. She thought of the way her father used to play the fiddle around the stove on cold winter nights. The way his fingers danced and flew across the strings. Her father had been a gentle man. Strong, yes, but not the brute strength Amber had shown so much disdain for. And the way he had pushed her out of the river . . . no one could argue he didn't have the mumma-bear instinct. Her mind fluttered to Phillip before she could dwell too much on thoughts of her father. She saw in her mind's eye the way he pulled her to safety from the writhing mob around the broken fountain. There were a few men she wouldn't mind seeing in armor. She thought of Connor's earlier letters where he shared his wish to be a knight one day. Why had that seemed so farfetched? She thought of the cruel beating Phillip had suffered at the hands of the guard pairs.

A few male guards might shake things up, she thought. Even if only to keep the guard pairs in check.

Before she knew what she was doing, she had risen from her bench and made her way over to the knights. Amber greeted her warmly and made space for her on the cushions lining the benches. Andromeda nodded curtly to her. Jacs knew the knight well enough by now to realize that this was her version of a warm welcome.

"I was eavesdropping," Jacs said unapologetically. "What's this about men becoming guards?"

"Just a rumor," Amber said quickly. "As if that would ever work," she scoffed.

"Why not?" Jacs asked innocently.

Amber shot her a look to see if she was serious. Andromeda replied bluntly, "They're just not built for it. It goes against their nature. Imagine a man in the heat of battle and his anger takes over. Then you have an unpredictable recruit on a rampage. A wildfire that puts himself and his team at risk."

Jacs nodded thoughtfully. "But surely with training and discipline they can tame that fire. Learn to control it. Couldn't their natural strength be an asset?" The knights looked at each other, then back at Jacs. She shrugged and continued, "It just seems a waste to deny half the population the chance to defend their Queendom based on their sex."

"Jacqueline, that's just how it is. Plus, can you imagine how distracting it would be for the guards to have a bunch of fit men walking around the training grounds?" Amber said, shifting forward in her seat.

Jacs laughed lightly. "I'm guessing the guards who like women get along just fine, so why would those who like men be less able to control themselves? What about you, Amber? If you don't mind my asking, are you more attracted to women or men?"

"Both," Amber said with a slight grin.

Jacs settled into the cushions. "And as you're a medal-winning knight and a role model to the realm, I'm guessing you're able to control yourself around your fellow females?" she asked.

Amber raised an eyebrow. "Of course."

"And you hold your troops to the same standard?"

"Naturally."

"So if men were allowed to train as guards, you'd have a greater variety of people to control yourself around, but do you think you could do it?" Jacs asked.

"Of course! That would be extremely inappropriate," Amber said, "and irresponsible."

Jacs swept her open palm in front of her in a, "well there you go" gesture. Amber looked uncomfortable but not completely convinced.

Andromeda looked thoughtful. "We'd have to change their style of fighting," she said after a time, "to optimize their natural strength and force. We train our women to harness their speed and agility. If—" she paused and stressed the word "—*If* men were trained to join rank, it might be an opportunity to expand our fighting styles." She tapped her chin, contemplative.

"It just . . . it doesn't seem right," Amber said doubtfully.

Jacs shrugged again and commented mildly, "To progress, we need to accept change. If we don't, we don't grow."

"Since when did you get so wise?" Amber teased.

Jacs smiled. "Riding with the Court changes you, I guess," she said mischievously.

Amber laughed, jumping on a change in subject. "That's right, you'll be titled this evening, I'm guessing?"

Jacs nodded and twisted a strand of hair around her finger. She marveled at the thought. Courtier Jacqueline Tabart. . . well, Courtier Jacqueline Daidala. Would a title change her at all? Or would they still just see her as a Lowrian basemutt when they found out the truth?

"Well then, we better get you ready," Amber said excitedly. She rose and held out her hand to help Jacs up. "And I know a certain

Prince who is probably wondering how deeply your eyes will sparkle toni-ight!" she sang with a wiggle of her hips. Jacs grinned despite herself and took her hand. Amber pretended to swoon. "My word, what a heavenly shade of green! My poor heart can't take it!" she cried.

Jacs swatted her playfully. "Shut it." She laughed.

Amber, Andromeda, and Jacs made their way toward the door. Jacs noticed Anya and Lena deep in conversation in one of the smaller pools. She caught Anya's eye and motioned that they were leaving. Anya nodded and waved her on, turning back to Lena.

The feast was, if possible, even more decadent than the first. Long tables had been placed end to end on the lawn and dishes upon dishes placed upon them. The King had decided that, as the hall was not in any state to receive guests, they would all eat outside. The evening was warm and clear. The stars began to blink awake, and countless lanterns had been placed around the grounds in their own constellations. Women and men in their finery strolled through the gardens in the moonlight, sat with laden plates at one of the many small tables scattered across the lawns, or stood in small groups to discuss the events of the day.

Jacs and the other contestants, their day's ordeal washed away and covered in silks and brocade, descended the grand stone steps from the palace to enthusiastic applause. Jacs felt like a stranger with her wide, asymmetrically split skirts flowing from her waist and her hair arranged in an intricate braided updo. She had pulled the viridian gown on her with such care, so nervous to even touch the fine yards of fabric that she was sure it was still hovering millimeters above her skin. Separated from her. Her splinted arm seemed to be the only reminder that she remained Jacs within her gown. That, and the ring on its thin gold chain around her neck. Its warmth was nestled safely under the complicated bodice. A companion for her heart.

Before the guests settled into the elaborate spread laid out for them, Jacs, Lena, and Anya were called forth to a golden stage that had been set at the top of the lawn to be dubbed Courtiers. The title given to those who have flown with the Court of Griffins. A title not bestowed in decades, now given to three women in one day. Altus Thenya, the white Griffin who had judged Jacs on top of the Court's mountain, stood beside the King and the Council of Four.

All those in attendance stood before the golden stage, and purple crystals dotted the clearing for those not present. Feeling the eyes of the Queendom on her, Jacs bowed deeply before Altus Thenya. The Griffin stepped forward, bowed its neck, and tapped its beak on each of Jacs's shoulders. Stepping back, it tapped its taloned foot on the stage twice and roared to the crowd, the sound echoing in Jacs's heart.

"Rise now, as Courtier Jacqueline Daidala. She who rides with the Court," The King said in a deep, resonant voice.

She stood slowly, caught the Prince's eye where he stood off to the side, and with a small smile to him, turned to face the audience. A cheer rose from those gathered before her like a wave. Smiling broadly now, she bowed to them and moved off the stage. Lena and Anya followed with a similar ceremony. Jacs cheered loudly for her friends each time and embraced them warmly as they stepped from the dais.

Altus Thenya took to the skies as the applause died away and the crowd gradually dispersed to help themselves to the feast and mill around the grounds. The name Courtier Jacqueline Daidala rang in Jacs's ears, and already she had been poured a second glass of champagne.

It wasn't until much later that Jacs was able to detach herself from the crowd of fans she did not realize she had accumulated and find a quiet moment on a balcony overlooking a small pond. The pond had been decorated with floating lanterns that reflected prettily on its still surface. The light created flickering shadows on the surrounding reeds. Jacs leaned against the stone railing and her gaze drifted up to the stars twinkling high above. She played with the ring around her neck distractedly, rubbing the pad of her thumb across the engraving.

Courtier in the Upper Realm, she thought. *What does that make me in the Lower Realm?* It was all so much simpler down there. No titles unless you earned the title of Master. No Dames, Chivs, Courtiers, or Lords. No special bow for special ranks. No. What did the Lower Realm have? Bookhead, Upper dog, basemutt. Jacs shook her head at the memories.

"I guess people find their own ways to put others in their place," she said quietly.

"May I join you?" Prince Cornelius's voice came from behind her, causing her to jump.

"I—I would be honored, Your Grace." She recovered quickly, tucking the ring in her bodice. Her empty glass perched on the stone banister next to her; she shifted it to her left as he came to stand beside her.

"How is your arm?" Cornelius asked softly. He rested his forearms lightly on the balustrade, concern creasing his forehead. Jacs's arm was still in a splint, but Master Epione had been optimistic when she wrapped it.

"A fracture. Apparently, all it needs is rest and time and it will be as good as new," Jacs replied. She did not have to mention the reality of needing to complete the remainder of the tasks with a splinted arm.

Cornelius shifted uncomfortably, as though unsure how best to comfort her.

"Beautiful night," Jacs ventured into the silence, gesturing at the grounds, her gaze returning to the constellations above her.

He cleared his throat. "Yes, it's amazing how many stars we can see tonight."

"Do you know any of their names?" Jacs tried to ignore the fluttering rhythm her heart made in her chest.

"Names?"

"Of the stars."

"Oh!" Cornelius shifted his weight and peered upwards. "A few. That one there is Orion with her belt." He traced the outline of the hunter. "And that one, that one is Cassiopeia. My mother always liked to tell me the story about her. She was used as an example of what a Queen should not do."

Jacs smiled. "I've not heard that one."

Cornelius rubbed his jaw with the back of his knuckles, remembering. "Well, in the legend, she was a very vain Queen. She claimed to be the most beautiful in all the land. Many of her duties went unfulfilled and neglected in favor of more selfish pursuits. Unfortunately, it was her people who suffered. Their cries for help were finally heard by the Goddess, who saw the selfish Queen feasting and dancing while her people starved. Next thing Cassiopeia knew, she's immortalized upside down in the heavens on her throne. To spend the rest of time with her skirts around her ears and the blood rushing to her head."

They both laughed.

"How unfortunate for her," Jacs said. "Although, to live forever among the stars, I imagine the view would be pretty spectacular from up there."

A dragonfly rose from a lily pad and cast a shadow across one of the lanterns.

"What was it like?" Cornelius asked.

"What was—?" Jacs said.

"Flying. What was it like to fly?" he clarified.

"Oh," Jacs smiled and closed her eyes briefly. She again felt the rush. "It was exhilarating. Like nothing I've ever felt before. Like I could land on a cloud or pluck a star from the sky. I know the situation was tense, but a part of me never wanted to come back down. I think I'm still waiting for my heart to . . . actually," she wound a strand of hair through her fingers, "for a fraction of a moment, I felt . . . free. Completely free."

They stood in silence together for a time. The sounds from the feast floated lazily toward them in the evening air. Light from the lanterns danced between lily pads.

"You were incredibly brave today," he said quietly.

Jacs was thankful for the darkness as the color rose in her cheeks.

He continued, his voice low. "And what you did yesterday in the fire. Jacqueline, that was remarkable. You are . . ." He paused to consider. "You are a force unto yourself."

She glanced up at him with a half smile and her feet took her one step closer, closing the distance between them.

"Your Grace, I only—" she began and didn't quite know how to finish her sentence. Her face felt hot. His eyes, deep blue in the moonlight, held her in place.

"And beautiful," he said, hesitant.

Hurriedly, she looked away. She felt rather than saw Cornelius watching her. Her pulse quickened and she tried to focus on the stars. She studied Cassiopeia as though looking at it hard enough would turn the Queen right side up. She needed to focus. She had a clear objective. She needed to focus on her clear objective. She could not afford to entertain school-girl notions of fancy when she still had two tasks left. But the Prince was looking at her.

She turned and met his gaze.

His eyes held a question. They were standing very close together—when had that happened? Her heart was pounding faster now. Surely he could hear it. Her mind started to race as if to drown out her traitorous heart.

I need to focus, focus . . . cus, kus, kiss.

Cheeks flushed from the champagne, or something more, she suddenly felt reckless. A boldness seized her. Her eyes flickered from his eyes to his lips and she felt herself drawn toward him. She was vaguely aware that they had stopped talking. The last smallest distance between them seemed a chasm, and tentatively, she reached out to settle her palm on a slightly worn patch of embroidery on his chest. His hand rose to encircle hers as though moving through water.

There was a moment's hesitation—the Griffin poised on the precipice—then their lips met, and she flew for the second time that day. Light, weightless, free. Her world was reduced to the feel of his hand grazing her cheek. She pulled him closer as the kiss deepened, ignoring the small pebble of guilt that settled on her heart, sure that its rapid pounding would be enough to shake it free. His hand was around her waist now. She took a step backward with him and shifted her splinted arm from the balustrade. Her elbow brushed against something cool. She heard a soft scraping, then the tinkling of broken glass as her empty champagne flute hit the cobbles below.

In a flash, the pebble became an anchor and pulled her back to earth. She opened her eyes. The lantern light flickered. She saw guards with torches. A woman crumpling. Images of a beaten and bloodied Phillip filled her mind, Mal on the banks of the river, the soft glow of purple from the corner of every room.

Then she thought of Connor.

Jacs gasped and pulled away, a hand covering her mouth.

"Your Grace, forgive me. I should not . . . I . . . I can't—"

"Jacqueline, it's okay. It was only a glass." Cornelius was smiling, he did not understand. He moved toward her but she took a step back.

"What?" Jacs said, momentarily distracted, then shook her head. "No! No, I shouldn't have . . ."

The smile slipped from his face. He frowned slightly, looked to where the glass had fallen, and back to Jacs. "It really doesn't matter, I'll have someone clear it—" he began.

"No, not that. I'm sorry, I shouldn't be here with you, like this, this was a mistake." The anchor grew and she felt its weight as though tied around her neck.

Cornelius stared at her. "Jacqueline, what . . .?"

"I'm sorry, I just— I can't afford this kind of distraction. Not now." She felt the heat rise in her cheeks and crossed her arms in front of her.

"Distraction?" Indignation colored Cornelius's question.

"From the contest!"

"Jacqueline, I'm not— I would never jeopardize a contestant's chances in the contest." He crossed his arms too. "Jacqueline, it's up to the Council, the Court, and the tasks to determine the rightful

Queen. For obvious reasons, any personal preferences of the royal family cannot weigh in on the final decision. It's all based on merit and performance. I can't affect your scores." He seemed desperate for her to understand.

Her eyes flashed as his brow furrowed deeper, this time in confusion.

Jacs turned away from the Prince's gaze, clenching her teeth in frustration. What was she doing? She could almost kick herself. This was not a vacation, not about her and her foolish fancies. This was never about her at all. She was the Lowrians' one chance at some form of representation and a few glasses of champagne and a lily pond were enough to let her forget that? She thought of her mother, she thought of her mentor, she thought of how his lips— *No!*

She shook her head. She could not make the Prince understand. She had come so far.

"Your Grace, my people are relying on me to stay focused on these tasks. I—" she fumbled for the words. She took one breath, then another, "I can't allow myself to indulge in personal matters. No matter how much I may want to. I just . . . It doesn't feel right."

He searched her face for a moment and smiled sadly. "I apologize, Courtier Daidala." He inclined his head to her. "I assure you; I will not assume such liberties again."

"Thank you." She wanted to say so much more but was uncertain where to start. He lingered a moment then nodded again and left her alone on the balcony. The lanterns flickered as they had a moment before, the breeze ruffled the reeds again, yet everything had shifted. She must not forget the world she came from. She was not Courtier Jacqueline Daidala. She was Jacs Tabart. No fancy dress could change that.

Restless, confused, and needing movement, she walked away from the balcony and away from the pond, heading toward the hedged garden. The music and the chatter from the feast disappeared as she walked through the overgrown archway and entered the dark moonlit world of the herb garden. She recognized the spot where she had first met Hera Claustrom and moved past the thyme beds into the rosemary. The familiar scent filled her with a longing for home so strong she had to stifle a sob. Sitting on a bench, running a sprig she had plucked through her fingers, it was a time before she had steadied herself enough to hear the quiet voices drifting through the fronds.

"So, you want me to forfeit? Is that it? You don't think I can actually complete a task by myself?" Jacs recognized Lena's hushed, furious voice.

"No! Of course no—" That was definitely Anya.

"So then you're just worried I'm going to slow you down? I did not ask you to stay with me!" Jacs realized they must be on the other side of the hedge. She did not know if she should listen or not, but Anya continued, and she stayed frozen in place.

"Lee, you know that's not what I—what if something had happened to you?"

"Don't 'Lee' me! I am not a child, and I need no protecting!" Lena's voice was almost unrecognizable with such hurt and disdain dripping from every word. There was a long pause before she continued. "If you're worried I'll slow you down, need I remind you that this is a contest, and a solo one at that. You owe me no favors and I certainly do not expect any from you. After all, I didn't even know you would be competing."

"Well how was I supposed to tell you that? You vanished! Without even a good-bye!" Anya hissed.

"That was not my fault!" Lena shot back.

"Oh, so someone forced you to just not say good-bye, or even tell me you were leaving? I had to hear from Elizabeth, that smug little stable hand. Do you know how humiliating it is to think you would confide in her over me? I thought—" Anya's rising tone was cut short by Lena's softer, now slightly pleading notes.

"No! Anya, it was not like that at all. You know that you—"

"And now you're here with Jacqueline. And she's . . . she's fine, but . . . she's just this woman who shows up out of nowhere and somehow becomes your confidant overnight," Anya said indignantly.

"I was helping her, you know that. She's all alone here. I just wanted to help."

Anya made a sound of exasperation, but Lena pressed on. "And Elizabeth is the stable hand, of course she knew I was leaving—she saddled my horse! But that does not mean I told her over you. She's just another servant, she was just doing her job."

"Just another servant." The words fell from Anya.

"Oh please, not this again. You know what I meant," Lena said.

"No, of course, it's fine. You have no reason to share your schedule with your servants. Why should I be any different? I just help with the bouquets in your foyer. Do you need a new arrangement, Your Elegance? Or will that be all?" Jacs heard a rustling of silk and a scraping of gravel and imagined Anya had sunk into a formal bow.

"Anya!"

"The daisies are gorgeous this time of year," Anya continued sweetly.

"Get up. That is not fair." Lena's voice rose above Anya's as the latter plowed on.

"Maybe some hydrangeas for the parlor?"

"Stop! That. Is not. Fair." Lena was breathing hard now. Jacs heard a breeze shift through the hedges. She strained to hear the next words, which came out low. "My mother sent me away for those months on a whim and did not permit me to speak with anyone before I left. I had a grand total of thirty minutes from the time she told me what was to be, and the time I was put in the carriage to stay with my aunt. What was I supposed to do? I tried writing, but she instructed my aunt that I was not to contact . . . not to contact . . . you." The last word was almost a whisper. Jacs's stomach dropped, and she exhaled slowly.

"Me?" Anya asked, perplexed.

"Yes. You," Lena said defiantly.

"Why?"

"You must know why. After all this time. After all we've . . . and for you to get jealous over Elizabeth and Jacqueline."

"Jealous?" Anya spluttered.

"Yes. Admit it," Lena said.

"I am not jealous!"

"Then what are you? Because right now, you are just . . . just cruel." Lena's last word fell like a stone in a pond and the silence radiated from it like ripples. "I cannot help our stations in life any more than you can. But at least I don't use it as a stick with which to beat you," Lena said quietly.

"Lee—I'm . . . I'm sorry. I guess I'm just . . . you scared me today."

"That was not my intent. I'm not your burden," Lena retorted coldly.

"Of course, you're not my . . . You know, it hasn't been the easiest time. You disappear for months, and today . . . you were so still." Anya's voice was very small.

"I was fine!" Lena snapped.

"You don't know that," Anya said gently.

"Well, I am fine now, look, walking around and everything." Jacs heard a scuffle of stones as Lena marched about.

"Lee, stop it! I swear——" Anya began, voice rising.

"See, right as rain. Listen, I do appreciate your worry, and I do not want to appear ungrateful for the help today, but Anya, we're not little girls anymore. I can lace my own boots, and if it is just going to cause you stress to watch over me, then don't. You do not need to, and I do not want you t——"

"I thought I had lost you," Anya said haltingly. The words broke from her piece by piece.

There was a loud cry of excitement from the main lawn, and the cicadas chirped as though afraid of the silence that followed. Jacs bit her lip and stayed very still.

Finally Lena said, "Well. You didn't. You haven't. I'm tired. If you will excuse me, I think I will go to bed. And I will continue in this contest. But I do not expect you to hold my hand tomorrow."

"Lee. Please?"

But the only reply was the soft crunching of footsteps on gravel. Jacs buried her face in her hands.

22

BALLOONS

After he left Jacqueline, Connor excused himself from the festivities. Suddenly he did not have the desire to engage with the lights and the laughter. A quartet could be heard near one of the larger fountains. The song was one he had heard before, but somehow it jarred in him as though played at a different tempo. His father's booming laugh could be heard from the edge of the gardens before the great lawn. He had no desire to join his father either.

Instead, he began to walk the well-worn trail toward the old oak tree at the edge of the Cliff. Although the night was dark and the moon still low on the horizon, he had no trouble getting to the river, his feet finding the familiar route that he had beaten out since he was a child. The water slid silkily along the moss and stones in the dappled moonlight.

He was about to turn right to follow the bank to where he knew the familiar perch awaited, when he stopped. He could feel the pull from his silent haven. Could feel the urge to shut himself away, but something Jacqueline had said made him pause.

My people are relying on me to stay focused on these tasks. There was something in that statement. My people. Surely "the people," or "our people" would have been a more natural way to phrase that. There had been such terror and alarm in her eyes. *Maybe you're just a bad kisser,* a voice in the back of his mind quipped. But it still did not account for the intensity of her reaction.

Poised between two actions, he scratched the back of his neck absently. He looked around the silent forest and then back up to the castle. *My people are relying on me,* she had said. Just as they were relying on him, and here he was running away to sit in the dark. His mother had told him years ago that his destiny was to become King or advisor. He knew which one he would prefer, and he wouldn't get any closer to it by hiding himself away. Shaking his head, he turned back toward the castle, thankful his father had not been there to scold him.

Cresting the lawn, he headed toward the place where he remembered his father to be. He came across the King, deep in conversation with Masterchiv Rathbone, Cllr. Perda, and Cllr. Dilmont.

The head of the royal guard seemed uneasy, but Connor only recognized the emotion in the slight shift in her feet and the few strands of ash-blonde hair that escaped her usual tight-braided bun. He had known Masterchiv Rathbone all his life, and knew she tended to scratch at the hair around her temples when distressed.

Cllr. Perda, in contrast, looked positively gleeful. Her sharp features stood out as though freshly carved from marble and her dark eyes glittered. Cllr. Dilmont demonstrated more restraint than her fellow Councilor and had an eyebrow poised in question; her spiky hair had recently been run through by her fingers and stood up straighter.

The King was speaking in a hushed tone and had not noticed Connor's approach. Masterchiv Rathbone indicated his presence with a nod of her head over his shoulder and the King spun around.

"Ah! It's you, boy," he said roughly and gestured for Connor to join their small circle on the edge of the lawn.

Many of the revelers were clustered closer to the castle where the lights were brightest. The band played a lively number and shrieks of laughter carried from the gardens. "Your Highness, maybe we should move this conversation inside?" Masterchiv Rathbone began, her eyes darting around the still night.

The King shook his head and waved her concern away. "This will be fine, Masterchiv Rathbone. Much better in plain sight than having our absence raise concern and curiosity."

"Has something happened?" Connor ventured. "Is it about the eggs?"

"The eggs? No! No, the Court are fine and, despite Dame Witbron's mishap, do not think any lasting damage will befall the fledgling. No, it's about the two Lowrian criminals that were caught days before the contest." The King scratched his chin absently.

"Caught doing what?" Connor asked.

"Why, trying to breach the Upper Realm. Honestly boy, where have you been?" Connor felt indignation rise in his chest as his father continued. "General Hawkins's patrols apprehended them before they could get their contraption to work and have held them in custody in Bridgeport. Only, this action is stirring up rebellion among the townspeople and the guards are having difficulty keeping the situation controlled."

Connor thought back to the riots he had witnessed a year ago and shuddered.

Masterchiv Rathbone interjected, "We have tried sending reinforcements, but that has also been met with resistance."

"Well, I stand by my desire to meet these two women," the King said roughly, a cold edge to his voice.

"But sire, do you think that wise? They attempted to fly to the Upper Realm, an act of undocumented but surely obvious treason, and they are then to be rewarded with a carriage ride up the Bridge? It's absurd!" Masterchiv Rathbone said, massaging her temples.

"I agree with His Majesty; let us meet these rebels. The design of their plan is one of dreams; the minds behind the plot must be extraordinary," Cllr. Perda purred.

"And they ought to be made an example of," Cllr. Dilmont said through lips that barely moved. "What better way to do that than during the selection of our next Queen."

"Precisely, and the longer they stay in the Lower Realm, the more likely the story of how they attempted to breach our land is to spread and inspire copycats," said Cllr. Perda.

"Well, we were lucky that General Hawkins had the foresight to burn that blasted balloon instead of parading it through the streets of Bridgeport," the King added.

"Balloon?" Connor's heart skipped a beat, and his mouth went dry.

"Yes, one of the criminals is an inventor, she created a large balloon that could carry a person in a basket beneath it. General Hawkins reports that she insists it was being used for a trial run before they attempted to carry anyone in it," Masterchiv Rathbone explained. "But trial run or not, the intent was still treasonous."

"Although we do not technically have a law to state that to be the case," Cllr. Perda said sweetly, her eyes glittering again.

"Councilor, with all due respect, this is the same inventor who built the clock tower from which the assassins dispatched our beloved Queen, Goddess rest her. I think it no coincidence that she is to be implicated in another plot against the Upper Realm," Masterchiv Rathbone replied forcefully.

Connor willed himself to sound nonchalant, although he felt his heart was echoing across the lawn. "What—" he cleared his throat and tried again "—What are their names? The criminals?"

"Names?" Masterchiv Rathbone pulled out a rolled piece of parchment and read off, "A Master Bruna Leschi and Ms. Maria Tabart."

Connor could scarcely breathe. He knew those names. Master Leschi's he had read countless times before. Tabart he had read just the once. Just on the first letter. He could never forget that first letter. Although it had followed a different first name. His mind reeled with shock as images of those names on parchment filled his mind in Jacs's careful handwriting.

"Was there anyone else involved? Any family members?" he asked as calmly as he could, although he knew his voice must have wavered.

Masterchiv Rathbone studied him carefully before replying. "No. The inventor's son was visiting a nearby village at the time of the event and claimed no knowledge of the plot. Tabart's daughter is, reportedly, visiting an aunt in Abysterra. A small unit has been sent to question her, but that could take several days given the distance."

"Have the scryers not found her?" Connor pressed.

"The daughter? No. Not that I am aware," Masterchiv Rathbone replied, then continued when she saw the look of concern on his face. "But that could mean any number of things, most likely she is simply not in range of a crystal."

He nodded absently. His mind whirled. A balloon. Jacs had designed countless balloons to transport her letters to him. Was she really not involved in this one? He knew the answer even as he asked himself the question. He knew her. She must have designed a balloon to carry someone up to the Upper Realm. But then why was she several days' ride from its launch? Something did not add up.

Cllr. Perda cut across his musings. "At any rate, tell General Hawkins to bring the two criminals to the castle. A mind capable of such invention should not be wasted in a Lowrian cell. Who knows? Perhaps she can be persuaded to redirect her ambitions."

"Of course, Councilor," Masterchiv Rathbone said reluctantly before bowing to those present and disappearing across the lawn.

"Now, Prince Cornelius," Cllr. Perda simpered as she turned to him. "I wish to speak with you about some of the contestants, namely the bravery and integrity demonstrated by Dame Hera Claustrom."

". . . What?" Connor had been watching Masterchiv Rathbone's retreating figure thoughtfully and pulled his mind as if through water back to the conversation.

"Why yes," Cllr. Perda continued, "it must have taken great strength to raise her concerns to one such as yourself, and greater strength still to do so against those with such favorable reputations." Connor began to respond but Cllr. Perda spoke over him, "and such compassion she demonstrated toward the poor Devon girl once her egg had been revealed to be damaged."

"I . . . suppose," Connor replied, unsure what Cllr. Perda expected of him.

"Gretchen and I were just discussing how beautifully she embodied both the strength and compassion you spoke to earlier today. Of course you would have noticed. In any case, you must be exhausted after such a day. I know I am looking forward to a better night's sleep tonight. Please excuse me, Your Grace. Good evening. Come, Gretchen." She dropped to one knee, rose, and followed Masterchiv Rathbone across the grass. Cllr. Dilmont mirrored her actions and fell into step with her.

"Right," Connor said quietly to himself. He scanned the garden idly. Many of the guests had similar notions and had gone to sleep, or else were heading back toward the castle. The few stragglers had paired off in quiet corners or revolved slowly on the dance floor. The band played a dreamy, languid melody. It drifted like a lullaby among the guttering lanterns. He saw Dame Glowra walk quickly out of the hedged gardens, Ms. Bishop following shortly after, their brisk pace juxtaposed with the molasses-like movements of the remaining guests. Jacqueline emerged last, quite separate from the other two and much more carefully. He frowned and looked away.

His father was watching him and followed his gaze. The corners of his mouth twitched in an almost smile. "If I were you, boy," he said gruffly, "I would work on tucking my heart a little farther up my sleeve. Especially during this contest."

Connor worked at a reply, but none came to him.

His father clapped him on the back and held him by the shoulder as he began walking with him toward the castle. "But Cllr. Perda is right: we will be of no use to anyone tired. Come, we have a long day ahead of us tomorrow." Connor allowed himself to be steered into the light of the castle while his mind continued to race.

"Father," he said before the two men parted ways toward their separate rooms, "when you meet the two criminals, I would like to attend."

The King smiled proudly. "Of course, son. We will deal with them together."

"Thank you," he said before bidding his father good night and heading toward his rooms. He felt emboldened. A plan in motion. He had to know. He had to find out what had happened to Jacs. He had to know if she was one of them.

23

WHAT LURKS IN THE SHADOWS

The tension in the bedchamber the next morning hung about everyone's shoulders. Jacs and Amber did their best to liven the mood. Amber, although unsure exactly what had happened to cause the coldness between Anya and Lena, had chalked it up to nerves and attempted to engage first one, then the other in polite conversation.

"So, Anya, do you think you will get to put your floristry skills to use today? I heard you used moss to help Lena out yesterday," she said cheerfully.

"That was Jacqueline's moss," Anya replied, pulling on her boots as though trying to push her foot through the sole.

"Oh," Amber paused for her to continue, then pressed on when it was apparent she would not. "Well, Lena, do you have any skills you hope to put to use today?"

"No," Lena replied curtly, brushing out her hair in the oval mirror.

"Lena, didn't you say the other day that you're a good swimmer?" Jacs supplied, Amber shooting her a grateful grin.

"Yes, but that does not mean I want to get wet today," Lena said, pinning her hair in place.

"Heaven forbid Dame Glowra ruin her shoes," Anya muttered. Lena shot her a withering look. A number of footsteps hurried past their door.

"I think we should go down for breakfast," Jacs said slowly. "Lena, let's see if they have eggs again today," she added, shooting a pointed look at Amber.

Amber's eyes grew wide, and she nodded knowingly. "And, Anya, hold on a minute, I want your opinion on something."

Jacs heard Amber inquiring about the merits of boots versus slippers for the next task as the door swung shut behind them.

"Well, that was painful," Jacs commented frankly as they turned a corner toward the room they had had their breakfast in the day before.

"What was?" Lena replied innocently. Jacs just stared at her, eyebrows raised. Lena met her glare for a moment, then looked away and admitted, "Oh, so you noticed."

For her friend's sake, she bit off the sarcastic comment that rose to her lips and instead simply said, "Yes. Are you okay?"

Lena blinked rapidly and shook her head. "I don't want to talk about it right now," she said quietly, reining herself in with visible effort. Jacs nodded. They were walking behind Verona and

Fawn, who had just emerged from their bedchambers deep in conversation.

"Can you believe my brother thinking he could try out to be Queen?" Fawn was saying, "The sweetheart. Poor dear came running up to me the day before I left wearing one of my gowns. Of course it was far too big for him, he only comes up to my knee."

"The darling!" cooed Verona.

Fawn continued, "So the little duck comes to me with these big baby blues and says, Can I be Queen after you?" The two women burst into delighted giggles.

"He didn't? Oh, what did you tell him?" Verona asked earnestly.

"Of course I didn't have the heart to tell him men aren't fit to rule whole Queendoms. What kind of beast of a sister would I be to say that?" Fawn sighed.

"There's no harm in letting the boy dream. What is he . . . six? He's got time to learn." Verona said as the two disappeared around the corner ahead.

"Okay, we don't have to talk about it," Jacs said quietly, picking up where they had left off, "but know that I'm here when you change your mind. Or even if you just want a hug." Lena nodded gratefully and said nothing. They walked the rest of the way in silence.

Jacs heard Anya's incredulous voice behind them. "Slippers do not have better grip! Honestly, you're a knight, you of all people should know that."

With breakfast eaten and, to Jacs's relief, kept down by Lena today, all nine remaining contestants rode on horseback behind the King and Prince toward the next task. Jacs was astride the same docile mare from the day before. The little mare—Peggy was her name— had seemed excited to see Jacs again. Although, Jacs reasoned, she had brought Peggy an apple from breakfast. It was still nice to receive such a warm greeting. Unlike the one she received from Cornelius. Jacs had felt her face burn when the Prince had greeted her with a stiff "Good morning, Courtier Daidala." She had refused to look at Amber, who she felt rather than saw give her a questioning look as he strode off without another word. Jacs rode between Lena and Anya to avoid having to share any details.

Now, she glanced at his back miserably. *Stop it*, she thought, *what else did you expect? You can't have it both ways.* To distract herself, she played with Connor's ring on the chain around her neck and looked at the thickening forest. The ground sloped away beneath her horse's hooves, and she instinctively leaned back. They were heading downhill.

"A lower part of the Upper Realm," Jacs mused. Peggy flicked her ears back briefly and bobbed her head against the bit. Jacs tightened her grip on the reins and ducked out of the way of some low-hanging branches. The trees were getting thicker.

The horses now rode in single file and warnings of "Branch!" could be heard down the line. Moss hung like fluffy green tendrils from the fern-covered branches. Tree trunks were smothered by crawling vines and large, flat, disclike fungi.

Anya rode ahead of her and stopped briefly to reach up and scratch the underside of one of these mushrooms with her fingernail. She marked a small happy face and turned to grin at Jacs, "*Ganoderma lucidum!*" she exclaimed happily as her horse, a speckled gray mare named Stogie, started off again down the hill.

"What?" Jacs called back.

"It's a type of fungus. You can tell it is because you can mark the underside like that. It helps with a lot of things, like stress reduction."

Jacs laughed. "Well, I think we all could have used some of that in our omelets this morning."

Anya ducked under a moss-covered branch. "Branch! Yeah, well, maybe next time." She chuckled. Jacs heard Lena clear her throat behind her. They continued on.

Finally the trees began to thin. Sunlight streamed cheerfully in long, triumphant rays through the canopy. It felt like a stranger in this dark, damp world. The horses emerged suddenly from the tree line into a clearing that resembled a sunken bowl. Thick, lush grasses covered the amphitheater like fur. Where they stood, the rim was littered with small boulders. The mossy boulders became larger the farther into the center they went, until they emerged from the grass like small huts.

Clustered together in the middle of the clearing were three cave entrances leading down into the large, jagged boulders. They gaped like toothless maws, waiting.

The horses arranged themselves in a semicircle at the edge of the trees. The King and the Prince moved to stand in the center of their group in front of the caverns. Dismounting from his own horse, the King motioned for them all to do the same and step closer. The air hung thick and heavy around them and it seemed even the King was nervous to speak too loudly in the stillness.

A number of attending servants hurried to collect the horses from the contestants. Jacs stood alongside Amber, Lena, Anya, Verona, Fawn, Hera, Andromeda, and Shane, facing the King and Prince Cornelius. She reached out her hands and held Lena and Amber's, feeling reassuring squeezes from both sides.

The Prince stepped forward. "Good morning," he said quietly, nodding to each of them. His eyes lingered a moment on Jacs. The trees seemed to swallow his words. "Today you stand on the threshold of the second task. Each of you demonstrating your right to be here, your right to prove yourself our next Queen."

The women stirred around Jacs like leaves swept up in a breeze.

"Yesterday," the Prince continued, "you were all able to demonstrate your ability to balance strength and compassion. You were not told how to do this, simply given the tools to show us. Today, you will be given a riddle to help you with the task. Whether you choose to solve the riddle or not is up to you, but the answer holds a clue that will assist your completion of the task ahead."

There was a soft murmur among the contestants that the Prince waited to subside before speaking again.

"You will also be given a lantern. Each lantern has a one-hour burn time. I can assure you it will not be enough to complete the task. Consider this—" he paused again "—today's task will focus on a contestant's ability to demonstrate intelligence. The ability to think clearly and critically is a trait Queen Ariel had in spades and is a trait important for any Queen to possess. No matter the scenario, she was able to keep calm and work through any problem. We will be looking for a contestant's ability to act with calculated reason despite the pressure their situation puts on them."

Jacs felt her peers shift uneasily beside her. She thought back to Prince Cornelius's story about how his mother had talked her way out of a highwaywoman ambush and almost smiled. Looking past the Prince, she took in the gaping mouths of the mossy caverns. She counted three entrances and wondered what lay beyond the shadows. Unable to describe it, she felt a coldness tugging on her mind, on her heart. As though the caves were calling to her. She glanced at the others to see if they sensed it too, but each contestant looked determinedly straight ahead.

The Prince indicated to a waiting servant to hand out the lanterns. The glen was silent while these were distributed. Jacs weighed hers in her hand; it was a simple black oil-fed lantern. It reminded her of a little house with four long windows. The windows were filled with horn rather than glass and Jacs knew it would not let off much light once inside the cave.

The lanterns were not lit yet, and she supposed they would only be lit once the task began.

Once each contestant had their lantern, the Prince continued. "You see before you three caves. These connect with a labyrinth that spans leagues under the earth. Three of you will enter at a time through her own separate entrance. It does not matter who enters first as the following groups will enter at regular intervals afterward and each contestant's time will be recorded. It does not matter which entrance you use as they all feed into the same labyrinth. Your task today is to find your way through these caves to the other side of the catacombs, where we will be waiting. Are there any questions?"

He paused again. No one said anything. He gestured for another servant holding a velvet pouch. She rushed forward and began handing a small roll of parchment to each of the contestants.

"These contain the riddle I mentioned, and the clue to escaping the labyrinth. You may open them once you are inside the caves.

"For their exceptional performance in the task yesterday, the following contestants will enter the caves first: Courtier Anya Bishop, Courtier Lena Glowra, and Courtier Jacqueline Daidala." He paused as Jacs and the others stepped forward, then bid them follow him. He walked Anya toward the entrance on the left, lit her lantern, and positioned her at the mouth of the cave. Lena was positioned in front of the cave in the middle, and Jacs in front of the cave on the right. The Prince busied himself with his flint as he lit her lantern and would not look at her.

Standing in the mouth of the cold, dark cave, Jacs touched his hand lightly as he made to leave. "Thank you," she whispered.

He looked at her then, and the tension left his face. "Good luck," he whispered back and gave her hand a small squeeze.

Returning to his place beside the King, he announced, "First group, begin!"

As if she had been pushed between the shoulders, Jacs started forward without looking back. A soft purple glow shone from the corner of the entrance. The purple scry crystal cast its sinister eye over her as Jacs stepped into the dark.

She wondered at how a glowing object could cast no light on the rock surrounding it. It almost seemed to suck the light from its surroundings rather than emit it. *There goes that backup plan,* Jacs thought. She had had a notion to use the crystals as a light source when her lantern ran out.

As she stepped into the cavern, the light from Jacs's little lantern barely reached the surrounding walls. What she could see was wet and slimy. The floor was a mixture of gravel and large slabs of rock interrupted by little streams. She could hear an incessant *drip, drip, plink* echoing all around her. She raised her lantern to the ceiling and saw what appeared to be a tapestry of stringy cobwebs and worms. She shuddered and lowered the lantern. The cold seemed to settle into her bones, and she had to fight a feeling of claustrophobia that began to well in her stomach.

Taking two deep breaths, she shakily unrolled her parchment to read the riddle.

I have keys without locks,
And I rest without sleep,
I have waves without tides,
These bars, no thief will keep.

Jacs smiled, the riddle calming her nerves. Reading the riddle over twice more, she put it back in her pocket. She held her lantern high and carefully started to make her way further into the depths of the cave. Her mind began to work.

It's all in the words, she thought, stepping between two boulders, *and each word must have a double meaning. By comparing the key with a lock, I automatically have to think about that kind of key, but it can't be that kind of key because it has to fit in with all the other pieces.* She knelt down and crawled under a low-hanging crag, stood up on the other side, and kept going.

What else has keys? Jacs racked her brain while trying to ignore the oppressive silence in the caves filled only by the steady dripping. *Keys, maps have keys, puzzles have keys, pianos have keys, it could be a metaphorical key like the key to someone's heart, or the key idea in an argument.* She decided to come back to the key.

The floor was broken up with a number of streams with stepping-stones spaced at varying intervals across them. Gripping the handle of her lantern tighter, she jumped lightly from stone to stone.

I'm not sure about the rest part. Okay, waves, she thought. *Waves could refer to sound waves, or shock waves, waves of emotion, waves of nausea.* She steadied herself on a wobbly rock, then jumped to the next. *And bars could refer to a counter, a tavern, a bar of soap, a sandbar in a river, a . . . a . . . a bar of music.*

Jacs paused, a slow smile fluttering across her face. *Hang on, music has keys, and rests, and waves.* She landed on the last stepping-stone and began to pant as the ground sloped uphill. She shifted her lantern to her splinted arm. Wincing with pain, she used her good arm to pull herself up. *That must be it!* she thought. "Music!" she said aloud. Her triumphant cry was muffled by the damp dark.

Jacs felt a stone form in the pit of her stomach. *But how does that help me?*

Still trying to puzzle out the supposedly helpful clue, she moved further into the darkness. It was not long before she came across a fork in her path and realized with a jolt that she would also have to find her way out of this labyrinth. *One puzzle wasn't enough, apparently,* she mused. A crystal glowed with a significant lack of luminescence in the center of the fork.

"Well, you're no help," Jacs said with annoyance. She did not want to take the wrong path, but was painfully aware that she did not know what the right path should look like. *How is music supposed to help with this?* she thought angrily. *Should I just sing the cave a song?* Surrounded by cold, wet stone, she could not think of anything she would rather do less. On a whim, she chose the path on the right.

The farther Jacs walked into the earth, the less hopeful she became. She could not hear anyone, nor could she see any farther in front of her than the little circle of light the lantern gave off. She would walk first uphill, then downhill. She crossed streams that all began to look similar. Once she came across a dead end barred by rocks, only to turn around and take a different route that led to the edge of a deep underground lake. She searched the shoreline for another path and had to retrace her steps when she could not find a way across.

Curiously, a small wooden boat lay on its side under an outcropping of rock, but Jacs did not like the idea of sailing into a void. She decided to keep her feet on dryish land.

Jacs quickly lost track of time, and every new fork in her path brought new frustration. She began scratching arrows into the rock at each junction to mark which ways she had already been. This appeared to help, until she turned a fresh corner and came across one of her arrows. She had been sure she had been walking away from it.

Jacs's thoughts gradually darkened, subtly at first, a nagging tickle in the back of her mind. Then slowly she began to realize that she may never find the exit. She would be down here forever. The crystals would be her only companions. The coldness she had felt in the glade crept into her mind like a thief. Surely, she should have come across another contestant by now. Even Hera would be welcome company. And who would care to come find her? How long would it take them to find her? To find her body? She shook her head to rid her mind of the images that had forced their way in and gripped her lantern tighter.

To keep herself calm, Jacs thought about the riddle. It has to be music, but what does that mean? Gingerly, she eased herself down a slimy boulder, and the world slid from under her. She lost her footing, splinted arm flailing uselessly, lantern dropping and bouncing down and away from her. The clangs echoing off the stone walls.

Jacs landed hard on her tailbone and slid the rest of the way down the rock to land at the bottom in a shallow pool of water. A short distance away, her lantern lay on its side and flickered feebly. She hurried to pick it up, her fingers grazing the handle when it spluttered and went out.

Everything went dark. Jacs's world became the sound of water trickling endlessly and her own thumping heart. A voice, her father's voice, whispered around her in the dark, *I'm right behind you.*

Panic welled inside her and she pulled herself out of the pool, clapping her hands tight over her ears. The voice couldn't be real. Her father was dead.

Sitting with the cold seeping through her body, gravel and pebbles beneath her, and an unforgiving tunnel of endless earth around her, she felt fear pierce her heart. Her breath became ragged, and she lowered her hands from her ears to cover her mouth. The voice continued to echo and reverberate softly around her, but she would not listen. She could figure this out. She forced herself to take stock.

She was alone. In the dark.

With no way out.

"Easy girl, easy," Jacs repeated to herself. "Easy, you need to figure this out. Despair is a pit that goes nowhere." Her father's words came to her in a flash, and she felt a warmth flicker in her heart. Suddenly she was five years old again, sitting on his lap, tears streaming down her face and a broken toy wagon in her hands. "We just need to fix the wheel," he was saying, "and we can't do that if we're sitting around feeling sorry for ourselves, now, can we?"

Jacs smiled at the memory and slowed her breathing. *Okay*, she thought, *what had Cornelius said? The lantern was not supposed to last us the entire journey anyway. I should not need the lantern. The clue is music. It has to be.* She rubbed her face with her unsplinted arm. *Music*, she thought. *Music, music, music.*

The dripping water was enough to drive her mad. *But do I want them to find me singing to myself in a cave?* Jacs turned that scenario over in her mind and sighed. *Well, the crystals don't transmit sound*, she thought, thinking about the silent mirrors and basins of water used for viewing, and there's no one around to look foolish to. Taking a deep breath, she cleared her throat, closed her eyes, and began to sing a nonsense song she had heard as a child. Quietly at first, then louder as she attempted to drown the panic that kept threatening to creep into her heart. Determined to keep the coldness at bay.

For want of a nail the shoe was lost
For want of a shoe the horse was lost
For want of a horse the rider was lost
For want of a rider the battle was lost
For want of a battle the Queendom was lost
And all for the want of a horseshoe nail

Something illuminated against her eyelids after the first few lines. Jacs opened her eyes and gasped. When she stopped singing, she was plunged into darkness. Tentatively, she began again, and saw to her amazement the ceiling of worms in their webs begin to glow. They shone like beacons of hope, running the length of the ceiling like someone had drawn the answer to the maze up there for her to see.

Her ditty became her battle song as she stood up, picked up the now useless lantern, and began marching down the tunnel, following the line of glowworms.

"For want of a nail the shoe was lost," Jacs sang as she slid between two narrow rocks. "For want of a shoe the horse was lost." She was smiling now. "For want of a horse the rider was lost!" At the next fork in the tunnel, she noticed that one pathway glowed more brightly than the other and followed the brighter trail. "For want of a rider the battle was lost!" Again, at a junction of three paths, she noticed one path shone brightest and followed her pseudo-stars.

"For want of a battle the Queendom was lost." Jacs was walking on a narrow trail above another underground lake with a spring in her step. She noticed idly that there were fewer crystals dotting this part of the tunnel, "And all for the want of a horseshoe na—"

It all happened in a flash.

As Jacs turned a corner, hugging the rock wall on one side, trying to ignore the still, black, bottomless lake that stretched off into the darkness on her other side, she came abreast with a small alcove in the rock wall and was suddenly aware of a presence beside her. She turned and saw a hooded figure step forward and push her hard in the chest. The shock ran through her and she felt herself stepping backward into thin air. She folded, feet scrambling for purchase, arms flailing and grasping at nothing, and fell.

Down, down she fell toward the wet, black nothingness that awaited below. Her scream was lost completely in its depths.

It all came rushing back to her, the memory flooding her mind as Jacs hit the surface of the frigid water and sank into the icy abyss.

Get to the bank, I'm right behind you. Her father's voice echoed in her ears. She felt the weight of the heavy coat. Felt it drag her down. Looked up and expected to see the ice stretching away above her, her father's fists hammering on its faceted surface. But there was nothing, just blackness. She was not wearing a coat. Her father was not coming to save her.

She kicked up. Hard. Felt the strength of a body that was older than the one in her memory, stronger. She was not a child. Her splinted arm clung to her side, reminding her of the present. Desperately she reached up and pulled water through her one good arm, her legs kicking out again. Her lungs burned. Her father's voice reverberated in her skull, calling to her, *I'm right behind you,* quieter now. She pushed it away.

Stroke.

Kick.

Almost there.

Jacs broke through the surface and sucked air greedily into her lungs. Warm tears mixed with the cold water on her cheeks. She swam toward where she had fallen and found a steep rock wall rising away from her shaking fingers. Treading water for a moment, she forced her breathing to slow.

Panic boiled in her chest. Rolled and writhed through her veins. The darkness pressed in on her as she clung to the rockface. There was someone above her who wanted . . . what? To kill her? That seemed a clear possibility. She stayed as quiet as possible, straining to hear anything from the path above, silent sobs racking her body, making her shudder more violently than the cold.

And still, that empty coldness pressed on her mind, weighed on her heart.

A lantern light flickered on the ripples from where she'd first landed and swept the water around it. Apparently satisfied, the light left the water, and Jacs heard footsteps make their way back toward where she had come from.

Keeping the rock wall on her right side, Jacs swam in the opposite direction and followed beneath the path to the other side of the lake. She tried to ignore the cold, the icy tendrils spreading upward from fingers and toes, threatening to still her limbs. She numbed her mind, forced herself to focus on each deliberate movement. *Kick, push, breathe, again.* Thoughts of what could be lying in wait below her teased the peripheries of her mind and she forced them out. *Kick, push, breathe, again.* Something brushed past her ribs and she bit her lip to keep from screaming. *Kick, push, breathe, again.*

Jacs clung to the facts of her senses. Her imagination wrestled against the sudden cage she had forced it into, waiting to interpret a sudden splash off to her left, a softer patch in the rock surface, or a flicker of light far ahead of her. The memory of her coat, her father, the ice prison threatened to consume her. His voice calling to her, welcoming her home. A part of her desperately wanted to listen.

To sink down to where he was. Safe at last.

Get to the bank, he had said. Sobbing, Jacs pushed herself onward.

Jacs finally felt the bottom of the lake beneath her feet, and she crawled onto the shore. Panting and shaking, she made to stand up when a hand clapped over her mouth and a familiar voice whispered in her ear. "Don't scream, it's Amber."

Breathing heavily through her nose, Jacs nodded shakily, and Amber let go of her.

"What was that for?" Jacs whispered fiercely.

"I didn't want you to scream and give away our position," Amber whispered back.

"What?"

"Shush, come here." Amber pulled Jacs to her feet and across the shore. Jacs noticed she had three sides of her lantern covered with a piece of fabric, allowing only a small amount of light out the front window.

"And you, singing away at the top of your lungs. Honestly. I'm just glad you popped back up," Amber scolded.

Jacs didn't reply, hugging her arms around herself, still trying to shake the memories that had seized her in the dark. Absently, she drew her necklace with Connor's ring from under her tunic and brushed her thumb across the engraving.

"Hello-o? Jacqueline, are you all right?" Amber peered closer at Jacs's face.

"I'm fine," Jacs said quickly, letting the ring fall to her chest, "just cold."

"What in Goddess's name were you singing for?" Amber asked.

"I did it for the glowworms. My lantern died. The riddle! Music! That was the point," Jacs whispered defensively.

"Yeah, yeah. But the downside of that is they know where you are. Although my lantern probably doesn't have much juice left." As if on cue, Amber's lantern flickered and died, plunging them into darkness again.

They both swore. Jacs was impressed by the creativity of Amber's profanity.

"Forget that for now, sit down," Amber said hurriedly. "I'm glad you're okay," she added as an afterthought.

"Thanks," Jacs replied. "Amber, what's going on?" Jacs noticed that they were huddled in an alcove, and she could not see a crystal from where they were sitting.

"Look." Amber pulled something out of her belt and whispered, "Lena Glowra." In an instant, Lena's image appeared on the surface of the mirror Amber was holding. She was sitting alone in the dark, arms wrapped tight around her knees, with her hands pressed firmly against her ears.

Although Jacs knew the tunnel would be dark, the crystal outlined Lena's figure in an eerie light for them to observe in the mirror.

"Oh, Lena," Jacs moaned. "Wait, why do you have this?" she asked Amber.

Amber shrugged in the glow radiating from the mirror. "I figure it's always good to know what your competition is doing. Especially after that stunt you said Hera pulled. And it was never technically forbidden in the rules so . . . ta-da!"

Jacs looked again at the image of her friend. "She didn't figure out the riddle. Amber, we have to help her!"

"Exactly, and not only that, you may not have noticed, but there appears to be someone down here intent on sabotaging the contestants. I only escaped because I heard the coward coming. You, obviously, were not so lucky.

"Lena here had her lantern stolen. Not by a hood, by another contestant. That Shane woman. She was waiting for her; poor duck didn't stand a chance. It was awful."

Jacs felt a cold anger stir in her stomach. She took a breath and asked, "How's Anya?"

In response, Amber said, "Anya Bishop" into the mirror. The surface clouded and Lena's distressed image was replaced by Anya's calm one. Her lantern was hanging uselessly in her hand, extinguished, but she must have been humming because while Lena's image had been a glowing outline, Anya was lit up under the glowworm trail.

"Okay," Jacs said, "okay, she's fine for now. We need to help Lena. Is there any way to tell where she is with this thing?"

Amber thought for a moment. "I'm not sure, but there must be, because how else would they find us if we get stuck and need rescuing?"

"Exactly," said Jacs, hopeful. "Try this." She moved closer to the mirror and said, "Find Lena Glowra." The surface clouded again and was replaced with the one they had seen before of Lena. This time, around the edge of the mirror, a light spun around and around until suddenly it stopped.

Jacs looked at it and then looked up at Amber in confusion. Amber took back the mirror excitedly and rotated it first clockwise, then counterclockwise.

The little light on the edge rotated around the mirror as it moved but stayed in the same spot in space.

"It's like a compass!" Amber whispered triumphantly. "Good thinking, Jacqueline! Let's go."

They stood up and, holding hands, followed the little beam of light guiding their way toward their friend.

Unfortunately, the light was not enough to allow them to see much in the dark, but they dared not sing too loudly and give away their position. After a few stubbed toes, however, each agreed to take turns singing while the other kept her eye out for any suspicious movement. Jacs was impressed with the knight's calculating eye and fluid movement through such difficult terrain. She commented on it once and saw Amber grin. "I've already got a beau, sorry."

Jacs laughed and playfully shoved her friend. "That's not what I meant by it."

"Speaking of," interjected Amber, "what was with the frosty Prince this morning? Did you two have a row or something?"

"Not exactly . . . It's complicated," Jacs said hesitantly as they took a left fork in the tunnel.

"It's not as if we don't have time," Amber said mildly.

Jacs sighed, eyes flickering around the cave. They passed a crystal and Jacs noticed the next one up ahead. "True, and actually it really isn't that complicated. We kissed."

"You kissed?" Amber began excitedly, then frowned.

"What?" Jacs asked, noticing the change.

Amber seemed unsure how to start and took a moment to gather her words.

"Well," she began, "that just seems . . . quick. You two aren't courting, are you?"

"No," Jacs said.

Amber bit her lip. "Now, I'm not saying this is the case. But," she hesitated, "I think you should be careful with that."

"With what?" Jacs felt the color rise in her cheeks.

"He's the Prince, right?"

"Obviously."

"And he gains more power as King rather than Royal Advisor, right?" Amber said patiently.

"Sure."

"And he can only become King if he marries the Queen. Do you see where I'm going with this?"

"No," Jacs said defensively, they both stepped around a particularly craggy section of the path.

"Jacqueline, you are currently outshining the rest of the contestants in this contest. You saved dozens of people in the explosion, and you became a Courtier in the first task. You're a likely bet to become Queen," Amber said, still in that same gentle tone.

"So, you think he's pretending to be interested in me because he thinks I'll be Queen?" Jacs asked hotly.

"No, I'm not saying that. We just shouldn't ignore it as a possibility," Amber replied.

Jacs felt the guilt and embarrassment from last night resurface. A part of her shrank away from the idea; she had made the move to kiss him, after all. But Amber's logic planted a seed of doubt in her heart. Shaking her head, she said in a clipped tone, "Well, it didn't go any further; it won't go any further. That's why he was cold this morning. I let him know that I wanted to focus completely on the contest. I was getting too . . . distracted."

Amber turned to smile mischievously at her. "Distra—"

"Look out!" Jacs cried. A hooded figure stepped out from behind a boulder and grabbed Amber in a headlock. Instinctively, Jacs threw herself at the attacker. All three of them toppled into the cave wall and fell painfully in a heap. Each struggled to stand up. The hooded figure became tangled in their robes and the two women stood first.

"Son of a mutt!" Amber growled. In one fluid movement, Amber knocked the hooded figure further off balance and shot her hand toward the now prone figure. Her fingers wrapped around their throat.

Jacs stepped back and cradled her injured arm, poking at a sore spot on her wrist delicately.

"What do you want?" Amber demanded. She shook the figure and Jacs heard their breath catch. Jacs reached to push the deep purple fabric of the hood from their face. She registered briefly the face of a boy about her age. His hair was short and black, his eyes filled with hate. He spat in her face. Jacs flinched but did not let go of his hood.

"What do you want?" Jacs echoed.

"You think either of you are worthy of the crown?" he hissed. "A soldier and a peasant?" He kicked out and attempted to twist free.

In the sudden silence, the glowworms extinguished their light, and the trio were plunged into darkness. Jacs heard Amber cry out and felt the fabric disappear from beneath her fingers. She hummed hurriedly but by the time her eyes adjusted to the new light, she saw his cloak whip around the corner.

Amber was coughing on the ground beside her, clutching her stomach. "The rat winded me," she managed after a time. Jacs looked again to where he had vanished and helped her friend to her feet. Her brow furrowed. They consulted the mirror again and pressed on.

"Lena!" Jacs cried with relief.

They rounded a corner to see Lena huddled in a tight ball, head between her knees, hands pressed tightly over her ears, just as she had been in the mirror. She had not heard them approach. Jacs shot a worried look at Amber, whose face had paled. They rushed over and crouched beside her.

"Lena?" Jacs said softly. Amber continued humming to maintain the glowworms' light.

Lena was muttering fearfully to herself and did not respond.

Jacs leaned closer and heard her repeating, "No, no, no. Not again, not again, never again. I said n-no."

"Lena?" Jacs tried a third time and tentatively touched her friend's shoulder.

The reaction was immediate. Lena shot backwards as if burned and screamed, "NO! Don't touch me." Her eyes were wild and did not seem to see Jacs or Amber. Did not seem to notice the light from the glowworms.

Jacs held her hands palms up and began speaking in a soft low voice, "Lena, Lena, it's me, Jacqueline. Your friend. I'm not here to hurt you, and I won't touch you again. This is Amber. Remember Amber? We're here to help. You're okay, you're going to be okay. We won't let anyone hurt you."

Recognition slowly stole into her eyes. Lena glanced from Amber to Jacs and covered her mouth with a shaking hand. Gasping back sobs, she struggled to her feet, and fell painfully into Jacs's arms.

"Oof!" Jacs freed her good arm and stroked Lena's hair. "Shhh, you're all right," she said softly.

Lena shuddered. "I could see it," she whispered, "it was like I was there. It was like I was back there. I couldn't stop it. It was happening all over again." Lena hiccupped and it was a time before her sobs subsided. Jacs held her tightly. Finally Lena lifted her head from Jacs's shoulder, took a step back, wiped her eyes, and smiled wetly at the two of them. "You have n-no idea h-how pleased I am t-to s-s-see you," she managed, moving to Amber and hugging her too.

"Sh-Shane attacked me. She st-stole my lantern and left me here," Lena said.

"I know, I saw. I'm so sorry that happened," Amber said soothingly, giving her a squeeze. "But we found you! So let's all get out of here—this place is seriously depressing."

"You saw?" Lena asked. "How?"

Amber showed her the mirror and she and Jacs took turns humming and explaining all that had happened. Lena's eyes grew wide, and she seized the mirror.

"Anya Bishop," she said urgently and watched as the surface clouded, and the image of Anya filled the mirror. She lit up as before and appeared alone in the tunnel. Lena slumped back, relieved. Then sat bolt upright as she looked at the image more closely. "She's hurt!" Lena gasped.

"What?" Amber scrambled to look too.

Jacs peered over Amber's shoulder. The bounce in Anya's step she had before was gone. Now, she was limping slightly and clutching her side.

"We have to find her!" Lena said, her eyes wide as she looked at Jacs. "Jacqueline, she's bleeding."

"She's going to be okay, she's strong," Jacs soothed. "We can find her like we found you, although she might beat us out of here." Her teeth were chattering, she was still soaking wet, and now that they had stopped was suddenly very aware of the cold. Lena seemed to relax a little.

Amber looked at Jacs worriedly, "Let's keep going. With three of us, we will probably be safe to sing to those glowworms."

"Sing?" Lena asked.

"The riddle," Jacs supplied. "The clue was music. If you sing to the glowworms, they light up and show you the way out."

Lena giggled, "I would have never gotten that."

"That's why we're here," Amber said with a grin. "Now let's get out of here before a hood finds us."

"A hood?" Lena asked.

"Yeah, there's a bunch of creeps in hoods sabotaging the contestants. You haven't encountered one?" Amber asked.

"The purple hoods? But they're here to help us, aren't they?" Lena said, bewildered.

Jacs and Amber stared at her.

"Yes, I tripped early on and my lantern went out, then all of a sudden there's a person in a purple hood right there relighting it for me." Lena shifted uncomfortably, "I was hoping they'd come back after Shane stole my lantern, but they never did."

"What? No. That can't be right. One pushed me off a cliff, one tried to sneak up on Amber, and one attacked both of us before we found you," Jacs said.

None of them seemed to know what to do with that information.

"This task just keeps getting weirder," Amber muttered.

"Should we check how the other contestants are doing?" ventured Jacs.

"Sure. To check they're safe," Amber said.

Lena passed back the mirror and Jacs said, "Hera Claustrom." Unlike the other times, the mirror remained black for a while. Jacs remembered the longer stretches of tunnel without crystals and waited. She was about to say the name again when it clouded over and revealed Hera walking alone in the gloom. She was approaching a fork in the tunnels. Jacs saw her lips moving and guessed she was singing to herself. She did not appear to notice the hooded figure following a few paces behind.

Jacs's grip on the mirror tightened and she looked up to see worry etched into Amber and Lena's faces. Her heart dropped. "Oh no," she moaned, "they've got Hera too—hang on." She watched as the hooded figure closed the distance between them, reached out their arm, and tapped Hera on the shoulder.

Hera jumped and spun around. Her song cut off, and she was plunged into darkness, the crystals picking up her glowing outline. Jacs watched, confused, as Hera's silhouette pushed the figure away from her in the darkness. The hooded figure glanced at the crystal, held up their hands in what looked like an apology, and pointed at one of the tunnels that veered off to the right in front of Hera. They jabbed their finger a few more times at the tunnel, then turned and walked down the passageway they had come, quickly disappearing from the view of the crystals.

A moment later, Hera was illuminated once again as she resumed her song. Clutching her chest, she looked about her, then hesitantly began walking down the tunnel the figure had pointed to.

"What?" the three women looked at each other. Not one of them understood what they had just seen. There was a loud clatter down the tunnel behind them and they all jumped.

"So, they helped Lena and now Hera?" Jacs frowned and said, almost to herself, "They're helping the Dames."

Amber looked uneasy. "Let's just get out of here," she whispered. The other two nodded in agreement.

"Find Anya Bishop," Jacs said into the mirror. The lights spun around the frame as they had for Lena and stopped to point back the way they had come. Jacs saw the same determination reflected in the faces of Amber and Lena as they set off again.

24

BROUGHT TO LIGHT

"We will have to disqualify Courtier Lena Glowra. She has failed to demonstrate the traits sought for in this task. She has just been rescued by two other contestants," Cllr. Gretchen Dilmont said firmly as she sat poised above the mirror and parchment. There were murmurs of agreement from the other Councilors, and Connor made a mark on his own parchment. The horses whickered and continued grazing in the glade a short distance from where Connor and his father sat. A small stream could be heard a short way off where it fed into the solitary exit to the labyrinth. The cave was smaller than the entrances had been. It was ringed with ferns and grasses that waved lazily in the breeze, ready to welcome the victorious contestants. Connor sat with his father at a small table as they had done the day before. Today they did not bother with a game of chess. Connor turned back to his mirror. He was cycling through each contestant and making notes of their actions. His father leaned back in his chair with his arms across his middle and his eyes closed.

"You could have designed shorter tasks, boy," he commented.

Connor chose to ignore him. He finished scribbling his latest note under Verona's name. "Father, who set up the crystals throughout this course?" he asked without looking up.

"Perkins, I think," King Aren responded.

"There are a lot more holes than there were yesterday, there are huge stretches of the course that contestants keep disappearing into," Connor muttered.

"The poor lad had to set up most of them by himself and you know how dreary those tunnels get. Does things to your mind. We're lucky he came out the other side." The King stroked his moustache and stood up. "Excuse me a moment," he said, before walking toward the refreshment table that had been set up for their benefit.

So far, Chiv. Andromeda Turner was the only contestant to have emerged from the tunnels. She was currently sitting next to the stream in the sunshine. She had been white as a sheet coming out of the tunnel, whispering of moving shadows, and was only now starting to get some color back in her cheeks. She spoke softly to Master Epione, who sat beside her.

The other three members of the Council were also present and sitting around similar small tables. However, Connor could not fail to notice that they checked their mirrors far less regularly today than they had yesterday, and Cllr. Portia Stewart even appeared to have dozed off. Cllr. Gretchen Dilmont remained vigilant, and Lena's was the second disqualification she had noted that afternoon. The first had been Dame Fawn Lupine.

"She refused to even open her riddle. By ignoring the advice given to her, she shows an arrogance unbefitting a Queen, and—ah, there you go, her lantern has been extinguished—dangerous. Such a waste, and a shame to lose a Dame. Disqualified," she decreed, as the other Councilors studied their notes and one by one agreed. Connor and the King followed suit. Connor beckoned for one of the guard pairs to approach and instructed, "Dame Fawn Lupine will most likely need to be helped from the caves. Make sure someone goes in to fetch her and help her back to the castle." The guards left immediately.

Beyond Courtier Glowra and Dame Lupine, two others had also been disqualified. Ms. Verona Julliard had not made it far into the caves before running back out again. She had taken her horse back to the castle with a few parting words. Connor imagined he would not see her again for a time. The most remarkable was Dame Shane Adella. She had been observed to attack several of the contestants. Her last victim had been Courtier Anya Bishop, whom she had ambushed and threatened with throwing knives, the scuffle resolving itself away from the view of a crystal.

That left five. Chiv. Andromeda Tuner, of course; Courtier Anya Bishop, who had since been observed to be well, if not a little shaken; Chiv. Amber Everstar, who appeared to be working with Courtier Jacqueline Daidala; and Dame Hera Claustrom. Connor looked his list over, forcing himself to spend an equal amount of time on each contestant.

Masterchiv Rathbone stood to attention a short way off. Her hand lay on the hilt of her sword, eyes searching the trees.

Connor caught Masterchiv Rathbone's eye and quickly looked away, thinking about what they had discussed the night before. His concern for Jacs rose in his throat. Masterchiv Rathbone's words came back to him, *most likely she is simply not in range of a crystal.* But how often were they checking? All it would take would be just one moment, one room she entered at one moment in time, and he would know she was safe. He looked around him. His father was helping himself to another pastry, the Councilors were engaged with each other or dozing, and the guards were scanning the woods and cave entrance for any sign of unwanted guests.

He picked up his mirror, unsure why he was suddenly so nervous. Steadily he said, "Jacs Tabart." The mirror clouded for a moment. Connor counted the space between the seconds, then refocused on— "Jacqueline," he whispered, disbelieving. There she was, walking alongside Chiv. Everstar.

He shook his head, leaned over the mirror and said, "Jacqueline Daidala," into it. The first image clouded over to be replaced with the same one. Jacs, Jacqueline, was now helping Courtier Glowra down from a particularly steep patch of rock. He could not believe what he was seeing.

He had not noticed his father returning, did not sense him peering over his shoulder to see what had caused his son's change of demeanor, until he had repeated, "Jacs Tabart," again into the mirror to be sure. As the mirror clouded to reveal the same image, he felt a hand on his shoulder.

"That name, boy. What name did you just say?" his father spoke as if scarcely able to breathe.

Connor jumped to his feet and hid the mirror, too late, behind his back. "I—I don't know," he stammered. "It was nothing." He felt as if the world were moving too fast, his brain unable to keep up with the new information he had just received, let alone consider how to process it with his father.

"Tabart, you said Tabart. That is the name of the Lowrian criminal. The one with the balloon. How did you know to say that name? How did you know the daughter's name?" King Aren snatched the mirror out of Connor's hands and studied Jacqueline in its surface. He repeated, "Jacs Tabart." The image clouded then came back into focus. He ran his thumb and forefinger around his mouth to his chin. With a voice that appeared to build in volume as his realization grew, he said, "You did it my boy! You located Tabart's daughter. And she's here! Infiltrating our sacred contest! The gall, the—the—the absolute outrage! The Tabart girl posing as an Upperite! Guards!" The King was working himself up into a frenzy; already spittle was flying from the corners of his mouth.

"Father, no we don't know that. Don't jump to—there are any number of explanations. It can't be her." Connor might as well have stood on his head for all the notice the King paid him.

Masterchiv Rathbone reached him first. King Aren barked, "Rathbone, it's the Tabart girl, she must have been in the balloon after all. She's in the caves. It's Jacqueline Daidala. She is to be apprehended. We cannot allow her to escape." The King rocked backward and forward on the balls of his feet.

If Masterchiv Rathbone was surprised by this news, she did not show it. She nodded curtly, "Yes sire." Then she said, "If I may, sire, we also do not want to stir a panic. The idea that a Lowrian could sneak into the castle so easily will surely distress the people. I suggest we allow her to exit the cave, move beyond the range of the crystals, and then we can seize her. Quietly."

The King wrung his hands and nodded. "You're right, Rathbone. See to it the matter is done discreetly."

"Always, Your Highness," she replied, and moved to instruct a number of the other guards.

Connor watched this all as a sinking feeling grew in his stomach. "No," he whispered.

The afternoon dragged on. Time meandering. Connor felt like a tightly wound spring. He checked and rechecked the mirror. He jumped at any word from the guards by the cave's exit. Even the slightest sound rang in his ears like boots scuffing rock. He had bitten his thumbnail until it bled. Everything appeared suspended, waiting for Jacs to arrive.

All the while, one thought chased itself around and around his head: *It's Jacs. It's Jacs. It's Jacs.*

He could see no way to reason with his father. No way to ensure he would at least get a few minutes to talk to Jacs, to get some sort of explanation. No way that did not also somehow tie him up in the plots of a suspected assassin. He could not think of that. It did not fit. Not Jacs.

He knew her.

Courtier Anya Bishop emerged sometime later to a subdued welcome. She looked around in confusion while Master Epione fussed over her scratches and one particularly deep knife wound. Connor heard snippets of her conversation with Master Epione.

"I honestly don't know what came over Shane. I've never seen her like that before. I mean it's not as if we know each other well, I've worked for her family on and off, you know? But she was not in her right mind. One minute we were walking together down the tunnel, the next she was jabbering to herself and accusing me of being one of Lord Adella's spies. If she weren't so frenzied, I would have had a much harder time, but as it was, I was able to pin her down long enough for her to snap out of it. Those tunnels though, they do something to you. Get right inside your head if you're not careful." Anya's voice wavered despite her forced bravado.

Master Epione instructed her to lift her left arm while she felt it for any tender spots. "Do you know if Le—Courtier Glowra is okay?" Anya asked mid-wince.

"She is doing better now, I've heard," Master Epione's brisk tone cut through the afternoon air, "However, she has been disqualified. She was quite distressed for a time. Lost her lantern. But she is safe now. Two other contestants found her and are helping her out."

"Oh." Anya's voice was small.

Dame Hera Claustrom emerged next. She seemed to be the calmest out of all the contestants. She allowed Master Epione to fuss over her but did not appear to be injured. Instead, she selected a small bunch of grapes from a fruit platter and settled herself on a number of large cushions on the grass near Cllr. Perda's table. She caught Connor's eye and smiled alluringly as she placed a grape in her mouth. He looked away.

After Hera came Dame Shane Adella. Connor stood to welcome her and give her the unfortunate news.

"Disqualified?" she shrieked. "You did not tell us what lurked within that labyrinth! No one should have gone in there unwarned. This is—!" But Connor did not learn what exactly it was because at that moment, a guard pair firmly steered her toward the awaiting horses to return to the castle. He heard the echoes of her indignation fade as she rode through the trees.

Finally the sounds of three women singing rose from the mouth of the cave.

For want of a battle the Queendom was lost
And all for the want of a horseshoe nail!

"Look!" an excited voice cried.

"Sunlight!" came a second.

"Finally!" The third voice laughed.

Connor saw Masterchiv Rathbone signaling the guard pairs around the perimeter. Silently, they all stepped forward toward the voices. Courtier Glowra came into view first and Cllr. Stewart was waiting for her. She pulled her aside and began talking with her in hushed tones. The younger woman put a hand to her mouth and nodded. Cllr. Stewart placed a sympathetic hand on her shoulder and led her toward Master Epione.

Connor stepped forward as Jacs and Chiv. Everstar emerged next. Both were wearing radiant smiles like laurels. Connor caught Jacs's eye and her smile faltered. She glanced over to where Lena was still talking with Cllr. Stewart, then met his gaze again questioningly. She moved toward him, but Masterchiv Rathbone gently pulled her aside. As he had been instructed, he met Amber and placed a hand on the small of her back to guide her away from Jacs. "Congratulations on successfully completing the second task, Chivilra Everstar," he said. He now had his back toward Jacs as if to block out what was about to happen.

He heard Masterchiv Rathbone state, as if reading a status report, "Jacqueline Tabart, you are under arrest for high treason against the crown."

Then everything seemed to happen in slow motion. Amber's eyes looked over Connor's shoulder and grew wide. Connor caught her as she started forward and turned his head. Jacs attempted to pull her hand free of Masterchiv Rathbone's grip. Masterchiv Rathbone twisted Jacs's good arm behind her in one swift movement. Panic and fear danced across Jacs's face as she attempted again to wrestle free. Lena cried out and ran to reach Jacs. A guard pair met Lena midstride and in two smooth motions, forced her to the ground. Anya ran toward the guards holding Lena and punched one square in the face.

More screams erupted around the clearing. Connor held Amber back as she struggled against him. His eyes met Jacs's and he saw her raw terror and confusion. She reached for him with her splinted arm. Masterchiv Rathbone caught that wrist and twisted it behind her to meet the other.

Jacs screamed in pain and dropped to her knees as Masterchiv Rathbone tied her wrists behind her back with a leather strap pulled from her waist.

Connor had not realized he had let Amber go, had not realized his feet had started to move until he had almost reached Jacs.

"Don't hurt her!" he roared and landed beside Jacs, whose head was now low on her chest. He noticed a familiar gold chain around her neck and saw with an ache in his heart a small golden ring hanging from it.

"Are you okay?" he asked, voice thick with emotion.

She looked up at him, face pale, and pleaded in a low voice, "You don't understand, I'm not a traitor. I'm not a traitor. Find a servant. He used to be a servant of yours, Your Grace. A servant named Connor, he's from the Upper Realm. He's at the castle, or was. He can vouch for me. He's known me for years. Find Connor. They're going to take me away, but I've done nothing wrong. Please! Cornelius, you know me." Tears shone in her eyes, and one made a path down her cheek. Masterchiv Rathbone jerked her to her feet. Jacs cried out with pain again.

"Your Grace, I am under orders from the King and the Council of Four to take care of this Lowrian traitor. Step aside so I may fulfill these orders," she said in a clipped tone.

For the second time that day he felt his father's hand on his shoulder. "Move, boy. Do not make a scene," he hissed in his ear before pulling him away from Jacs.

Amber had been restrained by another guard pair and was calling to Jacs from under one of the guard's arms. Lena was struggling against the guard still holding her immobile, while the second of the pair reeled from Anya's blow. Anya narrowly dodged as the reeling guard attempted to sweep her legs from beneath her, and turned her focus to the guard still holding Lena. More guard pairs started forward.

Everyone froze as Cllr. Rosalind Perda stepped forward and boomed, "Enough!" She paused and surveyed her surroundings with a forced calm, although Connor could see a vein on her forehead pounding. "Courtier Jacqueline Daidala has deceived us all. She is not an Upperite citizen. She is from the Lower Realm. She snuck into the Upper Realm and infiltrated our sacred contest. She is a traitor and has consorted with suspected assassins. May I present Jacqueline Tabart of Bridgeport. Her crimes are such that we have not before encountered, however, she will be dealt with accordingly. Masterchiv Rathbone, if you will." She gestured for others to make a path for the head of the royal guard.

"No!" a voice cried. It might have been Lena's. Connor touched a spot on his chest. It should have been his.

Connor watched, helpless, as Jacs was taken from the glade. She did not cry out, or say anything more. Rather, she fixed a blank stare at a point in the distance and allowed herself to be led toward the horses. The King's hand pressed heavily on Connor's shoulder.

No one appeared to know how to proceed. The scene reminded Connor of a stage full of actors who had forgotten their lines. Amber and Lena were both slumped in various states of shock.

Their captors released their binds and stood ready. Anya was struggling against the grip of another guard. The woman she had punched sat on the grass massaging her jaw. Lena staggered to her feet.

"Get OFF me," Anya spat.

"Anya, stop!" Lena pleaded. Her fingers clasped tightly together in front of her mouth as though fighting the urge to reach out.

Connor noticed the four Councilors speaking together in hushed tones. They all appeared to reach a consensus at the same time and nodded. Then Cllr. Beatrice Fengar stepped forward, the assortment of writing tools in her bun glinting in the sunlight. "Courtier Anya Bishop," she said in a voice that carried over the sounds of Anya's skirmish, "for your recent actions that demonstrate a shameful lack of self-control, you will be disqualified from the contest."

"No! You cannot do that!" Lena's cries interrupted any response Anya was about to give. Cllr. Fengar held up a hand for silence and continued, "Any further punitive action has yet to be determined. You will be detained until this matter is resolved."

"Detained?" Anya said angrily.

"No! Please." Lena had rushed between Cllr. Fengar and Anya as though to shield the latter from the former. "She was just—"

"She assaulted a guard, and in the presence of the royal family. Stand down, child," Cllr. Dilmont interrupted. She had moved to stand beside Cllr. Fengar. Her next words were directed past Lena, "Guards, escort Courtier Bishop to the castle."

"It's okay, Lee," Anya murmured, "I'll be fine."

Lena turned away from the Councilors and ran to hug Anya. The two women broke apart as the guard pulled Anya roughly toward the horses, the guard's second half a step behind, eyes sharp.

The King shook his head. "Messy business," he muttered absently. Connor could only look at him.

"A traitor! How awful!" Hera cried as she rose from the cushions and delicately smoothed her tunic. She moved closer to Connor and addressed him, a hand on her heart. "And to think, right under our noses. It is such a relief she was discovered so quickly!"

"She can't be a traitor," Amber muttered. She was no longer being restrained and had instead moved to comfort Lena. "She's not a traitor. With all due respect, Your Majesty, I know traitors. I've dealt with a few traitors in the field. If she had wanted to, she had plenty of opportunity to—"

"That concludes today's task." The King's voice cut across Amber's. "Congratulations to our three remaining contestants: Dame Hera Claustrom, Chiv. Andromeda Turner, and Chiv. Amber Everstar. The three of you will be competing in the final task tomorrow and will no doubt need time to rest and prepare. It is true we have had a distressing turn of events today. No doubt the knowledge that a Lowrian traitor moved so cunningly among us is unbelievable. I must impress upon all of you the importance of discretion. This matter will be dealt with appropriately. Until that time, I trust you all to avoid spreading incomplete or inaccurate information to the public. But let us all return to the castle."

Without another word, everyone moved to obey the King's command. Connor followed as if sleepwalking.

25

BEHIND BARS

". . . seven, eight. By one, two, three, four, five, six." Jacs muttered under her breath. She was walking heel to toe along the cold stone walls of her cell. Sighing, she sat back down on the plank of wood that was to serve as her bed. It took up almost half of the cell. She had measured every inch of the cell twice now. The bars were two fingers thick and spaced at one palm intervals. The bed was five palms from the ground, and the window was two palms by two and a half palms. She had to stand on her bed to reach the window. All this was of no comfort to her. Knowing the dimensions of one's prison cell does not change the fact that one is, indeed, in a prison cell.

How had it gone so wrong so fast? she thought. She cradled her splinted arm in the other hand and slowly loosened the straps. Wincing, she inspected her wrist. It was now a deep purple and began to throb horribly as she attempted to rotate it. Gritting her teeth against the pain, she carefully bound it again.

How had they known? Her mind worked through the thought experiment with a cold detachment. She worked as though elevated above her throbbing arm, above the dull, dark cell. Sitting in solemn silence, she studied the question as though inspecting each facet of a stone. *No one else knew, no one except my mother and Master Leschi.* Her heart began to beat faster. She knew they had captured the two women. She also knew that they would never have given her up. *Not willingly,* she thought with horror. Again, the vision of her mother crumpling filled her mind. She thought of Phillip, battered and bloodied. Her composure began to slip. She forced herself to breathe.

Suddenly eight paces by six paces felt impossibly small.

Breathe. She willed herself, her fingers gripping the wooden plank beneath her. They would not have given her up willingly. This thought spun inside her mind, threatening to drown her. How long had they withstood questioning? What had been done to them before they broke?

BREATHE, she thought desperately.

It was like sucking mud through a reed. There was not enough air in here. There was not enough space. She had to get out. She had to find her mother. She would surely die here. Nobody would know.

Suddenly Jacs was on her feet. "No!" she erupted. "No!" she screamed through the bars. "No. No. No!" She was pacing the room now. Three strides, turn, three strides, turn. "This is not right!

I have done nothing wrong. Nothing wrong!" she screamed again into the silence. Heard it echo around her like fists against the stone.

She heard a humorless chuckle from somewhere down the hallway and stopped to listen.

"They always crack," a voice said. "Some take longer than most, but sooner or later. . ." There was another chuckle.

Frustrated, Jacs screamed again and rattled the bars with her one good arm. She swore at the voice, which only made the owner laugh louder.

"The Lowrian language is so poetic," came a sarcastic response.

Fuming, Jacs sat back down on the plank and tried to slow her heart rate. She would not be goaded by this disembodied voice. There was a long silence as she focused on her breathing. She felt her heart begin to slow. Her mind began to clear.

After a time, she heard footsteps coming toward her cell. A murmuring. Someone new. The goading voice protested loudly and Jacs heard a sterner reply of, "That's an order." The voice reluctantly relented. More footsteps moved away, down the hall. A pause. She strained to listen. A heavy door opened and shut. Finally footsteps approached.

Jacs stood with her back against the far wall, bracing herself. The steps slowed, then stopped near her cell. She could not see their owner yet. She waited. Nothing.

Then a tentative, "Jacs?" It was a male voice. It was distorted and sounded unnaturally rough as if he were changing it on purpose, or had a very bad cold. Regardless of the voice, the sound of her name, her private name, stunned her.

Jacs slid down the wall and hugged her knees to her chest. "No one here knows me by that name," she whispered.

"I do," came the reply.

"Connor?" she ventured, disbelieving. Hope surged in her chest. The Prince had found him! But then . . . "I can't believe you came. After all this time—"

"Did you do it?" he cut her off.

"Do what?"

"The assassination occurred from your clock tower. Did you have any part in it?" The words came out in a rush.

"What? No! No, of course not! Did you not read any of my letters after that day?" she replied. She searched for an explanation. "A knife maker is not responsible for what is then done with the knife. I just designed the—"

"Then why did you come here?"

"Here?"

"To the Upper Realm."

"To . . ." Her mind was reeling. "To participate in the contest!"

"Why?"

"What?"

"*Why?*" The word was harsh, cold.

Jacs felt anger building where hope had flashed. Suddenly the hurt of his year of silence, the pain of all she had been through since, the curfews, the fear, the guards, the insidious purple glow in every home, and the indignation against his tone rose in her like a wave. She stood slowly, her good fist clenched and struck the stone behind her.

"Why do you think?" she spat. "I did it to give my people a chance. I did it to become Queen. Or to at least try. You have no idea. We are hurting. We are angry. We are despised by our own rulers. And we are dying!" She took a steadying breath. "At first I thought it was just because of the King, but it's everywhere. I've lived among the Upperites now. You're all the same. You have been fed this lie about us and it breeds and spreads and twists your hearts against us. I came to the Upper Realm to give my people a voice. And as soon as it was discovered that I, a Lowrian citizen, merely exist in the Upper Realm, it's condemned as an act of treason. What is my crime? What. Is. My. Crime?" She punctuated each word with a pound of her fist against the stone behind her.

She reached down the neck of her tunic and pulled the ring from where it had sat next to her heart since she had first begun building balloons.

Angrily, she ripped the chain off her neck and weighed the ring in her palm.

"But you wouldn't know any of this, would you Connor? Safe on your mountain. Where were you when the guards moved in? Where were you when my friends were being hauled in for questioning? Where were you when the taxes kept rising and my people were treated like little more than stray dogs? Where were you when people started disappearing? Where were you when I needed you?" Hot tears gathered in the corners of her eyes, threatening to spill down her cheeks, but she did not care, nor did she stop.

She looked at the circle of gold in her palm, its image blurred through tears, and threw it through the bars. It hit the opposite wall and rang softly as it struck the stone floor.

"I needed you," she said, hating how her voice wavered. "I needed my friend. I needed someone to talk to, to tell me it was all going to be okay. And where were you? I sent dozens of letters up, Connor. Dozens. And you could not even deign to give me a response. Didn't even have the courage to explain why you cut me off so easily. For a while I couldn't decide whether you were heartless or just a coward. Now I see you were both." She closed her eyes briefly and forced the tremor from her voice as she continued. "Did

I do it?" she repeated incredulously. "I saw her fall, Connor. I saw our Queen die. You can't imagine what it was like."

"Yes, I can." His voice, full of emotion, was not muffled anymore. Recognition shot through her like electricity, and she knew who would step into view a moment before he did.

"You!" she breathed. Prince Cornelius, Connor, was on the other side of the bars.

They stood staring at each other for a long time. Jacs's mind stalled in shock. Connor stood with his arms crossed, a number of emotions fighting their way across his face. Neither knew what to say next. This was not the reunion she had imagined all those years ago. It was not supposed to happen like this. Not like this.

"You know," Connor said stiffly, "it hasn't exactly been easy for me either. I was there. I saw her die. And I have had to spend the better part of this last year arranging a contest to determine her replacement. Do you know how to even begin figuring out how to replace your mother, your Queen? And knowing there was even a chance that the only woman you can ever remember loving could have been involved in her death? How do you write that in a letter?" He paused. "Maybe I was a coward! But I couldn't stand the thought of finding out it was you."

"Well, ta-da! It wasn't me. Which you would have known without asking if you had known me at all." Jacs struggled to hold on to her anger, but felt it slipping. *The only woman you can ever remember loving* rang in her ears. She decided to ignore it.

"I know." His voice was quiet, the fight gone. He bent and picked up the little ring. He turned it over in his fingers. "I should have known from the start." A loaded silence followed his words. He was looking at the engraving of the Griffin, passing his thumb pad across the image as Jacs had done a thousand times, his brow furrowed.

Finally he looked at her. "I am so sorry, Jacs. At the very least, you deserved an explanation, and I could not even give you that."

Jacs attempted to cross her arms, her splinted arm awkwardly settling under her other arm. "What's done can't be undone," she said bitterly, then dropped her arms to her sides. She felt the fight leave her. It was her turn to look away. Time stretched out until finally she met his gaze again. "But thank you," she added.

He smiled sadly and scratched the back of his neck. Slowly, she walked toward the bars. He looked at her, uncertain. She stopped in front of him. "I can't believe it was you. Why did you never tell me you were the Prince? In all our letters, all our conversations . . ." she trailed off only to pick back up. "We spent years discussing policy. I had no idea you were one of the few people who could actually act on it."

Connor shrugged. "Honestly, I guess I was just scared it would change things. It was simpler to be Connor. Just Connor, I guess." He stepped forward and rested his hand next to hers on the bars. "Did you really make a balloon big enough to fly you up here?" he asked in a conspiratorial whisper as a grin cracked the corner of his mouth.

Jacs began to smile too. "Yes," she said as they both burst into fits of stifled laughter.

"You are out of your mind!" Connor said after a time in amused disbelief, "I've traveled up and down the Cliff on the Bridge. To think of you trusting a balloon and some hot air to get you up. It's madness!"

Jacs wiped her eyes, "I have always found it funny how often madness and genius are paired. Maybe you simply can't have one without the other."

"Maybe," he replied, his mood turning somber. His gaze dropped from hers to rest on their hands perched side by side on the cell door. Jacs's eyes followed his. He cleared his throat and began, "You know, that day in the woods. The day we met?"

Jacs smiled at the memory of wet toes and awkward bows.

Connor still did not look at her as he continued. "That day by the Cliff. I had just sent a letter to you. A year too late, I know. But all the same . . ." He covered her hand with his, his touch a welcome warmth next to the cold metal bars. She felt a current course through her fingers and up her wrist as he softly ran the pad of his thumb across her skin. "All the same, you need to know that you never left my thoughts. Not for a moment. I can't change the hurt I caused you. I know that. You have to believe I would if I could. I let you down in the worst way I could have, and you deserved better."

"Yes, I did," she agreed honestly, then more reluctantly, "but I realize now that you were hurting too. I know what it is to lose a parent and I am so sorry you had to experience that, and in such a traumatic manner." Their eyes met. Jacs felt every word she could not say pass between them. "But to dwell on the past now is dangerous. You can't be just Connor; this is bigger than the two of us. My mother and Master Leschi have been captured and are most likely being punished for the same crime I will be punished for. You know we're innocent, but we look guilty. On top of that, someone was sabotaging some of the contestants in the catacombs this afternoon. That makes me think someone is trying to interfere with the contest. Who are the finalists?"

Connor told her.

"Anya and Lena were both eliminated?"

"Yes, Lena did not demonstrate the appropriate qualities, and Anya . . . well, she attacked a guard as you were being led away."

Jacs swore. "Amber, Andromeda, and Hera. Hera?" Jacs repeated with confusion.

Connor nodded.

Jacs thought again about the strange scene she had witnessed in the mirror. *Something still doesn't fit,* she mused. Unsure how to voice her concerns to Connor, she decided to wait. Instead, she said, "Two Upperite knights and a Dame. Connor, don't you see? My people have no chance of having a ruler with any desire to do right by them unless I compete. I need to finish this, and I can't do that rotting in here." She looked about her, her mind still whirling.

"But you've been disqualified!"

"I've been . . ." she began, then felt a match ignite in her heart. "No, no I never was! Connor, I was arrested, but they never declared I had been disqualified. I fulfilled the task's requirements, I solved the riddle, I made it through the tunnels, and I demonstrated the ability to keep—what was it? Keep calm under pressure. I know I did. I was never disqualified!"

"True . . ." he said slowly, "but they would just disqualify you when you try to compete; how does that change anything?"

"It changes everything!" Jacs replied excitedly. "It means I can still technically compete. It means I can still win!"

"But as soon as you set foot in front of the Councilors, in front of my father, they'll have you arrested again."

"Maybe, but you won't. You could vouch for me, insist I get a chance to finish what I started." Jacs twisted a strand of hair around her finger. "And they might not want to arrest me publicly anyway. They waited until after I had left the view of the crystals to arrest me. It makes sense, they probably didn't want to cause a panic. We can use that. All I need is enough time to complete the task." She seized his hands in hers through the bars.

There was a loud bang as a door swung open forcefully. Both Jacs and Connor jumped. She heard two sets of footsteps. One stumbling, the other assured. She heard a woman sobbing, a thud, a groan, and the sobbing subsided.

"Your Grace!" came a shocked exclamation. "I didn't think you would—or I wasn't informed of your—Please, sire. I have prisoners to put in cells. It's not proper . . . your safety . . . you shouldn't . . ." The guard paused.

Connor looked from the guard down to where his and Jacs's hands were clasped, dropped his hands, and stepped back from her cell. There was a heavy silence. Jacs could not see the guard or the guard's expression, but Connor looked uncomfortable.

"What . . . ah, what are you doing here, Your Grace?" came the guard's wary question.

Connor drew himself up and announced loudly, "I see you have your prisoner under control. Excellent work as usual, everything is as it should be up here." He looked about as though inspecting the walls. "I will leave you to your duties."

Connor looked at Jacs and said in a voice so low that even she almost missed it, "We will figure this out." He turned back to the guard and said pointedly, "You are to be commended on your due diligence, I will have your thoroughness noted to the King. Good day." He looked at Jacs once more and placed the ring on the crossbar. She palmed it silently, tucking the chain into her fist. Then he turned and strode away from the guard and left through the other door.

"Hear that? Commended to the King," the guard muttered smugly.

She waited a beat after Connor had left, then forced her charge into a movement that caused her to cry out.

"Oh, so now you have something to say?" sneered the guard.

The prisoner cried out again.

"We'll see how fast you hold on to your secrets after a few more sessions like that with the Councilors. You should be honored they deigned to oversee your confessions in person. Move along, come on," the guard said.

Jacs heard them approach her cell and took a few steps back from the bars. The footsteps came closer. Jacs saw the guard first as she passed into view. She was solidly built, and Jacs was surprised to see her working alone, accustomed as she was to seeing guards travel in pairs. But this guard did not look as though she were in need of a partner. Her short dark hair clung to her scalp in greasy wads. Each of her arms was as thick as two of Jacs's and despite the prisoner she hauled along with her, she walked with the confidence of a fist-reliant problem solver. Jacs noticed a deep red shining wetly on her gloves and tunic, and she had a fresh scratch along her jaw.

The prisoner she was half leading, half dragging down the hall behind her was dirty and covered in bruises and cuts. Bloodstains in various shades of red and rust were in patches on the prisoner's once-white garment. Her brown hair hung matted and limp over her face. The guard slowed in front of Jacs's cell with a twisted glee in her eyes.

"And here's the other basemutt," the last word falling from her lips like a curse. "Something to look forward to, eh?" She brandished the prisoner like a trophy, lifting her by the elbow, causing her to groan. The dark hair fell back to reveal a beaten but still recognizable face.

Jacs fell to her knees, not registering the pain that flashed through her as she collided with the stone. "No!" she cried. She pushed herself up with her wounded wrist and shot toward the cell door, reaching her arms through the bars. "No! What have they done to you?" She took in the swollen eye, the split lip, and the long cut that spanned from cheek to chin. "What have you done to her!" she roared at the guard, who merely smiled.

"Oh Plum, my sweet—" The words that escaped her mother's lips were small, and her fingers brushed Jacs's cheek. "You're alive." Relief flooded her pale face with color.

The guard pulled Maria up and away from Jacs. Jacs cried out. The cry was pulled from her as though someone had ripped her heart from her chest. She rattled at the bars, screaming. Her mother turned, and Jacs saw a blankness in her eyes that frightened her. She clawed at the hinges, at the lock, at the bars themselves. She threw her weight against the door once, twice. The sound echoed down the stone hall. They disappeared from view.

Jacs heard another cell door open and slam shut. Heard the guard's footsteps, the scraping of a chair, and a sigh.

"Mum?" she called.

"Oi! No talking," came the harsh reply.

Jacs swore at her, enlisting a few choice words she had picked up from Amber. She heard the chair scrape again, rough footsteps, then a loud crash as the guard slammed a wooden baton into the bars of her cell. She jumped back and glared at her, imagining several places she would gladly slip a knife. The guard glowered down at her menacingly and slowly approached the bars.

"Next peep I hear out of you, I take out of her hide, got it?" she growled, jerking a thumb behind her toward the other, now too silent cell. Jacs said nothing. Satisfied, the guard walked away.

Jacs slumped on the stone floor beside the bars. She began to shake violently and gathered her knees to her chest, covering her mouth with her hand as she attempted to stifle her sobs.

The night passed slowly and silently. Morning seemed reluctant to break. She tried not to imagine where Master Leschi was. Jacs lay on the floor next to the bars counting the stones on the ceiling, straining to hear anything, a cough, a sigh, anything from the cell down the hall.

26

ILLUMINATION

"Father, look at the facts—we have no solid evidence. What you are doing is wrong and you know it!" Connor was in his father's study. The fire was lit, the desk was littered with even more papers and books.

The King stood with his back to the room, his hand on the mantel as he gazed into the fire.

"Boy, the evidence we have links these women with the scene of the Queen's assassination and the infiltration of the Upper Realm. Something that has never before been attempted by a Lowrian citizen. We cannot ignore the connection." King Aren tugged on his moustache distractedly.

Connor was surprised their conversation had stayed as calm as it had thus far. He expected at any moment to be dismissed and searched for a new tactic to push this newfound ground he had gained.

"But Father, the people love her. She has done nothing to suggest her intentions are unfavorable. Sure, she was implicated in the clock tower—but you would not blame a knife maker for what someone chooses to do with the knife!" He echoed Jacs's words and forced himself to give his father time to respond. The clock ticked pointedly.

"Ah, the people love her, do they, boy?" Connor bristled at the implications in his father's tone. "In any case," his father continued, "the Councilors see no point in furthering her participation in the contest."

"No point?"

"She is not a desirable candidate, at any rate."

"Not a . . . Father, think of what her candidacy means! She can bridge the two lands in a way no other contestant can! She should be given the chance to complete the last task." Connor took a few steps toward his father's silhouette outlined in the glow of the fire.

"You would see a Lowrian crowned?" The words were soft daggers.

"If she won, yes. If she can prove herself worthy of it, yes. It is not up to me but up to her ability to demonstrate the qualities of a Queen. I would see her crowned over many others who have participated in the contest. I would see her crowned certainly over Hera. Why is she still in this anyway? She has demonstrated only self-interest and thinly veiled contempt for—"

The King laughed pityingly and turned around. "My boy, my poor naive boy. It is time. It is time I tell you what the last advisor to the Queen told me. This truth I should have figured out, just as you should have, long before it was revealed to me. It's quite simple, really. Hera Claustrom is still here because her mother is the Lord of Hesperida and has most of the surrounding counties' Lords comfortably in her pocket." He sniffed and continued, "She is still here because the Council knows they can use her and her mother's influence."

Connor took a step back. "What?"

"Without the support of the Council, the Queen is powerless. Without the support of her Lords, the Queen is penniless. So without either, she cannot hope to achieve anything. Anything of substance, that is." The King spoke as if explaining where the sun went every evening to a child.

"But the contest?" spluttered the Prince.

"Helps the people believe in the Queen. Gives them hope that any among them could serve their Queendom in the same way one day. Past Queens have always been Dames or Princesses. No exception. Did you not notice the severe lack of anyone not of status in the final rounds? Even Ms. Bishop became a Courtier, and Ms. Julliard has favorable connections despite not being a noble."

"You're not serious!"

The King shook his head, a patronizing smile played on his lips, "Do use your head. The Queendom would not have survived all these centuries if each successor was chosen purely by the contest."

Connor took another step back, his mind reeling. "Did Mother know this?"

The King shrugged, "She may have guessed, but I never told her. I encourage you to hold your tongue with the next Queen too."

"But people trust the contest, people believe in the contest!" Connor insisted.

"Exactly, and yet in the end, the Council decides." The King looked as though he had aged ten years in ten minutes; freed from the burden of this truth, he seemed to deflate. He spoke with a detached resignation. "Courtier Glowra was a hopeful candidate, well connected, much admired, easily influenced, but there was no way to pass her performance in the last task off as successful. The first task, maybe. But not the second. I suppose there is something to be said for the tasks themselves."

Something nipped at the back of Connor's mind, something Jacs had mentioned. "And the sabotage?" he murmured, almost to himself.

"The what?" The King took another step forward, away from the fire. Suddenly his features became distinguishable from the shadows in which they had been masked.

"There was talk of sabotage in the catacombs," Connor said carefully. "Was that to sway the outcome too?"

The King shook his head, confused now. "I knew nothing about sabotage." He paused thoughtfully. "But there is a lot the Council does not tell me. That does not matter much now. Hera will most likely be proclaimed Queen tomorrow. We cannot have a knight on the throne. So, I suggest you consider your next move. Use this knowledge to become an effective advisor. Or else despair in the futility of it all." The King walked to a cabinet and busied himself in pouring a drink.

Connor watched him, his lip curling. "If none of this matters, I can at least make sure my actions do," Connor insisted, and he stormed from the room in the direction of the servants' quarters. He almost did not catch his father's sigh and half-hearted, "That's the spirit, boy," as the door closed on the scene of the tired King, alone with his glass.

27

ASSEMBLY

The Queendom woke to the almost forgotten sound of rain splashing on cobbles. It had begun as a mist that hugged the evening lamps and shifted to sprinkling the trees with tiny diamonds and ruffling the surface of the palace ponds. As the sun rose, so too did the rain's intensity. It turned from mist to drizzle to downpour. Soon, buckets of water rattled the windows. Shutters were hastily closed, cushions quickly pulled from the outdoor benches. Horses were ushered into their stables and the water brushed from their coats.

Despite the torrents of water, the entrance yard continued to receive a steady flow of carriages. Serving women and men waited under awnings to rush out and receive each visitor. Palace guests shrieked and squealed as they ran across the open courtyards. Fires were lit, towels offered. A soggy and disgruntled mousing cat sat delicately on a windowsill licking her paws, watching the raindrops chase each other down the windowpane.

Edith felt as though she had been awake for hours. The castle buzzed in anticipation for the task that would determine the fate of the Queendom. It seemed such a silly notion to have to fumble through her key ring to find the correct key when history was to be made that day. Pulling her socks on had seemed equally as frivolous, as had pinning her hair under her cap. Did any action really feel monumental in the moment? Or was it only afterward when scribes had trapped the event with words that anything felt world-changing? But the Prince had been clear, and she had work to do, so she had tied her boots and adjusted her apron as she would have done on any given morning.

Pulling her shawl tightly around her shoulders, Edith headed down the chilly corridor. Shadows nipped at her heels, lingering from the night before. She passed tapestry after tapestry, portrait after portrait. She forced her imagination to behave, but she had the feeling the eyes in the portraits were watching her, ever on the alert. She saw the occasional purple glow from the crystals and ducked her head. She had no reason to be nervous. She was under the Prince's orders. Still, she hurried on, forcing the shadows away.

Jacs lay curled like a cat in the corner of her cell. The plank bed was no more comfortable than the stone floor, so she pressed herself to the bars to better hear. A faint, sporadic tapping of knuckle on iron thudded softly in the morning air. A pause, she tapped back *tap tap tap*, and waited. The reply came shortly after, the tapping more important to her than her own heartbeat. Back and forth they had tapped, Jacs certain that if they could just get through the night, her mother would be okay. Occasionally she would have to wait longer for a reply. In the silence, her heart would pound almost too loudly for her to hear anything else, then a gentle metallic tapping would emerge from the gloom and settle her heart for another minute.

Light seemed reluctant to enter the little window. It hesitated at the sill, inched into her cell, and seemed to pause too long before continuing. She tapped again, and waited.

Lena had not slept a wink that night and was dressed and ready long before dawn. Sitting in a chair by the fire, she finished writing her note to Amber and turned her plan over again in her mind. The room was much emptier now. Amber slept quietly in her four-poster bed. The two remaining beds in the room stood empty. As though called, she rose, donned her thick woolen cloak, and quietly collected her coin purse. Slipping the note into Amber's still hand, she silently opened the door and stepped out into the hall.

Tap tap tap. Wait. Breathe a sigh of relief. *Tap tap tap*. Wait. Breathe a sigh of relief. Jacs did not realize she had fallen asleep until she heard a tentative, "Jacs?"

Sitting bolt upright, her heart racing, she looked into the eyes of a woman she did not recognize.

"What? What is it?" Jacs said sleepily.

The woman held a finger to her lips and gestured toward where Jacs knew the guard sat somewhere down the hall. "Shhh!" The sound echoed down the passageway.

Jacs thought she heard a slight snore from the guard's station.

"I'm here to help. Wait here, and don't ask any questions," the woman hissed. Jacs nodded dumbly, wiping the sleep from her eyes and stretching a crick in her neck.

The woman disappeared. Jacs strained to see and hear in the darkness and silence. Quickly the woman returned with a ring of keys. She winked mischievously and unlocked the cell. The door opened with a deafening squeak that made Jacs gasp.

"Oi! What's going on down there?" a gruff voice called from down the hall.

With a warning in her eyes, the woman stepped behind Jacs, then grasped her hands behind her back and called, "It's just Edith, Maxine. I've been told to escort this lowerdog to different quarters for the third task." As she spoke, she made Jacs march out of the cell and toward the guard's desk.

"You have? Well, let me get the . . . hang on . . . where have the blasted keys gone?" Maxine replied.

"The keys?"

"Yeah, where in the—"

"Oh no, Maxine, have you lost the keys again? Masterchiv Rathbone will be furious."

"No! No, I ah . . . I just . . . well how did you get the prisoner out?" Maxine was searching her pockets, eyes darting, looking across the desk and around her station and then at Edith.

"Well, I was sent by the Prince! He would not send me without the keys, now, would he? And wake you up for nothing?" Edith placated.

The unfortunate Maxine patted various pockets on her person and scratched her head in wonder. "No of course not," she mumbled distractedly.

"Should I inform Masterchiv Rathbone?" Edith asked sweetly. Her hands were gentle on Jacs's limp and damaged wrists. She pressed her to walk forward toward where Jacs knew her mother's cell was.

"No! No! No, definitely unnecessary. I have them right . . . well, I won't hold you up if you have direct orders from the Prince. No need to mention this to Masterchiv Rathbone. None at all."

Edith smiled kindly. "Of course not. Thank you for all your help, Maxine."

Edith pushed Jacs past the guard, who was still patting herself down in a desperate attempt to locate her keys. They passed Maria's cell. Jacs saw her mother lying on the floor next to the bars as she had been. She stifled a moan and dropped down next to her. Edith squeaked in surprise and attempted to pull her back to her feet. The twist on her injured arm caused Jacs to cry out.

"Everything all right down there, Edith?" called Maxine.

"Fine!" Edith strained hurriedly. "Just tripped a little, everything is fine." Leaning low, she hissed in Jacs's ear, "Get up! There will be time to come back later; we need to move."

Jacs clasped her mother's hands through the bars and saw her mother crack a wavering smile. "I'll see you very soon, Plum," she whispered.

"I love you, Mum," Jacs whispered back and pressed her mother's bloodied fingers to her lips. Edith pulled her upright and made her move away. "I'll come back for you," she promised over her shoulder, reluctant to look away. Edith pushed her on again and they rounded a corner. The image of her mother was burned into Jacs's mind. She quickly blinked away tears and attempted to swallow the lump in her throat.

"She will be all right," Edith whispered. "I'll send someone to look after her. I cannot believe the state she is in." The woman made a tsking sound as though she had observed someone walk across a freshly cleaned floor with muddy shoes.

"Thank you," Jacs managed. Then, "Who are you?" She could not seem to phrase the question in a way that would not sound rude.

Edith dropped Jacs's hands and moved to fall into step beside her. "I'm Edith," she said, flashing a quick smile and quickening their pace to a brisk walk. "I'm Prince Cornelius's valet and friend. He sent me to find you."

"Oh!" Jacs exclaimed, relief loosening the tight bands on her chest ever so slightly. She recognized the name from Connor's letters. "And where are we going?" she asked as Edith led her down a narrow staircase and out into another corridor filled with similar cells to the one where she had spent the night. The sounds of a commotion reached their ears and before Jacs could think, Edith had flung out her arm painfully into Jacs's chest and pulled her back into the shadows of a cell alcove. Crouched in the gloom, Jacs strained to listen.

"You will release her," a familiar voice demanded.

"Courtier, with all due respect, I do not have that authority," came the tired reply.

"It's quite simple. As a servant of my household, she represents my family. I cannot have my mother hearing that a servant of hers is in jail. Or would you like to tell her? Lord Glowra has been in a foul mood since she heard of my disqualification, but I'm sure she will understand this little matter of your authority."

Jacs's mouth dropped open in shock; it was Lena.

"I can't just pardon prisoners," the guard who Lena was evidently arguing with said with forced patience.

There was a pause, then Jacs heard the unmistakable sound of a coin purse on wood.

"Well, I . . . er . . . right this way, let me just find my keys."

"And the paperwork?" Lena snapped.

"Right, ah . . . here you go," stammered the guard.

"That is very kind of you. Thank you," Lena replied.

Edith motioned for Jacs to follow down the way they had come. Jacs shook her head and jerked a finger in the direction of Lena. She strained to listen again but all she heard was the scraping of a chair and two sets of footsteps heading away from where Jacs and Edith sat hiding. The door at the end of the hall banged open and shut.

Edith whispered, "We need to go the other way. Maxine didn't ask questions, but she will, and there are strict orders that you are to be kept in your cell until the third task is over, Prince's orders or no. I'm sure your friend will be fine."

Jacs bit her lip and nodded. The two women waited a moment, then headed in the opposite direction down the hall.

Lena forced her steps to remain controlled and deliberate. She practiced making her face into an aloof mask and allowed the guard to lead her through the winding tunnels of the prison. Her heart felt as though it were ready to run off ahead of her. Why did this woman have to walk so slowly? She wrinkled her nose as the smell of mildew worsened.

"Ah, here we are," the guard announced finally. Lena felt suddenly apprehensive. She took a deep breath and approached the bars.

"Thank you," she said to the guard as she unlocked the heavy cell door. In the gloom, she saw Anya sitting on the small plank that had served as a bed, her back pressed against the wall and her arms wrapped around her knees. At the sound of the key in the lock, she jumped and attempted to push herself farther into the corner. Lena's heart froze.

"What did you do to her?" Lena said numbly.

The guard cleared her throat and said, "With all due respect, Your Elegance, there's little love lost on those who assault members of the guard. Those who do tend to be a little clumsier than most. I suspect she tripped. I will allow you to collect her and take her home. Good day." She bowed, turned on her heel, and left. Lena could hear the coin purse clinking against her hip as she strode back down the tunnel.

Turning back to the bars, Lena tentatively pushed open the door and stepped inside. Anya had a dark bruise blossoming over one eye and a cut along the bridge of her nose. Lena also noticed the red blossom that had appeared on her side yesterday had grown and spread.

"Oh, flower girl." She felt tears prickling her eyes. "I'm so sorry."

"Lee?" Anya was groggy and squinted in the light from the lantern. Lena hurriedly set it down in the corner. "How did you . . .?" Anya's eyes widened as if she had just realized she was there. "Lee!" Anya exclaimed and scrambled to her feet. She closed the distance between them and swept Lena into a tight embrace. "Lee, I was so worried about you. I should have been there in the cave with you. I'm so sorry. For everything." Anya's voice was muffled by Lena's hair. Lena felt Anya's breath near her ear and heard her voice break.

"Don't be silly, I should be apologizing to you! I was foolish, and I never should have—"

"No, you were right to be upset, I shouldn't have doubted—" Anya cut in.

"Well, you had valid reason, and you were right anyway." Lena attempted a laugh.

"I know you don't need saving—"

"I definitely was not capable on my own—"

They babbled over each other until they were both flushed and grinning. Lena pulled back and studied Anya's face.

"Those look awful," she said of the cuts and bruises.

Anya looked away and shook her head. "But what are you doing here?"

Lena frowned and gestured to the open cell door. "I came to rescue you," she replied.

"Rescue . . .? But why?" Anya cocked her head to the side.

Lena put her hands on her hips and glared up at the taller woman. "Because! Because I love you, idiot! I love you; I've loved you since we were girls, and even though you appear to be thicker than those bars about it, I don't care. I guess I'll just have to live with spelling it out for you. I love y—"

Lena's words died on Anya's lips as she was swept into her arms. Fingers entwined, breath quickened, and Lena felt herself lifted off her feet, legs wrapping around Anya's waist. Anya winced and stumbled a few steps, but only held her tighter. Lena lightly rested her forehead against Anya's and smiled. A lily bloomed in her chest, and roses on her cheeks.

"I love you too," Anya whispered and drew her in again. Her lips were soft.

A cough echoed down the hall and the women broke apart reluctantly. Lena dropped her feet to the ground. Her head spun and she cupped Anya's cheek in her hand. "We should go; I bribed the guard but it's better not to linger."

"You bribed the——?" Anya began, impressed.

"Come on!"

Anya nodded, took her by the hand, and they walked out of the cell together.

✧

Jacs and Edith made their way through the prison without much difficulty. The number of guards on duty was minimal, most likely assigned to overseeing the final task.

"Edith," Jacs said once they had left the oppressive stone building and headed along the cloister toward the main castle. The rain drowned out their footsteps and Jacs had to raise her voice above the drumming to be heard. "Edith, I need to attend the final task."

"Yes," came Edith's short reply.

"But I can't do that looking like this." Jacs waved a hand at her tunic, stained with lake water, mud, and blood. Edith's eyes flicked over her and lingered on the mess that was her hair. "I am fairly certain it will be hard enough to make my voice heard as a suspected traitor, let alone a dirty and disheveled suspected traitor," Jacs clarified.

Edith nodded and did not break her pace. "Of course," she agreed, "we'll make a quick stop." She glanced at the height of the nearly invisible sun outlined behind the thick gray clouds. "There's time for a wash too."

Jacs smiled, grateful, and allowed the brisk pace to quicken as they headed toward a servants' entrance along the side of the building.

The early guests continued to trickle into the Queen's throne room to stand along the walls. The later guests were given mirrors and guided into various sitting rooms on the ground floor. As before, each was given a small card with the names of the final contestants written on it. Three names and the title "Amanuensis." This last name could be used to see a written transcript of each contestant's speech during the final task. Each room was attended by several serving women and hot beverages were provided to ward off the chill that crept into the castle.

The throne room filled quickly, each guest jostling for a better spot, a better view. Each craned their neck upon entry as if on cue, to take in the enormity and magnificence of the space. The vaulted ceiling was decorated with dozens of frescoes depicting various scenes of triumph throughout the Queendom's history. In the center of the ceiling, a circle big enough to fit a small house was open to the air, lined with pillars, and covered with its own roof to prevent rain from entering the throne room below. The bottomless belvedere perched on top of the hall like a bell tower or steeple. Twelve pillars evenly spaced around the circumference left twelve openings that allowed for the Court of Griffins to perch and observe the proceedings from above. Now, twelve winged silhouettes stood in silent vigil over the gawking guests.

Impressive marble columns lined the length of indigo carpet that striped the center of the room, leading to the dais. The dais had three tiers. Four velvet-covered chairs sat on the first and lowest tier, two on the second, and the throne sat alone on the third. The throne was carved from a rich wood and polished to a shine. The back of the throne was sculpted to emulate a rearing Griffin, wings outstretched. The Griffin's feathers and talons were gold plated, and its eyes sparkled with sapphires.

Whether through a scry crystal's eyes or their own, the spectators watched as the four Councilors entered at one end of the room, walked down the long carpet, and sat in the four chairs on the first tier. Councilors Beatrice Fengar and Portia Stewart settled in the two chairs to the left of the throne, while Councilors Gretchen Dilmont and Rosalind Perda sat on the right.

Connor and his father followed the four Councilors shortly after and took their seats on the second tier. Connor felt the sapphire eyes bore into him, felt the eyes of the Court watch him, felt the eyes of the crowd and the glow of the crystals on him. He swallowed and tried to remember how to breathe normally. His father caught his eye and nodded once. He stood, and the low murmuring that had filled the hall was extinguished immediately.

"Good morning," Connor began. "Today marks the third and final day of the Contest of Queens. Today, our new ruler will take her place upon the throne to lead us with strength and compassion, with wisdom and justice into a prosperous age." He paused. An excited hum reverberated around the crowd and he waited for it to subside before he continued. "Contestants, please step into the center of the room."

At his words, the double doors at the far end of the hall opened. Chiv. Andromeda Turner entered first, her shoulders back, head level. Many of the crowd clapped as she walked the length of the room. Her long ash-blonde hair cascaded down her back, and her dark eyes flashed to the left and right of her as she approached the dais. She stood at ease, as was her training, and waited.

Chiv. Amber Everstar entered next, lively cheers erupted from her fans, and she waved happily left and right as she strode down the length of the room. Her brown hair was brushed back into a tight, low ponytail. She walked with a slight bounce in her step that made her appear taller than her actual stature. Her honey brown eyes glowed with determination and a small smirk crept into the corner of her mouth. She took her place next to Andromeda. Although she did not come up to Andromeda's shoulders, she stood just as proudly and radiated just as much right to be there.

Last came Dame Hera Claustrom. Where the two knights had marched down the purple carpet, Hera appeared to glide. Her blonde curls were arranged on top of her head in an intricate twist studded with jewels and held in place with a golden comb. Her attire dripped with the ornaments of her station. All three women wore tunics and leggings; however, Hera's tunic hung to her knees and was heavily embroidered with lace so fine and detailed, Connor imagined he could see the embroidered birds' wings flapping as she moved.

Hera joined the other two contestants and stood with her hands clasped in front of her, head high. Each woman looked every inch a Queen. The crowd had been following each contestant's entrance, and once Hera stood with the others, their eyes moved as one in the direction of the now closed doors. Expectant. The doors did not open again, and the crowd began to murmur their confusion. Connor winced inwardly; of course they were confused. The Council had decided to share as little information as possible.

Five women had completed the second task and fulfilled the task's expectations; five women had successfully exited the labyrinth, but only three women stood in the center of the room.

He heard a stomping from overhead and looked up to see members of the Court clicking their beaks and stamping their talons in outrage. *We disqualified the Courtiers,* Connor thought bitterly. He raised his hand for silence, but it took longer to come this time. When all had settled, he lowered his hand and continued. "Before you stand our three remaining contestants, one of whom will be crowned Queen of the Upper and Lower Queendom."

There was a screeching from overhead, too loud to be ignored. A number of voices in the crowd rose with names of the missing contestants. Questions hung heavy in the air. Connor faltered. He had received strict instructions from the Council in what information he was allowed to share.

Cllr. Perda stood and addressed the crowd. "For various reasons, these three women are our remaining contestants. Our only contestants. The only possibilities for our future Queen. The tasks have deemed it so. Let us continue."

The murmuring subsided slowly until the room was silent again except for the sound of rain and the low growls from above.

Cllr. Perda sat and gestured for Connor to continue. He tried to swallow around the lump in his throat and began again. "Over the last few days, these women have demonstrated many qualities that qualify them to rule our people. They have demonstrated courage, compassion, critical thinking, and a cool-headed determination that many of us can only dream to possess.

"Queen Ariel was known for her ability to sway the outcome of a war with her words. She had an incredible tact and way with language that allowed our people to flourish in peace and prosperity. She once told me that our land and our people are the most important priority; for our people we must sacrifice much of what we are as individuals. Today's task will require each of you to speak before us today. To speak before your people and demonstrate what you are willing to sacrifice to lead us."

Connor let the last sentence settle around the room before continuing.

"You will be taken to an antechamber to await your turn. The order of each contestant will be determined on the order they exited the labyrinth yesterday. Chivilra Andromeda Turner, you will speak first; Dame Hera Claustrom, you second; and Chivilra Amber Everstar, you will speak third." He paused again, took a breath, and said with emphasis, "It will be up to the people to judge who they would see lead them."

At this proclamation, the four Councilors, who had previously been engaged in quiet observation of the hall, twisted in their seats to stare in stunned silence at the Prince. This had not been part of the original task design. Cllr. Stewart bent her head and began whispering in Cllr. Fengar's ear, who nodded furiously and opened her mouth as though to interject.

"Once the speeches have concluded," Connor hurried on, "each subject will be given the time to acquire a mirror or water basin and asked to speak the name of the contestant they choose as their future Queen into it. This includes those viewing outside these castle walls, in towns and cities across the Queendom. Our scryers will be able to determine the winner from the volume of votes. Each citizen is able to only vote once."

Cllr. Gretchen Dilmont was staring at him with her mouth open, and the King looked at him as though seeing him for the first time. A proud smile stole across his face, and he shook his head in bewilderment. Cllr. Fengar fiddled nervously with the rings on her right hand. The contestants remained motionless, although Connor noticed Hera's eyes flash and a deepening in Amber's dimples. He raised another hand, and Perkins approached the three and led them to a chamber off to the right side of the dais.

"Chivilra Andromeda Turner will be given five minutes to collect her thoughts before stepping forward," Connor said as the door closed behind them. "I encourage you all to think on each participant's actions over the past few days and of which participant you see as the appropriate and worthy ruler of us all." He took his seat.

The crowd turned inward to discuss with neighbors this turn of events. The King leaned in and muttered, "I hope you know what you're playing at, boy."

Cllr. Perda, meanwhile, had risen from her seat and approached the Prince, "Surely you do not mean to have the fate of the Queendom decided by the plebeians?" she forced through gritted teeth. "There must always be a final authority on the matter and, I daresay, the Council stands ready to provide that."

"That is very magnanimous of you, Cllr. Perda, but I did not misspeak when I outlined the criteria for selection," Connor said blithely.

Cllr. Perda opened her mouth to say something more but thought better of it and sat back down. She and Cllr. Dilmont exchanged words too quiet for Connor to make out in the low rumbling buzz coming from the crowd.

After the longest five minutes Connor had ever experienced, Andromeda stepped out from the antechamber and took her place in the center of the carpet. The crowd quieted and waited in anticipation.

"People of our fair Queendom," she began stiffly. "I have served you since I became of age to serve. I am a woman of few words, but the words I have, I promise will always be used in the pursuit of justice and fairness for all. For you, I sacrifice my sword, the symbol of my training and discipline, the symbol of my rank, the symbol of my achievements in the field. I lay this sword at the feet of each subject I hope to rule and promise that it will only ever be used in your defense." Andromeda drew her sword, knelt, and presented her blade as an offering toward the throne. The crowd, upon realizing she had finished, burst into applause. She stood after a time, bowed her head, and was led by a servant to a seat at the edge of the dais.

Next, Hera emerged from the antechamber. She strode with certainty and stood poised like a dancer in front of the throne. She inclined her head to the Prince and then turned and faced the crowd. "People of our fair Queendom!" she announced with bravado; an excited thrum reverberated throughout the hall. "I am a woman of this Queendom raised among those who have always worked to better it. My mother, Lord Claustrom of Hesperida, has dedicated her life to bettering those in her county. Her charities are extensive, and she spends almost half of any profit our estate brings in on the community around her. I have had a blessed life and have been brought up in the lap of luxury because of my mother's daily sacrifices. For this Queendom, I sacrifice my inheritance. I sacrifice my lands and wealth, I lay it out for the people to benefit from, just as my mother has before me. Elect me as your Queen, and I will make sure our coffers floweth over evermore." A cheer rang up from the crowd as she bowed low, turned, and smiled at Connor, then took her seat beside Andromeda. She shared a comment with her that caused the knight to purse her lips.

The rain drummed out a heartbeat on the ceiling overhead and the crowd waited for the final contestant to step forward. Amber emerged slowly, her head bowed as she walked, taking her time, toward the center of the room. She took a deep breath, then lifted her gaze to the Prince. Her eyes were hard as iron, and Connor swallowed nervously despite himself. Clearing her throat, she never looked away from him.

"I am honored to be given this opportunity to participate in the contest to determine the next Queen. However, if I should win, I do not believe I could ever rule happily knowing that I may not be the true Queen this Queendom deserves. I demand the contestants Courtier Anya Bishop and Courtier Jacqueline Daidala be given their opportunity to prove themselves worthy, or else less worthy than myself, to be Queen. I will wait to give my speech, until this is performed." And with that, she planted her feet shoulder distance apart, clasped her hands behind her back, and bowed her head, waiting.

A shock ran through the crowd. The Councilors whispered desperately with one another; Connor looked at his father, who stared at Amber, bewildered. The piercing cry of several Griffins could be heard overhead. The eruption of noise silenced suddenly with the opening of the two great doors at the end of the hall.

28

THE FINAL TASK

Jacs, Lena, and Anya strode into the hall. Amber, standing stubbornly in front of the throne in wait, allowed a brief smile to cross her face at the sight.

Jacs held her head high, determined. Her hair hung in a straight tail down her back, and her clothes, though clean, were simple. Brown boots, cream tights, and a dark blue tunic. Lena was helping Anya, who walked with a slight limp.

Jacs caught Edith's eye where she stood to the left of the dais, and they exchanged a nod.

Her gaze shifted to Connor, seated beneath the throne, grinning broadly at her entrance. The crowd began to murmur, and from overhead came the piercing cries of Griffins. Jacs looked up in shock to see the ring of the Court brandishing their wings and stamping their talons in approval.

Connor held up his hand for silence and called across the hall, "It appears that you will not have to wait long, Chivilra Everstar, to have your request fulfilled." Humor colored his words.

Councilors Fengar and Perda had gotten to their feet, fury etched into each feature. "Enough!" roared Cllr. Perda, her eyes wild. "This is an outrage! These women have been disqualified from the contest. Their further participation is in violation with the laws that have governed our Queendom for centuries!" The other Councilors nodded furiously.

Jacs stepped forward. "That may be true of my companions, but I was never officially disqualified from the contest." She kept her gaze and voice steady.

"That's right!" said Cllr. Fengar, her voice wavering. "Courtier Bishop was disqualified for assaulting a member of the royal guard."

"And you, Jacqueline, were arrested for treason!" Cllr. Perda spat, brandishing a finger at her.

"But not disqualified," Jacs shot back.

"That does not—"

"Councilor, are you suggesting that we simply violate the laws that have governed our Queendom for centuries and prevent my participation in the final task?" Jacs watched as Cllr. Perda opened and closed her mouth several times. Cllr. Fengar looked to Cllr. Stewart, who shrugged her slim shoulders, at a loss.

"Well," came Cllr. Dilmont's tight-lipped reply. She held one arm across her body and the other perched by the elbow to allow her hand to rest under her chin. "Then we must rectify this oversight. You are hereby disqualified."

The crowd, who had been holding its breath, shouted both support and disagreement at these words.

"What?!" shouted Anya.

"You can't bloody do that!" Amber protested.

"On what grounds?" Jacs asked calmly.

It was a few moments before the hall was quiet enough for Cllr. Dilmont to continue. Her eyes flashed. "For your crimes as a Lowrian citizen."

Gasps fluttered around the crowd of onlookers and people began muttering. Jacs fought to make herself heard over the sudden flurry of sound. "My only crime is that I *am* a Lowrian citizen. And that is only a crime if you forget that I am a citizen of the same Queendom as all those here in the Upper Realm. I am of this Queendom. We are all of this Queendom. I have earned my right to be here. I have earned a voice in this contest."

Cllr. Dilmont glared at her.

Cllr. Perda moved around her chair and stepped toward Jacs. "You stand before us through schemes, tricks, and lies. You are not Courtier Jacqueline Daidala of Parima, you are Jacqueline Tabart of Bridgeport. You snuck into this contest to pervert its integrity." She moved toward Jacs slowly like a snake approaching a bird in the underbrush.

"I had no other choice! There is no other way for a Lowrian citizen to get to the Upper Realm. But my performance in this contest has been genuine. I could not have made it this far if I did not possess the qualities required of a Queen. Or do you refuse to believe a Lowrian could legitimately become Queen? I became a Courtier of my own merit, I completed two tasks of my own merit, I evaded those sent to sabotage us in the catacombs and scaled the Cliff between our two lands of my own merit, and now I will participate in the final task. It is my right." Jacs had begun walking toward the Councilor.

The Griffins roared their support and their cries reverberated around the chamber. Confusion rippled through the crowd. One half appeared to support Jacs's claim, while the other half sided with the Councilors. People were pressing forward. Jacs felt rather than saw Lena and Anya come to stand on either side of her. Amber joined their front, eyes darting from left to right.

There was a clatter from above and Jacs looked up to see a great white Griffin leap from its perch and fly through the hall. It landed heavily behind Jacs; wings outspread. She felt its breath on the back of her neck and tried not to wince as it roared at the Council.

There was a moment as the Councilors looked at one another.

"It appears Altus Thenya agrees, Councilors." The King, still seated, spoke softly, but every syllable seemed to ring to the outermost corners of the room. He appeared to be fighting an emotion within himself. Disgust and something close to anger flashed across his features as he regarded Jacs, but the regal mask came down, and he continued with his gaze averted. "This woman has risked everything to be here today. The Court believes she is worthy of a place among the finalists. If her motives were sinister, they would not speak for her."

Cllr. Perda regarded him levelly, then her shoulders slumped, and she nodded. "The Court has spoken," she said hollowly and walked back to her seat as the Prince stood.

"In accordance with the contest rules and the law of the Queendom, Courtier Jacqueline Tabart shall be allowed to participate in the final task. Perkins, please see the contestant to the antechamber to brief her on the requirements of this task. Chivilra

Everstar, I trust you are able to provide your response now?" he said.

Jacs turned and bowed low to the Griffin. She felt the familiar sensation of its beak in her hair. Rising, she squeezed Amber's hand and gave Lena and Anya quick hugs. She then turned, smiled at Connor, who winked at her, and followed Perkins to a room at the side of the hall.

"Of course," came Amber's reply as the door shut behind Jacs.

When Jacs reentered the hall, the crowd surged and boiled. She stood once again in the middle of the room, listening to jeers and muttered expressions of unrest. The resentment from the crowd felt like a tide barely held back by a dam.

Snatches of comments reached her ears, and she wished she could block them out completely.

"A Lowrian? Are they serious with this?"

"Basemutt."

"Such a joke."

She widened her stance and lifted her chin. The same white Griffin that had vouched for her against the Council returned to stand directly behind her now. She felt its warm breath. Altus Thenya was the reason the crowd kept the full force of their displeasure at bay. Emboldened by her silent sentinel, she drew herself up and cleared her throat.

"People of our Queendom," Jacs began. Although she had thought of nothing else for the past year, the reality that she was really there hit her like a wave and threatened to overwhelm her. She willed strength into her voice, willed her knees to steady, and willed her heart to slow. Her fingers found the Griffin ring at her neck, as warm as the breath of the real one standing behind her.

"I was born and raised in the Lowrian city of Bridgeport. Growing up, I would look at the Cliff and imagine what it would be like to travel up that Bridge. I wondered what the people were like. I wondered if they even ate the same things I did.

"Living among you for the past week, there were times when I forgot that I had traveled up the Cliffside. There were times that I expected to look up and recognize a member of my village in the crowd. I realize now that the differences I expected to see were fabrications. We are different, yes, but only in the same way that each of you is different from your neighbor. I have witnessed firsthand the brutality of prejudice's poison. I have seen decent and honest women and men beaten—and worse—because of people's assumptions about where they were born."

She took a steadying breath.

"I am from the Lower Realm, and I hear many of you using this fact to discredit my efforts to get to this point. How quickly did your attitudes change when you found out the location of my birth and upbringing?"

The crowd was almost silent now; only a few mutters could be heard.

"These slurs, these stereotypes, these attitudes serve no purpose other than to arbitrarily divide us. Upper, Lower, it's just a matter of location. The reality is much simpler: we all want to be accepted, and we all want to be treated with justice. I know that if our Queendom is to thrive and to grow, to provide these wants for all citizens, it needs unity. I am not saying that we should all be the same, for it is our differences that make us strong. I am saying that our differences need to be respected equally.

"This task asks us to demonstrate what we are willing to sacrifice to become Queen. I have already sacrificed everything. I left my home with the understanding that I may never see it again. My mother and my mentor are my whole world. They were apprehended after I had made it to the Upper Realm, and I . . ." her voice broke, she took a shaky breath, and continued. "Although I have since seen my mother, I could not be sure if I would ever see either of them again. If you want to know what I am willing to sacrifice for this Queendom, it is every breath I have left in me. It is every thought I have left in my mind. It is every beat of my heart. I am prepared to give all that is left of me to my people, because I know that together we can find peace between our two lands. Together, we can mend what has been broken. Together."

For a moment, all was still. Jacs felt her last word dance and float about the room. She bowed her head and waited for what was to come.

Lena was the first to clap. The spell broke, and others followed suit. Tentatively at first. Then, gradually, the hall filled with thunderous applause. The Griffins roared into the rafters. Jacs looked up and caught Connor's eye. The corners of his mouth twitched, and he inclined his head toward her. She turned and bowed to the Griffin, who ran its beak through her hair once more. Straightening, she made her way to the seat that had been placed for her next to the other three contestants. Amber clapped her on the shoulder.

Jacs scanned the crowd and noticed there were still looks of discontent, but far less than when she had first announced her Lowrian status. Lena and Anya were on their feet, cheering. The Councilors looked mutinous; Cllr. Perda whispered furiously to Cllr. Dilmont.

When the hall had finally quieted, the Prince stood. He held a mirror in his hand. Jacs noticed for the first time the small number of crystals lining the hall.

"You have now heard from each contestant. Consider carefully all you have observed in the past three days, all you have heard. The decision is in the hands of the Queendom. You will have three hours to vote for the contestant you would like to see become your Queen. We will reconvene at midday. Remember, to vote, simply state your name and the name of the contestant you are voting for into the mirror or basin on which you have been watching the contest. Their names again are: Chiv. Andromeda Turner, Dame Hera Claustrom, Chiv. Amber Everstar, and Courtier Jacqueline Tabart. Good luck, contestants."

The room erupted once more into applause and chatter. Everyone began filing out of the hall to cast their vote. Connor handed the mirror to Perkins before approaching the four contestants. Standing before them, he said in a much quieter voice, "You will most likely want a quiet place to await the results. You may return to your rooms, or one of the many rooms in the castle. I would suggest you enjoy the grounds, but they are . . . slightly soggier than usual today."

The four contestants stood and took their leave of the Prince one by one. He congratulated Andromeda and while his back was turned, Jacs felt a piercing grip on her upper arm. Stifling a yelp, she tried to pull free from Hera.

In a low murmur, Hera said in her ear, "You will learn your place, dog." Then louder, "My dear! What a shocking reveal. I hope it does nothing to affect your chances. That will be a long way to fall." She giggled lightly and released her grip. Gliding away serenely, she stopped to sink into an elaborate bow before the Prince.

Amber approached and wrapped her arms around Jacs's middle. "Good to see you!" she said warmly. "Prison does wonders for the complexion, it seems." She grinned.

Jacs laughed, rubbing her arm absently. "The cold and damp probably gave me a slight hue of death."

"Jacs, can I have a word?" Connor cut in.

"Of course," Jacs agreed, a flutter in her stomach. Amber turned to find Anya and Lena, winking at Jacs over her shoulder.

He led her to the antechamber. The door clicked shut behind them, and Jacs found she did not quite know what to do with her hands. Clasping them first in front, then behind her, she waited.

Connor did not appear to know how to start. He approached her slowly and stopped a few paces away.

"Thank you," Jacs said to break the silence, "for sending Edith to get me out."

He took her hands in his, "Jacs, you need to be very careful. Now more than ever. There are a number of people who do not want you here, and although I can try, I can't promise you will be safe, no matter the outcome."

"I know," Jacs said quietly. She looked down at his hands around hers. "But I'm so close."

"Just know, whatever happens next, I will do my best to keep you safe," Connor said.

She looked up and met his eyes with a smile. "It appears I can sometimes need help in that area." She took a small step forward. "But I've made it this far, I doubt it can get much worse, not with everyone watching. I'll be fine."

His brows creased in concern and searched her face for a moment. "Jacs, I'm serious."

"I know." She paused. "Do you know what they'll do with my mother? Or what they've done with Master Leschi?"

"Last I heard, they were awaiting trial. My father gave his word I would be present when the interrogation begins."

"What? But I saw my mother. I saw her in the cell near mine. She was . . ." The battered image of her mother filled her mind. "They hurt her. We have to get her out. And we have to find Master Leschi."

"Hurt? They wouldn't—"

"They did! I know what I saw." Jacs did not mean her words to come out so harshly. She pulled her hands from Connor's and ran the fingers of her uninjured arm through her hair. "If they have my mother, they can use her against me," she said quietly, remembering the way Maxine paraded her mother in front of her cell. "Can we go to the jail now; can we get them out?"

Before Connor could reply, the door creaked open. Cllr. Perda stepped into the room, followed closely by Cllr. Stewart. The former raised her eyebrows slightly at the two of them and said, "Cornelius, come. We need to review the changes you have made to the final task. Courtier, you will excuse us." She stepped back and waited expectantly. Cllr. Stewart nodded in a distracted manner, her thin neck appearing too frail to support her head.

Connor looked at Jacs and then back at the Councilors. He appeared poised for a moment on the brink of a decision, then Cllr. Perda's voice snapped again.

"We have very little time and much to alter, thanks to your . . . inspiration." She gestured impatiently for him to follow.

"Go," said Jacs in a voice she hoped would not carry to the two figures in the doorway. "I'll be fine."

With one last look of concern, Connor followed Cllr. Perda through the door. Cllr. Stewart moved to the side to let them pass and followed. The door snapped shut behind them. There was a pause. Jacs took a breath, straightened her tunic, and moved to leave the room.

"She went in here," Jacs heard Amber say as she stepped through the door.

"Jacqueline!" Lena said with relief.

Jacs smiled at the looks of concern on her friends' faces.

They embraced in the still emptying hall.

Amber, leaning against the wall, said with a smirk, "You know how to give a knight a run for her money."

Jacs grinned at her. "Well you were the one who wanted a fair fight."

Anya glanced nervously around the hall at the glowing crystals. Jacs noticed she threaded her fingers through Lena's. Lena caught Jacs's eye and beamed.

"Let's find somewhere a little less open to talk; we want to hear all about what's happened," Anya said.

Jacs agreed and added, "I have to do something first."

"Do what?" Amber asked.

"I need to find my mother," Jacs replied.

Anya and Lena both started talking at the same time.

"Your—" began Lena.

"But isn't she down—" said Anya.

"She's here, she's in a cell, and she's hurt. Edith said she'd send someone to help, but I need to see that she's all right. And if I can, I need to find Master Leschi."

Jacs forced her mind to stay on the task at hand and not think about the possible outcomes.

"Edith?" said Amber.

"Master who?" asked Lena.

"But I thought you were from the Lower Realm? How did they get up here?" asked Anya.

Jacs looked at each puzzled face, drew them all back into the antechamber and away from the crystals' eyes, took a deep breath, and explained everything. She told them about the balloon, seeing her mother and mentor apprehended, and her night in the prison. Her friends listened intently, and she tried to keep the details to a minimum. By the time she was finished, the confused visages had been replaced with looks of concern and determination. Jacs glanced at Lena, her eyes shining bright with eagerness to help, and recognized the same look she had worn the day they met. Jacs's stomach twisted with shame. Her next words faltered and died. Instead, she said, "Lena, I'm so sorry."

Lena's eyes widened slightly. "Whatever for?" she asked.

"What for? For lying to you. For not telling you the truth sooner. You have been nothing but kind to me and should not have found out the way you did." Jacs felt her cheeks burn.

Lena waved her hand dismissively, "Please don't, I understand why you didn't tell me. And I think," she paused delicately, "if I hadn't gotten the chance to know you like I do now, before finding out where you were born, it might have been hard for me to see you as a friend." She hesitated and looked uncomfortable, "I would have been wrong, and the lesser for not knowing you. But it's like you said in there . . . Prejudice is a poison that twists our hearts. So—" she took a breath "—I'm sorry too."

A loaded silence followed her words as neither woman knew what to say next. But where words failed, actions spoke, and Lena closed the distance between them, embracing her warmly. Jacs smiled and wrapped her arms around her slight frame, her heart light.

"Thank you," she whispered as they drew apart.

Finally Amber shook her head. "I can't believe you flew a balloon up here."

Anya snorted a laugh. "Absolutely mental."

"Well, necessity is the mother of invention," Jacs responded simply, a smile playing on her lips. "But I need to find my mother— if you're coming, we should go."

The four women hurried out of the hall.

Running through the corridor was much more difficult now that the castle was awake and bustling. Jacs felt weariness tugging at her bones and slowing her step. She forced herself to concentrate on retracing the path she had taken with Edith. *It was left past the hunting tapestry and up the spiral staircase*, she remembered. The small group walked quickly through the relaxed lull that had settled over the castle as everyone waited for the voting to conclude. Jacs did not give those she came across time to question her purpose.

The image of the blankness in her mother's eyes pressed her forward.

They passed an elaborate and ornate grandmother clock on their way past the entrance hall. Jacs checked the time: ten o'clock. Connor had said they had until noon. That gave them two hours to find her mother and return in time for the announcement.

The hallways they were traveling along changed from lavish to austere. They climbed up the stone stairwell to the floor Jacs remembered. She stopped before opening the door to the hallway.

"Okay, this is it," she said, panting slightly.

"What's the plan?" Amber asked.

Jacs hesitated. "First I just need to see that she's all right. I'm not sure from there."

The other women looked at each other. "Okay," they agreed together.

Jacs pushed open the wooden door and stepped into the hallway. Pressing a finger to her lips and looking at the others, she headed toward the second cell from the door. The cell she knew her mother to be in. She passed the first cell. Empty. She came abreast of the second cell and froze.

It too was empty.

Dark red splotches marked fragments of handprints on the bars and peppered the spot where she had been.

Anya tapped Jacs's shoulder and mouthed a question. Jacs gestured at the cell with wide eyes, a hand to her mouth. Her mind was racing. Why had she been moved? Where had she been moved? She heard a chair creak down the hall where she knew the guard's desk to be.

Suddenly, causing her friends to jump, she called, "Maxine? Is that you down there?"

"Yeah? Who's that?" came a gruff reply.

"What are you doing?" Amber hissed while Lena made frantic shushing motions with her hands.

Jacs waved them down, she rounded on Amber and said quickly, "Amber you're a knight, she's a guard, go ask her where Maria Tabart got moved. If she sees me, she might recognize me, and I've already been locked up once. Please, we'll stay here if you need us."

Amber nodded and turned to walk confidently toward the guard's desk.

"Maxine," Amber said loudly, "I heard good things about you from Masterchiv Rathbone. I'm Chivilra Everstar of the Springbank Division. At ease, guardswoman, there's no need to get up. Honestly, the contest has had this whole city in shambles, so I respect your adherence to custom. Listen, I'm not going to waste too much of your time, I know how busy you can get up here, I just need an update on the Lowrian prisoner, a Maria Tabart?"

Jacs grinned and shook her head in wonder at the other two. They heard Maxine's slow response as her mind caught up with her mouth. "Springbank . . . update . . . ah, right, the Lowrian, she was moved."

"Moved where?" Amber inquired.

"Why does the Springbank Divi—"

"Maxine, our next Queen is about to be announced. I was asked to make sure all protocol has been followed with regard to the Lowrian's movement. We can't afford any mistakes. I will ask you again, where was she moved and by whom?" Her voice was hard steel.

"Oh—of course! Cllr. Gretchen came with two guards to move her just after the third task. She didn't say where. She just took her. B-but that's not against protocol." Maxine sounded almost apologetic as she finished. Jacs imagined a bear apologizing to a housecat and felt pride for her friend surge in her chest.

There was the sound of a palm slapping on wood and Amber said, "Good show, Maxine." Her footsteps rang around the hallway as she returned to where her friends were listening. They headed out the door.

"What do we do now?" Lena asked as they descended the spiral staircase.

"I don't know. Why would they move her? Edith said she would send someone to check on her. Maybe they took her to Master Epione?" Jacs suggested hopefully.

"I don't know this jail system so it might be different from Springbank, but prisoners can get moved for a bundle of reasons," Amber offered.

"Like what?" asked Jacs.

"Well, questioning, time in the yard, time in confinement, trial, execu—" she cut herself off hurriedly "—and a whole number of other reasons."

"Wait, wha—" Panic fluttered in Jacs's chest.

"But if the Councilor came to get her, it must be for a more serious reason," Amber interrupted.

"But you said—" Jacs spluttered.

"And she wouldn't waste her time to escort someone for an execution," Amber said gently.

"Oh," Jacs said in a small voice.

"We'll find her," Lena assured her.

"Plus, there's a good chance that one of you two," Anya indicated Amber and Jacs, "will become Queen in the next hour. Then you'll have the power to grant her a pardon. That said, we should probably get back to claim that crown."

"Yeah, you're right." Jacs felt a tightness build in her chest and swallowed over the lump in her throat. "Let's get back."

29

LONG LIVE THE QUEEN

The rain had slowed to a drizzle, and the sun sparkled on the thousands of tiny droplets scattered across leaves and benches. Sunlight filtered through the high windows in the throne room. The Court had returned and was assembled in its lofty chamber, surveying the crowd below them. Many of the guests clutched mirrors and the air was full of speculation.

The four contestants stood side by side, looking up at the empty throne. The jeweled eyes of the rearing Griffin glittered. Jacs reached for Amber's hand and gave it a squeeze. She felt the firm response before letting go and clasping her hands behind her back. Her thoughts raced, and her heart pounded. She focused on the glittering eyes of the Griffin and felt her mind empty itself. Like sand trickling through an hourglass, her thoughts slipped away. A slow thudding, like the beating of wings, filled her ears.

Then Connor stood and began to speak. The steady rhythm in her mind drowned his introductions and she heard him as if from the bottom of a deep well. Shaking her head to clear it, she felt worry begin to tighten her chest again, like a coiled spring, and clutched her hands together.

Finally she heard him announce with a broad grin on his face: "My fair Queendom, it is with honor that I present to you, your Queen, as voted by both Upperite and Lowrian citizens, Her Royal Highness, Jacqueline Tabart . . ."

The rest of his sentence was engulfed in the uproar that followed his words. Jacs felt Amber clap her on the back. She heard the triumphant screeches from the Court, and saw Lena and Anya hug each other with broad grins on their faces. She felt the realization wash over her. Pulling Amber into a tight hug, she turned to do the same to Andromeda.

Hera had taken a step back and looked livid.

The Prince beckoned Jacs to step forward. Perkins, standing behind him and to his right, held a golden crown of wrought feathers and oak leaves glittering on a deep blue velvet cushion. Jacs made her way toward Connor; the hall seemed much longer than she had originally thought and the few steps required to reach him seemed to take an eternity. As she drew level with him, he indicated for Perkins to step forward. At another gesture from Connor, Jacs turned around to face the hall.

"Kneel with the knowledge that you now kneel to honor and to serve your Queendom." Jacs did as she was instructed, feeling hundreds of eyes and dozens of crystals on her. She scanned the crowd and saw a mixture of surprise, excitement, resentment, and confusion on their faces.

"And rise, Queen Jacqueline."

She rose, and the hall erupted in a discordant uproar. The cheers of celebration from the crowd and triumphant roars of the Griffins were woven in with screams of outrage. Jacs saw it all as though gazing at one of the many tapestries she had seen during her stay in the castle. All faces, all emotions entwined together to make a connected whole. She saw Anya and Lena embrace, beaming; she saw Amber stoically shake Andromeda's hand, she saw a number of feathers flutter down from above, loosened from their hosts' beating wings; and she saw mutiny etched into faces dotted around the room. Hera looked livid, and softly, below the noise echoing around the chamber, came the steady hiss of whispers from the Councilors behind her. She shifted her gaze to her right, Connor beamed at her, and she felt a warmth spread through her. She stood proudly as the crown was placed on her head.

The celebration moved from the throne room to the airy banquet hall. The hole in the wall from the earlier blast had been hurriedly patched, the water from the fountain and rain had been mopped up, and the debris had either been cleared or turned into creative additions to the furniture. It was almost possible to forget that an explosion had torn the room apart only days ago.

Before joining the revelry, Jacs was escorted to her new chambers to divest her commoner garb and don the vestments of state. Her arm was freshly bandaged, and the wrappings covered with a delicately embroidered lace. She stood on a stool in the center of the room in a complete daze as her new ladies-in-waiting flitted around her like moths around a flame.

Suddenly, there was a rap at the door, and the Council of Four was announced. The ladies fell silent and, as one, stepped away from Jacs with their heads bowed. The Councilors entered slowly, and each fell into an elaborate bow before Jacs. Jacs felt trapped by the heavy gown that now weighted her to the stool.

"Your Highness, if we could have a moment alone," Cllr. Rosalind Perda stated. It was not a request.

Jacs looked around her at the bowed-headed strangers and nodded.

"Of course," she faltered. "Ladies, please wait outside until I call you." The command felt thick on her tongue. With low bows and averted eyes, the ladies filed out of the room.

With the click of the door, the four Council members rose. Jacs awkwardly stepped down from the stool. Her foot caught in the hem of her gown causing her to stumble slightly. The four watched as she righted herself.

"An ill fit, it appears," Cllr. Perda mused.

"It fits fine, thank you," Jacs said, bristling. "How can I help?"

Cllr. Perda raised an eyebrow and indicated the other three members. "Your Highness, as you are Lowrian born, there are many customs you may be unfamiliar with. Are you aware of the Council's role within the Queendom?"

"I . . . not exactly."

Cllr. Dilmont's brow furrowed, and Cllr. Perda merely smirked as she continued. "Let's start at the beginning then, shall we? I am Cllr. Rosalind Perda, and these are Councilors Gretchen Dilmont, Portia Stewart, and Beatrice Fengar." With each name announced, the corresponding Councilor inclined her head. At her name, the various pens in Cllr. Fengar's bun clinked together like a bizarre wind chime. Jacs thought briefly of the wind chimes she had helped Master Leschi create, and of the wild assortment of instruments that always protruded from her mentor's hair. She was disappointed to note that Cllr. Fengar's face held little of the warmth Master Leschi's had. The assortment of tools in her bun glinted menacingly like weapons waiting to be deployed.

Cllr. Perda continued. "We oversee the upholding of tradition, policy, and cultural heritage of the Queendom. While the Queen stands on the helm of the ship, we are the sails, rudder, and wheel. The Council has always been instrumental in the choosing of the last Queens, and our successors will continue to protect the throne just as we have."

Jacs felt ice creeping into the pit of her stomach. There was something predatory in the glint of Cllr. Perda's eyes.

"You were a . . . surprising choice," Cllr. Perda said.

"And we do not surprise easily," piped in Cllr. Stewart, her voice a thin reverberation of Cllr. Perda's strong cadence.

"No, we do not," Cllr. Dilmont added.

Jacs frowned. "I was chosen by the people."

"Yes," Cllr. Perda said with slow deliberation, "but the interesting thing about that is where your votes came from. You see, we have spoken with the scryers. We looked at the votes. It appears the majority of your votes came from Lowrian citizens."

"Another surprise," said Cllr. Fengar.

"Quite right, Beatrice. Lowrians do not typically have an opportunity to vote in this contest. What with their . . . busy lives, they cannot be expected to find the time," said Cllr. Perda delicately.

Jacs's eyes narrowed at the lie; she knew Lowrians were not permitted to vote on any policies concerning the Queendom.

"I'm assuming Lowrians were allowed to vote this time?" she said.

"Yet another surprise," Cllr. Dilmont replied.

"Which puts you in a rather interesting position," Cllr. Stewart said, a giggle softening her words.

"How so?" Jacs asked, forcing an air of disinterest.

"Why, because it appears your supporters are an awfully long way away, and conversely, many closer to home are not pleased with your elevation." Cllr. Perda's grin widened.

"I see," Jacs replied, the ice in the pit of her stomach reaching her tongue and constricting her words.

"I'm not sure you do see—" Cllr. Perda began.

"I can assure you, I do." Jacs's heart thudded a warning in her ears. "But regardless of where my voters live, I am Queen." She took a breath. "I am Queen, and as Queen, I will ensure the prosperity of my Queendom, and silence those who threaten progress." She saw Cllr. Perda's eyes harden.

"Interesting," Cllr. Perda said, all warmth sapped from her tone. "I wonder how you would go about doing that?"

"Doing . . . ?" Jacs's voice wavered.

"Silencing those who threaten your idea of progress." Cllr. Perda fired back.

"Well—"

"Well?" Cllr. Perda said.

"As Queen—"

Cllr. Perda pounced. "As Queen with what supporters? You think you have power now that you have a title? Sweetheart, it's about connections. How many of the nobility can you count on to support you? How many of your guards can you count on to lay down their lives for you?"

Jacs scrambled for a response, but Cllr. Perda pressed on.

"How many informers do you have to reveal plots against you before it's too late? How many of your newly appointed ladies-in-waiting do you know to be loyal or even trustworthy? How many?"

The silence that followed her assault answered her questions. The Councilors were all smiling now.

"Why, if you can't even keep your own family safe, how do you propose to keep yourself or your Queendom safe?" Cllr. Perda said with quiet malice in her voice.

Jacs felt the ice inside her splinter, and a ringing filled her ears. Something the guard Maxine had said came echoing back to her. "Where is my mother?" Jacs hissed. "Where is Master Leschi?"

Cllr. Perda spoke as though she had not heard her. "Connections are everything in this world you so apparently know nothing about. I think you have already met some of our connections. Some of our associates? You already know their subtlety." At her words, the image of a purple hooded figure filled Jacs's mind.

"They were yours? The men in hoods?"

Cllr. Perda simply smiled more widely. "Unlike you, Lord Claustrom has always been able to provide for her Queendom. Land, money, extra womanpower. Her daughter would have made a much more useful Queen." She made a tsking sound.

"And the hooded assassins? On the clock tower?" Jacs's mouth had gone dry.

Cllr. Perda's eyes flashed, and her lips tightened. "As luck would have it, some of Lord Claustrom's connections have even taken a fancy to your poor frail mother. Others are very interested in the infamous Master Leschi."

"Where—" Jacs said.

"All we want," Cllr. Dilmont stepped forward, towering over Jacs, "is to uphold tradition, protect policy, and maintain the cultural heritage of our Queendom. By any means necessary. Any threat to the Council's plans will be met with force. And I'm not sure how much more force your mother can withstand."

"I'm sure we can come to some sort of arrangement where . . . everyone is happy," Perda said delicately.

Jacs felt panic seize her throat. "You can't—"

"Oh, my dear—" Cllr. Perda shook her head with mock sympathy "—of course we can. Now, let's get you to the feast. Big smiles, the Queendom awaits." And she held out her hand for Jacs to take.

Jacs had stopped breathing. She looked at each smiling mask and down at Cllr. Perda's offered hand. The moment stretched, slowed, and hung suspended between them. Cllr. Perda gave her hand a small, impatient shake.

In a flash, Jacs thought of Lena's hand helping her into her carriage, of Anya's hand beside hers as they toppled the pillar into the water fountain, of Andromeda's hand pushing her back down on the grass to rest, of Amber's hand around the throat of the hooded attacker, and of Connor's hand holding hers through the bars of a prison cell. She looked into the hungry eyes of the Councilor and felt her army rally behind her.

With a tight smile, Jacs clasped her hands in front of her and swept toward the door with the Councilors hurrying to follow in her wake.

"Of course," said the Queen, "and they have waited long enough."

ACKNOWLEDGMENTS

Holy smokes, this novel has been a true labor of love, and I think I will go to my grave pinching myself that it is now in print. What started as a bullet point on a bucket list at fifteen emerged as you see it now over a decade later.

First and foremost, thank you to the CamCat team for making this dream a reality. I will never forget the phone call from Sue at CamCat. After hearing the words, "We loved it. We want to publish your book," I had stayed completely silent and frozen until I heard Sue's voice on the other end of the line say, "You can scream now!" I don't think the written word can aptly capture the exact sound that came out of my mouth after that.

To my incredible editor, Bridget. Your enthusiasm is so inspiring, and your music taste is on point. From the little edits to the bigger overhauls, you were a dream to work with, and I learned so much from you. Thank you for seeing the diamond in the rough and bringing out its sparkle.

To the rest of the CamCat team that brought this all together: Maryann, the cover is stunning, and I will never tire of looking at it; Laura, Sophie, and Abigail with marketing; Helga and my copyeditors, Ellen and Elana, thank you for polishing this gem to a high shine. I know there are a lot more people behind the scenes who I didn't always interact with directly but thank you to you all! This would still be a document on my computer and several scribbled-in journals without you.

For my parents who have and always will be the first to read anything I write. There aren't enough words that can thank you enough for the life you have given me and the love you have shown me, and I am so proud to be your daughter. For my mum who is a Queen in her own right, and my dad who has spent my lifetime showing me what a true King looks like. You were my first storytellers, my biggest cheerleaders, and I love the stuffing out of you.

To my brother, who I love to the stars and back, you keep me grounded and get me out of my own head when I get stuck in there. And for the rest of my family, you are my roots and my foundation, thank you for giving me a solid jumping off point and a safe space to fall.

To my dear friend Andrew, who designed the map of Frea (and forced me to commit and actually name the world I had created). You're a light in a dark tunnel and one of the best friends I could be lucky in this life to find. Thank you for making my world feel tangible, for the cooking videocalls, for always lending an ear, and above all, for seeing me.

To Laura, thank you for all our chats. Your perspective, your insight, your sassy-molassy smirk, and for always bringing a sense of mystery and intrigue to my life. For Josh, to watch a master world/story creator at work every week is awe-inspiring, and thank you for having endless patience and for taking the time to teach me anything tech related. For Kara, you have a heart of gold, and I miss our lunch dates. To Jamie, for your strength, compassion, and incredible sense of humor. You have a beautiful ability to make others shine, and I hope you know you shine brighter than most. And to Krystian, for your kindness, your genuine heart, and for "Oh Jeez'ing" us through the rough patches. You guys make my life a party. Thank you for the memories, the adventures, and for bringing magic to my world.

To all my beta readers, your feedback helped shape this story into what it is today. Thank you for reading through its growing pains! As a wise fictional character once said, "While it is always best to believe in oneself, a little help from others can be a great blessing." To Nikki, for facetime book clubs, "Yasss Queen" bevies, and endless Austen analysis. To Sarah, for being the Aragorn to my Legolas (or, more accurately, the Merry to my Pippin), and for travels to castles, shires, and graveyards (after dark). I couldn't have asked for a better quest buddy. To Jesse, for all our chats, for keeping me on my toes, for matched wits and epic banter. And Jenna, for your radiance, your generous heart, and for thriving when others thrive too.

To the powerful queens (and kings) I have the great fortune of knowing, for your inspiration, your strength, your guidance, and your goofiness. I couldn't write about such incredible characters without some real-life role models to guide my pen. Thank you for your sparkle, my life would be much less vibrant without your colors in it.

To Karli, we made it! Ooh ooh! To Sonya, Jessie, Asha, Julia, and Sarah, for the quests of epic proportions, and for giving me more inspiration than I know how to write about. To Angelica and Katie, for the dance moves, the frosé, for putting a ring on it, and for showing me what true loyalty and perseverance looks like. To Erin, for the music. To Angelina, for the sewing chats. To Cecelia, for the mood, Madison minutes, and craft nights. To Michelle, for peddles, paddles, and Disney sing-a-longs. To Erin and my Yoga Kula, for the life lessons I didn't know I needed and for showing me community is made anywhere (even if we're all stuck in a lockdown). To Hilary, Lara, Kayla, and Kelsie, for the goodwill and fellowship. To Ashley and Kat, for the beers, movies, and Azula squad. To Leslie and Gordon, for knowing how to read the fine print. To Sammy and Joe, for ice cream and Springsteen. To Jo-Annie, Olive, and Chris, for making my life a little more gourmet, and a lot more exciting. To Matt, for tea, fairy lights, and for weaving Jacs and Connor into music. To James, for Spain and for showing me that a week can impact a lifetime—how good is Die Hard? For the wonderful hearts I have found around the world in Kate, Diana, Brandy, Kaet, Ellen, Whitney, Sara, Eva, Gemma, Syd, Gwen, Denny, Annie, Jill, Marilynn, Lesa, Karen, Jo, Jodie, and many many more.

To the storytellers before me who carried me to new places, introduced me to new people, and whose lessons taught me how to be okay in this world. You inspired me to create one of my own, and I hope mine provides even a sliver of wisdom, comfort, and inspiration to those who come after me.

To all the people I've loved and lost, all the people I've grown with or outgrown, all the fleeting meetings of magic and disaster, and the equal measures of light and darkness. For the people who entered my life and stayed for a moment, a season, or who are still with me now. It's the kaleidoscope of my experiences and interactions that has brought life to this story, and I can't regret a single laugh or tear that has led me here.

Finally, to anyone currently holding a copy of this in their hands. Oh my goodness, this is something I never imagined becoming a reality, and I want to thank you so much for being a part of it. Wherever you are in this life, I hope you're well, and that you meet each day heart first.

ABOUT THE AUTHOR

New Zealand-born Canadian Jordan H. Bartlett has lived on islands and surrounded by mountains; has fallen asleep to the sound of waves and train whistles. Growing up, home was the label given to family, not places, and stories of adventure kept her reaching toward the horizon. She grew up reading books about boys for boys and struggled to find that strong female heroine she could relate to. While empowered female characters are more prevalent in recent literature, they are often found in worlds dominated by men. Bartlett wrote *Contest of Queens* asking, "What if?" to create a world asking where females are the default gender and to show that no gender is perfect when in the power majority.

Bartlett has studied the areas of children's literature and the role of women in literature throughout history. It is through this affinity for fairy tales mixed with her desire to breathe life into compelling, unique, and ultimately flawed female characters in a world where they have not been tethered that she hopes to flip fantasy tropes and challenge gendered expectations in young adult readers—while keeping the levity of a fairy tale.

When she is not writing, Bartlett works as a Speech Language Pathologist and is a certified yoga instructor in Banff, Alberta. Any other free time is spent hiking, biking, and kayaking in the mountains and lakes of her backyard. She has devoured literature all her life and is honored to add to the world's library.

Find her short stories, fairytales, and art for
Contest of Queens
at
www.jordanhbartlett.com.

AUTHOR Q & A

Q: **What message/idea do you hope your readers take away from this book?**

A: That in all things, be kind. I hope that this novel shows that prejudice and division of people based on where they're born or what gender they are only makes us weaker as a whole. I hope that it makes people think about and reevaluate their own prejudices and how they impact others. I hope my book shows that at the end of the day, people are people. Give one group power and how they shape the world might look different, but there will always be those who are corrupt, and there will always be those fighting for what's right.

Q: What inspired you to write *Contest of Queens*?

A: A few things went into the lightbulb that went off in my head for this novel. The concept of a split-level kingdom (now queendom) has been in my mind since I was fifteen, as has the character of Jacs and her desire to make it to the Upper Realm. Both stemmed from the fairy tale retelling phase I was in at the time and my affinity for *Jack and the Beanstalk*. Many many years later, my Poppa became ill. There's not a lot you can do when you start to lose a loved one. However, my Poppa was an amazing storyteller, and when I was younger, one of my favorite stories that he would tell us was *Jack and the Beanstalk*. So something I could do to honor him was to write a story of my own, inspired by his.

The idea of a fantasy novel set in a matriarchal society came from a conversation I had with a dear friend of mine over tea. We were discussing how annoying it was that so many fantasy authors will create worlds with dragons and elves and whole new cultures and language systems but somehow decide to keep sexism and racism as a norm. The beauty of a fantasy world is that you can do whatever you want. You can create your own rules. Fantasy novels are a beautiful source of escapism, so why would I want to escape into a world where the societal narrative is the same (often worse) sexist bologna we deal with in our day-to-day?

Q: What aspect of your world are you most proud of?

A: Honestly, I really enjoyed creating and writing about the guard pairs and knights, which is wild because they weren't in my first storyboard and arose as a result of the worldbuilding that happened while writing the first draft. It was such a fun thought experiment to work out: okay, women on average are not as strong as men, how can they still be effective and intimidating law enforcers and a realistic military? And on the flip side, what would the narrative be that would exclude men from joining the ranks? I wanted to keep it as realistic as possible. I drew a lot of inspiration from the show *Avatar: the Last Airbender*, from research around martial art styles like Aikido that focus on outmaneuvering the opponent (rather than being stronger), and from the novel *Terrier* by Tamora Pierce.

Q: What was the most challenging part about writing a matriarchal world?

A: The language. Oh nelly, I was not expecting words to fail me, but the English language, I discovered, is patriarchal in nature. So many things I didn't expect needed to be renamed or reworded. Specifically the titles—many of the female titles we have did not carry the same power behind them. For example, in our world we have Lord and Lady, so to simply switch the power of these two would not convey the same message to the reader given the reader expectations, plus I wanted to leave it more open for same gender couples. That's where Lord and Genteel came from. Lord is gendered female, and Genteel is the gender-neutral term for a Lord's spouse. Also, balancing the language and the power dynamics in a heterosexual kissing scene was way more complicated than it should be! Who makes the first move? Who is being acted upon? How is it described? What are my world's expectations on how that should look?

Q: Who was your favorite character to write?

A: This answer changes day-to-day, because they all feel like a little piece of me, but I loved writing Amber. She has a gumption and confidence that was fun to capture on the page.

Q: Do you have a favorite quote? What about that quote attracts you?

A: This changes depending on what I'm reading and where my head and heart are, but right now, I have two favorite quotes. The first is from Patrick Rothfuss's novel *The Slow Regard of Silent Things*. *"To be so lovely and so lost. To be all answerful with all that knowing trapped inside. To be beautiful and broken."* I just love that duality. Especially in the last couple of years, the idea that we can be broken and still beautiful is really comforting, because if we've lived any form of life, we're all a little broken —but that doesn't have to mean we have lost any ounce of our value or shine.

My other favorite quote is from Brandon Sanderson's *Oathbringer*. *"The most important step a [wo]man can take. It's not the first one, is it? It's the next one. Always the next step."* I mean, this one was also said beautifully by Donkey in *Shrek*, *"keep on moving, don't look down,"* in Disney's *Meet the Robinsons*, *"Keep moving forward,"* and even by Winston Churchill, *"If you're going through hell, keep going,"* so it's probably a sentiment a lot of us need to hear in a lot of different ways, from a lot of different mouths. So if you, dear reader, need to hear it too, then here it is again from John Silver in *Treasure Planet*, *"You got the makings of greatness in you, but you gotta take the helm and chart your own course! Stick to it, no matter the squalls!"*

Q: **What was the most surprising part of the writing/
publishing process?**

A: Definitely all the incredible people I met along the way. I had
absolutely zero clue about the publishing process, and it's
almost laughable how I thought that the writing of the book
would be the hardest part . . . But so many people with busier
lives than mine were willing to take the time to go for coffee or
chat on the phone with me about the industry, give their
advice, and share their experiences. It's such a beautiful
community that I feel lucky to be a part of.

FOR FURTHER DISCUSSION

1. The contest is designed to find the right queen for the Queendom. Do you think it is a fair contest? Do you think there are biased aspects?

2. The citizens are led to believe the contest is infallible. Is ignorance truly bliss? Discuss.

3. Who do you think is/are the villain(s) of the story?

4. What is a central theme of this novel? Discuss.

5. What is the significance of both Jacs and Connor having two names? How does this affect the plot? How does this tie into the novel's theme of identity?

6. What does the novel say about prejudice?

7. How do the characters address gender roles? What are some beliefs held about women in this world? What are some beliefs held about men in this world? How are these beliefs true/false? How do these beliefs affect different characters?

8. Share a favorite quote of the book. What was it about this quote that made it memorable?

If you've enjoyed
Jordan H. Bartlett's *Contest of Queens*,
you'll enjoy
Brandie June's *Gold Spun*.

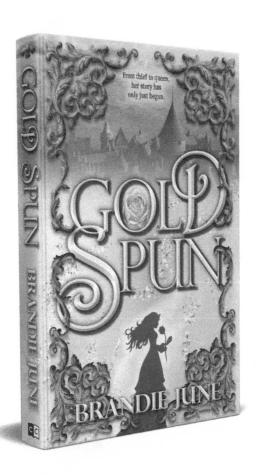

PROLOGUE

Prince Casper leaned against the ornately carved marble railing of the balcony as he finished the last of his coffee. In his five years as a royal hostage he had developed a taste for the very sweet cinnamon coffee so common in Faradisia, but always wondered if he would still enjoy the strong, bitter tea of Reynallis when he was finally given leave to return home.

If he was ever allowed home.

It had been weeks since his brother, King Christopher, sent him a letter. When Casper first arrived in Faradisia, his brother had written almost every day, praising Casper's courage and keeping him updated with news of home. Casper knew his brother was occupied with ruling Reynallis, aware that his focus was now directed at keeping their country safe from the dangerous fay. Still, he could not help the feeling that he had been sacrificed and forgotten.

Casper stared at the vast landscape of Faradisia, long rows of citrus trees and wide stretches of grassland that were only green during the few weeks of rain. The sole movement in the serene valley was a lone man on horseback, galloping toward the palacio. As he neared, Casper could make out the official orange and white garb of a royal messenger. Casper idly wondered what news the messenger was bringing, though he knew King Jovian would never share sensitive information with Casper. The Faradisian king treated Casper with great courtesy, but never forgot that Casper's first loyalty was to his home country.

Straining his eyes towards the horizon, Casper imagined that he could see all the way to Reynallis. It was foolish, he knew, but it was his habit since he came to King Jovian's palacio. He had been fourteen when he first arrived as an 'honored' guest. Not wanting to shame his brother or his country, Casper only allowed himself to cry in the very early hours of the morning, long before even the servants would come to wake him. He would creep out on his balcony and stare to the north, his heart aching for home. He had not shed any tears in years, but he still looked towards Reynallis every morning.

Sighing, he set down the slender porcelain mug, wondering what activities the day had in store for him. Though it was mid-winter, the southern kingdom of Faradisia enjoyed mild winters, a brief respite from their sweltering summers. Perhaps Lord Gerreld would want to hunt game or the ladies of the court would be interested in organizing a picnic by the hot springs. He might be afforded the finest luxuries the country had to offer, but his time was dictated by the whims of the Faradisian nobility, and his every move was subtly watched by half a dozen guards, even though he had never given King Jovian the slightest reason to doubt him.

As if reading his thoughts, King Jovian himself burst into his room, his rich orange and white robes flaring out behind him.

Casper startled, nearly knocking over his cup. The king never came to Casper's quarters, rather summoning Casper when he required an audience with the Reynallis prince.

"King Jovian," Casper managed, giving a short bow to the king, as he smoothed on his diplomatic grace. "I am honored by this unexpected visit." But the smile slid off his face as Casper approached the king, noting his grimace.

"Prince Casper, a messenger arrived this morning from Reynallis. I thought it only right that I be the one to tell you." King Jovian paused. For a wild moment, Casper hoped that Christopher was sending for him, that his clever brother had finally found a way to keep peace with Faradisia and summon him home. But the question died on his lips as he noted the deep furrow in King Jovian's forehead. Casper swallowed hard, a sudden knot of fear making him sick. He had to fight the desire to cover his ears.

"I take it the news is not pleasant," Casper said, forcing his words to remain calm even as his mind whirled, trying to figure out what could be so important that the king himself would deliver it.

King Jovian briefly looked away before fixing Casper with an unblinking stare. "No, it is most grave."

"The treaty?" Casper could not imagine his brother would do anything to destroy the peace he had worked so hard to create, but it was the only matter so important that the king would personally deliver the news.

The king shook his head. "This is not about the treaty."

"My family?" Casper's whisper was more of a prayer. He wished the king would correct him, but King Jovian only took another step towards Casper, confirming his fears.

"King Christopher was killed a fortnight back."

No, not Christopher. The floor dropped away from Casper, the rush of emotions making him dizzy. He stumbled to a chair, almost falling into it. King Jovian stared at him for a moment. Casper knew he was breaking protocol to sit while the king stood, but he did not think his legs would work as commanded. King Jovian gave a small nod and took a seat next to Casper, letting the slight go. Casper almost wanted to laugh, that it was mad that he was thinking about etiquette breaches right now.

But it was easier than allowing himself to accept the king's words. Anger, confusion, denial, and pain all swarmed inside him, making him want to scream. King Jovian sat by, staring at Casper with his shrewd eyes as Casper forced himself to regain some control. His brother would not want Casper to show weakness, even now. Casper inhaled deeply. *Pretend to be in control*, he reminded himself.

"What happened?" Casper's voice was even, if a bit husky.

"There was an attack by the fay off the Stigenne Road near the Biawood Forest. King Christopher was traveling back to your capital, but he never made it to Sterling."

"But it is too early for Christopher to be heading to Sterling. He never travels to Sterling till spring," Casper argued, as though that would bring his brother back to life.

"The messenger informed me that the fay had sent word they wanted to initiate talks of peace. Your brother was heading to Sterling early to commence such talks." King Jovian slowly reached into his pocket. "But unfortunately, it was a falsehood on the part of the faeries. They ambushed him."

Casper had never seen a fay, but knew with certainty they all had to be malicious and cunning if they had outwitted and murdered his brilliant brother. Casper swallowed hard, praying the rumors he had heard about the fay were not true. Were the Mother truly merciful, though, Christopher died with a sword in his hand, fighting. But if the Mother was truly merciful, Christopher would still be alive. He had to know. "And how did my brother die?"

King Jovian apprised Casper, seeming to weigh his words carefully. "The envoy told us dark magic was used. King Christopher appeared to have choked to death on his own blood." Casper imagined the scene, tasting bile in his throat. He needed to take care not to vomit in front of this king. "This was found pinned to your brother's body." King Jovian pulled out a folded piece of parchment from his robes and handed it to Casper.

Kill ours and we strike back. We do not forget.

Shock and fury warred inside Casper as he numbly held the death note in his hand. A few drops of dark rust stained the parchment. My brother's blood. The very thought of the fay's dark magic made him want to burn down the entire Biawood Forest, and all the fairies that lived beyond it.

"It does not make sense. We didn't kill any fay."

"The fay are a deceptive folk. They have no qualms about lying if it serves their purpose." King Jovian put his hand on Casper's shoulder, almost a fatherly gesture, but it felt wrong, awkward, and he moved his hand away.

Casper crumpled the note in his fist, wishing he was squeezing the neck of the fay that killed his brother instead. He silently vowed to never show mercy to the fay.

They did not deserve it. *Someday*, he promised, *he would avenge his brother*.

"We will have preparations made for your departure."

Casper looked up from the crumpled parchment to the king, feeling a sudden rush of gratitude. "Thank you, Your Highness, for granting me leave to attend my brother's funeral." It was not the homecoming Casper wanted, but at least he could say goodbye. He wondered how long the king would allow him to stay in Reynallis.

King Jovian shook his head. "You misunderstand, Prince Casper. Your sister will not be taking the crown."

Casper stared blankly at the king, not sure he understood. "But Constance is next in line." The fact of it was so ingrained in Casper, that he had never questioned it. His memories of Constance were more faded than those of Christopher; she had stopped writing him years ago. But the pain of being disregarded by his sister would be no reason for him to betray his country. King Jovian had treated Casper well enough, but he would never abandon Reynallis. "If you are suggesting I seize the throne, you deeply misunderstand me." King Jovian was clever, and perhaps thought Casper would be a more pliable king, having grown up in Faradasia.

King Jovian's raised eyebrows were the only indication of his surprise, or possibly his irritation, at Casper's accusation. "Prince Casper, you are in shock, so I shall forgive any accusations. Princess Constance has decided to decline the crown. You are to take your place as king."

All of Casper's diplomatic practice and training abandoned him. "You are jesting."

King Jovian rose, and this time Casper scrambled to his feet as well. "I do not jest, Prince Casper. You are free to return home. The situation from the initial agreement has clearly changed." *The hostage exchange,* Casper thought. "And I assume you shall send my niece back home when you reach Sterling," King Jovian continued. "Arrangements will be made for your immediate departure. I imagine you will want to reach Reynallis with time to prepare for your coronation."

"My coronation . . ." The word did not feel real to Casper. Coronations were held on the longest day of the year, and the summer solstice was in less than six months. There was no way he could mourn his brother and prepare to become a king in so short a time. "What reason did Constance give for passing on the crown?" Casper had never imagined anything would happen to his brave and brilliant older brother, but if it had, he assumed his older sister would be crowned queen. She might not care for him, but surely, she still cared for their country. Casper recalled her sharp tongue and efficient manner. Constance was no dormouse to scurry away from responsibility.

"The messenger offered no reason. Perhaps you should ask her yourself when you return home." King Jovian took several steps towards the door. "I will give you some time to collect your thoughts and ready for your travels." Right before leaving, he turned back to Casper. "And might I be the first to say to you, long live the king." And then King Jovian was gone, and Casper was left with his ocean of crashing emotions.

Once he was sure he was alone, he allowed himself to cry. *Home. King.* Casper wondered how he could possibly ever fill the void Christopher had left behind.

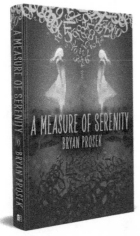

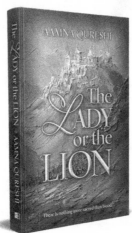

CamCat
Books

VISIT US ONLINE FOR
MORE BOOKS TO LIVE IN:
CAMCATBOOKS.COM

FOLLOW US

CamCatBooks   @CamCatBooks   @CamCat_Books